The O. Henry Prize Stories 2018

The O. Henry Prize Stories 2018

Chosen and with an Introduction by
Laura Furman

With Essays by Jurors
Fiona McFarlane
Ottessa Moshfegh
Elizabeth Tallent
on the Stories They Admire Most

Anchor Books
A Division of Penguin Random House LLC
New York

AN ANCHOR BOOKS ORIGINAL, SEPTEMBER 2018

*Copyright © 2018 by Vintage Anchor Publishing, a division
of Penguin Random House LLC
Introduction copyright © 2018 by Laura Furman*

All rights reserved. Published in the United States by Anchor Books,
a division of Penguin Random House LLC, New York, and distributed
in Canada by Random House of Canada, a division of Penguin Random
House Canada Limited, Toronto.

Anchor Books and colophon are registered trademarks of
Penguin Random House LLC.

Permissions appear at the end of the book.

**Anchor Books Trade Paperback ISBN: 978-0-525-43658-4
eBook ISBN: 978-0-525-43659-1**

www.anchorbooks.com

Printed in the United States of America
10 9 8 7 6 5 4 3 2 1

For Margaret Perry

As you set out for Ithaka

The O. Henry Prize Stories 2018 reflects the integrity, patience, and editorial skill of Diana Secker Tesdell as well as Anchor's art, production, digital, and publicity departments. The series editor thanks each and every person involved in making this book.

The editorial assistants for *The O. Henry Prize Stories 2018* were Fatima Kola and Darri Farr. We worked together in harmony and with respect for our differences in taste. Our conversations were a great pleasure.

The Department of English of the University of Texas at Austin gives *The O. Henry Prize Stories* a home and research libraries beyond compare and, with the Michener Center and the New Writers Project, provides support for the editorial assistants. The series editor thanks the university and especially Professor Elizabeth Cullingford.

—*Laura Furman*

A BRIEF HISTORY OF
THE O. HENRY PRIZE STORIES

Many readers have come to love the short story through the simple characters, easy narrative voice and humor, and compelling plotting in the work of William Sydney Porter (1862–1910), best known as O. Henry. His surprise endings entertain readers, including those back for a second, third, or fourth look. Even now one can say "Gift of the Magi" in a conversation about a love affair or marriage, and almost any literate person will know what is meant. It's hard to think of many other American writers whose work has been so incorporated into our national shorthand.

O. Henry was a newspaperman, skilled at hiding from his editors at deadline. A prolific writer, he wrote to make a living and to make sense of his life. He spent his childhood in Greensboro, North Carolina, his adolescence and young manhood in Texas, and his mature years in New York City. In between Texas and New York, he served out a prison sentence for bank fraud in

Columbus, Ohio. Accounts of the origin of his pen name vary: one story dates from his days in Austin, where he was said to call the wandering family cat "Oh! Henry!"; another states that the name was inspired by the captain of the guard at the Ohio State Penitentiary, Orrin Henry.

Porter had devoted friends, and it's not hard to see why. He was charming and had an attractively gallant attitude. He drank too much and neglected his health, which caused his friends concern. He was often short of money; in a letter to a friend asking for a loan of $15 (his banker was out of town, he wrote), Porter added a postscript: "If it isn't convenient, I'll love you just the same." His banker was unavailable most of Porter's life. His sense of humor was always with him.

Reportedly, Porter's last words were from a popular song: "Turn up the light, for I don't want to go home in the dark."

Eight years after O. Henry's death, in April 1918, the Twilight Club (founded in 1883 and later known as the Society of Arts and Sciences) held a dinner in his honor at the Hotel McAlpin in New York City. His friends remembered him so enthusiastically that a group of them met at the Biltmore Hotel in December of that year to establish some kind of memorial to him. They decided to award annual prizes in his name for short-story writers, and they formed a committee of award to read the short stories published in a year and to pick the winners. In the words of Blanche Colton Williams (1879–1944), the first of the nine series editors, the memorial was intended to "strengthen the art of the short story and to stimulate younger authors."

Doubleday, Page & Company was chosen to publish the first volume, *O. Henry Memorial Award Prize Stories 1919*. In 1927, the society sold all rights to the annual collection to Doubleday, Doran & Company. Doubleday published *The O. Henry Prize Stories*, as it came to be known, in hardcover, and from 1984 to

1996 its subsidiary, Anchor Books, published it simultaneously in paperback. Since 1997, *The O. Henry Prize Stories* has been published as an original Anchor Books paperback.

HOW THE STORIES ARE CHOSEN

All stories originally written in the English language and published in an American or Canadian periodical are eligible for consideration. Individual stories may not be nominated; magazines must submit the year's issues in their entirety by June 1. Editors are invited to submit online fiction for consideration. Such submissions must be sent to the series editor in hard copy. (Please see pp. 372–73, and www.ohenryprizestories.com, for details.)

As of 2003, the series editor chooses the twenty O. Henry Prize Stories, and each year three writers distinguished for their fiction are asked to be jurors and to evaluate the entire collection and write an appreciation of the story they most admire. These three writers receive the twenty prize stories in manuscript form with no identification of author or publication. The jurors make their choices independent of each other and the series editor.

The goal of *The O. Henry Prize Stories* remains to strengthen the art of the short story.

To Gina Berriault (1926–1999)

Gina Berriault is often called a "writer's writer," and one critic called her sentences "jewel-box perfect." Such praise is heartfelt and true, yet it makes Berriault's work sound dull and virtuous. In truth, virtue is the last thing Berriault's stories care about, and they are anything but dull.

In the short story, the writing is everything. Too much style, too many leaps in language for the fun of it, and the story deflates. Berriault's prose immediately awakens you, but if you look back to find out how she pulled you into her story, there's nothing obvious to tell you how she did it.

The opening of "Bastille Day," from her collection *The Infinite Passion of Expectation*, lures you in but waits to stop your heart until the very end. It begins at one in the morning in San Francisco when Teresa reaches San Gotardo, "the last bar on her round of bars this night of her fortieth birthday, July 14, 1970." Teresa is on an odyssey, a quest to find what it means to be forty. Others insist that the number has meaning, but "all her life, she'd refused to conform to popular delusions. With her, the sense of mortality hadn't waited to take her by surprise at forty. It had been with her always, a seventh sense, along with the absolute preciousness of life, hers and everybody's."

Teresa's odyssey differs from the Homeric original. For one thing, she's not trying to get home. (If anything she's running away from home, and her mate, Ralph, if only for a night.) The war in the background of the story is the Vietnam War, not the Trojan one. And in her description of herself, Teresa is neither noble nor heroic, nor does she encounter on her journey lotus-eaters, Sirens, or an angry goddess who turns men into swine.

Instead, the bar she enters is full of regulars, just as Teresa expected, and some strangers. All the characters—even the unnamed, the drunk, the foolish—are distinct and important, especially to themselves, evoking in their particularity Teresa's sense of how precious life is. There is a trio of women who especially intrigue her. A beautiful girl, whom Teresa names the fairy-tale woman, reminds her of being young and foolish, in a glad way. "A girl out of a fairy tale after she had come alive and become a woman and lost some teeth but not yet all her beauty." An old woman dances to Hawaiian music. A woman "neatly dressed in a gray suit and hat, her pumps dangling from her toes," sits at the bar spewing know-it-all reminiscences of her journalism career, laced with casual racist slurs.

A fight breaks out and is ended by a man with a quiet authority, whom Teresa recognizes. She knew this man, Mayer, from left-wing meetings, from a time when she, like the woman at the bar, thought she knew everything. He reminds her of her warm-fleshed youth. "She wondered if she had looked at him with desire, in the past. She had felt desire toward a number of men in that time when they had all conferred over how to right the world. Once in that time she might have made love with him in a dream."

The half-remembered possibility of desire stands in contrast to her feelings about Ralph, who, she explains later to Mayer, followed his own lengthy odyssey to becoming a professor. "'Well, first it was going to be Philosophy. He switched over to Economics and then he switched over to Modern European History. We felt it was all right for him to take so long. I had jobs. Anyway, I always felt he was like the favorite child of Time.'" She tells Mayer about their radical friends who became prosperous, who were blessed by Time: "'They just had to wait to get over their bleeding heart phase, if you know what I mean.'" Teresa does not see herself as a favorite child of Time. Time has gotten the best of her.

The fairy-tale woman, as it turns out, hasn't quite escaped either. She asks Teresa to walk home with her to show her guardian, a wealthy older man, that she wasn't out with a man. In the glimpse Berriault gives us, he is cold and frightening, and almost imperial. After the fairy-tale woman goes to him, Teresa and Mayer keep walking, until she realizes that it is now too late to leave the city.

"'I can't make it home,' she said. 'Over the bridge to Berkeley and another bus stop in the heart of darkness. Nothing's running this time of night. Or far between. I think I'm scared.'" She is scared, tired, far from home, and wanting someone else to take over. Her fortieth birthday is ending with her acting like a child.

Mayer takes her to his apartment. Teresa knows he wishes she weren't there. He's living in neat but reduced circumstances, just separated from his wife. They end up in bed, Teresa under the covers, Mayer on top.

"She listened to his breath change as he fell asleep. She heard his breath take over for him and, in that secretive way the sleeper knows nothing about, carry on his life." The word *secretive* is stunning here. Berriault emphasizes that the sleeper doesn't know the secret and neither will Teresa.

Often, short stories end on a rising note, with a new and abstract image that illuminates the story. Gina Berriault's endings are more often than not devastating, without a rising note to be heard. "Bastille Day" ends with Teresa once more alone, really alone, though inches from another person. Forty has brought her different intimations of her own mortality than she's had before.

—*Laura Furman*
Austin, Texas

Contents

Introduction

The subject matter of the twenty stories in *The O. Henry Prize Stories 2018* is so varied that even naming it feels reductive: a violent home invasion, an illiterate writer of letters from the dead, a retrospective homage to a failed marriage, an inconspicuous man in a very small town who bears witness to the great world's horrors.

It becomes second nature for passionate readers to identify and consider the elements of fiction: plot, language, characters, setting. Subject matter seems like the most obvious one yet is perhaps the least important in the long run. While an interesting subject might initially attract readers, it won't keep them there unless the formal elements are in balance.

For the author, subject matter is more complicated. Each element of a story can seem to have its own notion of its importance, so that the writer often feels in control of nothing. Add to this the fact that a writer can start with one idea of what the story is about and end by realizing that it's about something else entirely. Many authors say that they write to understand their own lives, so that even when a writer thinks she's creating a unique, completely invented character, she isn't surprised to recognize someone she knows lurking in the portrait—or even herself.

Nothing matters in the end except the story itself.

After you have completed a story in *The O. Henry Prize Stories 2018*, you might find you have two different answers to the questions "What is the subject matter?" and "What is the heart of the story?" And if you turn to "Writing *The O. Henry Prize Stories 2018*," you can see what answers the authors themselves have to offer.

Jo Ann Beard's "The Tomb of Wrestling" is spectacular in the fullest sense of the word: at once a spectacle and an impressive artistic achievement. Jurors Fiona McFarlane and Elizabeth Tallent chose "The Tomb of Wrestling" as their favorite story (pp. 347 and 350).

Here's a story in which subject matter and plot march with locked arms. A woman is alone in her house. An intruder enters and attacks her. They fight. One wins and one loses. Beard describes their battle in raw and realistic detail. And yet, as in any short story, there's a story underneath the story, and this understory is immediately hinted at by the second clause of the first sentence: "She struck her attacker in the head with a shovel, a small one that she normally kept in the trunk of her car for moving things off the highway." Surely every reader wants to say, *Who cares how big the shovel is or why she keeps it in her trunk? Get on with the fight.* The first clause is so strong that the reader wants to know what happens next, which is one definition of plot.

But we care about the shovel at least in part because the story is also about the particulars of the antagonists. We learn their names and stories, what each of them cares about, and how they came to be in the house at the same moment. We also learn where their minds are wandering, through passages that step away from the physical struggle. The mind never stops wandering, not even when the body is fighting for survival. Beard catches perfectly each character's strong will to live. By the story's end, the reader is fascinated as much by their mental ramblings as by the specifics of the struggle, and in this way "The Tomb of Wrestling" resembles what we call real life.

Marjorie Celona's "Counterblast," chosen by 2018 juror Ottessa Moshfegh as her favorite story (p. 348), is funny, wry, sad, and full of energy. The narrator tells about the failure of her marriage and what she was like as the mother of an infant. The action centers on the death of her father-in-law and her interactions with her husband and his sister. The most intimate relationship is between mother and baby. While many mothers can anticipate their baby's desire for food, a change of diaper, or sleep, our narrator is so attached that she feels little else but her yearning to be with her child. Adults make little sense to her; they're annoying and their motivations impossible to discern. She's set apart from her peers because of her desires, her unnamed and inchoate feelings that are the understory beneath the comedy of child care, in-laws, and her recurrent annoyance with her handsome husband, for whom life seems to be very easy. The last line of "Counterblast" is at first a puzzlement and then a revelation.

"Nayla" by Youmna Chlala begins with a place: "There was sun and then there was more sun and more sun. You can't imagine loss when it's sunny. . . . I was still in this camp in the desert, worming my way into acceptance while years—let's count them . . . something like $365 \times 6 +$ however many days—had gone by." The word *acceptance* has two meanings here: acceptance into another country, which every refugee needs, and acceptance by another person, which every person desires.

At a party, the narrator meets Nayla, her cousin Marwan's girlfriend, an ambiguous figure because she is a widow, and they become friends.

That summer, I practically lived in her apartment, a tiny place right above her late husband's family's house. I'd come over and we'd drink prosecco (pretending we were in Italy) and invent recipes together. We traded food for the bubbly wine with Ahmad, the liquor store manager. We made him fish fattoush; lamb-stuffed eggplant; pistachio, orange, and cardamom cookies; and vegetarian kibbeh with extra pine nuts.

Lucky Ahmad! Slowly the two young women come to trust each other, to share their losses and to confide what it is to be a survivor. The richness of their friendship in what is essentially a prison is perfectly conveyed by Chlala's gifted prose.

"Lucky Dragon" by Viet Dinh also begins with the sun, though this is a sun that betokens devastation: "The second dawn rose in the east, at nine in the morning." In the nonchalance of this first sentence, Dinh warns his reader that something is terribly wrong. The order of things is disturbed. The second dawn is no dawn at all but a nuclear explosion, a test by the Americans.

One member of the *Lucky Dragon* crew dies quickly and is buried at sea. The rest don't merely sicken and die; they first suffer horribly, including the ship's captain, Hiroshi, and his friend Yoshi. Some of the crew previously survived the Tokyo firebombings, others the battles in the Pacific. Hiroshi and Yoshi were together as soldiers in the Philippines and as prisoners of war. Together they transform into unrecognizable creatures as their skin scales and hardens. Dinh portrays not only their physical suffering but what their nation makes of them: first as victims, next heroes, finally as monsters. Their treatment makes a mockery of politics, nationalism, and military pride. In the end, Hiroshi and Yoshi have only death, the sea, and each other.

Michael Parker's "Stop 'n' Go" is a two-paragraph story whose emotional depth is masked by the banality of the main character. He is stoical, much attached to his habits, clothing, and schedules. His children have gone away. He no longer farms but still surveys his fields, now rented out to a company from out of state. We see his wife in her housecoat "wordlessly" making his customary breakfast. Nothing in the present quite makes sense to him. "Maybe I have outlived time," he thinks.

So far, so good. Maybe the reader thinks that, aside from Parker's elegant prose, this story about a grumpy old guy has nothing to reveal. Then, in the middle of the paragraph, everything changes. The old farmer's world seemed entirely local, but the reader learns that it's larger and more awful than it appears to be. With the words "in the war," we're taken back to his youth, back to war in another country, to being wounded, to a moment of unexpected desire, to seeing the worst that one human being can do to another, and then to seeing people whose ways are, to him, even more incomprehensible, more foreign and haunting.

Dounia Choukri's "Past Perfect Continuous" is another meditation on war and memory, but it's also a disquisition on time, as the title indicates. Here are war, time, and memory—her family's past and her present—considered by a young German woman. She comes from stolid women, "married to reasonable men with ice-blue eyes, men who only traveled in wartime." Her family is bent on forgetting and denying their country's (and their own) recent past. They yearn for the better days of a whitewashed past, whether embodied by Gene Kelly's dancing or recollections of past winters, which "aren't what they used to be!" The narrator, stranded in her adolescence, observes that "there's a particular loneliness to sitting down at a table others have already eaten at, flicking at hard crumbs and tracing the rings of cleared glasses with your finger." And then Aunt Gunhild, the narrator's Nazi great-aunt, makes a visit, much to the family's chagrin. She is "a smoker in a family in which women . . . didn't smoke" and a living ghost from the past, a living answer to the narrator's question, "But what about the

Second World War, huh?" The visit of her transgressive relative is inspiring to the narrator, an awkward thirteen-year-old, who's unprepared for what the future seems to offer—"breasts, bras, boys." In the atmosphere of her family's nostalgia for a past that never existed, she tells the reader, "Part of me wished for a past without the need to fill in the present."

Aunt Gunhild has lost the right to be nostalgic for her past. Through her visit, the narrator learns that time can be a false analgesic and that it's hard to learn time's lessons: "When the past sucks it just becomes a welcome lesson on how not to do things." "Past Perfect Continuous" is not only a story about German history, but it's also a tracing of a young girl's growth toward independence and a liberation as glorious and complicated as the fall of the Berlin Wall.

Thomas Bolt's "Inversion of Marcia" is also narrated by a young girl. Mary's on a family vacation with her parents; her older sister, Marcia; and the gorgeous and seductive Alicia, who is helping out "in exchange for a free trip to Italy."

Not surprisingly, complications ensue. The parents withdraw into their own problems, reappearing periodically to drive the girls to Naples and other sights. A painful triangulation develops as Mary observes her sister's increasingly sexual involvement with Alicia. Alicia's wardrobe and makeup, the attitudes she strikes, the cigarettes she smokes, all seem perfect and perfectly annoying to our shrewd narrator. Mary knows that she's about to lose childhood's freedom to the questionable joys of adolescence. She watches Alicia and Marcia like a disapproving hawk, hovering and waiting to be included.

Thomas Bolt's generous story is told with a bit of a novel's discursiveness, but he maintains the story's tight focus on Mary's quiet maturing and how she comes to understand something of the adult life she will soon undertake. She's torn between copying Alicia's ways and detesting them; between hating and loving her sister as Marcia moves through her first love affair; between thinking of her parents as distant monoliths and seeing their adult troubles as real and perhaps even forgivable.

Marwand, the Afghan-American narrator of Jamil Jan Kochai's "Nights in Logar," is on an expedition to find the fierce and unfriendly family dog, Budabash, who's somehow gotten free. It's a hot day, and the mission is a welcome distraction but also dangerous, even in the current lull or temporary "coma" in the American war.

Marwand is in the company of Gul and Dawoud, his almost-peer uncles, and his cousin Zia; the boys range in age from twelve to fourteen. Unlike Marwand, who's there on a visit from his home in America to his mother's family village, Gul is wise in the ways of Logar and declares that only four of them can go looking for the dog. Marwand's younger brother cannot be invited along. " 'More than four,' he told me and Zia and Dawoud as we sat between the chicken coop and the kamoot, 'and we'll look like a mob, but any less and we might get jumped or robbed.' "

Part of the reader's entertainment in Kochai's lively story is the mix of American slang with Pakhto, a duality that highlights Marwand's double existence. (On losing a bid to include his brother, here is his response: " 'Well, fuck,' I muttered, in English, and relented to the will of the jirga.") Marwand has two nationalities, two homes, two identities, and is at times comfortable with neither.

Even the missing dog is part of a duality. On first arriving, Marwand rushed to him, mistaking him for a favorite dog from years before. Budabash bites off the tip of Marwand's finger, proving that he is not the Mr. Kareem of old, not an American dog to be "hugged and petted and neutered" but "a mutant," perhaps like Marwand, neither one thing nor the other.

The four hunters see many things, and before long a numbered list of what Marwand sees reaches number twenty-one. They wend through graveyards and among slaughtered sheep, under mulberry trees and out in the open, over land possibly mined; they hunt until it is dark, darker than it ever is in the streets of Marwand's America. Whatever America means to Marwand, with its safety and its grand promises for his future, it remains hard for him to measure it against Logar, where there's a prayer and a story and an obligation to structure the days and nights and the familiarity of his family village.

The life of Trent, the twelve-year-old narrator of "How We Eat" by Mark Jude Poirier, is in its way as dangerous as Marwand's is in an Afghan village. Trent lives with his ten-year-old sister, Lizzie, and their mother, who insists they call her "Brenda" or "Bren." She's a self-righteous crazy woman with a hair-trigger temper who wins arguments with her children by shifting ground. She routinely blames them for her every trouble. Brenda has trained Trent and Lizzie to find money for her, and when they do, she buys a small quantity of fast food for them to share unequally.

Trent tries to take care of Lizzie, who is still innocent enough to disobey Brenda. His love for Lizzie and his attempts to care for her lead Trent into trouble with Brenda but also gain him a painful chance to escape.

In Lara Vapnyar's funny and moving "Deaf and Blind," the narrator views love, sex, and adult communication through the eyes of herself as a child.

Her mother's dear friend Olga visits Moscow as often as she can. The two women met when they were both undergoing treatment for infertility, which worked for the narrator's mother but not for Olga. Olga's husband, whom she doesn't love, remains crazy about her. The narrator's father leaves her mother, marries again, and becomes possessed by a new baby, neglecting the narrator. The situation is static until Olga falls in love with Sasha, a deaf and blind philosopher, who becomes an object of fascination for the narrator. She's learning about love in its eccentric and inconvenient possibilities, for, as her grandmother offers, " 'We don't choose who we love.' "

Stacey, the narrator of Jenny Zhang's "Why Were They Throwing Bricks?," is having problems with a different kind of love. For Stacey, and then for her younger brother, being loved by their grandmother is like being the object of a boa constrictor's affection. Their grandmother is used to getting her way and never gives up. Mixed with the story of Stacey's distancing of herself from her grandmother and her Chinese identity as she grows up in America is the story of her grandmother's own suffering. Unfortunately, that very real suffering doesn't make her grandmother any easier to love, though it makes Stacey—and her story—more nuanced and complex. The story's title evokes the grandmother's will and willfulness, and her separation from her surroundings. Wherever she is, she's an offended stranger. Stacey sums up the final dramatic scene of "Why Were They Throwing Bricks?" with characteristic bluntness: "you go on with your life, and you learn nothing, and you don't change at all."

Lauren Alwan's "An Amount of Discretion" is also ostensibly about delicate family relations. Aside from tension between Seline and her late husband's son, Finn, a college student, there's another fragile relationship at stake, between Seline and Jonathan, her dead husband.

Jonathan was an artist and teacher. He left a simple and clear will, in which he left all his work to the school where he taught for fifty years. Seline is executor of his estate. She's also an artist and a careful, precise woman. She has no children of her own, and while she isn't close to her stepson, she feels a duty toward him and a latent affection. "She'd never had much of a maternal temperament, yet on those weekend visitations and the annual two weeks each summer, she'd found surprising pleasure in the Lego building and story reading and the cooking of macaroni and cheese."

The story opens as she's preparing her house in Los Angeles, the perfect lunch, and herself in the right dress and jewelry for a visit from Finn, his girlfriend, Anna, and Anna's four-year-old daughter, Chloe. In the light of his father's death, Seline is no longer obligated to be kind and welcoming to Finn. She might, though, want to continue a friendship with him. Along these lines, she decides to give Finn the eight notebooks Jonathan used to record in words and drawings places, wildlife, and interesting botanical finds. The notebooks are full of exquisite drawings and quite valuable. Jonathan's will made no provision for such a gift, but as executor Seline is making the inventory and decides she can do what she wants with the notebooks. She feels an uncharacteristic desire to make up to Finn for past losses. It's also possible that she wants to bribe him into staying in touch with her. The notebooks would be an extraordinary gift of beauty as well as a moving reminder of his father.

The astute reader of the short story will know that Seline is creating a world of trouble for herself. Alwan's exact and thoughtful prose provides the perfect background for the surprising fireworks that the visit causes in Seline's quiet and careful life. Perhaps they're the right fireworks to launch her into widowhood.

Among the lessons life insists on teaching us over and over again is that everything dies. Thinking about our own mortality is bad enough, but there are losses that are worse. "Queen Elizabeth" by Brad Felver tells the story of a couple, Gus and Ruth, who love each other despite what seems to the reader to be a mismatch. In education and ambition, they are unequally yoked.

He grew up on his father's farm. She's from an upper-middle-class family in Boston and is afraid to pet a chicken. He's a carpenter who makes furniture by hand, lovingly carving and fitting together beautiful pieces of wood into useful objects that sell as works of art. Ruth is something else entirely—a mathematician. She studies stochastic—fittingly meaning "random"—

processes, and she lives with an affinity to "probability theory, random variables, and chaotic systems." They marry and have a child, Annabelle, and the three live on the farm he inherits from his father. Though Annabelle is much loved, Ruth thinks about herself: "Here she was: a mother, but was she anything else? Anything at all?" She's restless and he's content. She wants more but doesn't quite know how to get it without destroying their marriage. Then fate intervenes.

In the end, Gus and Ruth share a sorrow that's more dear and essential to each of them than their differences. Brad Felver's story is as lovingly crafted as the furniture Gus makes, and Felver leaves the reader with a haunting and bittersweet truth.

In "The Stamp Collector" by Dave King, the narrator wins "a small pot in the Massachusetts lottery." He and Louis, early in their affair, go to Europe, and "between Louis and the sudden wealth, [he] believed life had changed." Here's a short story that pulls its reader through with an easy, confidential narrative tone. We're immediate friends with the narrator. We want to know what happens next. Can money and love really change life?

By the end of the third paragraph, we spot signs of trouble on the horizon: Louis's formidable mom, the program Louis gets the narrator into, "all the bad years" to which the narrator refers as if we know all about bad years. We want to know what the money did to the narrator's life and how long the affair with Louis (and the money) lasted. We want to know to whom Louis was mailing sheets of stamps from all over Europe. We want to see more of Louis's mother, with her black belts in facade and condescension.

In a short story, the writer *has* to do it all right away—establish the tone, ensnare the reader, and make us want more. Dave King does all three just right in "The Stamp Collector."

"More or Less Like a Man" by Michael Powers is a gentle story filled with violence, a story about a brief meeting between two people who have no luck in love. One is a middle-aged

Slovenian woman who's fallen in love with the exact wrong man. She's an immigrant and so is he. Together, they're not just learning English but shaking it to see its roots. The consequences of her affair are unbearably painful.

She's on a plane to San Francisco in the middle seat between a man who is sleeping at the window and our narrator on the aisle. She remarks that she's fleeing. The narrator responds in a completely understandable way: "Okay, I thought, here we go."

But if anyone could use some conversation, it's our narrator.

Often in fiction, the writer chooses to provide a character's background information to the reader in one chunk of prose and then go on with the action. Michael Powers makes a different choice. Until the last paragraph, the only things we know about the narrator are that he dislikes talking to strangers on airplanes and that he's been to New Jersey. In the last paragraphs, the story blooms and the narrator reveals himself while returning us to the beginning, which we see in a new way.

Cassandra seems to be flirting with HM, hero of Jo Lloyd's "The Earth, Thy Great Exchequer, Ready Lies," nibbling his fingers and blowing nose kisses into his palm. She is a well-named horse, and when she turns to look around, HM knows that she is out to get his attention and keep it. Aside from his horse, HM is accompanied by the gloomy Shiers, "HM's most trusted employee yet tedious companion," and by Tall John, an all-around reprobate who considers himself "a second Adam, more free than a freeborn gentleman."

The title of Jo Lloyd's story comes from Thomas Yalden's poem "To Sir Humphrey Mackworth"; Mackworth was a politician and industrialist in the seventeenth and eighteenth centuries. It's difficult not to identify our hero HM with Sir Humphrey, whose later life was besmirched by a scandal but who lived to the then ripe age of seventy. Historical accuracy doesn't really matter, though.

The pleasure of Lloyd's story, aside from her successful imagining, is her use of language as she constructs both narrative and dialogue in a convincing idiom. She dances us through the tale of HM, "founding director and deputy governor of the Company of Mine Adventurers," as he attempts to verify for the company Tall John's claim that he's found "a seam of finest ore, right on the surface, fat and firm as floorboards."

Is Tall John's story too good to be true? Is it a test of HM's temperament and judgment? A trap? Knavery on the part of HM's enemies? Cassandra thinks so.

"The Earth, Thy Great Exchequer, Ready Lies" also delves into the ever-present British question of class. HM has the unfortunate habits of feeling sorry for himself and comparing himself to others. He wishes to be praised more than he is and wants to be recognized as financially successful and also charitable to the poor, a good provider, industrious, and in possession of "excellent judgment." He has what seems like plenty, yet he's self-conscious, touchy, and defensive.

At its end, the story opens up with a hymn that looks ahead to England after the Industrial Revolution when it's been turned by men like HM from the rich, dense fields and forests through which he rides into a dark place where "the stars, the planets, the moon herself are dimmed by the glitter of furnaces."

Tristan Hughes's "Up Here" is set in the contemporary countryside, where the narrator lives with his girlfriend, a naturalist in a "park that surrounded" them. She's made the decision that her dog, old and in pain, needs to be killed. "Her body was slowing, her insides were failing, her bones were going: she had to be careful about each move she made." The narrator, though he's never before done such a thing, volunteers to kill the dog himself. To pile on another difficulty, he likes the dog, old and sick as she is. He makes his promise partly because he's drunk and partly because "up here, it was the kind of thing you did for your lover. In other places, you might be expected to do other things."

He's in thrall to his girlfriend and the place where they live.

"I watched my girlfriend dive and swim. The elegant arch of her back, the easy grace of her swimming strokes—how beautiful and unencumbered she appeared, uplifted by the light and water. How lucky we were to live on a lake like this! How golden our lives seemed, lived so far away from anywhere!"

He's both lucky and unlucky, too tentative to call the place his own or to relax his nervous eagerness to please his lover. He soon discovers that nature doesn't care what he feels or does, another aspect of living in a beautiful wilderness. "Up Here" is a pastoral of sorts, a love story told in full awareness of how often failure greets those who solve their problems by moving to a paradise.

Brenda Walker's "The Houses That Are Left Behind" is also, at least in part, about place.

It's a Sunday afternoon. The narrator's cooking for her husband's children, who come weekly for a meal and a visit. Her husband's reading in the sun. Is this another paradise? Perhaps. But then the bell rings, and a young woman, weeping, tells them a ridiculous story. She gets them wondering—did she want to get into their apartment building? If so, why?

Walker's story is about places that used to mean something and about the consistency of uncertainty. Once there was a lovely new home, but, no, it was a house about to burn. There was a kind and helpful neighbor, someone else's husband, a lawyer on vacation, but, no, he was a stalker. Now there's a new place, a new home for the narrator and her husband, yet it's also a place where strangers meet for secret assignations—until the lock is changed, and then what becomes of them?

In deliberate and evocative prose that never asks to be admired but is, Brenda Walker relates the narrator's several lives and pasts before she arrived at the apartment where on a Sunday afternoon she's cooking for her husband's children. Those lives are one story, she's saying. The other story is the secret one that houses live without us.

Stephanie A. Vega's story "We Keep Them Anyway" is about another kind of mystery, the universal desire to hear from the dead and missing. Ña Meli arrives out of nowhere, almost uneducated, "poor among the beggars," perhaps a mystic, perhaps a charlatan. The neighborhood of La Chacarita is a collection of shanties made of "cardboard boxes and corrugated metal. . . . It clung to the lip of the river—muddy, smelly, filled with mosquitoes—like a howling, injured beast." Ña Meli offers the residents of La Chacarita an occasion for skepticism or hope. Her gift, or trick, is to write letters in a clear handwriting unlike her normal scrawl, using words she doesn't know, sometimes even in a language she doesn't know. The letters are dictated to her by those she calls her visitors.

Ña Meli lives down a dirt path from the narrator and offers him a message from his missing brother, "a small-time agitator." He passes up the opportunity, figuring that for Ña Meli's fee he could get a Coca-Cola or even an empanada.

Eventually, naturally, he succumbs to temptation. Little by little, he and Ña Meli become friends and stay close until she joins her visitors in death. Ña Meli is faithful to those dictating visitors but also feels an obligation to the living recipients, so she sometimes writes, " 'Burn this. Do not keep it,' " on the letters. "As Ña Meli wrote the letter for me I thought, *What good does it do me to know it was muddy after the rain and he slipped?*" The narrator warns her not to write dangerous letters, and she replies, " '*Imbécil!* It's not me. They visit me.' " One of the hazards of their lives is the political regime they live under, and Ña Meli is on the losing side.

There's no forced magical realism in "We Keep Them Anyway," rather there's the plentiful magic of reality. There might be no use, as the narrator argues, in knowing how someone you love died of torture, yet Ña Meli's visitors dictate the exact details and those left behind do want to know them. How deeply people love and miss the ones who've gone into death or the unknown—these everyday mysteries are the magical components in La Chacarita.

Throughout "Solstice," Anne Enright uses aspects of that twice-yearly occasion: darkness and light, beginning and end, that which we notice and that which we overlook, what we share and what we keep selfishly to ourselves, the intimacy and loneliness of family life.

"It was the year's turning," Enright begins. "These few hours like the blink of a great eye—just enough light to check that the world is still there, before shutting back down."

Ross makes his slow way home through sticky Dublin traffic. He meant to leave work early but didn't. The darkness of the longest night of the year catches him by surprise. Then he can't find his car in the office garage. "It felt like the end of things. Made you want your religion back." A muted feeling of wanting something back—religion, family, marriage, any source of lightness—suffuses the story.

Evening is no one's best time in this family. Ruth, the daughter of the house, is on her phone and won't get off it. Dinner's on the way, absorbing Ross's wife's attention. His ten-year-old son's contribution to their dinner conversation, which is about the death of their cat's mother—("'Animals believe in death'")—annoys Ross, and this provokes his wife. She's already annoyed with him: "His wife with a look that says, *Christmas is coming and it is all your fault.*"

It takes the morning sun's delayed entrance to unite at least part of the family. Father and son greet the new light in a united silence: "Nothing happened, but they know it was there. The tiny stretch of daylight that will become summer."

—*Laura Furman*
Austin, Texas

The O. Henry Prize Stories 2018

Jo Ann Beard
The Tomb of Wrestling

SHE STRUCK HER ATTACKER in the head with a shovel, a small one that she normally kept in the trunk of her car for moving things off the highway. There was a certain time of year in upstate New York when the turtles left their reedy ponds to crawl ponderously through the countryside, and wound up strewn like pottery shards across the road. The box turtles Joan could pick up with her hands; this was the shovel she had purchased to move the snappers to the ditches. Luckily, she had taken it from her trunk in order to straighten out her compost situation. The barrel stank so terribly that her neighbor had mentioned it, an aerobic smell of digestion, of tomatoes and corncobs and coffee grounds combining to form such a bright sharp stink that the neighbor, who lived down the road and was loaning her a gutter-cleaning attachment for her hose, suggested Joan start alternating small shovelfuls of soil with each bucket of food scraps. So the shovel was leaned up against the side of the house, right next to the kitchen door, a few inches of its business end buried in a torn-open fifty-pound bag of peat slumped on its side. She hadn't torn the bag open like that; it wasn't her style—she was a person who stowed a shovel in her trunk for rescuing amphibians. The bag had been torn open by her husband, a man who sometimes was so impatient he would tear right into the side of a package of bread if the twist tie was snarled. It was not the most appealing trait, and yet in this moment, glimpsing the gaping hole in the plastic, Joan felt a surge of protective instinct where her husband was concerned. She had to save his wife! So she reached down, lifted the ergonomic-handled, titanium-headed shovel, and stepped into her kitchen with it.

The stranger was standing with his back to her, staring into the refrigerator. In the split instant when he knew she was standing behind him, but hadn't begun to turn yet, Joan heard the mechanical whir of a hummingbird sipping angrily at the feeder. The hummingbirds had bad personalities, always trying to spear each other away from the trumpet vines and the feeders, their thumb-sized shimmering bodies aglow with bad intentions. She couldn't think how hard to hit him—it seemed first of all terrible to hit him but also wonderful. Inevitable. She had to do it or he would realize she hadn't died when he strangled her and would come after her again. Or one of the dogs. He seemed to hate the dogs, and the big one, Pilgrim, had attacked him and been kicked a number of times for it. It was brutal and routine, as though he were dispatching a duty that he neither agreed nor disagreed with. The dog had retired with a prolonged yelp to some dark area inside the honeysuckle. The little one, Spock, right now was whining and raking his toenails on the side door, making long feverish gouges in the wood. Joan could see the gouges in her mind's eye, some tiny part of her brain still attuned to home maintenance.

She decided in that split instant between the man's hackles rising, almost visibly, and his beginning the turn away from the refrigerator and toward her that she was going to hit him in the head with the shovel using every bit of force she could summon. She was a slight woman . . . or no, she wasn't; she had been a slight woman, but now, depending on how you defined it, she was middle-aged. Her arms and legs were still decently coltish, but her torso had all the nuance of a toilet paper tube. She had lost her beauty before she ever even knew she had it; looking at old photographs, Joan saw that she had been willowy, soulful, glossy haired the entire time that she was thinking of herself as stark, bug faced, lank.

She couldn't imagine using all her force; it went against who she was—female, for starters—but there was no choice. Having never hit someone with a shovel, or even with her fist, before, she didn't know what to expect with less than a full effort, or for that matter *with* a full effort; so it stood to reason that she had to let fly completely and utterly, otherwise what if it only stunned him, or pissed him off? She took a step forward, grabbing the very end of the shaft, the physics of it returning to her from something she had learned working at an art gallery many years ago.

"Let the hammer work for you," Roy had said to her, showing Joan how to hold the hammer near the end, allowing the weight of the head to add momentum to the swing. Roy had been pretty far out there, for an Iowan—he had kinky hair that rose straight up from his scalp like blond flames, wore sharkskin shirts and baggy cuffed pants, and made sculptures out of found materials; back then, big, complicated, beautifully crafted assemblages with baseball themes. He was the director of the gallery, and when he was excited would take off and run straight up the wall, leaving sneaker tracks that she had to paint over. When they were finished hanging the shows, he would climb up onto the tallest stepladder they had and jump it like a big pogo stick down the rows of track lighting, adjusting each lamp in turn so that the paintings were perfectly illuminated. After she had worked with him for five years Joan was forced to make a rule that he couldn't ride his bike inside her house.

So instead of choking up on the shovel handle, the way she might have automatically done, considering all the times her first husband had shown her how to choke up in order to really smack the Wiffle ball down the back sidewalk into the pitcher's face (their friend Kurt, stoned and graceful), she remembered Roy's advice, and the destructive, comforting weight of that old art gallery hammer as she swung it toward a nail. Joan lifted the shovel end as high as her ear, and put all her weight behind the swing.

Unbelievable, the small details you notice. He had a piece of individually wrapped cheese in his hand when he whirled around. She was actually embarrassed about that cheese, had put it in her shopping cart with the idle thought that she'd better not run into anyone at the checkout and have it revealed that she sometimes broke down and bought cheese food instead of cheese, just for the sheer laziness of peeling the cellophane away and slapping the orange tile directly onto the bread. Her husband couldn't believe she ate that crap—just yesterday, when she was making a sandwich with it, he had looked over her shoulder and said, "We can do better than that, can't we?"

So, the man was holding her secret cheese and swiftly turning around and the refrigerator door bounced against the wall and the shovel made a clanging sound, that's how hard she hit him.

It rang, titanium on bone, like a clapper on a bell. She might have thought that the worst sound would be a melon-like sound, but it wasn't. This was the worst sound a person's head could make—a muffled bell-like gonging, like a gravedigger hitting rock.

But maybe the melon sound would be better, though gorier, because what if the gonging meant that the man's head was preternaturally hard, that the shovel had met its match? Once when she had flipped a turtle and scooped it up, instead of retracting into its shell it lolled its head out toward her, upside down, opening and closing its beak fitfully. When she set it in the tall grass and flipped it right side up its feet came out lightning fast and it turned on the shovel. For an instant, she had felt the mighty turtle's strength and rage, right through the titanium and the wood handle. It had shaken the shovel like a terrier would shake a knotted sock before continuing on its prehistoric way, the tall grass shivering in its wake.

The man, the stranger who had her blood on his hands, who was still holding the square of cheese between his thumb and forefinger, didn't fly sideways to accommodate the spade thudding into his temple; that was what she half expected, him flying sideways into the cereal and wineglass cupboard, but her experience with this sort of thing heretofore was from cartoons. None of these thoughts were going through her mind, of course; they were more like synaptic realizations, pulses of understanding, except that understanding implies process. There was no process, no hesitation, because she was operating like a simple organism in that moment, one that is programmed to survive, like a sperm, or a hammerhead shark.

She had lived on a lake when she first came to New York, after Iowa and her divorce, before she met her new husband and moved into his sprawling farmhouse. Her rented cabin, the upper half of a duplex, had been set into the side of a hill and surrounded by tall reaching trees, elms and oaks and the like, creating a fringed green awning that cast everything into a perpetual dense shade. Every morning she woke to the sound of Round Lake slapping the legs of the dock down below; it was like cold astringent in the face, the loneliness of that sound after her busy chattering life in Iowa. Nothing to keep her company but her own self, and the soothing, flapping-moth feeling inside her skull that she registered not as depression, or as anxiety, but as a balance of both states—a kind of stasis that led to endless hours of sitting at a desk or standing on the varnished porch, staring down at the mossy path and the wavering blue lake.

She had never stood around like that before, just looking; in Iowa everything had been visible, exposed to the elements, there was no subtext, nothing to break the furrowed monotony but subtle geographical undulations, all the rows of corn suddenly banking in unison like a flock of birds, a DeKalb sign at distant intervals, the occasional yellow cat furtively walking along a ditch. Here in upstate New York there were the endless shadows, the low ceilings, the gloomy stone fences full of snake holes, trees bending over roadways, everything grown into everything else, warrenlike and confining.

One day the landlord's henchman had shown up to take out a tree and some brush. He spent half the morning sitting on a stump sharpening a scythe blade and then oiling, link by link, the chain in his chain saw, all the while listening to his earphones and drinking out of a huge, dirty cup with a snap-on lid. Maybe it wasn't coffee in the cup, or maybe it was coffee and something else, because he managed to make an error in his tree-cutting calculations. The tree, instead of falling directly down the hill, along a narrow unforested trough between the cabin and the water, fell on a slant, hitting the trunk of a neighboring oak with a resounding thunderous smack. That second tree had fallen against the trunk of a third tree, which landed with a crack against the trunk of another tree, until four trees in all had crashed to the ground with an enormous rustling noise, like big girls in petticoats tripping each other.

So when she hit the stranger in her kitchen, that's how she brought him down, like a felled tree. The ringing blow to the side of the head, the flat of the shovel against the temple, and he went over sideways, between the refrigerator and the counter, which was covered with the makings of that day's pathetic lunch, a leftover dish made with pale slabs of tofu. It had wobbled unattractively on the way to the table, but Joan had eaten it without paying much attention, absorbed in the newspaper. It had almost turned out to be her last meal; they would have found it in her stomach at the autopsy, tofu helper. A vegetarian from beginning to end.

As a Midwestern child, she had gotten to know food in its sentient state right in her grandparents' chicken-scratched yard. Joan had loved the white hens with their meditative clucking, red combs and yellow legs, rhythmic bobbing way of walking. Twenty feet beyond the chickens began the dirt field where the hogs were kept, the pink rubbery noses poked through the fence, the tiny wicked eyes, the little lean-tos they called home. The pigs had babies that Joan's grandfather would hold for her to pet, which she did, panicked and sorry, as they squealed in abject terror, the same syllable over and over, while their mothers snuffled and bit each other. In the next enclosure were the cows, standing on low mountains of manure, staring between the chewed planks of the fence, bright metal tags stapled into their ears. The color of the tags indicated at what future date the cow would be evicted from its body.

Joan's grandfather was a part-time butcher who drove a panel truck to people's farms and killed their animals for pay. It wasn't told to Joan, who had a hard enough time petting a baby pig who didn't want to be petted, but once she had glimpsed something strange, either at the grandparents' house or elsewhere: a group of blood-smeared shaved sheep in a dejected clump; a lost calf, tall with rickety legs and twine around its neck; and then a lamb on its side in the dirt, woolly legs bound together. The lamb had lifted its head and stared at Joan as she walked toward it, but right at that moment her grandmother began calling her, urgently, in a false lilting voice, the way you might call a puppy away from a busy road.

"Dearie, come here!" she cried gaily. "Come to Grandma!"

There had to be a rope around somewhere. Where? Joan was starting to feel the adrenaline leave her body. *He had tried to kill her.* For a second she almost swooned—her grandmother had called her dearie, she had been a little girl in a ruffled midriff top, somewhere she had a picture of herself in it squinting at the ground while someone in baggy trousers held a long fish up next to her. The fish was being held by the gills, and its tail was flexed just enough to show it was still alive; it was the same height as Joan. On the back, her mother had written *Keepers.*

She needed to immobilize him before he came around, if he came around. Rope, rope, rope. She was too afraid to leave the kitchen to go to the toolshed to look for rope, what if he woke up, what if she came back and he wasn't here. She'd seen it, everyone had: the blank span of linoleum, the moment of sick realization, the grab from behind, hands around the neck, the woman lifted from the floor, gasping like a fish. Joan raised the shovel and hit him again, this time a soggy, glancing blow to the shoulder.

He stirred and collapsed deeper onto the linoleum, like he was filled with sand. It reminded her of the old Friday night fights, dramas in which men in satin shorts alternated between pummeling each other in the stomach and hugging. Her father had been a fan, watching from a green armchair with the family's white terrier on his lap, eating ice cream from a mixing bowl, using one set of toes to scratch the top of the other foot. If Joan or her siblings wandered into the room and stood staring at the television he would describe what was happening as the guy fell backward onto a milking stool, or stood swaying, swollen head hanging down on his chest, or when the guy's spaghetti arm was lifted in its heavy glove by the referee. "He clocked him," her father would explain.

Joan had loved her father, a tender, hopeless drunk who stayed off the booze for long periods of time, confusing everyone and causing her mother to switch back and forth with him, between cheerfulness and relentless bitching tirades. It was a tumultuous household, as many were in those days, but it had the white terrier and a blue parakeet and Joan's mother not only made flannel nightgowns for her daughters but also made matching flannel nightgowns for their dolls, baked pies every Sunday morning, and put a plywood Santa in the front yard each December. Joan's father, when he was sober, was a classic backyard putterer; he knocked together bird feeders, staked tomatoes, hung buckets neatly from spigots, and sang to the children and anyone else who would listen, songs about paper dolls and drinking. Once, he got annoyed at Joan for bugging him while he was shaving and he took the towel from around his neck, gave it a twirl, and flicked it at her. It was so out of character he might as well have donned a hockey mask and taken after her with a carving knife; she sobbed until she was ill, and had to stay home from school that day, huddled on the couch in the darkened living room, watching reruns.

It seemed entirely possible she may have clocked this man to death; there was something too settled about the way he was arranged on the floor. He had cornered her upstairs, in her study, just walked in and said something offhand and expectant. "Here I am," or "Hey, I'm here," or "Okay, I'm here." For a good number of seconds she had been utterly confused, embarrassed that she couldn't remember who he was or what business he was there on.

"I'm sorry," she had said, haltingly. "I can't remember what we said." As though there had been an arrangement made earlier, for a man to come stand over her and grin as she sat in her soft chair with manuscript pages on her lap. When she started to stand, he stepped forward and gave her a gentle push backward, the tips of his fingers on her breastbone, and she sank back down, confused. Who was he, again?

And then, with a sudden zooming clarity, she realized he was a stranger who had come into her house and up her stairs and was now addressing her, pushing her down when she went to stand up. With the clarity came a tight, compressing panic. She made a noise and tried to scramble out of the chair, kicking at his legs. He took her by the back of the head and ran her into the wall; she lifted her hand to shield her nose, which nevertheless broke on impact. It was a totally visual experience, she didn't feel a thing—the sight of the forty-year-old wallpaper coming toward her, rows of parasols and roses followed by a bright yellow explosion, her own innocent knees for a second, then she was crouched before him, one hand holding her nose in place, the other raised in front of her, like a student asking a question in class.

Second grade, unable to raise her hand to ask Mrs. Darnell if she could go to the bathroom. Endless lessons, the opening of desks, lifting of books, rustling pages, chalk and eraser. The replacing of math book with language book, the stark impossibility of making it to the lunch bell. Unable to hold it and unable to ask, a drowning person in a warm, insistent river, eventually Joan just let go. As she stared fixedly at the blackboard, a hideous amber current moved steadily up the aisle past her desk, past the desk in front of hers, and then into the territory of the desk beyond that one.

That afternoon, after lunch at home, the ruined Brownie uniform stuffed into a laundry basket, the silent diplomatic companionship of her little girlfriends on the playground, she returned to find the floor around her desk miraculously cleaned up. Later, during art class, when everyone was milling about, tearing paper and mishandling paste, Mrs. Darnell crouched next to her and whispered, "Don't ever be afraid to raise your hand."

He took her outstretched arm and twisted it behind her, lifted it upward until she cried out and then held it there, stepping on her right foot with his thick boot, holding her in place. She tried to resist the impulse to wrestle her way out of it; his arms and hands were iron; it was like straining against the bars of a cell.

But he was tearing the muscles in her upper arm and cracking the delicate bones of her instep—if he would just let her arm go, if he would just pick up his boot! She writhed frantically, panting, and then she went still.

When Joan was with her first husband, they liked to get high, eat candy, and challenge each other to competitive games— say, jumping over the sofa from a standstill, pitching dirt clods onto a tin roof, or holding afternoon-long wrestling bouts in the tableless dining room of their farmhouse. This was during a time when her husband wore patched overalls and no shirt, and Joan wore cutoffs and a famous halter top made from two bandanna handkerchiefs tied together; they had a willow tree that looked like a big hula skirt, a collie dog, and a blue bong. Life was fresh and new, and they were learning everything: that dill pickles were actually small cucumbers, that oregano started out as a leaf, that going back to the land meant you should remove your top if somebody needed a hanky.

She and that husband were so perfectly matched in spirit and sensibility that they were like littermates, tripping each other, rolling around, hopping on each other's backs, getting rug burns. Sometimes, depending on the quality and quantity of the dope, they forgot themselves during their wrestling matches— Joan yanking on vulnerable areas and scratching, him clamping her head under his arm, poking a finger up her nostrils. Then they struggled in earnest, tugging and swearing, worrying the dog, until finally Joan's husband got fed up and pinned her. Just like that. Pressed to the floor and straddled, her wrists manacled in one of his hands.

It was always shocking, that utter helplessness, as though she were one of her own childhood dolls being laid to rest after a session of playing. When that happened, just for a moment fear would bloom inside Joan, dark and frantic, uncontainable, at the sight of her husband rising above her, foreshortened and monumental, like a tree growing out of her chest.

Years later in that marriage, they had grown so bored they went back to school instead of back to the land—he studied horticulture and Joan studied art history. Him in a greenhouse, pruning shears in his back pocket, folding back the petals of a flower. Her in a darkened auditorium, chin in hand, making thumbnail sketches of paintings in a notebook: clocks draped over trees; crutches holding up broken noses; a woman with bureau drawers set into her chest, knobs shaped like nipples. A single knotty carrot, a pipe hovering over the words *Ceci n'est pas une pipe*. She drew her husband's face, with their little brass pot pipe. *Ceci n'est pas un mariage*. In the black auditorium, a new slide clicked into place and Joan stared, pen suspended over her notes. Another Magritte metaphor: a room filled up with a huge garish rose, its petals bent back against the ceiling, walls, and floor. *Le tombeau des lutteurs*.

The stranger kicked her legs out from under her, flipped her onto her back, and sat on her chest, pressing her arms to the floor with his knees. He looked around.

The bookshelf, the table next to her armchair, the lamp, the cord to the lamp.

From that angle, her first husband had looked like Tom Petty, droopy haired and stoned, restored to affection for the pink-faced girl pinned beneath him—but this was a stranger, his hair dark and lusterless, flopped down over his forehead. He was hurting her, compressing her lungs, swinging his head back and forth, scanning the room in an exaggerated manner. For what? What was he looking for?

He leaned back to grope for something, shinbones pressing like rebar into her upper arms, and she realized she could shout.

Crazy. To make her last word be a dog's name.

PILGRIM!

The stranger took the yardstick, leaning against the wall, and laid it across her windpipe.

Ceci n'est pas une pipe.

Outside, Pilgrim pulled his head, shoulders, forepaws, and torso from a groundhog hole out by the back fence. He stood listening intently to the summer evening, nose lifted, and then turned his dirty face like a radar dish toward the house.

It was the same yardstick she had used earlier in the day to measure her stocking feet, each one in turn, to see if they were exactly the same size. She was more of a scholar than a mathematician—every time she measured she got something different—and managed to occupy herself for a pretty long time. The dogs were with her and she had measured their tails; the big black dog with a long nose and the intelligent brown eyes of a chimpanzee, and little Spock, thickset and amiable, with a triangular head that he could force like a wedge into all kinds of spots.

He had just that morning captured a chipmunk in the daylilies and carried it, squeaking, around the front yard. Joan had thrown open the window and leaned out, calling to the dog in a high, insistent, flattering voice. He looked around in alarm, and then up to where she was. He began wagging his hindquarters, lifting his ears high off his scalp, trying to figure out what she wanted.

"Come here, Spock!" she cried coaxingly. "Come here, boy!"

That long-ago lamb, lifting its head from the ground, had bleated at her, a drawn-out pleading, lonely sound. She only just remembered it. "Spockeeee!" she cried in a singsong, and then made as though she were running away from the window.

Spock dropped his prize and ran to meet her at the front door, panting.

. . .

Joan thrashed, arching like a fish tossed on the bank, and then quieted, focusing on getting air past the obstruction on her throat. She concentrated, gasping, staring past the stranger, who seemed impatient, almost bored. He bounced a little, pressing on the yardstick, when he thought she wasn't suffocating fast enough.

Pilgrim trotted around the house, nose to the ground, past the limestone wall, the lilac bush, a mound of disturbed dirt, the faint heady cologne of a cat. The bed of smooth river pebbles, a clump of hyacinths, and suddenly he ran into it, like a thick pane of glass—STRANGER—and followed it around to the front door, snorting frantically against the frame of the flimsy screen. STRANGER.

He sounded the alarm.

While Pilgrim was excavating the groundhog tunnel, Spock had been napping in the fern bed behind the outhouse, an unused shed with tattered flower-sprigged wallpaper and a worn plank with two sad holes in it. A garter snake lived in there, and some tiny large-eyed mice. Earlier, unbelievably, a possum had gotten up on the roof of it, via a little tree that could barely support its weight. Spock had been so invigorated by this he had taken down all the trumpet vines. The possum was still up there, inert and pink, and Spock was sprawled on his back asleep, large paws retracted against his chest, delicate fronds smashed flat beneath him.

The stranger exerted the required pressure without even glancing down at her, as though he could more or less do it by feel, like gliding underneath a chassis and tightening a bolt, gliding out again.

If the yardstick had been wood it might have broken, but instead it was metal with a cork backing. Flexible and inefficient, suffocating her, but slowly. It was as though her windpipe were a thin blue tube being wound tightly in gauze, layer after layer.

Let the yardstick work for you.

Roy and Joan in that long-ago art gallery, after hours, moonlight washing across a grove of pedestals on which they placed metal sculptures. Roy made up names for the amorphous polished blobs: "Underpants I, II, and III," or "I've Fallen and I Can't Get Up." He and Joan wore cotton museum gloves and listened to new wave music on the radio. They were lingering in the gloom, putting off going home to their respective spouses. A song by Elvis Costello came on, a ballad, irresistible. They danced in the dark gallery, white hands on each other's backs, singing along: *I see you've got a husband now.*

The metal yardstick pinched her neck and she saw glistening particles around the stranger's face, which had darkened, the room flattening up against his head like a cutout. Joan didn't exactly fake her own death; she simply left the scene of the crime—stopped resisting and faded backward into herself, like a fish swimming to the bottom of a pond.

Roy wasn't even around anymore. He had died of cancer. Joan looked for him in the murk. At the lake where she first lived when she came to New York, fat, tattered goldfish had risen from the depths whenever it rained to nibble at the drops, as though a big child were shaking food into their bowl. She used to watch them from her porch, slender glimpses of orange beneath the blue, varnished surface of the lake.

She should have been a painter; she always knew that.

Joan had seen a physics demonstration once where a bullet was fired into a slab of gel, its trajectory made visible by a jagged tunnel in the pale amber block. Just in that moment, gazing up at the matte brown of the stranger's hair, she heard it again, the sound of the report like a cap gun right next to the ear.

Joan had known someone who was shot, but he wasn't anywhere in sight; none of the people she might have expected to see were at the bottom of her pond. Mother? Father? Her eyes were wide, searching, but the only thing visible was her own hair, drifting in front of her like seaweed.

The stranger was startled from the task at hand; he clambered to his feet, tripping over Joan's body, and lurched against the wall. Pilgrim had hooked one of his muddy toenails through the screen and prized the flimsy door open a foot or so against its latch. When he let go, the bottom of the door snapped shut against the wood frame, creating a sharp report that reverberated through the house. He did it again, then gave up, threw all his energy into a baying, hysterical howl.

STRANGER . . . STRANGER . . . STRANGER.

Spock found himself in front of the house before he even knew he was awake. He bolted around in a joyous, dirt-churning circle, barking into the evening air.

On the roof of the shed, the possum opened one eye.

Too much commotion at once: the cacophony of dog yelps; the sharp noise, like two blocks of wood clapped together; the blurred sound of toenails being raked across a screen. The stranger glanced down at the body, boneless and vacated, mouth slack, eyes fixed and staring. More in common now with the carpet or the chair than with him. He looked out the window to the yard below. The black dog was trembling and baying, staring at the door.

In the woods behind the house, a silver coyote glanced up from what used to be a deer. The nearest neighbor, just getting home from work, stood next to his car for a moment, listening to Pilgrim and Spock, and then went on inside, where his wife was cooking dinner and his sons were watching the Three Stooges. Good old-fashioned black-and-white mayhem, and the after-work sound of meat frying.

The stranger stepped on Joan's outflung hand as he strode from the room.

Way back in the Iowa farmhouse days, Joan and her first husband had woken one morning to find they had survived a tornado. There was a wide swath cut across the cornfield next to their shed. The tornado had gone through a fence neatly, lifting it like a row of stitching from a hem, and then turned and run alongside the house, uprooting the soft-faced pansies and leaving in its wake a farmer's feed bucket, a muddy wind sock, and what looked like a waterlogged stuffed toy that turned out to be a kitten. Joan hadn't wanted to go to the cellar during the night because she had seen an obese toad down there, a horrible depressing creature who seemed to have eaten himself into a corner—he had grown so fat that his arms and legs didn't reach the ground; he was like a soft gray stone about the size of her foot, resting in a puddle of ancient exploded preserves. So they had remained upstairs on their mattress on the floor with the collie between them, getting up on their elbows every once in a while to peer out at the wild, whipping storm. At some point they had watched a ball of blue lightning travel back and forth between the house and the barn on an electrical wire, and had thought they might be going to die, but still they had lain in bed, unwilling to face the giant toad.

Joan hadn't let her husband bury the kitten that was flung onto their sidewalk in the tornado. At the last minute, while placing it in the hole, she decided maybe it wasn't really dead, and carried it out to the tall grass and left it there, just in case.

She came slowly back to herself, there on the floor of her study, lungs inflating and deflating until she could feel everything at once: crushed nose, thread of blood running across her cheek, the blue stem of windpipe.

The kitten had been gone the next morning, carried off in the jaws of whatever carries things off in the night. The sounds they would hear sometimes in that farmhouse, in the darkness, insane snarling fights, agonized cries deep inside the corn. From outside came the sound of Pilgrim's growling attack, a sickening thump. Joan pulled herself up to the window and looked out. The stranger was kicking her dog. Once, twice, off the flagstone stoop and into the shrubbery, yelping.

Then only Spock was visible in the early evening light, a white dog with a stick in his mouth, keeping just out of reach.

The stranger swept his boot sideways, knocking her geraniums off the stoop, homely Martha Washingtons, with neat scalloped leaves and lavender fringed petals. It was like kicking someone's grandmother.

Her neck, her dog, her flowers.

When she was a little girl, her grandma Bess had hung bed linens on the line down at Joan's height, letting them rest wetly on the clean grass as she set the pins, then lifting the line high with a notched pole until the sheets were off the ground, snapping feebly around in the breeze. Joan would walk in a kid trance through the damp white rows, a clothespin pinching each of her fingers, feeling the thin cloth against her face.

In the gloomy confines of that grandmother's living room was a mirrored coffee table made of cobalt glass that reflected Joan's face in a mesmerizing way, blue and desolate. She had loved that grandma, a silent, opinion-less woman from the unpopular side of the family. At Grandma Bess's house, there were no frightened farm animals, no knife-wielding butchers; she had her own gentle version of hens and chicks, cunning little succulent plants that spread in a low green flock across the cracked dirt by her back door, kept alive with periodic drenchings of dishwater. She used a rusted enamel dishpan with a rock in the center for a birdbath, and did her business out back in a shed. Once, eating dinner at someone's house with her parents and sister, Joan had piped up, remarking that her grandma Bess had the same kind of soup pot underneath her bed. That was one of Joan's famous childhood jokes, although she herself didn't get it at the time.

She peered down at her spilled geraniums, the curtain like a shroud against her face. The clay pots were broken into large pieces. She had spectral visions of herself on the front lawn—there was young Joan at her grandma's house, whirling through the laundered sheets as the sparrows landed on the rock and sipped at their bathwater; there was Joan crouching to look at the hens and chicks; there was Joan kneeling, gazing down through the blue coffee table atmosphere at her image floating below, disembodied and deprived. She had to touch her own mashed nose just to see if she was still alive.

The pain was dazzling, invigorating, like poking her brain with an ice-cold wire; she did it again, this time imagining a pair of shining tongs pushing alcohol-soaked cotton balls into her head. She'd read that in a story somewhere, a woman staring helplessly at a doctor as he packed her mangled nose with what felt like burning snow. Joan closed her eyes and pressed firmly against the shattered bridge, until she was rewarded with a surge of endorphins.

She opened her eyes.

He had been looking for something to lure the white dog, that's why he got in the refrigerator in the first place; he had decided to make a clean sweep of it, because he hated dogs anyway and the fact that the thick white one thought this was all a game— well. The stranger liked to play games himself, and this was one. Have a slice of cheese, dog, if you call this cheese.

In another Magritte metaphor, a man stares into a mirror and instead of seeing his face, sees the back of his own head. The dead woman behind him was noiseless, but he felt a shift, the still air giving way as the shovel was cocked back, and then he somehow was behind himself, seeing what she saw right up to the moment that the black bowl of the shovel hit the side of his head, at which point he heard not the sound of a gravedigger hitting rock but a sudden loud silence.

Joan had already killed something once, with her car, on a bitter night when snow was blowing into her headlights. A flash of antler, a shoulder thudding into the front bumper on the passenger side, and suddenly the animal was up on the hood of her car, sliding across it, into the windshield, and then off onto the ground, taking the side-view mirror and leaving a trail of fur. It was late on a black night, and Joan had been so startled that she screamed as she pulled the car over and looked behind her. There was nothing. Then something, a glimpse of turmoil, over on the gravel, the deer struggling to right itself, chin on the ground, trying to gather its legs beneath it. She began to tremble and cry, when suddenly the cracked windshield sagged inward and fell all around her, into her lap, down the front of her coat, like chunks of ice, and she drove on, into the windy stinging darkness, her face frozen.

Driving away from the dying deer was the worst thing she had ever done; it was how she had come to know herself as a coward, and for a long time afterward she had tried to atone by helping things off the road, either before they were killed or after, which is how she ended up with the little titanium shovel in her trunk. She used it now to reach across the man and push the refrigerator door closed.

. . .

His grandmother had been worn out from being married to a drunken gravedigger and raising six children and various grandchildren next to a sprawling cemetery. Just a backyard, a runoff ditch, and then acres of tombstones—some old, mossy ones with rounded shoulders and stricken, ornate messages and some modern, ranch-style ones in bright, rectangular granite inscribed with more circumspect messages. The old gravedigger himself ended up cremated, reduced to a pile of grit that seemed more like him than the previous version.

So, the gravedigger's grandson knew his way around a shovel, because they all did, or the boys anyway. They had to sit in the equipment shed during the service, an agonizingly slow and silent play that couldn't be hurried no matter what—there was always somebody who needed two people to help them walk; there was always a kid who lay down on the ground in his good clothes; there was always a pair of startling legs tottering in high heels; there were always old people who had to walk around saying hello to other tombstones before hobbling back to their car, getting in, starting it, and then fucking sitting there while it warmed up or cooled off. Only when the last car had finally crunched along the gravel road to the gate could they pick up their shovels and head across to cut up and throw dirt on each other while the old man cussed at them.

It was actually a nice thing to think about, the mysterious stately behavior of the black-clad people, the smell of rich dirt, the worms who didn't know they were cut in half. He let it keep him company now, wherever this was he was.

Joan had seen a number of dead things in her life, and although the man on her kitchen floor looked strangely flat and ruined, he didn't look dead. On his side, one arm lodged behind him, the palm facing up, the other arm slumped forward at the shoulder, elbow bent, the hand resting somewhere under the edge of the cereal and wineglass cupboard. She needed to get that hand, somehow put it with the other hand, and tie them together behind his back.

Rope, rope, rope.

All around her, things had come loose from their meanings and were washing in and out with her breath like tidewater: the planks of afternoon sunlight laid across the kitchen floor, the plaid dog leash looped over a chair, the garish paste jewels shimmering next to her lunch, cast by the prism hanging in the window over the sink. A giant rose, a single knotty carrot, a man in a bowler hat, his face obliterated by an apple.

Ceci n'est pas toi.

In fact, she had been a good-natured child, cartwheeling around the lawn, throwing the ball for the family's terrier, grinning gap-toothed into cameras, whistling, constantly with her arm hooked around the neck of one skinny cousin or another.

Her neck, her dog, her flowers.

Out the kitchen window, a heron stalked the edge of the pond, searching for grubs, jabbing its long beak into the mud and then tipping it up toward the sky, like a frail child playing with a sword. Beyond the pond, inside the woods, the coyote lay stretched out on the ground with a bone between his paws, like a dog. The bone had strings of flesh attached to it and fur, some of which he peeled off and some of which he went ahead and ate. He hadn't killed the deer, a truck had hit it, and it had crawled off into the woods and tried to bury itself.

There were crows trying to bother him but unless they came down he refused to be bothered. They were above him, squawking.

It sounded like the comedian he used to watch on TV, the big man who wore an overcoat and a pirate's scarf, and who traipsed up and down the stage, bent over his microphone, squawking in helpless rage at the stupidity of women. *Oh! Oh! Oh!*

You cuuuuunt!

Now his cemetery was dark, the tombstones like bones poking up out of the ground. The ones he had liked were the ones who died before their time—men in their thirties, women in their twenties, three-year-olds. Hurried along by farm accidents, childbirth, whooping cough. You could feel the unfairness hanging over the tombstones.

Once, he helped bury a coffin two feet long, ivory colored with chrome handles, which had housed a waterhead baby that died at birth. That's what people called it then, and that's how he had pictured it, a baby with a head made out of rainwater. The features, the ears, everything, a baby's head that looked like a clear glass jar, only it was water.

He felt like finding that baby's grave and stretching out, resting his head, which it seemed like he was carrying in his hands; he couldn't tell. It might be where it was supposed to be, but it felt like a balloon. Only solid. And with a bad spot, like a melon that had sat in the melon patch too long. This bad spot didn't feel like mush, though, it felt like rain. Or not like rain, like pain.

She had visited a morgue once, and seen someone with a bullet wound. In a hospice room, she had seen her mother, and later, in a room down the hall, her father; in a hospital chapel, she had seen a stillborn baby in its mother's arms. The bullet had created a precise, catastrophic hole that was deeply startling, even though she was prepared for it; her mother had been awake until the end, struggling and translucent, like a baby bird forced out of the nest; her father, picked clean by the vulture of cancer, had grown quieter and quieter, until even his heart devolved into silence. The baby had been lavender, and perfect.

. . .

Spock circled the house, checking all his posts, stopping to fan his leg at the corner of the shed, the stand of daylilies, both Adirondack chairs. Usually when the crows sounded like that it meant something was out there to eat, and he and Pilgrim would pace along their invisible border and try to see what it was and who was eating it.

He had mostly run out of urine but he still had his stick, one with a twig coming off it that if he turned his head would poke him in the neck. When he found the right spot, Spock was going to settle down and chew the twig off. For now, he just kept turning his head, letting the twig dig its own grave.

The kitchen was strangely beautiful. Joan looked down and saw flowers foaming at her feet last week as she took a short-cut through the Queen Anne's lace. Something weird was happening to time—it was swirling instead of linear, like pouring strands of purple and green paint into a bucket of white and giving it one stir. Now was also then was also another then. She saw Spock nosing through summer brambles with a stick in his mouth and her husband in the snow cutting a Christmas tree, making the Jack Nicholson face he always made when he had occasion to use the ax.

Honey, I'm home!

The hand that was under the edge of the cupboard, she needed to get that out of there so she could see it.

The stranger was somewhere else now. The tombstones were gone and he was in his chair, in the dark. It was late at night and the comedian was on TV, ranting and sweating through his overcoat. *Oh! Oh! Oh!*

He pointed the remote but he couldn't turn it up. His fingers weren't working.

You biiiiitch!

The comedian had been hurried along by a drunk driver, T-boned on his way from a gig. Gigged on his way to a T-bone. They used to catch frogs, he and his cousin Kyle, and do the most inventive things to them. Sometimes though, they just fished, and that was almost as fun, simply because of Kyle. Nobody didn't have fun when they were with Kyle, who ended up hurried along by mysterious circumstances involving diving off a bridge drunk.

Once, in physics class, Joan had seen footage of a bridge with a fatal design error: when it was stressed, the bridge began bouncing, then rippling and then undulating, flinging off tiny horses and wagons and canvas-topped Model Ts, until it literally came loose from one shore and began flapping, like a sheet on a line. She had never forgotten that film, the darkened classroom awash in boredom, the teacher's voice intoning, the jumpy scarred footage, and then the sudden electric shock of seeing something so interesting and bizarre. In school, of all places.

In retrospect, it may not have come loose from the shore, she isn't sure. But the undulation, the rippling forces hurling the carriages and cars, that part she didn't dream and she didn't embellish for herself. When Joan was growing up back in Waverly, Iowa, she once had the opportunity to attend the Miss Waverly pageant, when her mother's friend's son's girlfriend was a contestant. It was the most sophisticated thing Joan had done up to that point—the pageant was held in the high school auditorium, a velvet-curtained venue that nobody from Joan's elementary school ever had occasion to visit. The contestant, Connie something, was freckled and dazzling, with an ineffable quality Joan had never seen before, and it was fitting that she be up for

Miss Waverly. She wore her hair ratted high and folded into a French twist for the gown competition, and with teased bangs and a shining false braid that draped across her shoulder for the swimsuit. There wasn't a lot of talent coming out of Waverly—one girl in fact mixed a cake onstage, wearing a gingham apron and reading the recipe in a loud, theatrical voice—but Connie's mother had rigged Connie up in a black leotard and given her a long white chiffon scarf. Like, really long. All the lights were turned off in the auditorium and Connie ran out from the wings flinging the scarf before her, followed by a black light. You could see glimpses of her eyes occasionally as she ran back and forth, and sometimes a purple grimace from her teeth as she exerted herself, but mostly all that was visible was the rippling scarf as she flung it and ran after it, and flung it again. The place was speechless afterward, and then erupted into wild clapping.

For weeks after that Joan and her sister would put on swimsuits and race around the backyard with long scarves made from a ruined bedsheet, until they ended up sweaty and defeated, the strips of stained sheets growing lighter and lighter while their arms grew heavier and heavier.

Other things could be used to tie someone up, but what? Meaning had begun to swirl along with time. Looped over one of the kitchen chairs was a plaid copperhead, its face a silver clasp. It was like a scene in a book she had once read, where a dog was bitten and ran home over a terrible distance with the snake, huge and black, dragging like a leash. In the same book the rising river overcame a cage full of lion cubs, a man tried to asphyxiate himself, another man was trapped under a log and drowned as the tide rose, another man listened to criminally hip jazz, and another man lashed his severed forearm to a boat. Men, men, men.

That's what she'd been reading about when he barged into her study, the strange notions of the surrealists, with their unmoored minds and their brutal depictions of women. Limbs severed into doll parts and rearranged, high heels turned upside down and presented on a platter like a roasted bird, paper frills on their stilettos. Little girls with hair like kudzu staggering down a dark corridor, a reclining woman heaped with food and men posed with utensils, eating her abdomen and breasts. A tangle of women arranged by the artist—his mustaches sharpened into the kind of antennae catfish use to feel their way through the muck at the bottom of the pond—so their naked bodies created the impression of a skull. *In Voluptate Mors.* From pleasure into death.

Joan's family had fished for sport, sitting on banks, pulling worms apart like licorice and pushing them onto hooks, hauling out catfish and bass, discarding the junk fish by tossing them backward into the weeds to suffocate. Joan was forbidden to put them back into the water and would just crouch there, willing them to die. Sometimes, a long time later, one that she had told herself was dead would flop, just once.

In the distance, crows were screaming about something. They were trying to tell her to get out of there. Forget the rope. *Go! Go! Go!*

The women artists of that long-ago era were ferociously steel eyed, their limber bodies occasionally bent in the service of one photographer or another, but rarely did they smile, even at picnics.

No, no, no.

Time swirled in its paint bucket, and she saw her own family at play, her father in an undershirt and her mother in a billed cap, both of them grinning. In the background were bluegills, hanging from a stringer, each the size of a baby's hand.

Next to the front porch, under the arborvitae, Pilgrim pulled himself forward, through the bramble to the flagstone. There were knives in him that stabbed each time he moved and he growled at them.

The birds and the squirrels and the chipmunks had a certain feel to them, so did the toads, but sometimes other things would move through—a fox, a skunk, the black snake, un-shy and curious, probing its nose along the stone foundation of the house and then coiling into the depression next to the willow stump, inanimate, like something that might have fallen off the wheelbarrow. Spock was made nervous by the black snake and would whine under his breath until it moved on. To Pilgrim, the snake was nobody's business but its own, though he didn't feel that way about everything. For instance, the groundhog, or the man in the kitchen.

He had left his chair now and was moving through the darkened house, looking for something. The TV flickered in the corner like an aquarium. Whatever he was looking for, a tool or something, or a weapon he could use as a tool, was eluding him. Gliding under the chassis, tighten, tighten, gliding back out. Something Kyle said once, now that he's remembering Kyle: if he ever had a daughter he would name her Chassis, because it was pretty. They were talking cars, all of them, and everyone had turned around and stared at Kyle.

Once you understood basic physics, you could use things as tools that weren't necessarily tools. A screw turned just so into a block of wood would lift the cap off a beer bottle more efficiently than a church key, a strand of dental floss would slice a cheesecake more cleanly than the sharpest knife. Et cetera. He would never use the right tool if he could use a better wrong one. Unlike the old man, who would demand his Polish problem solver (i.e., the hammer), and then whale on whatever it was until it broke free or just broke. Which is how one of the boys got three of his fingers cut off at age eleven, during an episode with a tree branch caught in the mower blade.

Gimme muh problem solver, the old man had said. And then *Lift the gawdam thing*. And then whack, whack, whack, until the blade sprang free and finished its revolution.

It wudden spose to do that was what the old man said to the sheriff, who drove out to look around after the hospital reported that a boy was brought in minus his fingers. Afterward, the old man cut up about what had happened, to regain his authority. *I thought he was a bawling like that cuz he dropped his posies*, he said in a mincing voice. They were meant to laugh and they probably did.

Not much was asked of those kinds of men back then; all day surrounded by manure and recalcitrant machinery, they just simmered in their meanness. The women too—every egg his grandmother cracked had shit and feathers stuck to it, every shirt she scrubbed with her own knuckles and ran through the wringer came out of the wash still smelling like the old man. She knew how to improvise a tool too, maybe that's where he learned it. Everything from a wooden spatula grabbed off the back of the stove to an extension cord to the old wire rug beater, which the boys called the Doug Beater, after a particular incident that got it retired permanently.

His head sloshed, making him feel seasick. He was looking for—what, again? A tool? Something he could use to pry something else open. They used to try telling the younger boys they were going to dig the coffins back up and make them look, but it never really scared them. They knew better. It was just flat-out too much work.

Doug had almost got retired along with the wire rug beater. He looked like he'd gone through a threshing machine, and all for bringing a tree toad into her kitchen, which the older boys had told him to do. They tiptoed around for days, staying out of her way as she tended to the wet rags and what all else that she had to keep putting on him. Age seven.

The TV people were swimming behind their glass but he couldn't make out who they were. Or where this was exactly; it had the feeling of home but he couldn't really see that well, so it might be someplace else. He was used to being wrong in the head, but not wrong like this, where he was just wandering around in the dark. He moved closer to the TV and in its flickering light he saw scattered across the rug those long-ago posies, pink and red, with their grime-rimmed nails and their gaggous stub ends, as real and unreal as anything in a Halloween haunted house.

Suddenly, he remembered: stepping on her hand as he strode from the room, and how it moved under his boot like a snake.

When Joan was a little girl, her sister used to torment her by pretending to be dead, slumped in a corner of the living room sofa, mouth slack, eyes fixed and staring, Wally Gator on TV, their mother banging around in the kitchen.

"I know you're not," Joan would say at first, sitting down in an armchair with her snack; watching television, keeping peripheral tabs on the eerily still body across the room, getting more and more certain that her sister was alive but also more and more uncertain at the same time. "I'm telling," she would try.

Nothing but a clanging stillness from the corner of the couch, until eventually Joan couldn't take it anymore, the utter lack of sister where there used to be a sister, panic rising like a tide, lifting her out of her chair and floating her across the room, where her sister would inevitably frighten her so badly that a long piercing shriek would leap out of Joan, unfurling into the domestic air of the household.

"If I hear it again, I don't care who did what. You'll both get the yardstick," her mother would say, standing in the doorway with a spatula in her hand. She liked a yardstick because it had an efficient and democratic feel to it—both offenders could be attended to with a single whistling swat. It didn't hurt, although Joan nevertheless became frantic and had to be chased down and dragged back, pleading for mercy like she was being taken to the gallows. Her sister would bend stoically over the sofa and just before the moment of impact move forward so that the yardstick hit the other person first. She told this tidbit to Joan when they were in their thirties.

Let the yardstick work for you.

She touched him again with the shovel. Nothing.

A credit card as a door key, a hollow pen as a tracheotomy tube, a self-locking trash tie as a handcuff. Or using an already employed tool in an off-use way—a fence post as a sundial, a flag as a weather vane, a drinking fountain as a urinal. Or even better, turning a regular tool into a metatool—a crowbar to kill a crow, for instance.

Oh! Oh! Oh!

He'd never hurried along a bird, but he could see how somebody might. His head felt different now, huge and hollow, like a fragile eggshell that all the yolk has been blown out of, forced through a tiny pinhole, turning his head into a big white dome with an echo. In school once a teacher had used a pencil to lift a human skull, inserting it into the eye socket and then turning it while pointing out its various features. The front, the side, the back, and all the while the skull nodding slightly, balanced on the pink-eraser end of a no. 2. He had felt an illicit jolt right at the moment the pencil disappeared into the eyehole; the deep, almost shuddering pleasure of it. *In Voluptate Mors.* Maybe three or four times it had happened over the years, his disreputable life appearing unexpectedly in the middle of his reputable one, like a harlot coming forward to slip her arm through the parson's.

He was wedged somewhere, one shoulder wrenched up under him, the big hollow dome of his head resting against something hard. Wherever this was, it felt like he was filling the space completely, as oversized and momentous as Paul Bunyan. All he needed was his ax.

Joan and her best friend, age fifteen, standing alongside a hot blacktop road in bikinis and sandals, hitchhiking home from Linden Lake, a GTO pulling over and picking them up, the two guys leaning forward obligingly to let them into the backseat.

Joan was shy, but her friend had folded her knees into the space between the bucket seats and thanked the driver and his friend. "It was a heat wave out there," her friend said fervently. She had large green eyes, expressive high-arched bony feet, and hair the color and texture of straw. The passenger-side guy was shirtless, his arm resting on the open window. Joan, directly behind him, was getting a faceful of BO. She gathered up her long tangled hair and pressed it against her nose.

They turned off the main highway and down a labyrinth of country roads, winding slowly and talking between themselves as though the two girls weren't present.

"Should we rape them?"

"I don't know, what do you think?"

"It's up to you."

"How about if I rape one and you can rape the other one."

"Okay."

"Which one do you want?"

"Both."

"Me, too."

Even though Joan thought there was a good chance they were kidding, she was overcome with regret, there in the backseat listening. At her own stupidity, at how she hadn't understood what it meant to be not supposed to hitchhike but now understood it completely. Her mother in a blue pantsuit with a pocketbook hanging from her arm, saying, "Boy, I better never hear of that."

As her friend shrank backward, shy Joan moved forward, leaning between their seats and grinning.

"Let's get some beer," she said.

They didn't even glance at her. The car slowed and turned onto a dirt lane that widened into a dirt road and then went over a stream.

"We need beer, you guys! Is there a place around here?"

Nothing. And then the driver glanced back at her. "It'll be more fun," she said, "and we've got money."

The other guy turned around in his seat and looked at them pointedly, up and down. They were wearing nothing but bikinis the size of eye patches and damp T-shirts.

He snorted.

Just at that moment, her friend braced herself and began kicking the driver in the head, over and over, using her leather-soled sandals like paddles against his ears and the back of his skull. He hollered and swerved, and she began on the other guy, her legs churning between the seats, attacking his shoulders and head. He swung at her, she placed her feet against the back of the driver's seat and pushed with all her might, screaming and yanking at the guy's hair, until he ran the car into the gravel and opened his door. He was pinned against the steering wheel, struggling, as Joan's friend clawed at his head.

"We were kidding," the driver bawled. "Kidding!"

The other guy stumbled onto the ground and let Joan out. The friend pushed her way past the driver, grabbing his ear and screaming, "You fucker, I'll kill you!" as she clambered out.

They peeled away in a swirl of dirt, honking and extending their middle fingers. Total country silence as the dust settled and the heat resumed. Joan and her friend realigned their eye patches, walked a mile or so back to the hard road, and because there was nothing else to do, stuck their thumbs out.

. . .

The dogs could work in tandem when the situation called for it. From the flagstones, Pilgrim lifted his nose and sniffed Spock sniffing him. High in the oak tree the feral cat watched them. Tandem required teamwork and stealth, one of which Spock was good at and the other of which he was definitely not. He circled Pilgrim now, a white blob in the dusk, his stick dropped somewhere and forgotten.

He'd always thought about it later, what he wanted to tell Kyle that time everyone was talking about cars: that he himself liked Chamois as a girl's name.

The thing he never could get over was that Kyle ended up keeping cats. Two of them that he always made like he was torturing in his free time, Sinker and Pet Sematary, but they hadn't read the memo and continued to climb up onto his lap and onto the back of his chair, meow in his face for food, et cetera.

Cats can swim. They don't necessarily want to, but they can. Kyle could swim, too, but when push came to shove, he didn't.

People will surprise you. Like this dead woman, who didn't seem all that dead, in that she was poking him in the shoulder with something.

Joan knew for a fact that human beings were sturdier than they looked. She had watched her mother struggling, sinking and waxy, the aperture of her world growing smaller and smaller until she was staring at her family through a pinhole. Then the pinhole closed and there was nothing but the grip of her long graceful hands. Inhalations and exhalations, long sighing moans that seemed to be words, or parts of words.

This was back in the art gallery days, and Roy's mother had been sick, too, dying of cancer at the same time that Joan's mother was dying of cancer. Different kinds, different hospitals, and Roy and Joan sprawled morosely in their chairs at work all day, comparing notes. Sometimes they closed the gallery and went to the movies, where they would sit in the darkness and hold hands. One day Joan started crying and couldn't stop, another day Roy. Once, they blew everything off to go down the street after work and drink until they were beside themselves. They staggered to a local hotel and tried to get a room, but were not allowed. Neither could figure out why not—they shouted at the desk clerk, a young black woman who shook her head and walked away, then came around from behind the desk and escorted them by the elbows out the revolving door. They climbed into Joan's little car and drove up and down the empty pedestrian mall, honking and veering around the benches and stone planters. That's all that happened, though it became one of Joan's most vivid memories: the dark beery neighborhood bar, the beautiful old restored hotel, the kindness of the desk clerk, the late-night interior of the Volkswagen. A few weeks later, when she came home from the hospital after her mother's death, Joan sat down on the sofa and stared straight ahead for a long time, waiting for something.

Whatever she was waiting for never came, but Roy did. They sat in silence, eating the donuts Roy brought with him and drinking the coffee that Joan made. At some point Roy said, "I guess my mom won."

The first time had been a game—Pilgrim digging at the base of the stump with Spock positioned behind him, jumping up and biting at the loose dirt as it was flung into the air. Suddenly, the dirt took shape and the shape was a mole and Spock caught it, and dropped it. A flat lozenge of fur with no face and little flesh paddles for feet. Pilgrim turned it over with his nose, stepped on it, and bit it.

Done.

His mother had been fed up with him before he was even born, according to the legend, pounding on her own stomach wherever he kicked, Whac-A-Mole style. He remembered exactly nothing of her except a looming sense of dread and an expanse of cool gray. Apparently he crawled over top of one of her magazines and tore the pages, and she rolled it up and whipped him with it until he ended up living elsewhere.

I moved out when I was one, he used to tell people.

The cool gray was probably from when they took him up to her casket. Not because anyone gave a shit, but because they wanted to see what he would do. Which was nothing, just like now. Do nothing while they're expecting it and soon enough they won't be expecting it.

Out at the edge of the pond, the heron was poised on one stick leg, neck extended and head tilted, as still as a lawn ornament. In the heron's mind time didn't swirl or move; the past and the future were thoroughly blended into the present and the present was focused, like a gooseneck lamp, on the dappled bank. In the shallows were the flickerings of tiny fish, and right at the edge of the water a small delectable frog sat motionless, indistinguishable from the mud and grass as long as he didn't blink.

The bird's success was based on movement so slow it was indiscernible. The frog's was based on blending, and powerful back legs that could propel him with a plop two feet out into the pond. Should the need arise.

.   .   .

The second time they worked in tandem had been a squirrel. Spock didn't want to let go when Pilgrim grabbed it too, and for a moment it became a tug toy, until it made a sound like a kitten and then Spock did let go.

The third time they worked in tandem, the groundhog had been coming perilously close to the invisible fence. Pilgrim and Spock were at their stations, waiting, as he dragged his blubber back and forth between one mound of dirt and a neighboring mound of dirt.

When the groundhog finally made his mistake, they were on him, and just for an instant, before they dragged him in, the fence got involved too, vibrating through their collars in its own excitement.

The heron slept in an enormous laundry basket at the top of a tall tree. There was a certain point when it would be summoned up there by an invisible force that was both external and internal. The force was exerted at a specific moment, right before darkness settled its skirts over the pond.

He no longer looked like a sandbag. He was flat and still, but the air around him seemed animated. Joan stepped back, reached out, and put the blade of the shovel on his shoulder and pushed. Nothing, but it felt different somehow.

Light was penetrating his dark living room; it was grainy and swirling, amniotic. He felt rinsed clean and pure, like the baby with its head full of rainwater, getting ready to be born.

He moved his finger and it moved.

· · ·

Joan felt it more than saw it. Some subtle movement. The hand under the edge of the wineglass cupboard was awake.

The frog blinked a split instant before the invisible force caused the heron to open its wings and lift off. The frog was either in the pond or in the heron as it flew slowly past the kitchen window, long legs dangling, and Joan felt the gray shadow just as the dogs arrived at the kitchen door and threw themselves at the screen.

Somehow, lightning fast, the stranger had her by the ankle. Joan lifted the shovel like a sword as the dogs bayed at the screen.

When the mighty turtle had grabbed the shovel, Joan had to drag him across the grass for a few feet before he let go, and that's what she did now, tugging her foot until the stranger's arm was fully outstretched, his head lolled back, the hand like a constrictor around her ankle.

Turtles are not amphibians, as Joan always forgot. They are reptiles.

She leaned back as far as she could until she could just reach the screen door with the shovel.

Let the dogs work for you.

His grandmother had come out in the yard and picked up those long-ago posies from the ground, dropped them in a coffee can, and carried it back inside. He heard himself grunting now the way she did when she bent over, and he was being hurried along, tugged back and forth as the dogs worked in tandem, until he heard himself making a sound like a kitten. When the delicate blue stem of his windpipe was finally unwrapped, the stranger felt a great happiness overtake him. *In morte voluptas.* From death into pleasure.

Chances were he'd end up where Kyle had ended up, and nobody didn't have fun when they were with Kyle.

Marjorie Celona
Counterblast

We WERE ON THE PLANE, Barry and I, when he put his
wedding ring in his mouth and started flipping it around
with his tongue. This was six years before the divorce. We were
on our way to Barry's father's funeral in Cincinnati. It was the
end of June, muggy season in the Midwest. The ring fell, pinged
off the tray table in front of us, bounced off his shoe, and disappeared. We looked at each other. I was too tired to be annoyed,
my one-year-old daughter, Lou, balanced on my knee, a sweet
sheen of drool on her chin foreshadowing an incoming incisor.
Everyone was buckled. We were about to take off. Like worms,
Barry and I bent from our midsections, trying to see the floor,
our legs in the way. My husband leaned one way, I leaned the
other.

Barry Sr. liked to drink and he liked women, especially me.
He liked to hold me and tell me things about my husband. He
was a crier when he drank, tears running into his beard. *Barry is
so special, so very special*, he used to say, referring, I think, to my
husband's inability to hold down a job. Back then, my husband
was the kind of guy who was always on the cusp of doing something great. He was the kind of guy who had potential.

My husband unbuckled, and then the stewardess was there.

"My wedding ring," my husband said, still a worm, his head bobbing around my calves.

I could see the stewardess waiting to hear the bitchiness in my tone, the tired mother of a teething baby come alive, the dragon-hell-beast wife let loose. She looked at me and I said nothing.

At the time, Barry was so attractive that everyone wanted our marriage to fail. What Barry never understood was that 90 percent of his good fortune was because of his looks. No balding fatso walks into a bar and gets a free drink is all I'm saying. Right out of college, he got an agent for a book of essays he was writing about growing up with an alcoholic father. He had yet to finish a single one. But people wanted to be seen with Barry. They thought he was "going places." Barry, on the other hand, just thought people were kind. I'd put a lot of money on this: if my husband had been ugly, he would have been homeless.

Barry took off his shoe and peered into it. If memory serves, they were tan desert boots—we both wore desert boots back then. He took out the insole, peered in again. "I felt it bounce off my shoe," he said. I gave him hell-beast eyes.

The stewardess was on her hands and knees now, using a tiny flashlight to scan under our seats. She shimmied up the aisle, checking under the seats in front of us. I could see the backs of her thighs. "His wedding ring," she said, and everyone snapped to attention. She had big hair and seemed too enthusiastic. Everyone became a worm, bobbing. I felt so sad I could hardly stand it. The tiny engraving on the inside of the wedding band: our initials and the date it happened. I kissed Lou's fat cheek.

My husband took off his other shoe. I felt a sort of nondescript rage. He took out the insole. Peered into the shoe as though it went on for miles. He shook the shoe. He shook it again.

The people around us were bobbing, rooting, uprooting. The stewardess stood. She flipped her big hair. She announced to the passengers, though oddly not to us, that when the plane landed we would search for the ring. And we would find it, she said. My husband looked at me, and I saw that he was sadder than I.

"I bet you can't believe you married me right now," he said. "I bet you're regretting your life."

"I love you," I told him, but he was looking in his shoe again. "Stop it," I said. "Stop looking in your shoe."

"Hmm?" he said, peering into its inner depths.

"It's not in your shoe."

"I felt it go in."

My husband was the only person who had ever loved me as much as I needed to be loved. Everyone up to this point had loved me in a sinister way. My husband was the first good person I had ever met.

"It's either in the shoe, or not in the shoe," I said. "There's no secret cavity, no porthole to another time, no wormhole into another universe. Stop looking in your shoe."

"Hey," said the man behind us. "Hey, guys."

We looked over our shoulders, through the tiny gap between our seats. Lou was already looking at the man. He was bald, like she was at the time, and she gave him a big, gummy smile.

"Look," said the man. In his hand was my husband's wedding ring. "It was in my backpack."

"See," said my husband, "that's almost impossible. It would have been more likely for it to be in my shoe."

"Thanks," I told the man. "Wow. Thanks so much."

Lou protested in my arms. She had just been diagnosed with in-toeing, which was a fancy way of saying pigeon-toed, but only on the left side. We were supposed to put her in this thing that looked like a little ski boot, but we kept making excuses.

Barry Sr. died in his cabin in Kentucky. Cirrhosis of the liver. My husband was writing an essay about it. And a poem. The funeral was going to be a small affair—me, the baby, Barry, and Barry's older sister, Lonnie. Barry's mother had taken off years ago. I'd never met her. After her kids were born, Lonnie had hired a private detective to try to find her, but it was as if she didn't exist.

My flying phobia comes and goes, even now. I get tics when I'm stressed. The flying phobia is one of them. I also become ticklish, cripplingly so. But I wasn't too anxious on that flight to Cincinnati. Besides, if we had died, that's how I would have wanted it to happen: all of us together; a quick, lethal plunge.

In those days, my brain was a vortex, a sinkhole, a maelstrom. I was still nursing round the clock, hadn't had a period in almost two years, could gather my stomach in my hands and shape it into a loose doughnut, my belly button in the center. *Stop the planet, I want to get off!* was something I said a lot in those days.

Barry and I had brought too much luggage to Cincinnati, including a giant backpack with all of Lou's stuff that made Barry look like a snail. He was bumping into other disembarking passengers with it, and so I trailed behind him, baby in my arms, apologizing. Lonnie was waiting in a maroon station wagon outside. She was a large woman, as tall as Barry, with dark brown hair to her shoulders and frizzy bangs. She wore rimless glasses that magnified her eyes, jean shorts, and a Reds T-shirt. White orthotic sandals. She was fifteen years older than Barry and I. She was a no-nonsense Midwesterner. The kind of woman who doesn't flinch when a baby cries. The kind of woman who gets things done.

I sort of hated her.

The humidity found its way between my breasts, between my legs. Lou and I panted, pulled away from each other's sticky skin. Barry loaded the luggage, then the big backpack, and took Lou from my tired arms. I loved this about him, this masculine call to action—*I'll load the things! Sit tight, you woman!* I looked at Lonnie. I hugged her. I held her shoulders, then ran my hands down her body until I was holding her by the waist. It wasn't meant to be sexual. But somehow I got it wrong, and she wiggled away from me. "Whoa there, Edie," she said to me.

The only thing to say was, "I'm sorry for your loss," so I said it and then we got in the car. I sat in the back with Lou in my arms and let Lonnie talk at Barry. She told him all the family gossip—so many goddamned cousins, every one of them named Anna—while I stared at the shape of her head, how she and Barry had the same high cheekbones. I could see her hands on the steering wheel and they were Barry's hands, only smaller. The same weird, curved thumb. Lou had it, too.

While Lonnie drove, I pointed at things out the window to Lou, but she was interested in her feet. She could put her toes in her mouth. I loved her feet in a way I thought wasn't entirely normal. Did other people love their babies this much? I had searched the index of a parenting book for what to do when you love your baby too much but had come up with nothing. I'd wanted to write an angry essay ever since I'd had Lou. I wanted to give the essay to people like Lonnie, who believed in letting babies cry themselves to sleep, and thought that babies should sleep in cribs in their own rooms the day they came home from the hospital. But I couldn't shout at Lonnie now. Her father had just drunk himself to death.

"Oh, so you abandoned your baby?" I'd said when Lonnie told me her babies had slept through the night after doing "cry it out" for a week. I don't even remember why I'd called. I think I'd been having trouble nursing.

"It worked for our family," she said flatly.

"I've heard torture works, too," I said.

It had been our last exchange.

We wound through the hills of Kentucky, and then the Cincinnati skyline was upon us, looking—it always surprised me— like a miniature London. Lou had fallen asleep. Lonnie took a small detour and took us over the Roebling Bridge, my favorite bridge into the city. It was her Midwestern way of telling me I was forgiven.

The trouble was neither Barry nor I had made any money in almost two years. My pregnancy had decimated me. I'd vomited for nine long months. Other women went back to work when their babies were six weeks old, but I couldn't fathom it. I knew it was wrong to abandon Lou so young. *Stop the planet, I want to get off!* It seemed to me that the world was kinder to dogs than it was to babies.

Barry had a gig freelancing for the local alt-weekly but had trouble finishing articles. His desk was littered with yellow legal pads filled with brilliant half-written pieces, deadlines blown. We had seven credit cards between us, about sixty grand's worth of debt. I'd had a complicated delivery. Three days in the hospital. The fact that Barry couldn't look after us brought out the old equality-versus-liberation argument in me. To pay our bills I got a visiting professorship in women's studies, and I took Lou with me. I nursed her while I talked to my students about Germaine Greer. She slept in the front-pack carrier while I wrote on the blackboard about the construct of gender. She played with little wooden blocks during department meetings. When I was told this was unacceptable, I quit. I was so angry at the world that I could hardly stand it. I wanted grand gestures of rage. I wanted a sword fight. I wanted a beheading. I wanted ugly, ugly violence. Instead, Barry walked Lou around the neighborhood while I taught part-time at the community college. I returned home three days a week, breasts so big they barely fit in the car. I made fifty dollars a week. We were both hoping for some kindness in Barry Sr.'s will.

Lonnie had bought our plane tickets. She put us in her guest room—a cramped affair with a double bed and an old crib set up in the corner, though I knew we'd sleep with the baby wedged between us. I nursed Lou in secret. Lonnie dragged up a high chair from her basement and placed mashed sweet potatoes and shredded chicken and a cup of whole milk on the tray, and I pretended that my baby was fully weaned.

I lay on the bed in the guest room while Lou napped, her mouth around my nipple. She was snoring, and I stroked her forehead, her little nose. Photos of Lonnie's three children were all over the walls, so many photos that it looked like they had spent their whole childhoods at the photo center at Sears. All three of them—teenagers now—were in Canada with Lonnie's husband. None of them was coming to the funeral.

Though it was six years before our own sad parting, my husband and I were already surrounded by the carnage of other marriages. One by one, our friends found reasons to live apart— Fulbright years, sick mothers, sabbaticals, new jobs—until we were the only ones with rings on our fingers, the only ones wondering what to buy for the upcoming anniversary. I started looking at Barry as though he were a mole I'd found somewhere on my body. Where was the cancerous part of him, the part that would slowly kill me? His laziness seemed more like artistic selectivity in those days. We both believed a job would rob him of his time to write. Talent like Barry's, well, you didn't come across it every day, etc. I remember watching him sometimes, though, and thinking that if he were less good-looking, I'd never let him get away with it—the not working; the slovenliness; the one-sided relationships he had with people in which they'd give him things in exchange for being his friend, and aside from an hour or two of his lovely eyes blinking at them, he'd never give anything back in return.

Lou started suckling again, and I felt my milk let down. I studied the curve of her left foot. What if I never put her in the little white boot? What if I just let nature run its course? Would she be bowlegged on one side? Walk with a weird gait? A limp? Barry opened the door an inch and looked at me with a wide eye. He opened the door another inch. "Dinner," he whispered. For some reason, he had his shirt off.

I squeezed my breast, trying to get the milk out faster. Lonnie had nursed her babies on a schedule from the minute they were born, once every four hours, no more, no less. One time I had tried to space out Lou's feeds a little, and she cried so hard and so loud that I didn't stop shaking for hours. The way I felt when Lou cried was worse than the pain of childbirth. What would have happened if Lonnie had known I was still nursing? Nothing. Maybe one comment. Two. But I couldn't see that then. I was fighting with her in my head. I switched Lou to the other breast and whispered for her to hurry up until she was done.

I carried Lou into Lonnie's dining room, put her in the high chair, and waited to see what Lonnie would serve her. I was nervous that Lou would start crying and Lonnie would call her "fussy," a term that enraged me. I did not believe that babies just cried. I certainly had never cried for the hell of it. There it was: the anger rising in my chest. I had researched the "cry it out" technique after a few sleepless nights left me devastated with fatigue. You were supposed to let your baby cry for fifteen minutes at a time before you went to him. When he vomited, which he would eventually do from all the retching, you were supposed to clean it up swiftly and then continue to let him cry, lest he learn that vomiting was a surefire way to get you to hold him. If you did this for seven nights, your baby would stop crying out for you. I narrowed my eyes at Lonnie and imagined tossing the hot casserole dish of lasagna at her.

"Noodles," Lonnie said to Lou, and put a scoop on her tray. "Mmm." She had changed into her nurse's uniform—purple scrubs and clogs, socks with little hearts on them. I couldn't imagine being Lonnie. Working nights; threading IVs into veins; emptying bedpans. I felt oppressed if I had to make a phone call.

"Is she walking yet?" said Lonnie.

"A little," Barry said.

"My babies were early walkers," Lonnie said. "All three of them."

Lou picked up a long ribbon of lasagna noodle and flung it behind her.

"Oh," I said. "Lou."

"Don't worry about it," said Lonnie. "That's what they do. You should get a dog, Edie."

Lonnie's dining room was grandmotherly—floral wallpaper and dark wainscoting, black-and-white photographs of her and Barry's grandparents in tiny metal frames, a curio cabinet full of ceramic dogs. She told us she'd just gotten around to taking down her Easter decorations. I gave Barry a look to see if he found this as funny as I did, but he was scooping lasagna into his mouth with a kind of fervor. He was still bare chested.

Lonnie cleared her throat for Barry to stop eating. I gripped Barry's hand and reached for Lou's chubby, noodle-covered fingers.

"Bless us, O Lord, and these thy gifts, which we are about to receive from thy bounty, through Christ our Lord," Lonnie said. "Amen."

"Amen," said Barry.

"Almond," I said.

Lonnie's head was still bowed, and I saw that she was crying. I nudged Barry under the table, and he stood and held his sister's shoulders. "Hey, hey, hey," he whispered. Barry's chest was slick with sweat. I thought I'd turn on the air once she left. I hated people who didn't turn on their air.

"I'm okay," she said. She took her glasses out of her pocket and checked her watch. "Let's eat. I'll be fine."

Something about the lasagna—how it tasted so good, how it was so perfectly and painstakingly put together—made my heart thick with sorrow. I could see the black tidal wave of depression approaching through the dining room window,

cresting at the front of Lonnie's lawn, crashing over her bego-
nias, and then rushing toward me, over the cobblestone path
to the front door, over the welcome mat, the beige shag carpet,
knocking over the suede sectional and its matching ottoman,
and pooling at my feet. Ultimately it was not Barry's laziness or
good looks that ended our marriage, it was me. I waited until
Lou started first grade and then I calmly told Barry that I didn't
want to be us anymore.

"Before you leave, Lonnie," said Barry. "Show me where your
ironing board is?"

"In the linen closet." She cut her lasagna into bite-size pieces
with her fork and then shook Parmesan cheese over each piece.
I stared at Lou, who had transferred her dinner onto the floor.

"Whoops," said Lonnie. She disappeared into the kitchen
and returned with a wet washcloth. Lou grabbed her cup of
milk and tossed it. Lonnie rubbed the cloth over Lou's face and
hands, and Lou protested against the straps of the high chair,
threw her head back, and started to cry.

"Stop," I said to Lonnie. "I'll clean her up later."

"Sometimes, Edie," she said to me, "you have to let them cry
a bit." She turned back to Lou. "Now hold still."

I pushed Lonnie aside and took Lou in my arms. She rubbed
her lasagna-covered hands into her eyes and into her hair. She
wiped her face on my blouse. She was doing her distress cry, and
I felt my milk let down. I rummaged in my pocket for a pacifier
and pushed it into her mouth, and she plunked her little head
down on my shoulder.

"Oh," said Lonnie. "She still takes a pacifier?"

I thought of all I had to do in the next twenty minutes: take
Lou into the bathroom, run the bath, wash her, dry her, rediaper
her, get her in her pajamas, nurse her—all that bending down,
all that lifting her off the floor, all that rocking—and then the
long, sleepless night ahead of us. I thought of all I had to do in
the next two days: find a way to nurse Lou during the funeral,

find a way not to shout at Lonnie about being too rough with Lou, get Lou down for her naps, get her down in the evening, pretend the next morning that she had slept through the night, drink Lonnie's cheap supermarket coffee and artificial creamer, listen to her talk about nap-time schedules and pacifier use. And then, of course, there'd be the inevitable argument about how Barry Sr. had been a good man and a good father, how he had a "light" within him that only she could see. I thought of all I had to do, and I wanted to crawl under the table and cry.

"Gotta go," Lonnie said. She kissed Barry's forehead and waved to Lou and me. "I'll be back around four," she said, meaning four in the morning. "The funeral is at one tomorrow. I'll try to be up by ten."

"Sleep in," I said. "We can look after ourselves."

"I'll be up," she said. "I'll make pancakes for Lou."

The second she was out the door I blasted the air-conditioning. I let loose a monologue on Midwesterners' reluctance to turn on their air. I was talking to no one but myself.

"Can you just try?" Barry said. He had taken Lou from me, and she was crawling around the kitchen, leaving lasagna hand-prints on the linoleum while he did the dishes.

"I could, yes. I could try. I'm actually trying to try."

"Fuck," said Barry.

"I know," I said. "I'm in the wrong."

"She's a really nice person," Barry said. "I like my sister."

I picked up Lou and held her on my hip. "Sometimes Mommy is a jerk," I said in a squeaky voice. I wet a dish towel and moved it around the floor with my foot. "Mommy is sorry."

"You're being so aggressive," Barry said. He took Lou from me, and I saw that he hadn't been doing the dishes: he'd been turning the sink into a little bathtub. He wiggled Lou out of her clothes, then held her by her underarms while I took off her dia-per. He placed her gently in the sink, and I put my hand in the water to test it. The water was too cold, but I didn't say anything.

"She's had a tough time, Edie," he said. "She really misses Jerry and the kids."

"She should be with them then." I didn't want to talk about Lonnie's "tough time." Her husband, Jerry, had gotten a job in Toronto, and she had refused to go with him. Her kids had had so much fun visiting Jerry over spring break that once school let out they asked to spend the summer with him. They were all talking about applying for citizenship.

"She has a job here," said Barry. "All her friends. She's lived here her whole life. It's not easy to just uproot like that. Jerry didn't even ask her—he just took the job. Imagine that, me taking a job without talking to you. I respect that she stood her ground."

"Okay, sweetie," I said. I put my hand over his mouth so that he would stop talking. "Shh," I said.

"I don't know why you dislike her so much," Barry said.

"We really need to start putting Lou in that boot," I said.

"When we get home."

"We'll start then."

I found a beer in the fridge and watched my husband wash Lou. He filled a glass and tipped it over her head. He had found the bottle of baby shampoo I'd packed with our toiletries and was soaping her with it. He shaped her hair into a tiny mohawk. I wanted to tell him to protect her from the hard faucet by wrapping a dishcloth around it. I wanted to tell him that she was getting cold. He tipped too much water over her head, and she began to cry. I pretended that my feet were glued to the floor and that I couldn't rescue her from my husband's rough grasp. She looked at me with her sweet, helpless face, and I watched her little tongue quiver while she cried. Barry told her it was all right. He told her he was almost done. He lifted her out of the sink and looked around desperately for a towel. He was holding her directly under the air vent and she was shivering, and I couldn't help it, I snatched her out of his arms and ran with her into the bathroom, where I swaddled her in one of Lonnie's aquamarine bath towels and held her until she stopped crying.

"You make me feel like a horrible father," Barry yelled from behind the closed bathroom door, "when you do things like that."

Lou slept on my chest in the dark of the bedroom while I watched the news on Lonnie's shitty black-and-white TV. Her chin dug into my collarbone. Barry was in the living room doing angry push-ups. It was a little after two. I'd just fed Lou. I knew I should sleep. I could get maybe two hours before she woke again to nurse. I heard Barry setting up the fold-out couch. I thought about what I would tell Lonnie when she got home. He snores? I wanted to watch TV? The truth, which was that he was starting to sense I didn't want him around?

At that hour, every news story was about child abuse or murder. Some woman had decapitated her newborn in the neighborhood adjacent to Lonnie's. Men were murdering people all over the state.

Who would raise Lou if Barry and I died? Barry and I argued a lot about this and we had argued about it that night. He insisted that Lonnie was the only option. The thought made me dizzy with rage. I did not want Lou to grow up in suburban Cincinnati with a woman who did not question the world. I did not want Lou shopping at big-box stores, saying grace before meals, going to church on Sundays. I did not want her to hear a bunch of lies about how Barry Sr. had been a good father, when the truth was that he was nothing but a philandering alcoholic.

Barry and I thought of ourselves as intellectuals, as artists. We thought of ourselves as sensitive people, enlightened people. We wanted Lou to grow up going to readings and gallery openings; we wanted to reframe what she learned in school from a feminist perspective, to talk to her about the civil rights movement, gay rights, the whole bit. I didn't want someone like Lonnie raising my baby. I did not want my baby left to cry alone.

But there were no other options. I had lost touch with my own family ages ago. Like Barry's mother, I had decided to cease to exist.

"You fixate on something, and you let it ruin your day," whispered Barry. "You can nurse Lou in the bathroom." He pointed down a stone hallway past the church's coat-check room. I wore a black V-neck dress that I could easily pull aside for Lou and control-top tights that were giving me gas. The church was refreshingly cool. Lou didn't have any black clothing so we dressed her in a little chambray dress and white sandals. I waited for Lonnie to comment on her outfit but she said nothing. She had her hair in a tight bun and wore a black pantsuit, a gold cross peeking out beneath the blazer. She had on black running shoes, which she kept apologizing for. Barry held my purse while Lou and I went into the bathroom, under the guise of me having to change her diaper. I sat on the toilet, her little sandaled foot kicking the roll of toilet paper. She was too distracted to nurse, her eyes flitting wildly around the bathroom stall. My arms shook with her weight, and I felt the sweat forming on my forehead. I had slept maybe three hours. I gathered my breasts back into the dress and fussed with myself in the mirror while I held Lou with one arm. I kissed her forehead, then found Barry and Lonnie waiting for us in the vestibule. They were holding each other like children. Lonnie had her head on Barry's shoulder. I was not there for either one of them.

We sat in the cold of the church, in the front pews, Barry Sr.'s casket in front of the altar. The priest said a few words, and then it was over. I waited for Lonnie to stand up, reach into her blazer, and pull out a long speech about her father, but she sat there, unmoving. At the cemetery, we watched Barry Sr.

be lowered into the ground. Barry leaned against me. I felt his legs buckle and I thrust Lou into Lonnie's arms so I could hold Barry as he stared into the grass, on all fours. "Stop the planet," I whispered to Barry. I was trying to be funny. I was trying to lighten the mood.

"Not now, Edie," he said.

I could hear lawn mowers and the high whine of cicadas and Barry's breathing. The cemetery was the oldest in the city, inspired by the Père Lachaise in Paris, and was also an arboretum. I thought that maybe I wanted to be buried there, next to Barry. I still think I might, even though we live apart now. I have these horrible moments of regret that leave me catatonic, but Barry is with someone else, and, truthfully, I am more at peace now that I live on my own. Lou is grown, of course. She is a sculptor in New York City. Last year, she made $12,000 on one sculpture alone. I visit her two or three times a year. One time, she had too many glasses of wine and told me she can never get married because it would be too hard for her to have me and Barry in the same room. She said the thought of it fills her with anxiety, that she stays up all night trying to figure out how to organize the ceremony so that we feel that she loves us equally. I had to laugh. I told her when the day came we would behave. I told her she had to think of her own happiness.

When Barry and I stood again, Lou was asleep on Lonnie's shoulder. Lonnie was stroking the back of her head and whispering to her that she was the most beautiful girl in the world. It was stiflingly hot—already late afternoon—and Lonnie must have been dying in that black pantsuit. I saw how capable Lonnie was in that moment, how selfless. I brushed a mosquito away from her hand. I asked if she wanted me to take Lou but she shook her head. There were thunderheads on the horizon, and I wished desperately for a summer storm, something to blow the heat out of the city. I wanted crazy lightning. I wanted to count the seconds between the thunder and explain it to Lou.

Barry Sr. was buried, and we were headed toward the car, but no one seemed to be in any rush to get there. "You know something, Lonnie," Barry said. He had taken off his blazer and was rolling up his sleeves. He shielded his eyes from the sun. "I thought Mom might've showed up today."

Lonnie repositioned Lou onto her other shoulder. Lou's body was entirely slack, her mouth open. She made a little sighing sound, and I felt my milk let down. I think I was afraid to put her in the special boot because I was afraid it would make her cry. I felt so frightened when Lou cried.

"Oh, I don't know," Lonnie said.

"I'd like to see her again," Barry said. "Even if she doesn't want to see me."

"I can think of a few things I'd say to her," said Lonnie, and I smiled, liking her in the moment.

"So," Barry said. He was leaning up against Lonnie's car now, fiddling with a button on his shirt. "Hey, so, did Dad leave a will?"

"Oh," Lonnie said. "Let's not do this now." She looked at me and then at the front of my dress, which was soaked through. "You're leaking, Edie." She dug in her pocket for a Kleenex and passed it to me. "Takes a while to dry up, as I recall."

My breasts were so engorged it felt as though they were full of rocks. Lou was stirring in Lonnie's arms, and I knew she would wake up hungry and start crying.

"Did he leave a will or not?" said Barry. He stepped toward his sister, and they looked at each other like two schoolyard bullies about to brawl.

"I'm just going to say it," said Lonnie. "He wrote you out of it last year."

"He did?" Barry had his hands on his hips. He craned his neck toward Lonnie. "I don't think he did that."

"Well, that's what he did." Lonnie pulled Lou off her shoulder and handed her to me. "She's waking up," she said.

Seconds later, Lou was wailing. She reached for the front of my dress, yanked it open, and started slapping my breast with her little hand. "Okay, okay," I said. I wrestled my breast back into the dress and tried to get her pacifier into her mouth, but she grabbed it and flung it into the grass. I could hear Lonnie telling Barry that he should have expected this. He had not been there for his dad. Lonnie had been the one to keep him company all these years, the one inviting him over for Sunday dinners, the one driving to the Kentucky cabin and rolling him over so he wouldn't choke on his vomit in his sleep.

"It wasn't my job to look after Dad," Barry was saying, yelling now over Lou's cries. A couple of people hurried past us and I tried not to think about what we must have looked like to them.

"Maybe if you'd visited more, helped out a little, Barry," Lonnie said. "What did you think would be in the will anyway? Millions of dollars? Some property we didn't know about? He left me the cabin. That's it. It's probably worth about forty grand. He told me he'd given you about that much over the years."

My dear, handsome husband. It was the first time I'd ever seen him not get what he wanted.

Lou's cries were intensifying into a high-pitched wail that made me feel as though my bones were going to shatter. She reached into my dress again, her body rigid and angry. She threw her head back and screamed.

"He never met Lou," Lonnie yelled. "You never brought her here. He never got to meet his granddaughter." I couldn't tell if she was talking to me or to Barry.

I could feel Barry's eyes on me. I had been the one who hadn't wanted to visit. I couldn't handle the thought of being around Barry's family with a baby. I was so anxious in the months after she was born that it felt like a kind of psychosis. I had told Barry that it would kill me to travel with Lou, to break up our fragile routine of napping and nursing. I had manufactured a panic attack, my arms out in front of me, shaking and crying.

"Just nurse her," Barry shouted at me then, red faced. "Nurse her, Edie."

"We only nurse sometimes," I said to Lonnie. "She's more or less weaned."

"Christ," said Barry. He walked back toward Barry Sr.'s grave. He was gone for what felt like a very long time. Lonnie and I sat in the car with the air-conditioning on high while I nursed Lou. We listened to the radio. She did not say a thing.

"What's he doing?" I asked.

"Apologizing to his father," Lonnie said. "Who knows. They never got along."

I thought of Lonnie and Barry Sr. in the Kentucky cabin, sitting around the kitchen table, talking about me and Barry. I had to admit, I was disappointed about the will.

"What are you going to do with the cabin?" I asked her.

"Keep it for the kids, I think," she said. "I don't know."

By the time we got home, the front of my dress was stiff with dried milk and sweat. Lou and I went into the guest bedroom and we lay together, her in her diaper, me in my tights. She needled me in the stomach with her chubby foot, then kicked out her leg and flailed it around, slammed it down on the mattress. I held her hand and kissed her forehead. I closed my eyes. I promised myself I would put her in the little white boot when we got home. She was supposed to wear it for six weeks. The doctor said the pigeon-toeing was mild and would be easy to correct. It was because of her position in the womb. I had carried her wrong, unwittingly.

Barry came into the bedroom and I felt myself tense. He lay behind me and put his hand on my waist. Lou was playing with the curls in my hair.

"It's like you guys are having an affair," Barry said.

"We are," I said.

I am sorry for the way I am, I wanted to tell my husband. I am sorry for my narcissism and the peculiar way I navigate the world. I am sorry that I haven't said one kind thing about the fact that you lost your father. I am sorry that I need things to be just so, that I cannot relax and do things any other way but the way in which I do them. I am sorry that I need so much time with Lou. I am sorry that I try to control my environment and everyone around me. I am sorry that I feel things so intensely and that the intensity of my love for Lou creates a kind of counterblast of rage for all other things. I am too full of love and thus I am too full of sorrow. In the quiet of the morning, when Lou is nursing and the blue of dawn begins to appear, I am grateful that you, Barry, are in my life. I whisper to Lou that she will grow up with a good father, with a father who loves her, that she will not roam the earth looking for a man to love her as much as she needs to be loved. The terrible things that happen in the world will not happen to Lou. I will not let them happen.

I could hear Lonnie on the phone with her husband in the other room. She was telling him that the church had a new stained-glass window. She said it had been a nice day, not too hot. She said the neighbors still hadn't finished their deck.

I wondered why she didn't tell her husband that she needed him. That she had needed him and her children to come home for her father's funeral, that she needed him now. I wondered when it got to be too much for a person like her, if she had ever thrown a plate against a wall and demanded anything, or if not moving to Canada was the best she could do, the only way she could assert herself. Jerry had met someone else, she would find out a few weeks later. When we heard the news, Barry and I lay in the dark of our bedroom and talked about how we were the only people left in the world who still loved each other. Our house then was funny. One story, just two small bedrooms for the three of us, a little stone patio out back with a portable Weber grill. I say "funny" because Lou can hardly believe that we ever lived in a place so small. Before she left for New York City, she and I shared a five-bedroom house with an outdoor pool and a hot tub on the wraparound deck. I have done well for myself as the dean of arts and humanities at the college here. I'll retire next year. I sit in the hot tub at night under the stars and wonder how Barry is doing. He never did find work, though he did finally publish the book of essays. He married this woman, June, who owns some kind of successful business, and they have a nice condominium downtown. They had their honeymoon in Paris. I found this out online, of course, though Lou would have told me if I asked. She refers to June as her stepmother, and I feel a little shock every time she says it.

After Lou was born, the agreement was that Barry and I would have a second child when Lou turned three. He did not know that the thought filled me with such anxiety that I lay awake at night, imagining nursing a newborn while Lou called out to me from the other room. The idea that I could not be fully present for Lou—I knew I was only capable of being a good parent to one child—Barry could not understand it. He couldn't understand why I wouldn't want to have another baby with the man I loved. He couldn't see how tired I was already, how a person like me probably shouldn't have had a baby in the first place. Lou turned three, then four, then five. When I divorced Barry, more than his absence, I felt the absence of all that anxiety. When I told him this, he did not speak to me for a very long time.

The only time I feel like talking to anyone is late at night, after I've showered off the chemicals of the hot tub water and am sitting at the end of the bed in my bathrobe, my hair in a towel. I'd like to tell someone about my day, the funny things that happened, the things that were remarkable. This person was Lou for many years. I do remember Barry Sr. talking to me about the loneliness of the elderly shortly before he died. He said he was alone because he deserved to be. I imagine I'll die here, in my bed, and that Lou will notice after a day or two that I haven't called. I have my and Barry's wedding rings in a velvet box in a safe-deposit box downtown, bequeathed to her. I've told her they might be worth something one day.

After Lonnie divorced Jerry, she came to stay with Barry and me for a few days. She hardly said a word. She seemed to hold herself very still. I remember her sitting across from me in the kitchen of our little two-bedroom house, drinking a tall glass of Baileys with ice. Lou was opening and shutting one of the cabinet doors—her new favorite game—while Barry watched TV in the other room.

"My youngest had to wear one of those," Lonnie said, eyeing the counter, where Lou's special boot sat, still untouched. "I'd forgotten about it until now."

"Was it hard on her?"

"I don't remember," Lonnie said. "She was so little. I think it took some getting used to. These things feel like a huge deal at the time, but they're not. Not in the grand scheme of things. Just put it on and carry on with your life."

She looked at me from behind her rimless glasses. I took her hand then and asked her if she would take care of Lou if Barry and I died. "Yes, Edie," she said. It was not the emotional moment for her that it was for me. Barry must have heard us because he was suddenly in the doorway, the remote in his hand.

"You know I will," she said to both of us.

"What's going on in here?" Barry asked.

"We're putting the boot on Lou," I said. I picked her up, then motioned for Barry to pass it to me. It was white with green Velcro straps that fastened around her ankle and just below her toes. I slipped her foot into it, adjusted the straps, and I waited.

"Well?" I said to Lou. She was examining it.

"She'll live," said Lonnie.

The trouble was, I wanted more than that. I wanted more from the world than survival.

Youmna Chlala

Nayla

THERE WAS SUN and then there was more sun and more sun. You can't imagine loss when it's sunny. Everything reflects, the sides of buildings, dirty, dusty windows offer half a version of a sad tired face. You squint and rooms appear tilted, the sky unbearable, and then when—like a turtle, worm, or whatever it is that burrows—you wrap thick heavy blankets around the curtain bar, dust flies everywhere. So you sneeze and secure the blankets with giant paper clips, metallic tape, anything that feels like it will protect you from the brightness for a long time.

This is how I felt for the first few days of my twenty-first year. I was still in this camp in the desert, worming my way into acceptance while years—let's count them . . . something like 365 × 6 + however many days—had gone by. By the end of the week, Mama pulled down the blankets and dragged me to my cousin Marwan's birthday party. He relished his legal ability to drink, although as I told him many times, legality did not matter here.

Mama spent most of the night in the living room with my aunts while Marwan and his friends entertained them by try-ing to dance the dabke with a group of terribly synchronized tabla drummers. Already tipsy by the time we got there, Marwan introduced us to his new girlfriend, Nayla. I noticed that everyone else seemed to approach her cautiously or envelop her in an airy swoop that simulated the grandeur of a hug without bodily contact. She didn't smell bad or look disheveled or unkempt. There were no obvious signs of repulsion. I asked my mom what was going on and she said: *She's a young widow*, in the hushed tone of a terrible fate or a shameful secret. I immediately thought of a spider and recoiled. So when Nayla sat next to me on the sticky linoleum kitchen floor and offered me the wobbly part of her spinach quiche, I hesitated. She insisted. I took a small chunk with my hands as if like sisters we had always shared food.

The music was loud in the kitchen, a mix of bootleg DJ Khaled and De La Soul. Nayla and I stayed on the floor, legs extended, bare feet against the cabinet, eating. I picked out the almonds from the rice and gave them to her. She whispered that they were a cheap substitute for pine nuts. We agreed that bread is the best utensil and that olives without pits are disgusting, as if manhandled by a machine. By the end of the night we were friends.

Nayla worked part-time as an engineer. She fixed boilers, heaters, and pipes. She made sure all the internal parts worked: the heart, the liver, the organs of a building. She spoke of codes like a spy. She had a clipboard with stacks of paper that she flipped through and wrote on only in pencil. I never saw her erasing. There were numbers and barely legible words along the margins. Her soundtrack was the scribbling scratch of the pencil. When she was surrounded by the rest of her crew, mostly men who liked to yell into the air rather than speak directly with one another, she seemed feminine, like a feline cartoon character who bats her eyelashes when she wants something. She wore short skirts or belted long shirts along with the white hard hat she carried looped around her gaudy large gold purse. She didn't wear heels but her shoes seemed demure, dignified, and actually, as I often told her, totally old-lady-like. The leather was never scuffed or dirty.

That summer, I practically lived in her apartment, a tiny place right above her late husband's family's house. I'd come over and we'd drink prosecco (pretending we were in Italy) and invent recipes together. We traded food for the bubbly wine with Ahmad, the liquor store manager. We made him fish fattoush; lamb-stuffed eggplant; pistachio, orange, and cardamom cookies; and vegetarian kibbeh with extra pine nuts. Ahmad had a huge family who liked to be fed by anyone other than the aunt in charge of cooking, who vacillated between old-school kushari and a weird version of rice pilaf.

We'd go out dancing until late, and it just seemed easier to sleep over. We shared the crickety pullout bed in the living room, and I'd help her fold its giant metal legs in the morning as our Turkish coffee gurgled on the stove. We ate breakfast together, dipping stale and barely thawed bread into bowls of homemade labne drowning in olive oil. Then we gulped down one more coffee before we each went our own way.

Nayla never talked to me about her husband. I didn't know how long they were married, if it was arranged, if they had been super in love, or how and why he died. This was a time when so many of us had lost someone close. There was an unspoken rule not to talk about them, as if it would put you at risk. Like you only existed because of their absence. I only knew what he looked like because the first time I came over she pointed to a single photograph hanging on the refrigerator door and said, *That's him. I keep it up here for them*, pointing down at the floor that separated her from his parents and siblings. The magnet was weak and each time she opened and closed the door, the photo swayed a little. His cheeks were reddened by the sun or wind. He had on sunglasses so I couldn't tell much about his eyes, his aura.

He wore a collared striped blue and white T-shirt. He seemed preppy, healthy, what youth was supposed to look like.

Marwan, on the other hand, had a face only a mother could love, as my mama often said, teasing her own sister. When I saw him at family gatherings, I tried to get him to reveal something about how he felt about Nayla so that we could dissect his words as we chopped onions and pulled parsley leaves. She seemed to really like him, though I couldn't understand how he compared to the beautiful man who haunted the kitchen.

I enjoyed my role as a spy until Marwan told me that he liked dating her because he'd never have to commit. Clearly, you can't marry a widow. I told him that was insane and archaic and backward and stupid. In an instant everything changed. He stood up, got really close to me, and yelled: Why don't you leave my girlfriend alone! Are you a lesbian or something? And I said, Yeah, so what? Then he told me I was going to hell and a whore and anything he could think of that would make me feel shame, and when I didn't blink he pushed me hard, both his hands flat against the center of my chest. I didn't fall or fight back, instead that night I told his sister, who really was a lesbian: Don't ever tell him the truth. It's not worth it.

The next day, Nayla and I were supposed to make a flourless chocolate cake for Ahmad's daughter's birthday. We were promised a bottle of champagne in return. I kept trying to find the right time to tell her what had happened with Marwan. We stood in the kitchen grating dark and heavy bars of chocolate. Facing each other across the wood counter, we each had a cheese grater set up like a monument in the center of the plate. We leaned with all our might into them to shred the cocoa.

I was restless and set everything down and began to fumble with the record player on the side table. There were no records in sight. The lid was always closed. I opened it and found a layer of dust.

Why don't you ever use this thing? I asked, and Nayla just stared at me silently. I suddenly remembered the small grave-yard next to the east fence and the line of vinyl records shoved into the ground next to a headstone as if they were guards. And without thinking, maybe as a way to fill my mouth with words of forgiveness or to be a distraction or maybe just to undo this unintended opening, I began to talk about my sister.

I never told you that I have an older sister, I said, entering a strange world where I uttered what I thought. My life up until that moment had been suspended, like when it's really hot out-side and muggy and you know it's going to rain, that all of this humidity will break and burst water from the clouds, but you wait and you wait under the graying sky and it doesn't happen. Until it does, much later, at night when you no longer mind because you're safe at home.

Nayla didn't respond and looked down at the chocolate shreds. I opened the refrigerator and grabbed the fig cookies (that she kept cold so that they crunched when she bit into them) and continued to talk.

We don't know where she is. She ran away before they brought us here. My mother rarely mentions her name, only on her saint's day or birthday. We have a ritual where we sing happy birthday to each other. Mama even bakes a cake and we blow out a single candle together, and Mama mumbles something about how she hopes that she is out there somewhere enjoying herself and blow-ing out candles.

The more I talked, the more I moved around the kitchen like a grazing hungry animal. I stuffed three cookies in my mouth. I went to the stove and stuck my fingers in the melted butter, dipping them into the oozing pale yellow liquid.

She is alive, I said, and licked my fingers greedily.

Have you heard from anyone who might know anything about her? She pulled the butter away and poured it into a bowl.

No, but I know it, I said, following her and putting my slimy fingers in the crystal brown sugar.

She pushed my hand away swiftly and I went in again and she grabbed it and held it. Yes, I understand, she said with a firm grip.

We have a bunch of her clothes here with us because we thought we might as well bring them, I continued.

Where do you have room to keep them?

In the suitcases lodged between the closet and the ceiling. Mama takes them down every few months and changes the lavender bags and cedarwood, checks for moths, and then seals them and slides them away.

Do you ever go through them? she asked, and picked up the chocolate and grater that I had left behind. She moved slowly so as not to scrape her fingers against the metal. I could see the small muscles in the backs of her arms working.

When we were growing up, I used to always steal her clothes. Now they smell stale and terrible.

Well, yeah, it's obviously the cedarwood, she replied.

She poured the blend of almonds, forming a landmass inside the glass beaker, and said: He drowned, in the pool. Can you imagine making it here and then something stupid like that happens?

I stared at her and she kept her gaze down. It was silent. There was only one window and it was never open because it was too hot. We were sealed in.

I've always hated these pools. Too much chlorine! I said.

Nayla looked up quickly, and I smiled and walked over to her and she hugged me, hard and close, for what felt like a long, long time.

Let's go now, she whispered.

Where? I pulled back.

Swimming.

Are you serious?

Yes. Let's go.

Mama thinks that Nayla has a straightforward tone about everything because she's an engineer. I think it's because she's sad. Mama says there's nothing straightforward about sadness, it's full of ebbs and flows and that I'm a ridiculous romantic even about sadness.

We dropped everything: sugar, almond, butter, chocolate, pans, cups, measuring spoons, eggs, and left it all for the ants, as Mama would say. We ran in the midday humidity all the way from her apartment on the south side to the reservoir in the north. We charmed the guard with a box of Turkish delights (which we both hated), and he opened the mesh metal gate, giving us only twenty minutes before his supervisor showed up.

We held hands, closed our eyes, and jumped in—right into the cold, unsalted water without even taking off our sweaty clothes. We emerged smiling and triumphant. Nayla said she hoped that our grimy bodies wouldn't taint the water that we were going to have to drink. I floated on my back and watched the still bright sky, wondering if Nayla could see into bodies the way she could see into buildings.

Viet Dinh

Lucky Dragon

I

THE SECOND DAWN rose in the east, at nine in the morning. Hiroshi had never before seen such radiance. It rivaled the sun. He stood on deck with Yoshi, and the light crushed them beneath its purity. Hiroshi closed his eyes, but even so, the brightness pierced his head. The other crew members clamored to see this strange, unexpected light. But Hiroshi returned to the tasks of the day. He consulted Sanezumi about their current bearing. He examined the nautical charts, the curves and byways of the ocean unfolding beneath his forefinger. Last night, he dreamt of a large school of tuna, a flotilla so dense that the ocean became blue-black from their scales. Their eyes flashed like diamonds in the waves. Each time the crew pulled in the nets, the smallest of the fish dwarfed him. They entered the hull without struggling, their flesh tender and firm, bellies thick and marbled with fat. When he woke, Hiroshi knew that it was an omen. Dreams were unreliable things, sinuous and slippery as eels, but morning had not yet come, and he felt the gentle listing of the boat with a single coordinate in mind: *east.*

But soon after the second dawn, Sanezumi pointed at a line of chop on the water's surface. The water recoiled, and before Hiroshi had time to react, it was upon them. The wall of air thrust over the boat, an avalanche of sky. Their clothes trembled as it passed. The men shouted, necks tense and strained, but nothing penetrated the ringing deep in their ears. Hiroshi's feet vibrated. His men gestured at the distant blaze blossoming from the horizon. Many had lived through the Tokyo firebombings—Masaru's left arm was gnarled with scars—but Hiroshi instead remembered the Philippines. His unit had gotten trapped in its position, and he hunkered down in a trench, face pressed against the mud escarpment. Mortars whizzed overhead; shrapnel fell like ice. The Americans were approaching. He felt their progress, a drumbeat in the earth. Only he and Yoshi and a handful of others were still alive. His comrades had sprung from the trench, guns raised in defiance, and were cut down before they had taken ten steps. Hiroshi should have been with them. In the creaking and moaning of the ship, he sometimes heard the voices of the fallen, calling to him from subterranean depths.

After an hour, the fire had cleared from the sky, but now came the rain of ash. It smelled of electricity. The men watched, mouths agape, awed by flakes the size of flower petals, warm to the touch. It clung where it landed, and when Hiroshi wiped it off, it disintegrated into a glittery sheen. It whispered underfoot. Yoshi flapped his arms, sending forth white plumes, as if he were dancing in a snowstorm. Some men held out plastic bags to catch it as it fell. Hiroshi looked to see from where it had come, but if the sky had once been clear and blue, it was now a peach smear. For a few minutes, the rain was a wonder, a miracle. But ash continued falling for the next three hours. It came down so heavily that the boat seemed mired in fog. The men dared not open their eyes. They left footprints where they walked. The ash gathered on the surface of the water, forming gray masses. The crew retreated inside, waiting for it to stop.

"It's inside me," said Yoshi. "It itches."

Hiroshi exhaled. Residue inside his lungs. He sneezed out pebbles. "You're imagining things," he said.

"I feel it in my chest," Yoshi continued. "Underneath my skin."

That night, the men were too nauseated to eat. In Sanezumi's quarters, Hiroshi rested a hand on his navigator's back. Sanezumi couldn't even keep water down; after each swallow, he retched, and the water rushed out of his mouth and dribbled onto the floor. *You'll be fine*, Hiroshi told him. But in the middle of the night, Sanezumi began vomiting blood.

II

They spent two weeks at sea, slowly chugging back to Yaizu. Hiroshi radioed that they were returning home, that an unspecified illness had overtaken them, but they could not move any faster. The crew scratched without end. No one slept. They rolled on the deck, unable to ease their burning. They ate as little as they needed to to survive. Kaneda, the cook, served them rice watered down to a milky broth. Even so, nine days after the fall of ash, Sanezumi died. The crew debated whether to preserve his body or put him to rest. It wasn't auspicious to keep a corpse on board, some argued. But others demanded respect: *If you had died, what would you have us do with your body?* Yoshi insisted on a sea burial. It was Yoshi's tatami mat in which Sanezumi had been rolled, and it was Yoshi's blanket that draped Sanezumi's body down in the cold hull. "He lived at sea and died at sea," Yoshi said. "It's only fitting that the sea take him back." The next morning, they gathered on deck, steadying themselves as the boat bucked and shuddered in the waves. They bowed their heads, and Hiroshi heaved Sanezumi's body over the side. For a short time, he trailed in their wake, but Ryūjin seized him, embraced him in foam, and took him to Ryūgū-jō.

The men feared that they would follow Sanezumi into death. But when Hiroshi saw the single character—*kori*—glowing on the horizon, he knew that they were saved. He steered toward the *kori* until he could see the wall of the ice house on which it was painted. The other members of the fishing co-op waited on the dock to gather and unload the catch. Miho was waiting to greet him. Sanezumi's widow was there as well, and when they delivered the news, her wails filled the sky, and the other women crowding around her in a rustle of silk and sympathy could not keep the sound from clutching her throat.

The next day, Hiroshi and Yoshi went to the Shizuoka prefecture doctor, who looked at Hiroshi's body and clucked his tongue inside his mouth like a wood-boring beetle. The doctor prodded his skin with a metal rod. Across Hiroshi's chest and legs, roseate patches had spread, the centers peeling off in thick flakes, and underneath, skin the shade of twilight. The doctor shook his head and suggested that they try Tokyo University Hospital. Their appointment was scheduled for a week hence. "In the meantime," he said, "try vigorous bathing."

Miho drew Hiroshi's bath and poured water on his body. He winced as it sluiced over him, washing away the ash and salt in his scalp. But when Yoshi went to the *sentō* to bathe, the boisterous chatter near the main tub stopped when he entered. The tub emptied of people when he stepped in.

"At least my skin has stopped itching," said Yoshi. A small comfort, at best.

At their appointment in Tokyo, he and Yoshi were greeted by a reporter from *Yomiuri Shimbun*. He bowed and introduced himself as Nakamura. He held a slender notebook. Pens were clipped to his shirt pocket. "A student informed me of your condition," he said. "You were near the Rongelap Atoll on March 1, correct?"

"That is correct," Hiroshi said.

"Ah." Nakamura lowered his voice. "We believe that your illness may have been caused by an atomic bomb that the Americans detonated on the Bikini Atoll."

Were they still at war? Hadn't they already been thoroughly humiliated?

"A test," Nakamura continued. "A hundred times as powerful as what had been dropped on Hiroshima."

It made sense now: fallout, a black rain that sickened those with whom it came in contact. Yoshi's arms drooped at his sides, as if they were boneless. "If I may," Nakamura continued, "I would like to accompany you during your examination. Your struggle is the nation's struggle."

Hiroshi nodded, as if there were any other answer to give.

III

Hiroshi no longer recognized his own face. This was not the fault of the photographer—he truly could not recognize himself, not even in a pool of water. His skin had dried and cracked and rehardened into an unfamiliar form. His cheeks were broken into grooves and crevices. The flesh had discolored to the color of algae on the side of a boat. The black-and-white picture could not capture this color, but he saw it on his hands, his legs. He rubbed his finger on the newspaper until his stippled image smeared, and he had merged into shadow.

He horrified Miho—he knew it. She washed her hands constantly. She handled his bowls and utensils as if they were made from lightning. She flinched from him, avoiding even accidental contact. He slept on the floor in front of the door, like a dog.

The doctors had said that he wasn't contagious, but what did they know? They hadn't been able to arrest the spread of the illness. Even now it crept down his neck, onto his back. Specialists on radiation sickness from America had flown in. They waved Geiger counters over his body, and the wands crackled like sap-rich pine on fire. The poison was so endemic that it was inseparable from his being.

The government had towed the boat to Tokyo, quarantined where nobody could reach it. It still emitted high doses of deadly, invisible glow. Even so, as captain of the *Lucky Dragon*, Hiroshi's responsibilities now bore down on him more heavily than before. Hardly a day passed without a news agency coming to interview him, flashbulbs popping in his eyes, microphones recording every breath. Every picture promised a new deterioration—*Look what the Americans have done!* But not to him alone: his entire crew. They had all been similarly afflicted, but Hiroshi was the only one who had been photographed.

Nakamura showed him letters from around the world: China, Russia, South Africa, and so, so many from America itself. *You are in our prayers*, they said. *Our heart goes out to you.* Many included money, the stray bills here and there growing into a considerable sum. *Yomiuri Shimbun* had established a fund for the crew, but the money addressed to Hiroshi was his alone. He shared what he could, but this did not stem the tide of resentment. *You should have joined Sanezumi*, he imagined his crew saying, their hearts full of mutiny.

Yoshi remained steadfast: their bond was thicker than blood. They had seen things more horrible than an extra flap of skin growing between their fingers and toes; they had witnessed things more disturbing than the red sores appearing along throats like slashes.

During the escape attempt from the No. 12 Prisoner of War Camp in Cowra, Hiroshi watched his commanding officer, Sugiro, remove a fork from his boot. The tines had been compressed, like fingers inside a tight mitten, and scraped along the concrete floor until they had sharpened to a point. Amid the machine-gun fire, the alarms and klaxons, the screaming to run left, right, forward, Sugiro unbuttoned his shirt from the bottom, parting it as though he were opening a curtain. On his bare stomach, he pressed the point of the fork into his skin until it dimpled and bled. He dragged the fork down, then to the left, using both hands to keep it steady. Hiroshi bore witness to his bravery, his determination, even as Yoshi hissed at him to hurry, to run. The prisoners of war had taken a gun tower. Now was their chance.

Sugiro kept his face inexpressive, his mouth twitching only as the fork caught on something tough, gristly. But Sugiro cut through it and passed into someplace else, a place without walls, barbed wire, sandbags. What did he see when his eyes rolled heavenward? He knelt to one knee before collapsing, his pants cuffs and bootlaces blackened with blood. Only after he had fallen did his mouth relax into a smile, a blissful release.

Hiroshi tried to smile now, watching his reflection in his bathwater. Miho had added salt—the only thing that soothed his sores—and the undissolved crystals lay at the bottom of the basin like sand. His lips refused to form the shape his mind commanded. His face was no longer his own.

IV

Hiroshi had not spoken to his father since the war had ended, and he had not expected Nakamura to contact him, but the past was beyond his power to change. Nakamura had wanted a quotation, and his father said this: "I have no son. He died during the war. My son would have died rather than allow himself to be captured."

Forgiveness would not come in this world, nor the next, but

after Nakamura ran the quotation, Hiroshi's shame was exposed for all to see: he was a failed escapee, one of the ignoble. He had returned to Japan with his head hung low, chin attached to his chest. He walked, eyes locked upon the ground, as jeers fell upon him, as if from heaven itself: *Coward. Traitor.*

Then something further unexpected happened: someone wrote to defend him. Countless others had condemned him: FALSE HERO; A CELEBRATION OF COWARDICE; A SHAME UPON OUR NATION. But the letter supporting him—A VICTIM TWICE OVER—filled Hiroshi with not so much hope as a fleeting, momentary peace.

"Look at this," Hiroshi said to Yoshi, handing him the newspaper.

Yoshi set it aside without reading. His lips were as thick and rubbery as caterpillars, his skin the color of new moss. "We were cursed even before we went to war," he said. "Our skin matches our souls."

"Nonsense," Hiroshi said—though he sometimes thought the same thing.

Yoshi spread his robe to reveal how the skin on his stomach had separated into scales, each as hard as a turtle's shell. "I wake up each night with my mat in shreds." Yoshi tapped his abdomen. "I bet it could deflect bullets," he said.

"It's still skin," said Hiroshi.

"If we were bulletproof," Yoshi continued, "think of what we could do."

This new Yoshi worried Hiroshi. Yoshi had always been solitary, but now the village people shook their *omamori* when he approached, and none would look him in the eye. None of his former shipmates, none of the workers at the fishing co-op. He remembered the old Yoshi, whose eyes widened each time they reeled in a catch, wondering aloud how much these fish would fetch at Tsukiji Market. The old Yoshi stroked the sides of the tuna, thanking them for providing him a roof over his head and a mat on which to sleep, and when the fish stopped struggling, he licked the brine off his fingers.

The new Yoshi's fingers fumbled with his robe, the rough claws and scales fraying the cotton. He ripped the sash, loosening it. He bared his chest, where the scales were as thick as a thumb and cupped the area above his heart. From his pocket, he produced his old service revolver.

"Shoot me," he said.

"Don't be foolish."

"It's a test. If the bullet bounces off, then this is a blessing. If I die, then you will have simply hurried me to my next life."

"I will not."

Yoshi dropped the gun to the floor. "I am unworthy of your friendship," he said, contrite. "Your loyalty."

Hiroshi placed a scaly hand on Yoshi's shoulder. He remembered their escape attempt from the POW camp. Hiroshi had covered the barbed wire with his blanket and flung himself over it. They clambered over the wall surrounding the prison, where Hiroshi found a dead Australian guard at his feet. He'd been bludgeoned, his forehead collapsed. The other prisoners spread out, and floodlights scoured the surroundings, picking out shadows fleeing into the nearby farmland. The prisoners had shed their maroon caps, which were scattered on the ground like pools of blood. The guard couldn't have been older than eighteen. Another boy pulled into war. Hiroshi felt at the guard's waist until he found his gun.

Yoshi ran ahead blindly, flailing his arms, deeper into the darkness. Searchlights arced above their heads. Yoshi's movements were panicked, like a small animal caught in a snare. Hiroshi caught a glimpse of Yoshi's arm, his neck. Yoshi stumbled and fell, and Hiroshi aimed the gun at where Yoshi scrabbled in the dirt. A quick and honorable death. He could kill Yoshi and then kill himself, and when their bodies were returned to Japan, his father would wet his lips with water and cover the family shrine with long sails of white paper. His mother would hold the *juzu* in her hands, repeating a sutra for each bead, before offering incense to him, once, twice, three times. Yoshi would never even know that the bullet had come from him.

Hiroshi, Yoshi whispered, *where are you? Don't leave me alone.*

Close behind them, the prison guards called to each other. No matter where they ran, Hiroshi knew that their recapture was imminent. If they were captured with the dead guard's gun, they would be executed on the spot. Why was one death better than another? What was honorable about smashing in the skull of an Australian boy who was still too young, perhaps, to know pleasure? Had he died for his country so that they could honor their own? Hiroshi clasped both hands around the gun and flung it as far into the distance as he could.

I'm here, Hiroshi responded. *Keep going. I'm right behind you.*

V

Masaru took a job in an American sideshow. THE HORRORS OF ATOMIC WAR. The poster showed him surrounded by oval cameos: midgets, bearded ladies, legless men. He made a good wage, the villagers said, and he sent back money to his wife, who moved up in the village's esteem. Miho overheard this at market, where she was overcharged for even rice, flour, and salt.

Nakamura had invited Hiroshi to appear on television, but he demurred and referred Nakamura to other crew members. They were men untouched by cowardice, and public opinion of them had swayed from disgust to pity, and now, to sympathy. It was possible that people thought differently of him too. Perhaps they were willing to forgive his conduct in the war. Strange:

when he was a man, he had been a monster; now that he was a monster, he was once again a man.

Hiroshi's hair had fallen out, and the top of his head was hard and smooth as a helmet. Deep creases scalloped the length of his forehead, a permanent ridge of worry. Scales ringed his body like ruffles of armor.

Yoshi laughed at the news of Masaru. "You know," Yoshi said, "that his wife used to never touch his burned arm? Now she lives high off his deformity."

"We've had offers too," Hiroshi said. "They will fly us to America."

"Haven't the Americans done enough?" Yoshi said. He raised his arms, as if surrendering. "You know what people call us? They say we are *ningyo*. Mermaids! Already some of the villagers think that if they eat our flesh, they will live forever." He rapped his knuckles against the carapace on his chest. "Maybe they will break their teeth on me."

"*Ningyo* are omens," Hiroshi said. "To catch one is to invite misfortune."

"It's too late to throw us back," Yoshi said. He lifted a scale on his arm. The flesh underneath was gray and bumpy, like lizard skin. "What do you think I taste like? There's enough of me to feed the village for a week."

"You? You're as stringy as week-old beef. And if you taste the way you smell, no one would be able to stomach you."

"We could be a boon to this village," Yoshi said. "Remember the story of 'Happyaku Bikuni'? One bite of me and everyone would have eternal life. They would hail us as heroes." Yoshi flexed his hands, the webbing as translucent as kelp. "Or maybe our flesh will poison the village folk, and they will know what our pain is like."

"Why do you say these things?" Hiroshi said. "Why can you not be at peace?"

"Look at us," Yoshi said. "Better to have died in Cowra all those years ago than to live like this today." He exhaled—a wheeze, a gasp. "You should have shot me," Yoshi said. "You should have pulled the trigger."

VI

Yoshi hanged himself. Hiroshi found him—maybe Yoshi had meant for Hiroshi alone to serve as witness to his bravery, but the truth was that no one else visited him. He had fastened one end of his obi to the pine beam bracing the ceiling and looped the other end beneath the scales on his neck, where the skin was still soft. A green forked tongue lolled out of his mouth, and his eyes were yellow, glassy, streaked with red.

Hiroshi did not cry out when he saw Yoshi's body dangling there, nor did he cry as he tried to cut his friend down. But his webbed hand could not hold a knife; his fingers were too stiff and clumsy. He slashed at the cloth with his talons until it frayed and snapped. Yoshi's body crashed onto the floor, and Hiroshi cradled his friend, scales scratching against scales. Hiroshi's eyelids had atrophied, but his nictitating membrane flicked ceaselessly to keep his eyes moist.

Soon, people gathered outside Yoshi's door, looking in, hiding their words behind their hands. The crowd grew as news spread, and it seemed as if the whole village were looking in. Hiroshi didn't move. Let them look. They had wished us dead—let them look at the result. He no longer had ears, but he heard them whispering, *If it's dead, we should have the body.* He heard Miho gasp. *How could you say that*, she said. *That's his friend. That's Yoshi.*

Monster's whore, they replied.

Enough. Hiroshi lifted Yoshi's body and walked outside into the night. The villagers trailed him, holding aloft torches. Miho was among them. He smelled the detergent she used to purify herself. Here they were: a procession of monsters.

The villagers shouted, *Give us his body. Give him to us.*

If you want him, Hiroshi said, *come take him from me.* He gouged a nearby tree with his claws, and none of the villagers dared pass the patch of splinters he had made.

Hiroshi did not know if Yoshi's body would burn, as leathery and resilient as it was. And it would be impossible to bury his body in secret. What if it tainted the land where it lay? Hiroshi walked to the beach with Yoshi in his arms. Miho stopped at the sand. She placed his sandals at the start of the path back to the village, as she used to do when he went swimming. *The water is too cold for me*, she used to say. *But you go on.*

Hiroshi stood at the ocean's edge, the water sluicing onto his feet. He thought once again of Sugiro, the commander who had committed hara-kiri. Perhaps it had been the brave thing, the honorable thing. But Hiroshi had seen a new world blossom, a world born of light and fire, and this world no longer had a place for the proud, the defeated, the disgraced. The old world held on to its illusion of bravery, like the cowardly men up on the hill brandishing their torches, as if they had driven him toward the sea themselves. But all Hiroshi had to do was turn and open his mouth—his square teeth had fallen out weeks ago, replaced with triangular shards—and the men ran off like curs.

He no longer felt the cold. Even waist-deep in water, he felt no unease. Indeed, it seemed comforting. The tide pulled at his body, urging him forward. Yoshi's body was buoyant, and the sea lifted him out of Hiroshi's arms. But there could not be even the remote possibility of Yoshi floating back onto land. A *ningyo* washing up on shore was an omen of war, and they had both seen their fill of calamity. Hiroshi ventured further, deeper, until the light from the stars vanished.

He sensed the thrumming of fish around him: the mackerel low on the ocean floor, a squid curling its tentacles around an unlucky clam, and a school of tuna bustling about, mouths open and hungry. He breathed and exhaled through the slits in his neck. He propelled himself, undulating his torso, and as his eyes adjusted to the darkness, vast forests of seaweed unfurled before him. Fish darted out of his path. He released Yoshi's body. He swam forth, examining the endlessness of the new world, and Yoshi followed in the pattern Hiroshi cut through the water, almost as if he were himself swimming. *Yoshi*, Hiroshi wanted to cry out, *where are you? Don't leave me alone.* And Yoshi, now given to the ebb and flow of currents, called to him, *Keep going. I'm right behind you.*

Michael Parker

Stop 'n' Go

EVERY DAY BUT SUNDAY he dresses in the uniform of his former profession: khaki-colored work clothes, steel-toed brogans, a thin windbreaker zipped to the Adam's apple if there is a shadowy sweetness in the morning breeze. He rises before dawn, lights the pilot of the kerosene stove, lets the dogs out, careful not to slap the screen door. He sits at the kitchen table drinking instant coffee, black, for an hour until his wife rises and fries breakfast wordlessly in her housecoat. Neither of his sons wanted to take over the farm and his daughter moved up to Raleigh to work in a bank and he doesn't understand a good three-quarters of the things he hears people say. Commercials on television perplex him. There doesn't seem to be any logic to them, they begin in the middle and it's never quite clear to him what it is they're even advertising. He stands in the back-yard looking out over the fields he leases now to an outfit out of, by God, Delaware, working a pick between his teeth, dogs at his feet. Maybe I have outlived time. Soon there will be no such thing as dew, the thing he once had to rouse himself early from bed to beat. Get it done before the sun burns the dew off. They'll do away with that, too. In the war he had been walking through a French forest pretending he was back home quail hunting in Beamon's woods with his cousins when he took two bullets: one through the palm of his hand, another in the shoulder, shattering his clavicle. The Germans pinned them down at the edge of a field for sixteen hours. Mortar rounds exploded the trees above him, turning tree limbs into tiny, deadly slivers. It grew dark and so cold he bit a wadded-up sleeve to quiet the chatter of his teeth. He lay there hoping he would freeze to death before he bled out because he had heard a frozen man just fell finally asleep. But some old boy came along, picked him up and slung him over his shoulder like a sack of fertilizer, took him deeper into the woods. He laid him down and stripped off his clothes and bound his wounds with tourniquets and fetched from somewhere a medic who told him they couldn't risk the light needed to clean his wounds but he had a choice between a shot of morphine and a shot of Scotch. He said he'd take the morphine and ten minutes later the same medic came back as if he'd not been there before and asked him the same question and he said he'd take the Scotch. By that time the old boy who'd hauled him back from where he lay dying had taken his own clothes off and zipped two bags together and, because of the heat coming off that boy's body, here he was, pondering the disappearance of dew. He'd only been with his wife, one woman in seventy years, and all he had to compare the feel of her body to on a morning when the windows were frosty and the radiators clanked on was that boy, who was big but all muscle and hairy. It felt like a sin to still retain the memory of the roughness of the boy's cheek when in the night it grazed the back of his neck but this wasn't the worst thing, nor was getting shot at and lying alone in the cold and dark trying to choose which way to die. After he spent six weeks recuperating in England, they sent him to a psychiatrist and the psychiatrist asked him was he scared to return and he said hell yes I'm scared, wouldn't you be? The psychiatrist shrugged and said to the sergeant who'd brought him over there, Nothing wrong with this one, send him back. Later, by the time he got back across the water to France, Hitler was dead. He figured the whole thing was over and he could go on home but they sent him to supervise the POWs whose job it was to clean up Dachau. He saw a lot of things during that detail he'd just as soon forget, worse things than when he was getting shot at, but it wasn't what they hauled out of there that got to him. For weeks after they'd liberated the place, men and women were camped outside the gates. Roma, someone told him they were called when he asked what they were doing there still. Gypsies. They ain't got no home. Here's as good as anyplace to them. Every morning his captain would come along with an interpreter and tell these people they were free to leave, but the next morning there they'd be, sitting around a fire, dirty, skinny as saplings, eating the C rations they gave them.

When the sun has burned off the dew, he climbs into his pickup and motors, slow as a combine, the half mile down to the Stop 'n' Go. He knows it is just spite that keeps him from climbing out of second gear, spite for the traffic bottling up behind, all in a hurry, eager to get to that someplace, he doesn't know where or care, somebody told them they needed to be.

Dounia Choukri
Past Perfect Continuous

"THE PAST IS SO FAT, no one would ever know if you slipped a lie into its armpit," said Aunt Gunhild. She actually used a more colorful body part, but then Aunt Gunhild was a jaywalker and a smoker in a family in which women, unless they were dead Nazi great-aunts from Hamburg, didn't smoke. Not on the outside—they puffed on the inside until their throats burned and tears welled in their eyes. Our women braved north German winters in clumpy shoes that gave them chilblains. They married early and stayed married to reasonable men with ice-blue eyes, men who only traveled in wartime. When the rest of the family had already gone to sleep on starched sheets, they would sit in the halo of their own silence and mend the wear and tear of clothes as wounds on their own skin. By the time their faces were as threadbare as their husbands' last fine-rib undershirt, their past would be woven into a fixed memory, the first spring after the war or that summer when the goat had clambered up the stairs and nibbled on the sleeping children's chins.

If the past is another country, then it must be lenient toward trespassers.

"There will never be the likes again!"

My father's words, his finger in the air whenever Gene Kelly tap-danced across the TV screen, Kelly's esthetic apple buttocks as sexless as Grandma's groceries bouncing around in the bag when the streetcar makes a turn.

"Those were the days!"

Every kid takes away one main lesson from home—one dish that is cooked and recooked until you've seen it in all shades and textures. Your life's meat and potatoes.

THOSE were the days. Those WERE the days. Those were the DAYS.

There's a particular loneliness to sitting down at a table others have already eaten at, flicking at hard crumbs and tracing the rings of cleared glasses with your finger.

But what about the Second World War, huh?

Were those the good old days?

No, but when the past sucks it just becomes a welcome lesson in how not to do things.

Thirteen is a great age for lessons.

It's an age like a witch trial. You sink or you sink.

Sink, sank, sunk, I recited, learning irregular verbs. These irregularities sounded so final, like a Roman emperor holding his thumb at twelve, nine, then six o'clock.

Stink, stank, stunk.

Some of the kids in my class had started stealing things. Little things like pencils, erasers, candy. It was a daring contest, won by Laura, the girl with the biggest breasts who pinched the other girls' breasts and shouted, "Honk, honk!"

I too had started stealing stuff here and there, but not the kind that could get you into trouble with the Polizei. No, I would cross the border to another country and like a tourist smuggling home street signs, I would strip down bits and pieces that weren't meant for taking.

I couldn't steal from my grandfather, who cut out pictures of airplanes from newspapers and magazines to paste them into neat albums that he locked away in a cabinet with a tiny key. The war had made his mouth very small and flat, and he only opened it to eat and to complain about lottery numbers.

The room to my grandmother's past wasn't locked. She told me about swinging milk cans on the way home, ten-pfennig lemonade on Sundays. I looked at her photographs while she rolled up her support stockings. She was part of the purpose generation. She couldn't sit for more than five minutes without mentally cooking the next meal or weeding flower beds. Every visit at Grandma's, I stole bits of her past, checking under the pillow of her memory, then working on the seams until I found a little worn tear in the lining and slipped my finger inside the stuffing.

"Before your granddad and I got married, he got leave from the front and that's when I knew love for the first time." Grandma's neck blushed and she searched her pockets in the oblivious way Leonard from next door played pocket pool. I had always thought of her as a sexless flower. She needed no gardener to manure her roots, clip her blooms.

"What do you mean?"

Grandma didn't reply. She stared into the distance where I assumed she was projecting her past in all its perfection—all sexual organs hidden under the covers.

Ours was still a family of prudes. We went to the beach with our swimsuits already sticking to our skin underneath our clothes.

"You made . . . love?"

"There was a war on and I didn't know if I'd ever see him again."

Grandma got to her feet. "And now I have to get dinner ready."

The way she said it made me think these two facts were linked.

If Granddad hadn't survived the war, Grandma wouldn't

have been cooking us any dinner because none of us would exist now—except for Grandma.

One by one, the ingredients of the meal wafted into the living room.

I waxed German and philosophical as I analyzed Granddad. Potatoes. Granddad was the remainder of a real person. Red cabbage. He'd been sent home from the war like a parcel some stranger had torn open and pilfered before sending it on its way again. Meat. The precious part of Granddad, his heart, had gone forever. It couldn't be found again—like the silverware Grandmother had buried near a tree when the Russians had marched in and couldn't find again after the war.

"Dinner is ready!"

The ingredients of a good meal are like members of a biological family—opposites by nature.

Aunt Gunhild appeared in our family like a new, polarizing character spicing up a tired TV series. She was Grandma's cousin. Their mothers had been sisters and they had both married men called Wilhelm, but these Wilhelms had lived in cities far apart. I thought it would have been much cleverer if they had both stayed in Berlin and married men with different names.

These two Wilhelms were the sum of my knowledge about Aunt Gunhild.

It took a lot of carefully dosed questions to coax answers out of my mother, who, as a child of the purpose generation, liked to create work where there was none by ironing the family's underpants.

"Why haven't I heard about her before?"

Mom told me that Aunt Gunhild had moved to the Black Forest years ago. "Out of sight, out of mind." The iron hissed and my mother wielded it like Thor's hammer across my father's fine-rib briefs.

That's when I knew.

My mother didn't approve of Aunt Gunhild, a single woman,

who cooked only for herself. A woman who didn't send me a girl's weaving frame for my birthday but a bill powered by two fat zeros.

My mother protested. "You can't accept it! It's too much!"

Every night I took out the bill and felt its power crackling like electricity. Money could turn on a lamp or it could turn into a lamp. Unlike time, with its compartments of tenses, beginnings and ends, go-went-gone, money was truly liquid.

Aunt Gunhild invited my grandparents, my mother, and me to the north coast, where she had rented a holiday house for a week. We played cards in the evening and the rough wind was roaring and rattling louder than Aunt Gunhild's smoker's cough. The nights were black squares in our windows.

When we were nestling in our deck chairs on the terrace, Aunt Gunhild gave me *I see you* smiles. *I see you* smiles make the eyes of the person who sees you so small that you know they don't really see you with their eyes but with their heart. That's cheesy, but true—like that song "Lili Marleen" that was sung by Nazis, Allied troops, and Grandma.

During our stay, Aunt Gunhild made me little presents and stuffed my pockets with money. I wanted to steal from her badly, but my mother was always around. All I learned was what Mom told me while we were out beachcombing. Mom wanted to walk arm in arm like the other mothers and daughters on the beach, but she was carrying her memories like a vendor's tray around her neck. "You were so much cuter when you had pigtails!"

It's impossible to bond when a vendor's tray keeps jabbing into your ribs. Also Mom didn't want to sell Aunt Gunhild's past in exchange for a shiny lavender seashell. She only told me that Aunt Gunhild's husband had not returned from the war. He had given her his last name, put on a uniform, and got himself blown to bits right away.

Blow-blew-blown.

My fingers traced the edges of the seashells, their coats empty and hard like Granddad, who always stayed back at the house because the soft part of him had been stolen in the war.

As Christmas approached, there was talk of Aunt Gunhild coming to stay with us for the holidays. My mother's mouth smiled, but her eyes were as cold as the hungry north German winters she'd braved as a postwar child. The winters in which your veins showed like cracks on ice and you pushed ice around your mouth, turning it into a Christmas roast, a Bundt cake, or a fruit drop. Ice was the poor man's liquid then.

Aunt Gunhild usually spent the holidays on duty at the hospital where she was working as a nurse, but this time she wanted to celebrate with her family. I imagined her in the nurses' break room, sleeping with her eyes open, taking long drags and watching the smoke unravel like her lonely psyche.

Dad and Aunt Gunhild were like chemicals that didn't mix—no matter how hard you shook the test tube. He avoided her, his eyes searching the TV set for more than it could give him. Aunt Gunhild had strong opinions about many things and sometimes her opinions were so strong that they erupted in a smoker's cough and loud voices that pulled me from sleep. The night before, Aunt Gunhild had come charging topless into the living room to ask Grandma for her hairspray. Dad had called for Mom, ashen, pieces of salted peanuts clinging to his lower lip, hanging open like the flap of my piggy bank when I was listening to the crackling of the bills.

That's when I knew.

The emperor's thumb was at six o'clock.

Aunt Gunhild wouldn't be invited again.

Fall-fell-fallen.

No more *I see you* smiles and caramels.

Then, one night, I stepped out on the balcony, and she joined me.

The air smelled like soggy leather shoes. The temperature was too mild for snow.

"Winters aren't what they used to be!" Mom had said, her ice-blue eyes melting a little with regret.

Aunt Gunhild lit a cigarette and flipped the HB packet on the ledge. It was a brand that nobody else I knew smoked.

"HB—Hanging Breasts," she said with a hoarse snicker.

"Thanks again for the ski suit," I said. Not that I had ever been skiing, but the suit had the right sort of flashy pink Mom would never have bought me. At thirteen I felt unprepared for most things. Breasts, bras, boys. The ski suit's soft shell had the silky sound of Allied parachutists landing behind enemy lines in war movies.

I loved it.

We looked at the stars.

"Do you have a boyfriend?" Aunt Gunhild asked, her lips twitching a little as if she were counting the stars under her breath.

I thought about the boy I'd stopped being friends with this summer. We'd grappled with each other like we had since kindergarten. Suddenly he'd been on top of me as if I were a raft on a river he'd wanted to explore.

"Uh, no."

"What do you want to do with your life?" she asked, still counting the stars, her voice sounding like gravel crunching under the feet of dinner guests as they walk out into the night.

I shrugged. Life scared me. Part of me wished for a past without the need to fill in the present, but I was too ashamed to tell her that.

"Did you always want to be a nurse?" I asked, thinking that a house has more than one way in and that a thief needs to be flexible.

"Not at all. You're so very lucky to be growing up in this day and age."

Her raspy voice and the shadow of her rotund, blow-dried hair shut me up. Something had happened to Aunt Gunhild.

Her past—it had been stolen a long time ago.

It was like flicking through the newspaper only to find that someone has cut out the article you were looking for. Who had done this to her?

A true thief, not some thirteen-year-old collector of pressed flowers, but someone who knew what they were taking, ripping out the plants roots, juice, and all.

Aunt Gunhild nodded at the stars, scattering ash while her cigarette glowed like an afterthought.

"Stars are the perfect landmarks," she said. "They never change, but every time we look at them, we see them with different eyes. We can measure the distances we've traveled inside ourselves. Isn't that wonderful?"

I gave Aunt Gunhild an *I see you* smile, and then I looked through the glass door, seeing the solemn constellation of my grandmother, mother, and father on the living room sofa.

Aunt Gunhild left with Grandma a few days later and we all went back to our normal routine like a string quartet sitting down after an interlude. School was due to start again, and I looked through my things, trying to prepare myself for Laura, the boob pincher, and the hollow-eyed World War II soldiers lying on the side of the road on page 135. Question: Why is it important that stories are recorded for the future?

It was then that I started missing things. Little things like pencils, erasers, a rubber ball.

I asked my mother if she'd seen them, expecting icy-blue eyes for not taking care of my stuff. Instead she steered us toward the two uncomfortable rattan seats no one ever sat in—it was here we'd had our birds-and-bees talk a few months back.

Mom: What do you know about sex?

Me (blushing): Err, everything one needs to know.

Mom: Good, then tell me.

Did she think that unpleasant topics might be absorbed by uncomfortable furniture?

"We didn't want to tell you, but Aunt Gunhild took some things," she said. "Cheap little things like tea candles and so on."

"How do you know it was her?"

"She took some stuff when she was visiting Grandma in the spring. It's all very childish. We think she might be a kleptomaniac."

Aunt Gunhild never visited again, but every time I opened my closet, I caught a flash of pink in the corner of my eye, like fluorescent roadkill. The ski suit hung limply in its corner, a deflating memory, soon too small for me. I was liquid too, adjusting to my different bodies, new gravities.

The following year, the Berlin Wall came down in a fall so mild that January brought hazelnuts and primroses.

The present was another country.

Strangers were hugging strangers in the streets. There was dancing. Every person was a crowd, and the crowd was one country.

My parents cried about their past.

It was history.

Everything was liquid.

Thomas Bolt

Inversion of Marcia

Y<small>OU AWAKE</small>?" Alicia asked. No answer.

I opened my eyes: Alicia stood there in the dark, watching my sister sleep. After a minute she leaned over Marcia's bed and whispered, "Hey. It's chilly. I'm getting in with you." Bracelets jingled. The bed squeaked. I heard her kiss my sister's cheek and say a few words in Italian, probably a joke. They began to whisper, too quiet for me to hear.

Great. Now if I made a noise they'd say I'd been *pretending* to be asleep so I could lie in the next bed and listen. I kept so still I wasn't there at all, and thought about building a tiny house in the woods one day out of silvery lumber; about how Dad kept missing the turnoff and driving us through the same ancient arch; about painting my nails, which were disgustingly bitten and chipped and had last been painted in the United States. (I'd happily try some random Italian color, but we were out in the country, sort of, and you couldn't walk on these roads.)

Marcia whispered something and they laughed. Fine: I didn't want to know.

Mom called this place a villa, but really it was a cross between an old hotel and a school. There were sandpapery towels and glass doors with golden coats of arms, but also rows of coat hooks and a library. Anyway, Dad's friend Ian had gotten us a deal, and it was obvious why, since we were the only people here. But you could see the Gulf of Naples from your room (unless it was the Mediterranean). It looked close enough to walk to, though I was the only one who wanted to try.

The whispering went on and on and on, like rain falling so softly you wonder if it's rain at all. I woke from a wild dream about kids with flashlights racing through a construction site: still dark. Marcia's bed was empty. That interested me: where else was there to go?

The big tiles were cool underfoot. You could feel how old they were, uneven and smooth.

At the end of a long hallway, I saw their backs: they were standing out on a balcony, sharing a blanket. I wondered what they were doing till I saw the smoke.

My feet were freezing, so I went back to bed. Anyway . . . we'd only been in Italy a few days and already it felt completely normal, as if *this* was the way things ought to be and it was everything else that was strange. I'd never been out of the United States before; never heard of Cuma, where we were staying. My dad said it was where the alphabet came ashore in Italy, but he said things like that. Whatever it had been thousands of years ago—famous religious center, Greek colony, biggest city in Italy—it was off the main highway now.

So was I: I'd been "asked" not to bring my computer, and my phone was the wrong kind, so I couldn't even *text*. Mom and Dad probably thought it was "healthy for Mary to take a break," but they didn't under*stand*: it was like my friendships were these tiny twinkling lights and they'd yanked the plug. I put my earbuds in and skipped from song to song until I realized I didn't want to listen to anything, not even silence: I listened to the wind. Where was it coming from? Probably the whole building was infiltrated by any breeze that really took an interest.

We were going to Pozzuoli and Pompeii—both close by, out there in the dark somewhere; then back to Naples to see more churches and museums, shop, and eat more amazing food; then north for a bit; and back to Connecticut. Simple, but fine with me. I liked it here. Even the villa was interesting, all curves and scrolls, with odd little balconies. Our room looked out onto an orange grove that was just *there*, and the trees—with real fruit you could actually eat—grew on a sloping, stepped hollow that exactly followed the shape of the amphitheater buried underneath. Beyond that some olive trees that got a faint silvery look when the wind blew, something industrial, a stretch of absolute darkness, a few lights, and the black of the sea (unless it was the gulf). Across the water was Naples, a crazy city with traffic worse than New York. The pizza there was completely different from anything we had in Norwalk or even the city, but it happened to be perfect: these people knew *exactly* what they were doing. All you had to do was forget what you already knew and just *go along with it*.

Marcia was really taking her time. Getting high, fine—but Alicia was in *college*; my sister wasn't even sixteen until next month, so it was a little weird the way they were hanging out so much. And a bit insulting, since the way Alicia probably saw it, there was no one else to hang out with but *me*. I closed my eyes. I could always sneak down to the library and pick through the beach novels, old board games, random histories ("the emperor's pallor worried his advisers"), guidebooks from before I was born, and rows of serious scholarly thingies bound in red or green, by or about people like Chrysippus, Lucretius, and Philo of Megara. There was even a book called *The Tenth Muse: A Life* (as if muses were real? I loved it). Whole shelves were in Latin or Greek, some with no English at all . . .

They were never coming back.

Actually, Alicia was all right. She had this little philosophy book that proved that whatever you thought (though she had *no* idea what *that* might be) was wrong—as much a part of the past as whatever was in those red and green books. Her blond hair was cut short in a way that made her seem almost tough, but had a cute flip to it. Her lips were big and soft-looking like a wilty flower, one of those huge blossoms with droopy clinging petals, so she'd start to look all pretty and romantic—but then would say something hilarious and sharp and her eyes would squeeze almost shut, and if she laughed she wouldn't make any noise at all. She had a nice body—her breasts were very proud of themselves. Anyway, you have to be careful not to dislike people for no reason.

I turned on my side. When I opened my eyes it was bright out; Marcia hadn't come back.

No sign of Mom and Dad. I followed the smell of coffee down to the kitchen. Alicia and Marcia sat at the end of the long table reading my guidebook. They looked up as if it were *their* kitchen and *their* book and I'd interrupted some secret discussion, and would I please go away? I screamed like the goddess Alala until they turned to stone and cracked and crumbled to dust and sifted away, poured myself a glass of blood-orange juice, and sat twisting my bracelet, the one I loved, with the irregular beads of blue and amber glass. "Good morning?"

Alicia yawned. "I need a shower." She winced, pursed her soft, soft lips, and took about four years to slide her leg off the bench. It was like watching someone do physical therapy—only her disability was laziness. She smiled at me and skipped off up the stairs.

Marcia lifted her tiny cup. She had Alicia's lipstick on, deep red with flecks of blue-black sparkle. "Hey," I said. "Where are Mom and Dad?"

The dark lips formed a smile. "Like it? It's called Glitterjack. She'll let you try it. Just ask."

"Thanks?" I wasn't going to ask. "Hey, are they going north without us or something? Did Mom say anything?" For some reason we were skipping Rome, and Rome was what I really wanted to see—though the way Dad kept getting lost, we might end up there anyway.

"Actually . . . Alicia's going to stay with us for a few days. In Dad's friend's place, in Siena."

While our parents took off for Florence, Ravenna, and Venice: *great*. And my role would be to make my sister, who was barely *nineteen months older than me*, feel sophisticated and adult, just by being myself. She'd done her fingernails, too: she looked Alicia's age.

"We'll have the car. She'll drive us anywhere we want. After all, she's our *babysitter*." Marcia poured herself the last of the coffee. "Oh—sorry. You're welcome to make more." She slid the faceted metal pot my way. "You know how, don't you?"

"I thought you drank coffee with lots of sugar and milk."

"When I was *ten*. I like espresso; it's bitter, like my heart. Oh, by the way, we're going to see the Sibyl of Cumae. Her cave's *still there*—cut into the living rock."

"Thanks for the information you got from my guidebook." I headed back upstairs.

"And we're going out for *cinghiale*," she called after me. "Wild pig! Alicia says it's delicious."

"Alicia should know," I said, but not out loud. You don't have to say everything you think.

Dad was standing in the hallway, jacket on, studying a map. He said to get ready and get in the car: we were going to walk around on a flat volcano! "Bring water," he shouted. Mom put on a floppy straw hat, got her bag, and we walked down. Something kept making her smile.

On the way, Alicia told us about the old brick sauna that looked like an oven, and the place where you could camp (*really? I could already smell the sulfur*). We parked and went up.

PERICOLO • DANGER

said a warped yellow sign. Alicia and I laughed: the *sign itself* was smoldering. Steam drifted by or rushed up from under the dirt. Hot spots kept shifting, leaving safety barriers tilted and twisting, about to be swallowed up, or neatly fencing off some harmless stretch. I stared at a distant pit of bubbling muck and tried to get used to the *smell*. "It's literally on fire."

"What do you expect?" Marcia said. "It's a volcano."

Sky was *so* blue. Alicia stretched out her arms and whirled around. I squinted and smiled. Mom put on her movie-star sunglasses.

"So . . . this is a caldera." Dad studied my guidebook. "And these are . . . fumaroles?"

"Sounds like a fancy dessert," Mom said. "Forget the guidebook, Peter, look around!"

He blinked and smiled, but he did look: I could see he liked it, too.

I picked up a rock and wandered toward the lake of boiling mud. Alicia stood by a repositioned fence, nose in the air, wrists against her hips, hands turned out, neck elongated, like she was posing for a fashion shoot. She wore black jeans and a dark red sleeveless shirt that was actually perfect. On her bicep was a neat, needle-thin tattoo, plain punctuation:

$$? > !$$

—whatever that meant. Still, her posture *was* a little odd: like she was a model, but a really clumsy one. I couldn't decide whether she posed like that on purpose or couldn't help it.

Must have been unconscious: I saw her do the *exact* same thing an hour later in the Pozzuoli town square. A soccer ball rolled by—followed by a curly-haired boy (dark blond, tan, blue shirt) who looked my way for a second with bright-dark eyes. Amazing, though, to see the palm trees near the ancient columns: pretty obvious where the whole *idea* for columns had come from, right down to the leafy decorations on top.

The restaurant was big and empty and had a wood-burning *forno*. The people who ran it were crazily busy but nice. Dad joked about ordering a dormouse glazed with honey, stuck with poppy petals; Alicia slitted her eyes and murmured, "Petronius." Since the menu was a choice between noodles with a gamy sauce and some kind of local mushroom, I asked for a sandwich. While everyone ate flat pasta with wild-boar sauce, a.k.a. *pappardelle al sugo di cinghiale*, and went on about how it was the best meal of their lives, I picked at a huge piece of crusty bread and a hunk of cheese. Dad offered me wine, but I said "No, thanks" before Mom could object.

Marcia sucked a long noodle into her mouth and looked up to see if anyone had seen. It was sad: we used to notice things together—find the *meow* in *homeowner*—and laugh till we couldn't breathe. We'd be having fun together now, but apparently we'd been to the beach with Alicia's family when we were little and had both "adored her." We hadn't even *seen* her in six years, but it made sense to them: Alicia could "help out" in exchange for a free trip to Italy.

We all got tired at once. Sulfur clung to the weave of our clothes, a disgusting smell that might never wash out. There was no escaping it—as if it were somehow *inside* you.

No one spoke on the drive back. Marcia fell asleep. We passed an unlit villa—old, crumbly, streaky, and gorgeous, like lots of things in Italy. Even the darkness seemed ancient. This road had older roads underneath; people had lived here, lied to each other here, cried, prayed, fought, spoken languages no one living even knew, and died, and now we were here: just for a second, it was our turn.

Headlights swept over trees. I caught Alicia staring at me, her head a little to one side: she didn't look away. Instead, she got this irritating look of satisfaction, as if she'd let me in on a big secret in perfect safety, because it was something I would never understand.

"Didn't you take the left fork last time?" Mom asked.

Tall, shadowy, with weeds and bushes growing out of it, the ancient arch passed over us.

Dad didn't reply, which meant he was either angry or super frustrated. I'd been chewing so quietly that the last thing Alicia expected to emerge from my lips was a pink bubble the size of a grapefruit. I let it deflate and wrinkle back into my mouth. Even the *gum* tasted sulfury.

Then there we were, back on the ancient pavement, gliding through the arch again, wondering how many more times we'd see it tonight before we could collapse into our beds. (Or whichever bed we planned to sleep in, anyway.)

No note. I checked the rooms: everyone was gone. Alicia had left a neat little pile on her pillow. The name on her International Driving Permit was Mary Alicia Minnen—we had the same first name? I sat on the edge of her bed and untangled a wonderful charm bracelet: silver telescope, bronze acorn, enameled ham, tiny hourglass with real sand in it—nice. The velvet pouch I guessed was her makeup bag was jammed instead with prescription medicines. Wow. Why so many? Their names made me think of those late Roman emperors who issued coins, marched around the frontier for a month, and died without visiting Rome: Verropax, Mortorian, Afflexitor, Numerian, Cerulazapam. I picked up her music player and touched the button:

> If you work hard and get counseling
> You can turn your life around, but . . .
> I don't fucking WANT TO!
> I don't fucking WANT TO!

· · ·

Sleep in and everyone abandons you. I showered and put on jeans, a dark red shirt, and a thin charcoal cardigan with one tiny hole in it. Touched my lips with the Lipdust Matte Stick I'd brought, so my shirt and lips were almost the same red; and that was it. I couldn't *go* anywhere, but at least I was dressed. I couldn't drive, there was no place I could walk to, I didn't speak Italian; but that was just a situation. I felt like I *knew* this place. You don't have to kiss someone to know *exactly* how the kiss would be. When that boy in the soccer shirt walked past, guiding the ball without ever seeming to touch it, I didn't *know* him at all, but I knew what it would be like: his breath hot, his lips a little chapped, his mind on something he couldn't describe. (It's amazing how defenseless people are.)

I slipped through my secret passageway, a cloakroom that joined the LOUNGE to the LIBRARY: narrow hall, long shelves, row of hooks. I liked the stillness, the way the old books smelled. I sank into a chair and tried to follow the mental adventures of Diodorus Cronus.

Alicia and Marcia bubbled into the lounge next door, laughing and talking. I turned the page but didn't read. "No, but his villa was *walking distance* from here. When they put him under house arrest, he threw a suicide party. Just a normal night with friends—except he let himself bleed to death." Alicia, talking about some guy she knew—or some musician or director she only knew *about*. I couldn't hear Marcia's voice. "Anyway, he liked *you*. Did you catch what he said? In English it'd be something like: 'I want pictures of you to decorate my dreams.'"

I read on over their laughter: I didn't really get the Master Argument.

"I'm not a good example," Alicia said. "I was having sex before I knew what sex was. Mostly older men who 'thought' I was twenty—and I was your *sister's* age. She's pretty, your sister."

"She's afraid someone'll *think* she's pretty," Marcia said clearly.

My chin touched my chest. I blew air across the pages of my book.

"Oh, come on . . . you two look alike! Big brown eyes, olive skin, brown hair . . . long-waisted—"

"My eyes aren't 'brown' at all. They're hazel, actually. See?"

I was sorry I'd looked in Alicia's pill bag. At Solfatara she'd dragged me over to the old brick sauna and shown me where to stick my hand, into a gap in the brickwork: *hot*. Quite hot, but I could stand it. *Okay, now move your hand a tiny fraction higher, and keep it there.* What? It was so hot my hand just jumped away on its own.

My sister squealed in the next room. "You're playing with something dangerous." She was out of breath.

"What am I playing with?"

"Me."

They went quiet. After a minute I got up but didn't leave. I felt ticklish all over, like when someone tells a ghost story late at night and stops at a scary moment and everyone *listens*.

"You lose," Alicia said. "Now you have to do what I say."

A muffled laugh. "All right—this one. Wait: does it actually work?"

"Oh, it works. It's a kiss timer. We'll have until the sand runs out: no more, no less."

"That's not much sand." Silence. "Barely a pinch. Anyway, no. You'll mess up my lipstick."

"I'll mess up your *life*. Did I say you could stop? You lost: pay the price. *Andiamo, amante.*"

Leaves rustled overhead; wind flung my hair around. I hiked past the excavation, sat down on some crumbly steps, and spoke mock Italian to Luca, one of the dogs. Trees creaked. It was already getting dark. What a waste of a day! Where were Mom and Dad? Why bring us to Italy and disappear? One star out. No, that was Venus: slightly blue and very, very bright.

I went in. Whatever had happened was over and they'd slid the wooden doors open. Marcia was telling Alicia that Mom and Dad had lost a lot of money, taken out a loan, and were trying to start a new business. Huh? What money? What business? Was she making it up?

I went down to the kitchen and turned on the tiny TV. Weird ads, then girls in miniskirts and lots of makeup singing jingly love songs and smirking. I trudged back up: now the lounge was empty. I sat and wrote postcards to Kristen Wilbeck and Anita Alvarez, and thought about writing one to Anita's brother, which made me so nervous that I had to stretch out on the rug and close my eyes for a minute. Even so, I was smiling.

Alimar and Malicia dropped onto the couch and started leafing through magazines. I ignored them. *Whaaaat?* Now Marcia was wearing Alicia's socks, the ones with the helmeted cartoon Martian. I wrote another postcard, got some tiny thing wrong, and had to tear it up.

"Ooh. I *want* that," Marcia said.

"The handbag? The skirt? . . . Or just the model?"

"Very funny, Lee." Every time they laughed, I ruined another card—and they laughed at *everything*, as if they were high. Wait; they were definitely high. I could smell it. Fine . . . Whatever Alicia did, my sister was right behind, like a towed boat.

"Wow . . . the Tetrarchs live on in the old 'marching *K*s' Krispy Kreme logo. That's the Nicomedian Augustus on the left." Alicia sat up. "Hey, Britta Choatelle! I used to work for her."

Marcia leaned over the page. "You *know* her?"

"I don't know anyone. *Britt* knows a lot of people. I was her assistant for three weeks once, while her real assistant was sick. It was pretty crazy: she has this *huge* space in Chelsea—"

I felt like asking them whether celebrities and scenesters were the only people worth knowing, but they'd be all "Of *course* not," whatever they really thought. I copied my words onto a fresh card, and wrote two more before they distracted me again, reading a love letter out loud and laughing. It was apparently from some man Alicia barely knew. Marcia laughed so much I had to leave: it was *not* her normal laugh.

I moved my postcard operation to the MAP ROOM, which no one else had discovered—or so I'd thought. An actual letter lay on the table half-written, next to Alicia's little notebook.

Dear E, hope you just dumped me and aren't ill. Either way, I miss you. I miss the way you used to bring me toast and juice (with a lemon slice) on your old Bakelite tray, the one with the rooster on it. I miss your black kimono and how you never smiled (not before coffee, anyway). I miss the hand-lettered newspaper you wrote out on rice paper that morning, just for me. I miss the complicated board game with the dozen dice and the awful penalties we dreamed up, and I miss your laugh, all soft and papery like a hornet's nest falling in the woods. I miss fucking you. I miss kissing your throat, I miss nuzzling around to find the source of your smell, I miss that old shirt you used to wear, I miss seeing you without your glasses. By the way—

By the way, in the morning, once we got outside, it was almost warm. It had rained, a dirty wash that left a spatter of silt on everything. Dad tested the fine grit between finger and thumb and told us it came straight from the Sahara—picked up in a storm and blown across the sea to coat the hood of our rented Zeus. "A sirocco." And, for a moment, everything seemed fine.

At the museum in Naples, we all stared at Hercules, at the hard curves of his muscles, at his tremendous marble buttocks, and were impressed. "Why does he carry that enormous *pickle*?" Marcia said, and giggled at her own dumb joke, one I guarantee every child makes. (His club *was* exactly like a pickle, but so what?) She had too much mascara on, but looked good—really good. Alicia ignored her for once, absorbed in some lustery glassware from Pompeii.

"What are you thinking?" Mom took my hand. "You're like your father—he could lie on the floor for hours and stare down at the dust. What do you see? Are you having a good time?"

"Yes," I said, and squeezed her hand and let go.

We feasted on *filetti di baccalà* and marinated zucchini and *gnocchi alla Sorrentina* at an amazing restaurant near the water. My father raised a glass to the stuffed boar's head on the wall, its neck still draped with last year's Christmas tinsel. On the drive back, Alicia held her philosophy as steady as she could under the trembling clip light. As a reader she seemed completely different—serious and at ease. She read as if she slowly took things in without rejecting or accepting anything right away. If she could really do that, she was wonderful.

The arch loomed up and passed over. We made the loop ten times, following the same exact route; the eleventh time, the villa was just *there*. We crunched to a stop. A dog barked off in the dark, near the olive grove. This place was nothing like Connecticut.

Mom headed for the villa, walking fast, holding Dad's phone, which was all lit up.

Dad got out and stood petting the dogs. Bracelets jingled as Alicia bent over to adjust the ribbons on her shoes. Her breasts almost came out of her top; I heard the juicy little click of metal as her tongue arched and the steel bead in her piercing touched her teeth, but Dad just went on patting Luca. He hardly noticed her, and I loved him for it: no matter how she dressed or what she did, he ignored her completely, without trying to at all.

Marcia went right to our room, so Alicia and I ended up in the kitchen, drinking supercold mineral water. She swung her feet up onto a chair and cursed. "Left my philosophy in the car."

"Lots more in the library. Try Philo of . . . someplace? Not Parmenides, there are a bunch of loose pages. And, I only read a little bit, but Lucretius is *awesome*. One of the red books."

Alicia slumped down, tilted her head to the side, and gave me a look like: *I wish you were prettier. The way you look really depresses me.* But all she said was, "You seem older than your sister sometimes." (*Thanks?*) "Anyway . . . you can have my book if you find it, Mary. In a way it's the only thing I really own; but I'm pretty much done with it." She kept looking at me, and for a second I could see how tired she was. "I'm only evil part-time," she said. "Aaand, like most people, it's when I'm thinking fairly highly of myself." She went up to her room.

I got out my flat little zip bag and wrote a Vesuvius postcard to Bethany Taylor and one to Maya James, and spent a long time drawing Hercules and his club to send to Todd Chan. It got messy and the club looked too weird and I threw it away. I made another drawing that was sort of worse, but decided to send it anyway, mistakes and all, because *why obsess?* Also, the ribbons on Alicia's shoes were actually *beautiful.* You had to give her that.

Marcia wasn't in our room. The clothes she'd had on were strewn on her bed. The floor was solid—no one could hear a thing—so I popped my earbuds in, put on crazy music, and danced.

I said, "Morning!" but Mom didn't seem to hear. I went back in after my shower: she sat brushing her hair. She stopped with the brush still in; leaned forward little by little; the brush dropped. All I could think of to do was leave: I closed the door as quietly as I could.

It had rained again and was cool. In the kitchen we ate *pizza bianca* and delicious little yogurts in glass jars, and peeled the fat, round oranges a landscaper at one of the villas had given Alicia and Marcia, who'd risked their lives to take a walk along the road. Handsome, Marcia said, but married, with a newborn baby named Eleonora Orfanelli.

Mom came down and sat with a cup of tea. She smiled, like she was trying very hard to be herself. "Mmm," I told her. "*Frutti di bosco* is the best flavor in the world."

"I miss bacon," Marcia said.

"Seriously? Since when do you even eat bacon?"

"I don't. I miss its being *available*." New earrings: rubies like tiny drops of blood.

"They do have bacon here, honey," Mom said. "Pancetta. It's better than our kind, in some ways." Marcia looked at me: *We have pancetta in Connecticut.*

Dad showed us a photo of an octopus relaxing in a bed of seaweed, taken just a five-minute swim from where we sat. Alicia reappeared in an olive-green raw-silk sheath and wooden jewelry. *Where* was she getting her clothes? Midnight shoplifting expeditions? Waking up to find the outfit she'd dreamed about in a neat pile at the foot of her bed? Anyway, she looked sophisticated, completely comfortable. She smiled at me.

We spent an amazing day exploring Pompeii, but got lost coming back: Mom drove us straight through Naples, into the craziest rush-hour traffic I'd ever seen—in and out of tunnels, along the waterfront, and then onto a huge highway . . . heading *away* from the coast. Dad gave up and handed me the map. I got us as far as Cuma, but the villa was *gone*. We glided again and again past old walls, shivery bamboo groves, dark restaurants, palm trees, signposts, tiny trucks, sudden forks in the road— but any choice we made took us back through the arch. No one spoke. Once, I was sure we'd found the way—but there we were, on the Roman road again, the archway rising up ahead. Alicia said it used to carry a new highway laid out by the emperor while Pompeii still smoked under pumice and ash. "We're on the even *older* road it replaced." I didn't think so; couldn't be sure. I rested my forehead on the glass and closed my eyes. We would all dream of gliding through that arch: recurring dreams.

I woke and lay listening to Marcia breathe in the other bed. Almost dawn: you could *hear* the quiet; nothing moving at all, just still things waiting. Then Alicia's voice, somewhere nearby—on the balcony of an empty room, or stretched out on a couch in the hall. Of course, *her* phone worked. But when did she *sleep*?

Down in the cool, dim kitchen, I sat with a glass of blood-orange juice and watched the sun touch each tomato on the sill, until all five seemed to be lit from inside. I stared at the bulletin board until it blurred, thinking of things that might happen in my life, turning them over like curious stones, bits of surf-smoothed glass, slivers of shell. So many choices I might make; so few I really would. I went back upstairs and slept for three more hours.

There was a note from Mom in the kitchen: she'd taken Marcia out for breakfast. I poured a glass of cold peach tea, went to the library, and grabbed a book about satyrs. They had tails and pointy ears and were incredibly horny. As the book put it, "They bring the wine, provide the music, and misbehave." Ha! I *loved* the vase paintings: in one, a tame and pleasant satyr pushed a lady in a swing, but they had horse-size erections everywhere else. *Hilarious.*

Alicia came in, stretched out on the couch, and swung her feet across my lap. "Is this old place really safe, do you think? I mean, if there were a fire, where would we go?" With a silent finger, I showed her: there were signs on all the walls, everywhere in the building.

"And if there's not a fire?"

I didn't bother to roll my eyes. I wanted to say: "You can take a break, Alicia. There's nobody here but us." Instead I sucked cold, sweet tea through my sparkly straw.

Her eyes moved all around the room. "Can I tell you something?"

"I guess." I turned the page. "Wait. Are you wearing my mom's per*fume*?"

She tilted her head. Of course she was too smooth to say anything, but I knew that smell.

"So, I had this *thought*," Alicia said. "About pornography. That the people who make it aren't trying to imagine or portray actual people, but only a situation. Then I realized: philosophy is pretty much the same. Right? Back in a sec. Then I'm going out again."

"Wait, wait, wait. Isn't being a person a situation, too?" (Also: exactly how much porn did she think I watched?)

Alicia swooped back in and set something down with a *click*, as if she'd put me in check: a lipstick. I said, "Oh . . . thanks!" but she was already gone.

In the bathroom upstairs I screwed the color out, almost touched it to my lips, and stood like that, thinking. Somewhere a wild wind was peeling signs off walls. Somewhere a girl my age was practicing her sport with a serious trainer. Somewhere millions of strangers were doing billions of things I'd never know about. And, in the mirror, a girl who was me and no one else stood waiting for something to happen.

Nothing did. I screwed the color in, capped it, and dropped it in my pocket. (Not today.)

"We had breakfast at Baia Castle!" Marcia called up from the entranceway. She wore a floppy straw hat and a sky-blue shirt, and looked completely happy. "We went window-shopping, too! Ugh, dude, those Shroud of Turin beach towels are in poor taste."

Mom looked worn out. She said our dad was waiting to take us to the Sibyl's Cave.

"—and of course the arch," Marcia joked. "Mary, the castle was *amazing*. You *have* to go. Wish I'd brought Rollerblades."

Mom said she would stay behind and have a nap. Her smile was small and tight; you could tell she'd stop smiling as soon as we left.

Dad took a detour to the Birdless Lake to show us the Entrance to Hell, so we got to the Sibyl's Cave right before closing. The men at the gate weren't going to let us in, *especially* after Dad told them in his flimsy Italian that it was their *job* and they *had* to, but Alicia stepped forward, pushed her soft lips out, and asked them, *Please, per carità?*

The gate swung open. They didn't even let us pay.

We spread out over the site. It was late, so we were more or less alone. Alicia jogged ahead, sprinted to the end of the cave, and stood there, arms outstretched: her mouth made an *O*. The Sibyl's scream went on and on and on: echoed down the rock walls and left everything quiet.

Alicia dropped her arms and laughed.

On the path to the acropolis I ran into Dad; we walked up together. "Having a good time?"

"Yes," I said.

We climbed all the way up to where the temples had been and looked out over the gulf. Far below, three people on horseback galloped along a beach. Sun was about to set: in a few minutes we'd all have one less day (obviously). Dad seemed to want to say something, but didn't. We just watched the horses, and a speeding, bucking motorboat way out on the water that made no sound at all. Maybe he wanted to tell me why he and Mom were so preoccupied, as if they had to remind themselves that they were here with us at all? Or why Mom was so upset?

I didn't ask; he didn't say. It seemed like those were the rules.

We sat down on a slab. "About Marcia," he said. "Hey. I know she must seem a little annoying these days . . . but please don't take it personally."

"Oh—I know." I looked over, but couldn't tell what he was thinking. "I love these long bricks. And the color of the water. I guess the marketplace would have been up here, too?"

"Exactly: the agora. You know, the last king of Rome died here. Julius Caesar spent time in Cumae, too. And, after Hercules finally caught him in the snow and hurled him into the sea—"

"Dad? Sorry. What were you going to say about Marcia?"

"Oh . . . I just don't want you to feel outnumbered. But your sister's at an age where, sometimes, you feel so *ready*. Whether you really are or not."

We looked off at the water: the boat was gone. The horses and riders were specks. *Ready or not, here I come.*

"You'll get your turn, Mary. Soon enough—too soon for me!—but for now, please don't take it to heart. Shall we head back down? I don't think the others are going to make the climb."

And in not so many years, first Marcia's room, then mine, would be as empty as these archaeological sites, and things would be different for all of us. Maybe we would love our parents just as much, or even more, but we wouldn't need them at all. We went down the hill.

My sister grabbed a sheet, tripped on it, ran out of the room naked. I stepped back, mouth open. Marcia's bare feet pounded down the hall. A door slammed.

Alicia was naked, too, but she didn't move. "It's okay," she said slowly. "It's all right."

I closed my mouth. (Why was *I* the one blushing?)

Alicia kept giving me the same steady look, but I could hear her breathe. "Okay? It's no big deal. We were playing around."

I was *shaking*. I tried not to shake. "I couldn't find Mom or Dad. I was just going to ask if you wanted something to *eat*."

The Italian boy went on getting dressed, taking his time, as if he were in his own house. His skin was smooth and very, very tan. His lips curved like a statue's. He didn't look at me.

Wait—no—he wasn't a boy at all! He was one of the landscapers from down the road, the one who'd given them oranges, the one whose wife had just given birth to a little girl!

Alicia held her bra like a cat's cradle, looped it over her arms, shrugged into it, fastened the strap, adjusted herself. Shaved bare below, she did nothing to cover up. She seemed amused.

He was way older—twenty-seven, twenty-eight. He had a *family*. The door clicked shut and he was gone.

"You okay?" Alicia asked. "Are you okay?" She came closer, her eyes on mine.

My face kept trying to smile on its own, which made me hate myself a little. "Am *I* okay?"

"Oh, Mary, I know you won't say anything, of course, you aren't like that at all, but I want to thank you anyway. So here's your reward." She leaned in like an actor in a film and gave me a long, soft kiss on the lips. The kiss went on and on, as if we weren't both girls, as if—

Oh.

"It's the Tyrrhenian Sea," Alicia whispered, so only I could hear. "I found a map."

We were squished into the car. Mom was driving, Dad was up in front, and they were talking about some "symposium" they had to go to all of a sudden. They were going to dump us with Alicia, leave us stuck in Siena without a car. Oh, there'd be "plenty to do." I watched the traffic. Alicia's arm was warm against mine, our bare skin touching now and then, as if it were a test to see if I'd pull away. I didn't: I wasn't playing her game, whatever it was. Why should I? The road was actually interesting—what I could see of it. On curves, Alicia leaned into me.

Her lips had tasted like grape jelly. Then there she'd been, back across the room, getting dressed, putting her earbuds in, hunting down a playlist as if nothing real had happened and nothing meant anything and that was that. All night I'd tasted traces of that kiss, felt it all over, and now (I could feel my cheeks go warm) I needed a few minutes or days of the kind of privacy that probably only shipwrecked people get. Not because I was embarrassed—because the whole thing had sprung open at me without warning and folded away before I'd had a chance to know what it was. I could still feel that kiss.

Sun flashed on Alicia's piercing. She liked showing it off—catching the little barbell between her teeth, arching her tongue so the steel bead gleamed—but, honestly? It was a little gross. I closed my eyes. Sometimes there isn't much to do but wait. Maybe things will improve: maybe not. You wait.

Alicia was nudging my sister. "That sign again. You're famous."

Marcia laughed. "Yeah: famous upside down."

Okay, and that man's wife? Their newborn baby? Are they part of your stupid private joke?

Long day in Naples; night rushed by. It still felt so *different* here. Even when there was nothing special—a highway, some industrial landscape, cars—I loved it. And that dark blue shadow against the darker sky was Vesuvius, the volcano that destroyed Pompeii.

Wheels on gravel woke me. Dogs barked. I avoided everyone and went straight to bed—so of course I couldn't sleep: I lay in the dark thinking of every single time I'd ever been shallow or mean or afraid, or hadn't paid the attention someone or something or someplace had deserved. Would I even *like* college when the time came? From the little Alicia said, I imagined people socializing chaotically while ideas slid by like roadside scenery. Though maybe a real idea would just insist, like that gap between the bricks at Solfatara, where you can't keep your hand in the serious heat for even a *second* before it shoves you back.

Marcia was in Alicia's room again. I wondered what the octopus from Dad's photo was doing right now, this second, tonight. Undulating out there in the dark, moving exactly like the water at first, then suddenly *not* as it reaches for prey, all of its suckers flared.

I read Lucretius until late—his philosophy was all about *sex*!—and finally got sleepy. When I went to the bathroom, Dad was down the hall, his back to me, talking on the old phone you had to put a token in. "I don't know what else I could have done." He listened. "Soon."

God. I'd overheard a thousand conversations on this trip and actually *had* maybe *two*.

I woke up late. Suitcases stood by the door and the whole place felt different. I ate breakfast alone; sat watching a spider with pale, transparent legs investigate the hinge of Mom's suitcase. Dad came in. With care, he took the spider up on the brim of his hat and flicked it lightly onto the nearest sill. "*Siamo pronti?* Time to pack, Mary, we're going north."

I gave him a hug and he patted me on the head, just like he always had—even when I was a baby, probably. Only this time I was feeling nauseous and hollowed out, so it didn't really stick.

We said good-bye to the dogs and got in the car. Dad tried to drive through the archway one last time, for fun, but we couldn't find it. We passed a CUMA sign with a red slash through it, meaning *No more Cuma—ciao!*—and were on the road.

Alicia's bracelets jingled. I let my forehead rest against trembling glass. I *loved* the umbrella pines: I'd seen them in paintings and always assumed they were cartoony, made-up things—but they were *real*. Italy was real. A cloud passed out of sight and into my mind, where it floated slowly on, dimming a little as I closed my eyes and we rushed up A1, the Highway of the Sun.

When I looked over, Alicia and my sister were holding hands. I couldn't see my mom but I knew she was staring out of the window, seeing the same trouble everywhere we went. I wanted to reach over the seat and pat her, but she would only tell me to put my seat belt on.

"I can't *believe* they gave this place *two stars*," Marcia said. I had to agree: the room was disgusting. You couldn't bathe without brushing against the toilet, which was *inside* the shower, and the bathroom ceiling was black with what Mom called "terrifyingly mature" growths of mold. Still, when you stepped outside, there was Siena. Dad and I climbed to the top of the old tower and saw the city spread out like living geometry; Piazza del Campo opened like a fan.

We all met up at a pizzeria on a steep narrow street. Marcia wore a thin white sweater over a wine-red dress that was practically see-through—Alicia's, of course. Mom didn't even notice. "I need a nap before we do the Duomo," she said. In the hotel's tiny lobby, the TV was on. An American actor whirled to face the camera and shouted: *Che cosa fai?*

"*Non lo so, idiota*," Alicia told the TV, and gave me a quick smile. She wore a perfume that smelled like lemon peel and grass and some spice you couldn't be sure was there or not, but I was honestly getting a little tired of her. Something about her was maybe a little cruel? What I'd thought when she'd kissed me (or a bit after, once I could think again) was mostly, *why?* It was like sitting in someone's car and revving the engine, then not bothering to take them anywhere.

Back in the tiny room I shared with Mom, I lay on my bed reading. Dad came in and said something that made Mom jump up. "No. Absolutely not. I'm not letting you out of my sight!"

I got up and left. I didn't hear what he said back, but it sounded like he was trying to be quiet and patient in a way that wouldn't calm you down at all.

Marcia and I went for a walk. We wandered all over Siena, stopping to look at the yellow pottery or figure out which *contrada* we were in—we loved all the different coats of arms. We didn't really talk, which was nice. After an hour she headed back; I stopped at a newsstand. Some of the magazines had little presents shrink-wrapped onto them—change purse, lotion sample, diary. I flipped through a flimsy gossip magazine: An ad for lingerie. Rings. A baby carrier. A wristwatch encrusted with every color of jewel. Gardening soil. Goofy furniture. Puffed-up, perforated weight-loss pants. Little muffins sealed in bags. Ugly suede wedges. Biscuity cookies that looked like little gears, that you somehow had to buy at the pharmacy? Amazing furniture. A special fitness shoe that would definitely injure you. A crystal ball (though the ad was for something else). Oh, and the articles all seemed to be about old men in bathing suits and topless women with lots of makeup on. The pictures were amazing: an ominous old man gripping a young woman's duffel bag. A woman in plush purple sweatpants talking on a jeweled phone. And I recognized none of the celebrities, which made me feel FREE.

Mom and I both went to bed early. I slept pretty well—until a man screaming for quiet woke everyone up. Down the hall somewhere, an Englishwoman went on shouting at her daughter. "I should *not* be doing this! I should not be cleaning *your vomit* from *my* car keys!"

¡Cállate! ¡Quiet! screamed the Spaniard in the next room, ten times as loud.

Mom put a pillow over her head. I put my earbuds in, set an instrumental track on endless repeat, and went back to sleep with wild jazz in my head.

Alicia and I lived in a big old house in Rye, near the amusement park, playing a game with complicated rules. We had to act like we were married; but, since the whole point of marriage was to get the upper hand, you could never relax or be nice.

When the wind blew, the house creaked like a ship. She sang while she loaded the dishwasher: *O, O, they call me Jack-A-Roe.*

I was glad to wake up and leave the moldy hotel forever.

We moved into a neat little *appartamentino* in the newer part of town. Our parents took off right away, saying they'd be back in time for dinner, which no one believed. I put Mom's sunglasses on. Pushed my bottom lip out as far as it would go, just to see how far: pretty far.

"Teach not thy lip such scorn," Alicia said. Silent, unsmiling, like a cop who was half machine and half man, I swiveled and turned my dark lenses on her. She laughed.

Marcia was in the kitchen painting a hunk of bread with Nutella. While I waited for her to offer me some—since that might take forever—I poured two glasses of mineral water and put one in front of her. "When we get back," she said, "I'm getting a labret."

"A lab rat?" I felt my nostrils widen: the gloss on her lips smelled like grape jelly.

"A *piercing*. Right here. A little silver loop over my lip. Alicia says it's good for kissing."

"Alicia would know. God. You're consuming that whole thing? What would Mom say . . ."

Marcia chewed intently. "You really don't get it?" She licked her fingertips. "Our parents are breaking up, Mary: divorcing, separating, ending things, moving on."

"No, they're not."

"They're probably working out the details now."

"Shut *up*. You sound like something on TV."

"Yeah . . . okay . . . My brain weighs as much as an adult's. Yours won't for at least another year." She took a giant bite of the loaded bread and walked away, leaving her mess behind.

I wanted to shout: "I'm not a dumping ground for your MOODS." Instead I rested my cheek on the marble counter and breathed. Anyway, it wasn't true. Nothing was going to change.

Was it? I reached for the sparker wand and clicked out sparks. *Spark-lick. Spark-lick.* Bizarre: Why didn't they just have pilot lights? Why didn't we just have wands?

I put the Nutella away: I didn't want to get blamed and have a fattening-foods discussion with Mom. Of course, I'd seen Marcia at her worst—puffy face, matted hair, blotchy skin, so thirsty we'd had to feed her ice from a spoon. This was all because I *knew* her—I really did—and she was trying to become somebody else.

She sat on the living room couch, her head on Alicia's shoulder. I didn't go in.

The car keys lay in a bowl on a table by the door. Hey, the compass on the key ring was real! I looked out: our car was right there, so Mom and Dad hadn't really gone to Monteriggioni . . . Unless they'd taken a bus?

"I said, 'Don't even ask me,'" Alicia was saying. "'I'm no judge of what's normal.'"

So, there was the car. I was tall enough. I understood the signs. It was an automatic.

"Anyway," Marcia said, "*she's* supposedly very nice. We're going to be there for at least one night while my mom and dad do . . . whatever they do when they abandon us."

I slipped my jacket on, stepped into my shoes. Stepped out of them again and looked into the living room: they were reading an old church magazine and giggling.

"Listen to this! 'Dance, which works to arouse the senses, can never be pure.'" They laughed.

I didn't. Because, actually, if you were honest about it, wasn't it kind of a serious thing, to rouse the senses? Just because it's easy to do at first didn't mean it would go on being easy. THE BODY SEEKS THAT WHICH HAS WOUNDED THE MIND WITH LOVE.

I stuck my head in. "Hey. I'm going out to walk around a bit. See you."

Alicia looked up: they went on talking. I snagged her license on the way out. *Ciao, ragazze!*

It was quiet in the car. I sat gripping the steering wheel. People my age could probably drive here anyway—couldn't we drink wine? Have sex? Be emperor, if all that started up again?

I strapped myself in, adjusted the seat, played with the mirror until I could see behind me. The engine started right up. I let it run for a bit, pressed down on the brake, and shifted: a jolt of power told me I could move. No one was around. *Ready or not . . .*

I pulled out—whoa, too fast. I went easier on the gas, made a turn, and there I was, driving through streets full of cars and people! No one noticed or cared. I went faster, faster, until I had to stop and pressed the brake too hard: a truck in the mirror came suddenly close.

After that I was a little too careful, too slow; cars collected behind me, but somehow no one honked. I got nervous, pulled off onto a side street, and sat breathing. Sky brightened. Trees rushed and went still. A lean, toast-colored cat trotted by, leaped up onto a wall, and picked his way along: a Siamese. The engine ran on. A woman in a window went on brushing the hair of a doll with brief, fierce strokes. The doll was the size of a child, the woman ancient. When the sun caught her eyes I saw she was blind.

No tourist would come here. Maybe *this* was what Italy was really like. (Though I had no idea, of course.)

I turned the car around. It took me an hour to get back, but, just as I pulled in, a tiny truck backed out of our spot. *Whew.* I parked, cut the engine—and remembered to shift into P.

Mom and Dad were back. Alicia and Marcia sat slumped under a blanket, watching TV. I dropped the keys into the bowl. No one even noticed I'd been away.

. . .

I put earrings in, little buttons made of gold. Mom and Dad were going to dump us at the country house of some couple we'd never met, so we were dressing up. Why not make it fun?

Alicia, busy pinning up part of her hair, offered to lend me a skirt.

"Don't bother," Marcia said. "She'll never wear it because of her ugly legs."

I just looked at her.

"What? You said so yourself!"

"After I flipped my bike, and was all bruised and scabby? Anyway, I have tights. Thanks, Alicia." The charcoal skirt was wonderful: *lana cotta* lined with silk. It was nice to wear something so adult. Even Marcia said I looked five years older—*"Non è una gag."*

Mom stared at us, but said nothing. She and Dad drove us *way* out into the country, pulled up at a big old farmhouse— part stone, part brick, with pinkish uneven roof tiles—waited for us to get out, and just drove away.

No one answered our knock. No one answered our pounding, either. Was it even the right place? We stood there like idiots.

Around the side we found a door propped open with a chair. Alicia called *Hello!* and led us into a huge kitchen with uneven ceiling beams and an arch at one end. Shrivelly sausages hung next to strings of peppers; big piles of American mail lay on a long pine table in the sun.

"HELLO?" No answer. A pot steamed and rattled on the stove.

We stood waiting like children in a fairy tale.

A man with shoulder-length gray hair came in, smiled, mock-bowed, and welcomed us. He wore sandals and comfortable pants. His loose black polo shirt didn't minimize his belly at all, if that's what he was after, but he was very polite; we sat and had *acqua minerale* with lime slices in little unadorned glasses. We'd expected a whole family, but Milt Melling—he made us call him Milt—was all alone: his wife had just taken off for Milan with their nephew Giorgio, a boy my age (probably perfect for me). Milt asked us what we'd thought of Naples and Pompeii, and we talked about ancient villas, each with its hidden interior open to the sky.

"Wouldn't work in Connecticut," he said, "except as a metaphor."

Alicia smiled. Milt leaned in close and took her hand "to get a better look at your *charms*," as he put it. I'd seen that smile in a fresco. Her red lipstick smiled back.

He inspected Alicia's bracelet and looked up happily. "But this is the real thing!"

His face was red and puffy, as if he spent too much time in the sun. He was older than Dad, but she *definitely* flirted back. It even seemed to give her energy in some weird way.

He released her hand and turned to Marcia. *I* was being ignored, as usual. I stared at a bowl of artichokes, the long stems still on them; reached over to pet his black, silky cat, who got up, stretched, and moved to a sunnier spot with a view of vineyards, hills, distant dirt-colored buildings. The pot rattled away. Milt got up and turned it down.

"We'll need a few things from the village," he said. "Anyone up for a walk?"

Alicia and Marcia volunteered. Milt gave them a map, a bag, a list, and some cash; they went off holding hands. I sipped my mineral water, but, man, I *still* didn't understand Diodorus Cronus. Lots of things are possible. Once something has happened, sure, its having happened stays true. But all the things that have failed (so far) to happen are not untrue, or not untrue *yet*. You have to come to a definite end before you can say: *Well, here's the list of things that never happened; their possibility was always just an illusion*. Ah! Just thinking about it (or trying to) was like swimming underwater, straining to hold your breath till you touch the wall. And what if the things that hadn't happened (yet) but might were *not* for that reason unreal or false, but only balanced in some unknowable state of potential? *The pre-real. The ready.*

Milt uncovered the pot and stuck a long fork in. He quizzed me over his shoulder: Had I known Alicia long? Did she go to school? Where? What was she studying?

"Hats," I wanted to say. I could feel the steam on my face from across the room. He covered the pot, opened the fridge, and put a bottle of pale green wine in front of me.

"A nice, crisp Greco di Tufo. Do you know Greco? One of my favorite whites: medium dry, a little tart." He gave me a slow grin. "I have some prep work to do. Why don't you open it and pour us both a glass."

Wait: he thought I knew how to open a bottle of wine? The corkscrew he put in my hand was dark with age, heavier than it looked. I peeled back the foil, put the tip against the cork, and did what I'd seen my parents do but never tried. I knew you had to get it in deep, so I aimed at the center; it kept slipping off. Then it went in, but at an angle. I leaned over and got a grip. The farther it went in, the more it straightened: a little pressure and the cork came out.

He set two plain glasses down. "You know, Greco may well be ancient. Pompeian graffiti allude to it—and here it is, straight from *Vesuvio* to our table. I have a Lacryma Christi as well, also white, or, as Marlowe calls it, 'liquid gold . . . mingled with coral and with orient pearl.' " He smiled like an old statue. "Nothing to prevent us from sampling both."

"Oh, no, this one's fine," I said. "Thanks!"

I forced my hands steady—I don't know why they seemed to want to tremble—and poured two glasses out, with just an inch in mine. Moisture condensed on them right away.

Before I could even move he claimed *my* glass, filled it all the way, and raised it to toast me.

I'd never been toasted before. As our glasses clicked, I probably even blushed. I took a sip, just to taste: made my nose wrinkle. But it was nice to be treated as a person for once.

Milt sat down with a little cutting board, kitchen scissors, and some herbs. He finished his glass and poured himself another. "Something's up with your sister," he said. "Am I right?"

I definitely blushed. Was it *that* obvious? I took a sip: watery and strong, cool and tart. I had to force myself not to make a face, but I didn't have to talk if my mouth was full.

He snipped at an herb. "Did you notice Alicia's charm bracelet? The hourglass?"

"Oh, the kiss timer?"

"Ahh. Then you've divined the secret." He snuck the bottle's snout into my glass and poured me more wine before I could even say yes, all right, sure, thanks: *glig glug glug*. "It's an old trick, you know. It looks like your time would run out right away, but there's a pinch too much sand." A broader smile. "So it *never* runs out."

"Cute." I took a sip. Though I didn't really get how you could kiss while looking at a tiny hourglass on your wrist? And anyway, why would you? When you like someone enough to kiss them, don't you just want to keep on kissing? I would kiss until I caught fire.

He went back to the sink. "How long have those two been an item?"

"Not long," I said—not what I'd meant to say at all.

He turned and gave me a happy look. I took a quick gulp of wine. I wanted to kick myself under the table, but I wanted to laugh, too! Though it really wasn't funny. (Yes, it was!)

Milt put out a red plate with a slumped-over little loaf of goat cheese surrounded by these amazing pieces of bread toasted up in olive oil, and started asking me all about myself—which was weird because he always seemed to be *insinuating* something, and I didn't even know what he was getting at? So I just kept swallowing little mouthfuls of wine while he chopped and stirred and whisked and told me funny things about his neighbors and the local towns and the history of the region, and something about Renaissance philosophers and the local wine, and someone called Gallino Nero (another emperor?). I was about to mention Diodorus Cronus when he topped up my glass again, *exactly* to the brim. It was like a test: could I avoid spilling it? I had to lean over the table and take a long, slurpy sip before I could even *lift* the glass.

He watched me, smiling. I got very quiet, which seemed to amuse him even more. He kept asking questions; I kept taking long, slow sips. It was actually kind of fun. I drank the last of my wine and tried to smear goat cheese on a piece of toast but it was cakey and crumbly and wouldn't smooth out so I made a mess of it and ate it in one bite: delicious!—but of course I'd left my glass unattended: it was full again. He *had* to know I wouldn't drink a *third* glass of wine (fourth? fifth?), but maybe he was just being ceremonious. Or wanted me drunk so he could drag me off somewhere. I made a note of where they kept the knives, because *fuck* that.

Anyway, how had he even poured it so full without spilling? You could see the surface tension making a dome. Plus, I couldn't *reach*. I had to climb halfway onto the table to bring my lips to the glass—slipped; caught myself and laughed. He laughed, too, but I hadn't spilled!

The glass sweated. I could smell the wine. I bent over, kissed the rim, and slurped.

He stopped stirring to stare. He didn't deserve those blue, blue eyes. Of course, if everyone only had what they deserved, the world wouldn't be so easy to recognize. I sat back in my seat and drank the rest. "Funny," I said, a little out of breath, "how people with good luck can usually manage to—I don't know. Muster up a feeling that they deserve it?"

Milt made a grave tilt of his head. He poured more wine, but

I *liked* it now—I mean, I was *totally* used to it. He started to ask another question, but it was my turn: "So . . . Milt. What do you actually *do*?" Because I was finding his whole existence a little hard to understand. Was he on vacation? Like, all the time? I mean, he mostly cooked and drank wine?

Once again there was that little smile. "I suppose you could say, having failed at the things I wanted to do most—and having succeeded at something I did not want to do at all—I'm taking time out to rethink my life. For the moment, that means I cook, shop, tidy up, run errands, open and close the blinds, and find my days quite busy enough. I travel a little. I read. Friends come to visit, or we visit them. Do you mind if I put on music?"

I shook my head. He went down a hall and up some stairs, leaving his little smile in midair.

I lolled back in my chair, chuckling to myself without making a sound. Whatever he was cooking smelled good, but it was *hot* in here. I got up, unbuttoned my cardigan, and snooped around a little—sloppily, not caring at all what kind of mess I made. I almost tripped—over nothing. Found a hand-carved walking stick topped with a sort of pinecone; traced the vines that wrapped around its shaft. *Ha!* I loved *D'Aulaires' Book of Greek Myths.* Lots of mail from investment funds. Fancy invitations. But where was the *bathroom*?

Leaning, laughing, I swayed down a dim hallway that was all books, touching spines with my fingertips. In the bathroom, framed pictures showed Milt's wife (amazing cheekbones, ponytail) and Milt himself from years and years ago; he'd been handsome, which explained a lot.

I sat on the toilet and let my head drop back, mouth open, not needing to move. Actually, I felt pretty good. With a loud, scratchy sound, a needle touched vinyl and fast old asymmetrical jazz came on—wind instruments going wild, drums all feathery except for an occasional punch.

As I flushed I saw I'd forgotten to close the door. Whoops! I grabbed the doorframe: the hall tilted away. I *liked* this place. I wanted to explore. Was it really a farmhouse, like Mom had said, or random buildings, yoked together at various times . . . ?

Milt stood at the stove, stripped to the waist. His potbelly glistened with oil and sweat. It was *huge*—bigger than I'd thought—and very tan.

"Mary. Would you care to see what we're having for dinner?" I swayed there for a second, but had no choice: tucked my hair behind my ears and came up just out of reach of the rattling steam, willing myself not to wobble. I was a brimful glass, trying not to spill my *self*.

Milt's face shone. He poked his fork into the pot, speared something enormous, raised it, and held it dripping for me to see. The huge lump of flesh—a disgusting pinkish gray, pores everywhere—flattened down to a rounded tip.

Oh—gross. It was a tongue. *An enormous tongue.*

"You've had tongue before, of course." He cut a slice from the tip and held the steaming bit of meat, pierced with the point of his knife, right up to my lips.

Actually, it smelled all right: like corned beef. I took it in, worked it over slowly, and swallowed. It was okay, once you got over what it *was* (if you ever did).

I floated to my chair and sat down with a thump. The glass I'd left empty was full to the top. I stared at the sweating green wine and wondered what would happen if I had even *one more* taste. I was going to throw up anyway. Were Marcia and what's-her-name *ever* coming back?

People keep offering me tongues.

I snorted, almost spilling; leaned over and took a long, slow sip.

"Delicious with a little Dijon," he said. "Or the local *senape*, when you can find one sharp enough." He dabbed his face with a cloth. "Hot work, this." His eyes were incredibly blue. "You don't like Alicia much, do you?"

"No, no, no, sometimes I do!" I said loudly. "I don't *know*. I think . . ." (I forgot to talk for a minute.) "She steeps herself in her own psychology."

He laughed so hard he had to wipe his cheeks. "The shape of your lips," he said, "is really quite something. You have an audacious little mouth, Mary. But you know that, of course."

I rolled my eyes, picked up my glass, held it in front of my face, and looked at him through it: he was fatter, greener, smaller. I liked the Wine Milt better. I peeped over the rim.

"No. It isn't even Alicia—not as herself. It's just . . . she's having this effect on my sister." I swallowed more than I'd meant to and coughed. "We went to Solfatara," I explained.

My glass was empty. A chilly new bottle stood in front of me, unopened, complete. Milt came up behind me and leaned in to whisper something secret, but didn't whisper; didn't move away. Just *stayed* there, close enough to smell. Before I could think I felt his hand slip down to my waist, his lips brush my ear, his tickly fingers reach in under my hair—

I ducked under the table and *ran*. Books, bathroom—I slammed into a cabinet and set it rocking. In a side room with dark furniture, a woman sat in the glow of a computer screen—sparse white hair, an ancient face, a profile like the Duke of Urbino, but with headphones on. I scrambled up more steps, turned again, and raced down a second hallway, lined with vinyl records. The hall went on, narrowing as it went, until there were no more records, no more shelves, only plain white walls spotty with dirt or mold. An empty jar rolled after me. Would the hall NEVER come to an end?

A narrow arch led down to a rough-walled room where, past brown quilted jackets, through a glass-paned door, there were hills and sky. I dodged a sink, jumbled a lineup of rubber boots, twisted an old iron key back and forth, and kicked and kicked and kicked the dried-out door until I forced it wide enough to squeeze through: free.

I half-waded, half-limped across a freshly planted field to a country lane, which I trudged along till I could breathe again. It was getting dark. Burrs stuck to my clothes. A dog barked somewhere. I pulled a leaf from my hair, tucked my chin down, and kept walking.

They left me alone with him? Really?

Milt didn't follow: he probably just smiled, topped up his glass, grabbed the big fork—

I vomited into a ditch. Vomited again. Remembered, too late, to pull back my hair.

Mom and Dad were in their room with the door closed, but we could hear everything: Dad insisting he had "business" in Rome, Mom saying, "Fine! Then I'm going with you. Leave Alicia the car. She can drive the girls down to Terracina. We'll meet them in a few days."

Dad said something very quietly, and that was it: they came out of the room with their bags.

"Dad," Marcia said. She was reading a gossip magazine. "Who's Vittorio Bazzini?"

"Why, dear?"

"He's gross and old and has a saggy potbelly, but the woman he's been seeing (not his wife, though she's nice, too, apparently) is incredibly pretty."

I sat on the couch and watched my parents move around, their eyes never meeting. *The emperor's pallor worried his advisers.* Alicia, in a rust-brown silk wrap, turned cushions over, looking for a lost bracelet. "Can I speak with you?" Mom asked. They went off.

I unzipped my bag and took out the rock I'd picked up at Solfatara: it still smelled exactly like that day, like sulfur and sun, already memory. The emperor carried the bags out to the taxi, Mom kissed us good-bye, and they were gone.

Alicia threw her wrap at Marcia, spread her arms, whirled around, and sang: "WE'RE FREE!"

I'd seen her naked before, so no big deal.

I sat on the cemetery wall, hugged myself, and turned toward the sunrise: didn't help at all. Edges were brightening, making it *seem* a little warmer, but we were freezing. We were lost. We hadn't slept. Alicia and Marcia had gone off to have a smoke and maybe make some kind of plan, but Alicia just kept kicking the side of someone's mausoleum. She wore dark lipstick and more eye makeup than I'd ever seen her use. She looked fantastic. It seemed to amuse her that so many things had gone wrong: the worse things got, the funnier she thought it was—and she was the one in charge. She went on kicking, *scuff, scuff, scuff,* her short skirt flipping up. The weathered marble sparkled like sugar cubes. (I used to sneak those cubes home from restaurants and lie very still while a temptingly crisp shape dissolved in my mouth, uncrunched.)

First Alicia had driven us all over Italy. We saw some amazing things, but our theories about where we were stopped making sense. We circled and circled an enormous crater lake and then got lost in some dusty industrial countryside. We stopped in a random hill town to pee and finally got to eat, in a long, fluorescent basement filled with local soccer players in uniform. After dinner we explored the town on foot, down to its narrowest, most dead-end street, until we were ready to lie down on the cobblestones and sleep; Alicia couldn't find the car keys. We spent hours searching everywhere in the dark, getting lost, arguing, circling back, and found the keys hanging on a nail outside the locked restaurant. The car wasn't where we were pretty sure we'd parked, so we hiked all the way to the *other* edge of town, ran from a barking dog we never actually saw into somcone's vineyard (a bad place to run in the dark), and ended up watching the sun come up from inside a little shop that hadn't technically opened, drinking espresso and staring at a mortadella the size of a man. Alicia thought we might be able to see the car from higher up, so we climbed all the way up here, but no. Of course not.

I popped the last mint into my sour mouth. My skin felt sticky and I needed to pee. Were we *ever* going to sleep? I yawned. A humpbacked dog trotted by, nose to the ground: wiry fur, big teeth, spindly legs . . . I had to laugh. Maybe being amused when things go wrong was a good approach. Strange how the wild boar either had *no* neck or was nothing *but* neck: just a massive head with legs and a tail. It was *definitely* a boar: certain animals have that medieval look. Pelicans don't seem modern either; the ones on coats of arms seem as real as any photograph. What did wild boars eat? Acorns? Mushrooms? Girls from Connecticut? I closed my eyes and tried to will myself warm. Alicia had not only lost the *car*, she'd lost the keys *again*, in a stream we were crossing. We'd ended up groping about in freezing shallows for quite a while before Marcia held the key ring up on a wrinkly thumb. They were going to lose me next.

I took a walk to get warm. Some of the tombs were actual little houses where you could visit your dead relatives. It seemed like make-believe to me, a child's tea party with bodies instead of dolls, but the Romans had done it, too; they'd even poured wine into a special hole in the grave.

Wine. Had Milt thought I *liked* him? Oh God. That couldn't be it. More likely he'd been too lazy and self-amused to care who I was at all.

I wandered past slabs, headstones, a pedestal with a sort of stone bathtub on it, and more little houses: NANONE. BIZZARO. CARBONE. STELLACIO. Old marble, slightly rough to the touch; stone vases empty, or full of dirty plastic flowers, or dried-out husks of real flowers, or fresh flowers just beginning to droop.

It was quiet, except for my steps and the wind. I didn't even feel tired anymore—though I *really* needed to pee. Just not enough to risk it in the open, with wild boars running around. D'ELIA. VECCHIONE. PARADISO. MAROTTA. Surprising breezes would sweep past, fade suddenly. I tried but couldn't really picture the lives these people had lived, whoever they were: COLLOMOSSE. CRISCI. DELLE DONNE. I didn't know enough: about the past, about this place, about these people. I could hardly imagine my *own* life, much less theirs. PAVORONE. ACQUAVELLA. DOCILE. One slab looked comfortable enough to stretch out on, close my eyes, and rest like a marble angel in the sun . . .

I heard them both—their voices suddenly *there*, my sister sucking in smoke in a dramatic way, letting it out endlessly. I could tell by the harsh way she breathed and gave dull, one-word replies that she'd been crying and was miserable. *Why?*

Alicia was saying, "That's silly. You're beautiful. You're intelligent. You'll find someone."

"I already did."

Wind rushed the trees. Marcia tried to laugh bitterly but only coughed. Alicia murmured something, but it was none of my business: really. I tiptoed away, turned a corner, and went on. Old slabs blanked with shadow, blanked with sun. A row of tombstones sparkled: DETUCCIO. FICINO. VERDONE. CHIAROLANZA. Maybe I could loop around from the other side, so they'd at least see me coming. Or just take off, head for Venice or Sicily. Why not? They wouldn't notice for days. AGITI. SICONDOLFI. AUTULLO. LA LANCIA. This adventure wasn't going to turn out well. But how do most things turn out? They all end here: grandparents, parents, kids, whole families, nothing left but old buttons and bones. Skeletons in boxes, dressed in rotten clothing long out of style. Atoms and the void.

I turned, walked for a bit, turned again. A cigarette burned on the edge of a slab.

They sat on the front step of a mausoleum, backs to the

bronze-barred door. They leaned into each other and seemed to be whispering. No, they were kissing. *Really* kissing.

"Nothing I haven't seen in a movie," I said in a flat voice that didn't sound like me.

Dogs were barking: two, three, maybe more; faint but getting louder, coming this way.

Alicia and Marcia didn't look up. Alicia's hand moved under my sister's shirt.

I chose a big white tomb (DA PORTO), grabbed the window bars, and hoisted myself up to the roof. The barking got louder. A man shouted nearby. Marcia and Alicia stopped, stared into each other's eyes from an inch away, and went on kissing.

Bristling, its jaws wet with foam, the wild boar ran right past them. Gravel chips flew.

Alicia shrieked. I saw Marcia's open mouth, heard only squealing barks.

Dogs formed a ring, but the wild boar whipped around, its snout glistening with snot and grit—and went for one of the dogs. Like an explosion, they all spun away—but circled back right away to face the boar. Dense and muscular, it broke through the line and took off fast. The rush knocked Alicia down. In a second the animals were out of sight.

She leaned over and spat. A spittle thread hung from her lips and disappeared.

"Alicia? Allie, are you okay?" Marcia crept out from behind a tomb. "I think they're gone."

"Um," I said from above, "I wouldn't be too sure—"

More loud barks; an awful yelp. The boar made a strange cry, sharp with agitation and rage.

Marcia was gone. Alicia crouched down, her back to a tomb, and looked around rapidly.

More dogs rushed by. The boar screamed again, sounding almost like a monkey or a man.

A worker in a blue jumpsuit jogged past; a tall man followed, taking his time. His stiff gray hair looked oddly like the boar's; a rifle hung from his shoulder by a strap. He was eating an apple. The sounds moved off with them.

Alicia sat on the gravel, knees to her chest. She raised her head—as *another* boar swept past.

"Alicia!" I called. "Up here!"

She ran to my tomb, jumped up, grabbed at the roof, and tried to claw her way up.

"No, look, it's really easy—use the window. Put your foot— grab my hand!" She almost made it; fell back. "Come on, you can do it. Take a breath."

With a stunned, angry look, she made a running leap, gripped the roof, got a leg up, and slid off before I could catch her. Her lip was bleeding.

Bits of gravel stuck to her cheek.

"Use the bars. Put your knee on the window," I advised. My knuckle was raw; Alicia was shaking. Twenty dogs poured in, shouts and barks came from all directions, and the sky was so wonderfully blue! Italy was *by far* the best place I'd ever been.

Another boar rounded the corner, leaning hard, going nearly sideways. Alicia ran, tripped on a step, and crawled off rapidly on her hands and knees.

My mouth was open and I was making noise. I didn't know *what* noise at first: I might have been screaming for help or crying, but I was *laughing*—laughing so hard it hurt. From the roof I saw more men in coveralls, an old farmer limping along, dogs rounding corners only to run into other dogs, and—appearing and disappearing here and there—a blur of brown bristle with live little eyes, enraged or frightened or both.

"*What* are you laughing about!" Marcia screamed. "She could have been trampled or bitten or gored! They could be taking her to the hospital *right now*! We all could have *died*!"

I couldn't help it. I was aching. *Aching!* Face wet, nose running, hardly able to breathe, I *couldn't* stop laughing: just *couldn't*. My face must have had the shape of the empty mask they hang over theater doors. At the edge of the roof, stooped over, shaking, I laughed.

Marcia yelled, "He's back. He's coming! RUN!" but I couldn't even see, which made me laugh harder, though I was so tired of laughing and so needed to breathe . . .

With a quick scrape like a match being lit, the cemetery reeled away: I hit gravel, hard. Lay on my back looking up at blue, blue sky. Carefully, bruise by bruise, bone by bone, I sat up.

After a minute Marcia came up and leaned over me, breathing heavily. Her face was wet: she'd been laughing too. When we looked at each other we started to laugh again; tried not to, but only started laughing harder, though every laugh was its own stab of pain. And of course Marcia was my sister and I was hers; it didn't matter if we liked each other or not. So, that was that—except for the sound of gunshots, far away. I'd been hoping the wild boars would escape somehow, and get on with their lives; and who knows, maybe they did. But probably not.

I wondered what it was like to think in Latin. My suitcase having been packed, I sat out on the cozy modern balcony, leaned back in my chair, and picked cloudflowers. Traffic passed below, or didn't pass; I heard its sounds but saw only sky. I felt *good*: though I was going to miss all this. I even missed driving through the arch, which Alicia had been wrong about—I'd checked.

Harsh lipstick. Wouldn't look at me. Even the way Marcia *stood* now was weird. Her slip dress was on backward and she wore Alicia's socks, the ones with the maps of Portugal. She picked up a terra-cotta Buddha and put it back on the shelf; headed off to the kitchen, walking slowly, tilting to one side, the way our grandmother had the year she died. It made me feel like being nice to her, though she hadn't been nice to me. Anyway Marcia had to be feeling what I felt, that Alicia's power or glamour or charm was just *gone*: as if she'd been disproven.

I went inside. My jaw felt heavy, delicate as glass. It rested on my chest as if on a velveted display in some old museum. Without moving my chin, I picked up the remote: on BBC News, people carried bodies from a blast-scarred building. An angry woman vowed revenge. It occurred to me that I didn't even know what side I'd be on if I had to choose; though probably the woman hadn't had a choice herself, but it was weird: she was Alicia's age. In her situation, I'd be screaming and cursing, too, obviously—but what then?

Alicia had taken the barbell out of her tongue. She hardly spoke, unless to say something like "I'll bruise if you touch me. Sorry: I think I'm ill." All she seemed to want to do was sleep.

Someone—and this made me really sad—had taken a pair of pliers and crushed Alicia's hourglass. She'd shown me the little wad of wreckage, the twisted silver, the burst glass, and just looked at me. There were tears in her eyes, but she'd refused to cry. Anyway, we both knew it wasn't me.

Marcia was busy emailing everyone using her *phone*—it would cost more than our house when the bill came. I skipped from channel to channel until I found an old American movie dubbed into Italian. A boy hid in a school bus from some kids who wanted to beat him up. *Now what? How do I get out of here? What do I do?* But I knew the answer: you just have to wait.

I poured a glass of wine and sat with it. I'd never had wine all on my own. I took a sip: it was a different kind, dark red, and I absolutely *hated* the taste. It was practically poison, it could do you harm, you had to force yourself to like it—so of course it was part of being an adult.

Dad drove us to the airport. No one talked. Mom would be staying on for a week (if you believed what she and Dad kept

telling us in serious tones), so she could "wind up some important business in Rome." When I finally saw the sign they'd been
joking about—

INVERSIONE
DI MARCIA

—no one even noticed. We passed old walls, umbrella pines: I
was going to miss Italy.

There was snow all over Connecticut—filthy mountain ranges
at the edges of parking lots, lumps and crusts still glittering
in the woods—but it was easy to be back: I went to school,
hung out with friends, used my phone and laptop like a regular
person, and glided along in the familiar strangeness of being
myself. I tried to take things as they seemed to want to be taken,
which wasn't quite so easy anymore. In school, on the bus, at
volleyball, during meals, I'd think of random things that had
happened (or almost happened: always more of those), and the
oddest moments would come back: My sulfury chewing gum.
The sparker wand. That irresistible arch. My taste of hot tongue.
How easy it was to drive. The old man in Terracina (when we
finally got there) who wanted to know why we'd bombed the
town in 1944, *after* the Germans had left, and killed his girlfriend. He showed us a colorless, scallop-edged photo of a girl
my age and looked intently at each of us in turn.

An older boy—in Marcia's class, actually—started calling
me. I wasn't sure about him, but we texted all the time and
talked for hours very late at night. Or we'd be silent and listen
to the connection, which had its own sound sometimes, like far-
away surf. I'd lie on my back, fingers laced across my stomach,
phone propped up by my ear, and fall asleep listening to him
talk.

I still drink the occasional glass of wine.

Of course Mom *did* come home from Italy after a week and everything was fine, or seemed that way to me. They would *never* get a divorce—I was right about that.

Once there was no one around to impress, Marcia stopped being so mean, but we're not close; maybe I know too much. Anyway, I just went ahead and decided that I would treat her as an adult and expect the same, which means we don't talk a lot right now unless there's a reason.

In April, Alicia's mom fell asleep while driving on the turnpike. After the funeral, Alicia left school, moved to Texas, and got a job as a bartender. Maybe she read her philosophy book on breaks. Maybe the book was right, at least as an approach to certain things? Or anyway better at asking questions than forcing a definite set of answers. I actually do hope she's okay. I wouldn't mind getting to know her again someday, once she figures out how to be herself without driving herself crazy, and how to get along in this weird civilization of ours without giving up her own idea of life (probably most people need to figure that one out).

I'd been sure she was going to mock me without mercy when they found me sitting by the road in Tuscany, a vomity, grubby, drunken mess, but Alicia had dropped her bag in the grass and put her arms around me, vomit and all; when she let go, she was crying, too. "I'm so sorry," she kept saying. I refused to go back to that house, and she agreed, and Marcia had nothing to say about it, so we all sat by the blue metal gate to someone's farm, ate the bread and olives and apricots they'd bought, and laughed about all the wine and the boiling tongue and my introduction to the kind of thing every woman has to deal with in one way or another—which isn't fair, gentlemen. Really.

Of course I'm exactly the same as I was before, only maybe I understand a few more things. And when you understand a thing it's yours, even when it stays a little bit out of reach. When

I think of our trip now—about how it felt to be kissed for the first time; to stand on the spot where a huge temple had been; to get a pretty good sense of why a panicked nymph, her bare feet pounding the dirt, might beg to be transformed into a tree; or just to pass through an old arch again and again, until the villa, our beds, our belongings, even our *selves*, began to seem mysterious and out of reach—I feel a kind of nostalgia for the future. It's like knowing that something quite important is already mine, but having *no idea* how to get to it. Or anyway how to *wait*. The way a bus driver probably feels at the start of a shift, passing her lover's house along the route. I mean, seriously, I'm ready. Put a red slash through it, let's get on the road.

Jamil Jan Kochai

Nights in Logar

B UDABASH GOT FREE sometime in the night.
I didn't know how. Just that he did and that we needed
to go and find him. Me and Gul and Zia and Dawoud out on
the roads of Logar, together, for the first time. This all happened only a few weeks into my trip, my family's homecoming,
back when it only cost a G to fly across the ocean, from Sac to
SF to Taipei to Bangkok to Karachi to Peshawar all the way up
to Logar, where, at the time, though the American war wasn't
dead, it was dozing a bit, like in a coma, or like it was still reel-
ing off a contact high from that recently booming Afghan H or
opium or kush, leaving the soldiers and the Ts and the bandits
and the robots almost harmless, so that all that mattered then
for a musafir from America was how he was going to go about
killing another hot summer day.

The First Jirga

Gulbuddin said it'd be a four-man operation.
He said it in Pakhto because my Farsi was shit.

"More than four," he told me and Zia and Dawoud as we sat between the chicken coop and the kamoot, "and we'll look like a mob, but any less and we might get jumped or robbed."

He sat at the head of our circle twirling one end of the thick black mustache his older sisters were always trying to tear from his lip because it made him look too much like the beautiful Turkish gangsters from their soap operas.

Gul was my little uncle. About fourteen. The oldest of our bunch.

"What about four and a half?" I asked, thinking about my brother.

"What did I *just* say, Marwand?"

"More than four is a mob," Dawoud answered.

"But an extra half might come useful," I said.

"Not the half you're talking about," Dawoud said, squatting at the farthest edge of our circle, taking up too much space.

Dawoud was my other little uncle. Around twelve. Same age as me.

"Listen, fellas," I went on. "Five is a good number. Five pillars. Five prayers. Five players on a basketball team."

"Only five?" Zia asked.

"Well, is it four and a half or five?" Dawoud asked.

"Football is better," Zia said. "In football everyone gets to play."

"What do you think?" I looked to Zia, my cousin, but he just shrugged his skinny shoulders and pointed the barrels of his fingers at Gulbuddin. "Chik, chik," Zia said, "pow, pow," and pulled his triggers twice.

Gulbuddin nodded at Zia and pressed down on the air with his hands. His eyes, green like duck shit, shifted from his hands, to the gate, to the courtyard, where the rest of the family still slept. We quieted down.

"We'll put it to a vote," he said. "Raise your hand if you want Gwora to come along."

Only my busted hand went up into that morning chill.

"Well, fuck," I muttered, in English, and relented to the will of the jirga.

Initial Encounters

Wallah, the first time I saw big Budabash standing three-legged beneath his apple tree, pissing on the bark he was chained to, I thought he was the no-name mutt I met and tortured and loved the first summer I came back to Logar.

My memories of this dog, who I secretly named Mr. Kareem, haunted me all throughout grade school, since it was in third grade, when I learned how to read, that my American teachers also taught me dogs were supposed to be hugged and petted and neutered, but never beaten or tortured.

So on the afternoon of my second homecoming I arrived in Logar eager to see Mr. Kareem, even though I was already carsick, pockmarked, jet-lagged, and sweating floods in a black kameez and partug, two sizes too small, which my moor made me wear just before we crossed the border. When we entered my moor's compound for the first time in six years, a flood of sparkling dresses and scarves and vests swallowed me up as I stepped through. I had so much Farsi hurled at me all at once; I didn't know what to do with it.

They asked me if I was hungry, if I was sad, if I was tired, if I was thirsty, if I was happy, if I was scared, constipated, lonely, sick, confused, nauseous, stupid, smart, always this dark, always this cute, always this skinny, always this hairy, this tall, this quiet, nervous, shy, lost.

I said yes to every single question.

They asked me what I wanted more than anything.

"I want to go and see Mr. Kareem," I said.

None of them knew what I was talking about.

Sag, I said in Farsi, I want to see the dog.

They blew up with laughter, cursed me and my moor, and dragged me out of the room.

In the orchard, as soon as I saw Budabash pissing on his apple tree, I broke off from my family and rushed his circle with nothing but sabr in my heart and love leaking out my fingertips (wallah!), and it was only after he crouched and lunged and swallowed forever the very tip of my finger, that I saw in his eyes, in the heart of the eyeball, that Budabash, the new dog of the orchard, the province, the millennium, was not a dog at all, but something more like a mutant.

The First Maze

Just outside the big blue gate, the road we walked curved upward into a bend that led into a maze of interconnected clay compounds. If you didn't know your way, Gul explained, or if you didn't have a guide, it was easy to get lost. After Gul led us out of the maze, we found ourselves on the main road. It was made of a hard, dark clay. Rows of chinar and a thin stream ran along its edges. In the fields near the road, farmers tended to their crop. "That's where Budabash went," Gul said, pointing at nothing in particular, pointing, it seemed, at the whole country. Then he started down the road.

While Dawoud paced ahead, sniffing for Budabash's scent, Gul stopped from time to time to ask a farmer if they'd seen a big black dog roaming about.

Zia hung back with me. He held my good hand and pointed out the sights.

"That's Haji Ahmad's," he said, pointing to an orchard, "and those fields belong to Mullah Imran. And that trench there is where little Zabi stepped on an old mine. Lost his foot."

"In the name of God, Zia," Gul called back, and slowed down

and wrapped his fingers around my right wrist, just above the gauze covering my finger and palm. "You got everything wrong. The orchard belongs to Mullah Imran's dad, who's still living, so Imran owns nothing yet, and the fields are Haji Ahmad's, and little *Nabi* got his foot run over by an army truck, not little Zabi. Little Zabi is fine. We played cricket with him a month ago."

"We did?" Zia asked.

"Yes, bachem, go ask Dawoud."

Dawoud walked ahead by himself. No one liked to hold his hands because of his warts, so he always had them busy. I tried to do the same thing, but the fellas were persistent. "This is what friends do here," Gul kept trying to explain.

"Zabi still got both feet," Dawoud shouted back.

"See," Gul said, and pointed to Zia, "all this guy knows are hadiths. You listen to me, Marwand. I'll tell you what's what."

And he did. He told me where we were and where we were going. He told me the names of the roads and where they would lead. He told me who died where and whose grave and flag and stick and stone belonged to who, and he told me the names of the trees and the fields and the plots of land. And as he held my hand, he pointed me one way and could tell me what way that way was and he could point the other and tell me what way that way was too.

But, still, he couldn't tell me—for sure, at least—where Budabash went or why he ran away in the first place, though I had an idea.

Ah, but before I forget, here are a few more things I saw that day:

1. A cobra
2. Six kids, ages ranging from four to eleven, walking toward that cobra
3. A cobra, its skin stripped, its flesh bared, pelted to death by six kids

4. Laborers in the fields covered in mud
5. Laborers in the orchards covered in mud
6. Laborers, covered in mud, building a wall out of the mud that covered them
7. A little girl, about nine, walking with her donkey
8. The fields
9. My cousin or uncle (both?) Babrak, who stank of hash and couldn't recall my name
10. Two strays that looked like what Budabash would've if he'd actually been a dog
11. Two American helicopters
12. Four kids playing cards in the corner of a field, betting walnuts and marbles
13. Four kids running from the stones we threw
14. Fifty-two cards left behind in the corner of a field
15. A man with a gun who might have been a T
16. One drone (I think)
17. 1,226 white lilies
18. The wheat shaking in the wind
19. Ten million pounds of clay
20. One true God
21. No Budabash

Some More Rocks

A few hours into the search and we still had no real lead. Zia prayed his Dhuhr prayer without any sign from God. Gul interrogated almost everyone he saw, but heard nothing from a soul. And though Dawoud couldn't sniff out Budabash, his nose did eventually latch on to the unmistakable scent of cheap hair gel, butchered meat, and unrequited love.

At Dawoud's signal—and Gul's confirmation—we leaped behind some chinar, into the sloping path of a river bend. A guy with his mouth masked in a dusmal and his hair slicked back into a weapons-grade pompadour came strolling down the trail.

"Who's that?" I asked.

"The butcher's son," Gul whispered, and then gently placed a stone in my hand.

The butcher's son was walking the trail very slowly, carefully, and, luckily for us, unarmed. Dawoud gathered stones from the stream and set them at our feet, and just before we chucked them, we lifted our own scarves over our mouths, at the same time, like bandits out of an old John Wayne flick, and we rubbed the stones in our dirty little fingers, huffing quick breaths that shook the tatters of our masks, and then there came this moment between the holding of the stones and the ambush itself, when I was watching the butcher's son walk the road, watching him and knowing what was coming for him, knowing what he didn't know, would only know when it was already too late, and I felt so bad for him and for me too, wallah, because although I knew that the stones were coming, I didn't know why, and in that way, the butcher's son and I were the same.

Then we chucked.

Later, I asked the fellas why we did what we did, and they looked surprised that I didn't know, that I was that much out of the loop over in America, but having taken part in the ambush I thought it was my right, you know, to be informed.

Luckily, they seemed to agree.

The Tale of the Butcher's Son

Really, the story of the butcher's son was the story of Nabeela Khala. She was my moor's younger sister, the third out of six girls, and as the oldest of the unwed sisters, also the next in line to be married. Problem was Nabeela wasn't the prettiest girl in the family or the slimmest or the most polite. Word was she could slaughter a steer, chop down trees, and whup on her nephews. At a wedding, during a machine gun celebration, she'd snatched her brother's AK and unloaded the whole clip before going back to the ladies' side of the wedding to dance her ass off.

Nabeela was getting dangerously close to unmarriageable when the butcher's son came calling. He was handsome, light skinned, with a head of hair like Ahmad Zahir and a pair of eyes like an English movie star. But also poor. Very poor. A butcher's kid, and a failed butcher at that, so Baba, taking Abo's advice, proceeded to reject his offer. But the butcher's son, of course, came back.

The first three or four times a guy comes over to ask for a girl's shawl, the father is supposed to reject him no matter what. But if you get rejected more than seven or eight times, the suitor has to start thinking about his honor, and most of the time, he'll give up and move on. The butcher's son had already been rejected some twenty times. He came over almost every Friday with his only pair of clean clothes, a dingy little waskat, his hair combed back, and his heart beating in his hands.

Meanwhile, Nabeela—to everyone's surprise—had fallen madly in love with him. The last time he was rejected, she locked herself in a room and threatened to cut her wrists with her scissors, to hang herself with her dresses, to eat dirt until she vomited and died. Eventually, Rahmutallah Maamaa had to knock the door down with an axe, take up his sobbing sister in his arms, and drag her out of the room. After handing his sister over to Abo, Rahmutallah Maamaa began to shout at her, demanding that she allow Nabeela to marry the boy and end the madness. Abo stood square to her much larger son and cursed him and his lack of honor. So Rahmutallah Maamaa, saying nothing to anybody, went and got his rifle; walked all the way to the butcher's house near Waghjan, in the middle of the night, with the Ts and the Marines loose and everything; and he knocked on his door and Rahmutallah warned the butcher that though their families had enjoyed many years of peace between themselves, and though they'd had no issues in the past, if he could not control his son, then the peace built up between the families would very soon, and very suddenly, come to an end.

He said that to him and then he left.

The threat worked for a while. But, about a week before my family arrived, the butcher's son came back again, ready, it seemed, to die for Nabeela.

"That," Gul explained, "is why we ambushed him."

The Carcass

Around Asr, the sun dipped into the late afternoon.

Gul was getting so desperate for some sign of a clue, he suggested that we pray, and although he was very clearly trying to bribe God with our Salah, Zia was so ready to play the part of the imam, he didn't seem to mind.

We made wudhu, one by one, in a nearby stream, and laid out our scarves on the dirt. Zia made the call to prayer, Gul said the iqama, and the three of us stood behind Zia and we prayed to Allah together, but by ourselves.

I had a list.

My list was in English, though it should have been in Arabic or at least Pakhto.

First, I prayed for Allah to forgive me and to save me from myself, and I prayed for him to assist me and my buddies on our journey because I knew that's what Gul wanted. Then I prayed for my parents, my moor and agha, for her mind and his body. I prayed they wouldn't have to be so lonely all the time. I prayed that my brothers might become men, Mirwais especially, who I thought might become a snitch or a coward, though in many ways I couldn't admit, he was much braver than me.

Dawoud was praying on one side of me, fidgeting and cracking his knuckles and scratching his elbows, but I went on with my list anyway.

I prayed for my baba and abo, for my akai and athai, for all maamaas and khalas, and for my amas and my one dead kaakaa, Watek, and for all of my cousins, and I prayed for the health of the girl I might marry someday, and I prayed for the health of all the mothers on the earth but in Afghanistan especially, and I prayed for the men in the village who took care of their families and prayed all their prayers and watched over their neighbors and worked all day in the sun and never beat their wives and never sold their daughters and never snitched on their people and never joined the Americans and never hurt anyone they didn't have to hurt, because I swear to God those sorts of men existed in Deh-Naw, in Logar, in the country. I swear to God.

A few villagers joined our line: farmers from their fields, laborers from their homes, and shepherds from their trails, until there were maybe thirty men or so praying behind Zia as he was wrapping up his final rakah.

I went on.

I prayed for all of my family and all of my friends and for all of the innocents and the martyrs, and I prayed for so many people and so many things that, wallah, just as Zia was turning his head to say salaam to the angel sitting on his right shoulder, Raqib, the recorder of good, I prayed one more time for Allah to bring us home, safely, so that I had no time left to pray for my enemies.

When Zia finished greeting Atid, the recorder of sins, and turned around to make his dua, he was only flustered for a second by the size of his congregation. He then recited a lovely little dua in what I assumed was perfect Arabic. Afterward, some of the men who had joined us in our prayer recognized Zia as Rahmutallah's son, and they asked him what we were doing so far from home.

But before Zia could answer, Gul spoke up first, telling them that we were chasing after a dog, and a young shepherd stepped up and informed us that his flock had recently been attacked by something resembling a dog. He led us along a stream, the way we had come, to a clearing in a pasture where his flock was allowed to graze, and where he'd been briefly distracted by the erratic flight patterns of an American helicopter, and by the time he brought his attention back to his flock, his sheep were dripping red, and so, following one sheep after another, each of them getting more and more bloody, he came upon the source of the carnage: at first, he thought his poor little lamb had exploded from the inside out. That was until he saw the red paw prints leading away from the carcass.

We thanked the shepherd and promised to bring the dog to justice for the murder of his sheep. At which point, we started to follow the tracks, deeper and deeper into the valves of the country.

The Second Jirga

Budabash's tracks disappeared just as we got to Watek's marker.

So did his scent. Dawoud sniffed and sniffed as the sun dipped into the late afternoon but got nothing.

Watek's flag didn't look much different from any of the other flags littering the makeshift graveyards and the dirt roads all over Logar. It hung red and torn from a wooden rod. Stones gathered at the base of it. Ash too. It was the loneliest thing I had ever seen.

Near the flag there was a mulberry tree planted specifically in honor of Watek as a sadaqah. We gathered underneath it, catching our breath, rubbing our feet, and eating the toot from the branches, which belonged to Watek and so belonged to no one, or else, belonged to the whole village. We were so hungry and the toot was so sweet, we ate too much, too quickly, and our mouths got sticky from the juice. Gul said he was going to wash his face and he gestured for me to follow him. Past this hedge of chinar, we slid down a slope of clay into the bank of the canal.

"You know what happened here?" Gul asked me.

I told Gul I didn't, which was true.

"You don't know what happened to your Watek Kaakaa?"

Watek was Agha's little brother. He was executed during the war by the Russians. He died really young, a kid practically. A shahid of the highest purity. That's all I knew.

"This is where it happened," Gul said, pointing to the earth beneath his feet as if that was the exact spot, as if we squatted right where he was standing when the Russians slit his throat or shot his face or filled his heart with lead.

The shade from the chinar fell slantwise against the bank of the water where we knelt.

He must have fallen in the water, I thought, it must have carried him.

"Shagha never told you that story?"

"Sometimes bits and pieces. But never the whole thing."

"No one hears the whole thing."

"Just bits?"

"Just pieces. Shagha'll tell you the story piece by piece. And you'll have to put it together yourself, and when you do, you have to come and tell me too. You understand?"

When we walked back out on the road, we found Zia and Dawoud whispering to each other. The two of them had created a secret pact in order to gather the strength to call for a second jirga, demanding that we, as a clan, a tribe, a nation, reinitiate our former council and vote on whether or not we should abort our prolonged mission.

"It's getting dark," Zia argued.

"I'm getting hungry," Dawoud added.

Gul wasn't buying it.

"Gul, you been saying a little farther, a little farther," Zia said, "but you can't force us unless we vote on it. Me and Dawoud want to head back. You're the only one who wants to keep going."

"Marwand wants to keep going."

"Marwand wants to go back."

"Well, what do you say, Marwand? You want to go home?" Zia asked.

"Or you want to go on?" Gul added.

The three of them looked to me for an answer and, wallah, I was trying to come up with one that might make everyone happy, but the toot juice in my belly wouldn't let me think.

"What's your vote?" Gul asked.

And just as my guts were about to give up and give in, I shouted, "Ghwul!" as loud as I could, and ran off through the chinar.

Hidden in between some bushes near the fields on the other side of the bank, I squatted and waited. Down the road the voice of a child called out the adhan from the speakerphone of a mosque's citadel, and even with the static and the echo and the cracking of his pitch, it sounded so sweet in the fading light, with the fields darkening, and the crickets chirping their songs.

When the adhan finished, Zia stepped through the chinar and started to pray his Maghrib Salah near the stream. "Asalam-alaykum Rahmutallah wa Barakatu," Zia said to the angel sitting on his right shoulder, and just before Zia turned his head toward the angel on his left shoulder, to say his final salaam, I, too, peeked past my left shoulder, through Atid, God's first snitch, and clenched my guts and watched the dark fields at my back, whose every single stalk of grain was trembling back and forth and side to side, while the whirlpool in my belly spun wildly into itself.

And all at once.

Zia finished his salaam.

I shat my flood.

Atid wrote this down.

The wind parted the wheat.

And a shadow leaped from the field, toppling me over, like a pile of rocks.

Night

Gul came bursting through the chinar, shouting half phrases in Farsi and Pakhto: "Zia, goddamn it, Zia, Budabash, Zia, fuck, Zia, Budabash, Zia, quit praying, Dawoud, sniff, get to sniffing, sniff the Budabash, Budabash, and where the fuck is Marwand?"

I was still hiding between the bushes and the fields, desperately trying to wipe the shit off my clothes. I worked quietly, without breathing, and as soon as Gul left with a curse and a huff, I hobbled over to the canal with its water cool and clean and pure, took a deep breath, and hopped in.

Gul must have heard the splashing.

"Marwand . . . ," he started saying before he spotted Zia a little ways up the canal, still facing toward the Kaaba, his hands before his face, his head bobbing to the tune of a song we couldn't hear.

Standing in the stream, I looked to Gul as Gul looked to Zia as Zia looked to God and I could see that Gul was being torn at the moment between his uncle's inclination to beat the shit out of Zia for ignoring him and his long-held, almost primordial, Afghan's esteem for the act of worship, whether faked or not.

Gul ordered me to stay and wait for Zia, but it took such a long time, I remember, for him to finish his prayers. At first, I sat beside the stream, watching him, waiting for him to finish, trying to guess which head bob, which dua, which surah, would be his last, but he just went on and on until I got tired of it and went back toward the road and sat beneath Watek's tree.

It was cold on the road by myself as wet as I was.

About two seconds later, Zia came crawling through the chinar, finally finished with his prayers, and sat right next to me. I gave him a suspicious look like, "I see you." And he, in turn, gave me an expression of innocence as if to say, "God sees all," which was true, you know, but, still. Probably, I could have pressured him, made him explain why he kept on praying his fake prayer when Gul needed him most, but part of me, I think, didn't really want to know. Besides, Zia was all I had left, and I was all he had left, and so, even though I stank horribly of toot-shit and mud, Zia unfurled his patu and wrapped it around me and him both.

To pass the time, Zia asked me for a story.

The roads darkened. The crickets chirped. The donkeys brayed. And everywhere there was a smell of smoke and sadness. Me and Zia huddled underneath his patu, underneath the mulberry tree, underneath the sky.

We watched the flag of Watek's marker and smelled the ash and listened for every footstep of every killer in Logar: the psychopathic white boys, the ravenous bandits, the Ts and the gunmen and the drug runners, the kidney kidnappers, the robots in the sky, the wolves from the mountains and the coyotes from the rivers, the witches in the cesspits, the djinn in the trees, the ghosts from the graveyards, and the monsters in the maze.

I whispered to Zia, "It's so dark."

"You scared?" he asked.

"It's just that back in America it doesn't get so dark because we have lights going on all night in the streets."

"But who pays for the fuel?"

"I think taxes."

"You miss it over there?"

"No," I said, "fuck America. I rather be here."

"Wallah?" he said. "Don't lie in the night, Marwand. Snakes will hear."

"Well," I said, "maybe not right this moment. But in general."

"So you are scared."

"Maybe a little."

"All right," he said, and asked me to give him my right hand, which I did, and after carefully unwrapping the gauze still clinging to my skin, he traced for me—with a single finger—his evidence of God's existence.

In some way or other, I knew we would be saved, either in the night or in the days to come, that it was only a matter of when, not if. At some point, we both fell asleep, and for the first time in a long time, Zia forgot to pray.

Mark Jude Poirier

How We Eat

THE THRIFT STORE Brenda drags us to today is on Kolb, far on the east side towards the Rincon Mountains, just past the Lucky Wishbone Chicken with the pulsating sunburst sign. Like every thrift store, it stinks of dust and mothballs and dirty diapers and bad breath and dead flowers. It smells like the floor of Brenda's car.

My sister, Lizzie, and I search pockets, while Brenda scans other aisles for stuff to sell at the swap meet. It's Thursday, late morning, and I'm nervous about missing another day of school. I'm in the sixth grade at Lulu Walker. I'm twelve, so it's 1992. Lizzie is ten but she's only in third grade because they held her back. For social reasons. She bit a kid and broke the skin. Lizzie is taller than me.

Brenda's our mother but she forbids us from calling her "Mom." We're allowed to call her "Brenda" or "Bren," though we never call her "Bren." She says she looks too young to have kids as old as us. She has big eyes, and hair like hay because she uses Miss Clairol too often. The Natural Medium Golden Blonde has stripped our kitchen sink of its shine.

We started searching pockets a few years ago, and we've found a lot of different things, mainly in men's clothes: money, condoms and condom wrappers, keys, sticks of gum, notes, credit cards, checks and check stubs, driver's licenses, receipts. I once found the top of a set of dentures in a jacket. The most money I found was sixty-eight dollars in a pair of dirty jeans with a chew can ring worn into the back pocket under the plastic Wrangler patch. I gave eight dollars to Brenda and I kept the three twenties for myself. I rolled the bills tight and hid them deep in my underpants. Brenda always checks our pockets when we get to the car and sometimes she slides her finger around our waists to see if we're holding out.

From the chest pocket of a pair of paint-splattered white overalls, I pull out a Polaroid, overexposed, but clear enough that I see its subject is a turd floating in a toilet. I feel like I shouldn't have seen it. I shouldn't have even touched it. Someone put it there so I would be freaked out, and I look around for the perpetrator, who I imagine to be a stringy-haired man planning on abducting me, torturing me, and sawing off my limbs, which he will put in four different dumpsters. Last week, the police found a woman's arm in the dumpster behind Skate Country. I saw it on the news. They showed the gaudy, jeweled ring that was on the middle finger. Now I'm terrified, and I blame Brenda. If we don't search the pockets, she tells us she's doing her best, and why should she if we're not, then she ignores us, sometimes for hours. The image from the photo is branded into my mind, and after I slide it back into the pocket and wipe my hands on my shorts, I can still see the bowed, feathery turd. I wish I were in school, even in math—though the teacher, Miss Burk, is a cruel woman who yelled at me when I first arrived in her class because I didn't know how to divide fractions. Her left hairy ape wrist is cinched by an incongruously dainty women's Timex that never fails to unsettle me.

. . .

Lizzie hasn't found anything, and I can see the fear in her eyes. Brenda will be disappointed. Other than the Polaroid, I found only a flimsy, wrinkled one-dollar bill in a pair of shorts. We begin to look through sport coats when Brenda marches over, the high-heeled sneakers she stole from Value Village squeaking like dog toys on the glossy floor. In her cuffed denim shorts, her legs are too thin and her butt looks deflated. I wish she'd gain weight. Sometimes I worry she might collapse and crumple into nothing. "This place is picked over," she says. "What did you find?"

"We can stay longer," I offer.

"So you didn't find anything," Brenda says. Her shoulders drop as her face does.

I hand her the limp dollar bill.

In the parking lot, before we get in the car, Brenda crams her hands in Lizzie's pockets, then mine. Her hands are like wild animals, quick and unpredictable, and when she feels around my waist, she nearly touches my dick. She smirks and says, "Still nothing," referring to my lack of pubic hair, which is none of her business even if she is my mother.

There's a pair of red, glittery shoes on the asphalt in a puddle of something gravy-like, and I imagine the lady who wore them: a hooker with a ratty wig and melted makeup, and she's crying and hurrying to her car, which is junkier than Brenda's silver 1979 Ford Fairmont sedan. She kicks off her uncomfortable shoes so she can walk faster. This woman just saw the photo of the ring from the severed arm in the dumpster. The ring belonged to her friend, another hooker. When we lived on Miracle Mile, Lizzie and I used to watch hookers through a cluster of desiccated palms from the safety of our apartment's balcony. Most of them were sunburned. They fought each other.

They yelled a lot. Some didn't wear wigs or much makeup; they looked normal, like Brenda—but not so skinny—or a teacher, or someone you'd see in the supermarket buying margarine. Lizzie could watch them for hours, her eyes wide and her mouth agape. She watched them like Brenda watched TV, and she knew their names: June, Daniella, Shannon, and two Cindys.

The backseat burns my legs so I shove my hands under my thighs. I don't complain about the heat. What's the point? The AC is broken and it costs, like, four hundred to fix it. The lighter still works, and Brenda smokes a Winston. The smell of her lighting it is pleasant, like chopped wood and white paper and birthday candles. But soon the cigarette stinks up the car, even with all four windows rolled down and the hot wind blowing in and swooping clumps of Lizzie's pale hair.

Lizzie stares outside and picks at the last of the crusty impetigo on the side of her chin. I have it, too. It itches and hurts and cracks. Brenda says we wouldn't have it if we'd just wash our faces more often, but we only have strawberry shampoo at the apartment right now, and it burns. I wash my face twice each day I'm at school. If there is any, the golden soap from the dispensers there stings, but not as bad as the strawberry shampoo.

Nirvana comes on the radio. I love them. I even looked up "mulatto" and "libido" in the dictionary. But Brenda changes the station and begins to hum-sing to the Eagles: *'Cause I'm already gone, and I'm fee-ling strong . . .*

My money stash is Ziplocked, the baggie taped to the inside of the toilet tank lid at the apartment. On a cop show that used to play in the afternoon when Lizzie and I got home from school, I saw drug addicts hide their heroin and needles in the same place. At this point, I have $126. I figure if the toilet's running or clogged or something, Brenda won't fix it; she'll make me do it, so it's safe.

. . .

After we cross Craycroft, Brenda pulls into a McDonald's near a sprawling brick high school I have never noticed. We're in line at the drive-thru, three cars back from the intercom, which sits in fiberglass Grimace's mouth. Brenda tells us, "I need you to find eight cents." She digs in her purse, pulls out a thickly matted hairbrush and places it on the passenger seat so she can dig deeper. Lizzie and I are running our fingers in the space where the back of the seat meets its bottom. I find the buried middle seat belt, which is hardened from years of baking, but no coins. Then Lizzie finds a dime, and I hate her for it, but only for a second.

"Good girl," Brenda says. "Give it here."

Brenda never thanked me for the dollar I found back at the thrift store.

I know not to ask for what I really want: six Chicken McNuggets, a vanilla shake, a cheeseburger and fries. I know Lizzie wants all that, too, though the shake she wants is strawberry and she'd only eat the breading off the McNuggets. But we didn't find enough in the pockets. That's the rule.

Brenda orders three cups of ice water, which are free, and two hamburgers. The hamburgers are two for ninety-nine cents—with tax, a dollar seven. When we arrive at the window where we pay, Brenda also asks for a plastic knife, and a handful of ketchup packets. She likely has about twenty packets in her purse already.

I'm hot with shame as the McDonald's guy hands Brenda a bag with the hamburgers and the ketchup in it. He then passes her the waters, small, one by one. He smiles and thanks Brenda. She doesn't thank him. He sees us in the backseat and I can sense he pities us, even though his own life is probably crappy. I want Brenda to speed away, but she takes her time cutting our hamburger in half with the plastic knife, licking a stray morsel of meat from the top of her hand. There are several cars behind us, and I can sense that the McDonald's guy wants her to move, but she doesn't care. It's her moment to control the world.

Brenda eats her hamburger as she drives. My hamburger half has the two pickles, so I give one to Lizzie. She puts it on her half; she doesn't just pop it in her mouth. I know Lizzie would have given me a pickle if she had gotten both. The ice water tastes like wax and a bit like orange drink, but it's good and clean. I take a small bite of the half hamburger and chew and chew, savoring the onions and sugary ketchup, until it's almost liquid, and then I swish it around before I swallow. Lizzie and I do this for every bite. We do it at Burger King and Whataburger and Arby's, too, even when we get full meals. When we were younger, we'd play mother bird and baby bird, and I'd spit the chewed McDonald's into Lizzie's mouth. Then she'd take a bite of her McDonald's and do the same for me. We played it a few times before Brenda caught us and swatted me in the neck with a rolled-up magazine.

Brenda tells us she wants to hit another thrift store. She says it tentatively, like she's asking our permission, but she isn't. I knew when we climbed into her car this morning that it would be a long, stifling day and that Brenda might not feed us and we'd have bad headaches by the afternoon. Lizzie had a social studies test about Mesopotamia today. I helped her study last night and she knew all the terms—Tigris-Euphrates river system, the Bronze Age and the Iron Age, the Parthian Empire. But Brenda doesn't care. We could have gone to school and Brenda could have gone thrifting by herself, but she hates being alone.

I check the sunbaked pay phone in front of Goodwill. Nothing. Just inside the store, by the entrance, there are a few gumball machines, and as Brenda hurries towards the back, Lizzie and I check them. "Oh," Lizzie says. "Trent, look!" She's turning the knob on the one that dispenses rubber balls and she keeps getting free balls without having to pay. She hands them to me: two blues, a bright green, and a swirly one. I look around. No one's watching us. The small placard behind the glass calls them "Super Space Balls," and features an image of a purple ball that has bounced thousands of miles above Earth, which looks puny in the background. How fake, I think, but I continue to load my pockets: green, yellow, red, red, sparkles, blue, swirl . . . Then I hear Brenda yelling: "Trent and Lizzie, now!" Lizzie looks over her shoulder when she hears Brenda, but she continues to turn the knob. "Now!" Brenda yells, and I hear another lady tell her to shut up.

"We better go," I say, and I pull Lizzie by her shoulder.

"I want to get another sparkly one!" she says, batting my hand away. She's chewing the side of her mouth like she's concentrating.

Soon, I'm forcing my hands into pockets of men's jeans. One pair smells like gasoline; another, like cigarettes. If they're Levi's, I check the red tag on the back pocket for the capital letter E, which means that they're old, and Brenda can sell them to the Japanese man who comes to the swap meet every few months. There are no old Levi's today. Brenda will soon learn that Lizzie's still at the gumball machines, draining one of them of its contents, and I'm nervous. So I search faster. A nickel. A nine-volt battery. A to-do list that begins with *pick up Jenn at 4*.

When I'm rushed like this, the urge to piss is overwhelming, so I weave through the overloaded racks of clothes towards Brenda. She clutches a metal *Welcome Back, Kotter* lunch box. She's grinning widely. She tries to remain calm, but I recognize her leaking excitement. "I bet I can get forty for this," she whispers, like I'm her coconspirator. "At least thirty-five." This makes the back of my neck tingle in a pleasant way that warms and tickles my inner ears. I like being on her team. I like it when she finds a treasure and holds firm on a price when swap meet people try to haggle her down.

"I need to go to the bathroom," I say.

"That's it?" she says. She's angry. "I don't know why I even bother." She scratches at the inside of her thigh. The pinkness means she's already been scratching a lot. "I drive all over and search and search," she whines, "and finally I find something good and you can't even congratulate me or thank me."

"Sorry," I say.

"And you're welcome for lunch."

"I probably said thanks."

"I was waiting for it and neither you nor your sister said it."

I was the one who found the dollar that paid for the hamburgers. But I don't gripe.

"I hate it when you force me to call you an asshole," she says, "but you're an asshole, Trent." Now she's practically crying, and I really have to pee. "A mother shouldn't call her son an asshole, but you're an asshole."

A woman with a mop of dark curls turns her head from a shelf of mismatched dinner plates and coffee mugs. "Keep your family's business to yourselves." She wears a pink bandanna around her neck. Her teeth are small and sharp, like grains of rice.

Brenda hands me the lunch box and takes a few steps towards the woman. "We're trying to have a conversation here," Brenda says. She sniffs and tilts her head sideways.

"You don't want to fuck with me," the woman says. She wears an oversized black Kenny Rogers concert T-shirt. The letters that spell "Kenny" are puffy and red. She also wears baby-blue terry cloth gym shorts that feature her legs, which are thick and tan, not fat but not muscular—like big hot dogs.

And very quickly, the two women are pulling each other's hair, scratching and hitting each other. "Bitch. Cunt. Fucking whore." I don't know who says what; I can only think about my bladder. Brenda looks over to me and says, "Help me!" The lady has Brenda by the hair and she's kicking her in the knees.

I don't help my mother. I can't. I'm frozen and it feels like a nightmare, like I'm about to wake with a start. Maybe part of me wants Brenda to feel pain and lose this fight. I watch her reach behind her back for anything. Her hand lands on a waffle iron from a shelf of housewares. Its frayed black cord swings in an arc as Brenda clobbers the woman with it. The woman's hair is soon drenched with blood. Brenda steps away and places the waffle maker back on the shelf. The woman wipes her neck, watches in disbelief as blood drips from her hand. She wobbles, and tumps. Her body makes a double wet slap on the floor.

This all happens in about twenty seconds but it seems like an hour. I just stand there, holding that lunch box by its handle, wondering when Brenda will be arrested, barely noticing the warmth trickling down my leg and soaking my droopy tube sock.

I feel intense relief unrelated to my bladder.

Brenda digs her nails into my shoulder and pulls me through the aisles towards the front of the store, grumbling, "Baby! Wetting your pants!" We pass two teenage girls, one of them wearing thick-framed glasses, both of them looking through men's flannel shirts. The one in the glasses says, "Oh, my God!" when she sees I've wet myself. The other says, "Shut up! He might be special!"

Brenda keeps pulling me, gripping my shoulder tighter, guiding me out the emergency exit, which buzzes loudly and makes my stomach drop.

"We didn't pay for this," I say, holding up the lunch box.

We wade through the heat pumping up from the asphalt until we reach the car, where Brenda rifles through the trunk and pulls out a *Tucson Weekly*. "Sit on this," she says as she pushes my head down and forces me into the backseat. "Where the hell is your sister?" She looks back towards the store. I notice a scarlet scratch flaring from her ear to her throat. "I can't go back in there," she says. "That crazy bitch started it." I can't remember who actually did start it. "I don't like to cuss," Brenda says. "You know that." She sits in the driver's seat and starts the car. "You make me cuss."

"What about Lizzie?" I say.

"Shut up," she says. "God!"

She speeds out of the parking lot. The tires even squeal.

"But Lizzie is stuck in there," I say.

"Sometimes mothers have to teach their kids a lesson."

As we pull onto Flowing Wells, I stare at the corny rendition of Mr. Kotter pointing to an F he wrote on Epstein's quiz, and I imagine that Lizzie's looking for us. Her shorts' pockets and hands are full of rubber balls. Maybe she has made a basket out of the front of her shirt to accommodate them all, exposing her belly to everyone, but not caring. Now Lizzie must be panicking. She searches everywhere for me and Brenda, calls for us. Maybe she sees the woman on the floor. Or the woman's blood. The police will be there any minute, and she hides, squats under a rack of dresses until she's discovered by the strange man with long, stringy hair, the same man who put the turd photo in the overalls. He's been tracking us all day, waiting for Lizzie to be alone. "Wow," he says, "those are great rubber balls." And she follows him to his car and rides with him to the desert, to a concrete foundation of a house that was never built, a stage, and when Lizzie realizes what's transpiring, she'll drop the balls, and they'll bounce and bloom outwards and look like a big, happy firework before they roll off the edges and disappear.

This story, these images of Lizzie and the strange man, take residence in my gut and sit there like a tumor, so when we stop for a red light at Prince Road, I open the door, jump out of the car, and hurry down the dirt shoulder back towards Goodwill. My wet shorts chafe my thighs. Part of me wants to stop and drop down there in the dust next to a drained Big Gulp and a smashed Sammy Hagar cassette, but I keep moving, and even start to run.

Lara Vapnyar

Deaf and Blind

THIS DEAF AND BLIND MAN, my mother's friend's lover, was on his way to spend the evening. His name was Sasha. My mother's friend's name was Olga. I had known her since I was a baby, so I considered her my friend, too. She was beautiful. More beautiful than my mother. She had a long soft body and pitch-black hair that reached to her waist. My mother and I also had dark hair, but ours was messy and thin and forgettable, while Olga's hair made people stare at her. Olga lived in a town on the Black Sea, but she visited Moscow often and she always brought a gift for me. My favorite was a necklace made of seashells. I loved to put it on and dance, while Olga clapped and sang. "Poor Olga, she's so good with kids," my mother would remark. I was only a child, but I was very close to my mother, so close that I couldn't help hearing the smug note in her voice. "Both of them really wanted a baby," my grandmother explained to me, "but only your mother was able to have one."

My mother and Olga had met while undergoing fertility treatments at some sort of experimental program in one of the Moscow clinics. Inpatient, two weeks long, run by a mustached woman in military boots. The patients had to sleep in the same room and undergo procedures together. There were five of them. All women in their thirties, all (for some insane reason) Ph.D.s. My mother's Ph.D. was in math, Olga's in philosophy. Olga's subject was perception. My mother's was negative numbers. Their beds faced each other, so they had no choice but to become friends. They shared food, books, stories, jokes. My mother told me that Olga wasn't that funny herself, but she always laughed at my mother's jokes. After a couple of days, they began sharing urine. The mustached woman demanded that all the patients produce urine samples every three hours. They were required to pee right before going to bed, at eleven p.m., and then set their alarm clocks for two a.m. and five a.m. My mother took the two a.m. shift. She would get up and pee for herself and for Olga. And Olga did the same for her at five a.m. That way, they could both have a half-decent night's sleep. Neither of them cared that this could destroy the validity of the mustached woman's research. "Olga and I are pee sisters!" my mother loved to say. I was jealous of her. I hoped to have a pee sister of my own one day.

By the end of the program, my mother and Olga had confessed to each other that their marriages weren't happy. Olga explained that her husband loved her like crazy, but she'd never felt more than affection and respect for him. She wanted to know what it was like to love somebody "with every fiber of your being," the way people did in books. She was sure that she would love her child like that. My mother told Olga that she did love my father with every fiber of her being, but she wasn't sure if he loved her back. She had a feeling that he was getting tired of their marriage. She hoped that having a child would bind him to her.

They both lost in the end. Olga's treatment didn't work. And my mother had a child, but my father left her anyway. I was five then. By the time I was seven, my father had a new wife and a new baby. That baby was often sick. Every time my father planned something with me, like going to the children's theater or the zoo, the baby would get sick and he'd have to cancel. The good thing was that every time he canceled he promised something else, something much more exciting than the thing we had to skip. I would think how lucky I was that I couldn't go to a concert, say, because now I would get to visit a theater! And when the theater was canceled I was promised the circus. And then the circus was canceled, too, and I was promised something really special: a cross-country-skiing trip. We'd take a train to the countryside and spend the whole day together. We'd ski through the woods with backpacks full of food, and we might even see some winter animals. I thought what incredible luck it was that my baby sister had been sick for the concert and the circus and the theater! And we would go really soon. My father said next weekend. "Next weekend" turned out to be an elusive time frame. The weekend after next was technically "next weekend," too, and the weekend after that, and the weekend after that. "You're breaking her heart!" I heard my mother scream on the phone. She was wrong, though. I was okay with all that waiting. I knew that one of the next weekends would have to be "next weekend." I didn't doubt my father even when winter officially ended. "Everybody knows the March snow is the best," my father said, and I repeated it endlessly. "My father and I are going on a ski trip soon. We're just waiting for the best snow." Meanwhile, the snow in Moscow was melting at a discouraging rate. "There is still plenty of snow in the country," my father said. In the middle of March, a neighbor's sick dog died. I asked my mother, "Why won't my baby sister die, too? It would make it so much easier for everybody." She scolded me, but I overheard her recounting the conversation to my grandmother and laughing.

My father and I did eventually go on that ski trip. It was March 31, the date when the snow becomes simply perfect for skiing. All expert cross-country skiers know that. "See, there is snow!" my father said when we got off the train. I could hear that he was both surprised and relieved. We put on our skis and went into the woods. We didn't ski for long, because the snow, though pure and brilliant, was too sticky. After a few minutes, a layer of about two inches of it was firmly attached to our skis, so we couldn't really glide; we had to walk on our skis as if we were wearing platform shoes. We didn't see any animals, either. But it was still a magnificent day. My father showed me how to make a campfire in the snow, and we made tea using snow instead of water. We drank that tea crouching by the fire, laughing like crazy whenever one of us lost his balance and fell backward into the snow. On the way home, my father said that we would do it again every year on March 31, the date for the best snow. He also told me that I should never wear my backpack on the train, because I could accidentally hit other people with it. What I needed to do was to remove the backpack before I boarded the train and carry it in front of me, or drag it by one of the straps if it was too heavy. This stuck with me. I always take my backpack off before I board a train, even if it's a tiny backpack. I don't remember any other life lessons from my father.

When I got home that night I told my mother that I loved my father more than I loved her. That was true, but I don't know what cruel demon possessed me to share it. Perhaps I blamed her for failing to make my father stay with us. Perhaps I sensed that she blamed me for the same thing. Anyway, if she regretted her fertility treatments that night, I would certainly understand her.

Olga happened to be in Moscow on March 31 of the next year. She was hoping to spend some quiet time with us and to tell my mother about Sasha. Instead she stumbled onto a scene of total disorder. I was sitting on the floor, wedged in between the large wardrobe and my mother's bed, sobbing and refusing to come out. My mother, my grandmother, and my grandfather were taking turns trying to reason with me, using different tactics ranging from bribes to threats to reassurances that my father loved me very much.

Olga didn't adopt any of my family's approaches. She assessed the situation, then marched into the bedroom as if nothing were out of the ordinary, as if I weren't shaking in the corner, red faced and covered in snot. She announced that she and I were going to make orange ice cream. She was holding a string bag full of oranges in one hand and a large brick of the best Moscow ice cream in the other. She meant business. I didn't have the strength or the desire to argue with her. Plus, I'd never made or eaten orange ice cream and couldn't possibly say no to that. I crawled out of my hiding place, and it was only then that Olga alluded to my distressed state. She said, "Go and wash your face, dear. We don't want snot all over the ice cream."

Here is how you make orange ice cream: You halve the oranges, carefully scoop out the flesh, and remove all the skin and pith from the segments. Then you mix ice cream with the cleaned, diced pulp, spoon the mixture into the empty orange halves, sprinkle some shaved chocolate on top, and put it all into the freezer. Our small freezer had no space, so we had to temporarily remove a whole chicken and a block of lard. Olga said that it would take at least an hour for the ice cream to set, and that the best way for me to kill the time would be to read a book. My grandfather was napping on the sofa, my grandmother was cooking dinner, and my mother and Olga went into the bedroom to talk. I took out a book and sat down on our living room carpet to read, but after ten minutes or so I was knocking on the bedroom door, asking if an hour had passed. "No!" my mother yelled. "Go away!" It took me four more attempts before they finally came out. I saw that Olga had been crying and my mother looked shell-shocked, but I didn't care. I was too excited about the orange ice cream.

It didn't disappoint, the rich ice cream with sparkly orange crystals in round cups so cold they made your fingers ache. I tried to make it many times as an adult, but every time it came out bland and runny and desperately silly. Back then, though, I thought it was magical. I proclaimed it the best food I'd ever tasted and hugged Olga with all my might. I did wish for a mother who was more like Olga—kind, pretty, and smelling of oranges—and less like my own mother, who was angry and losing her hair. But I was eight now and my capacity for cruelty had diminished, so I decided not to share this with my mother.

"I have to tell you something," my mother said to my grandparents and me as soon as Olga had left. "And you'd better sit down." My grandparents were putting the dishes away, and I was crouching on the floor, trying to build a castle with the empty orange cups.

"Olga has a lover," my mother said. That got our attention.

My grandmother gasped and my grandfather froze with a wineglass in each hand.

"His name is Sasha."

My grandmother pointed at me to remind my mother of my censoring presence, but my mother just shrugged. She never had a problem with my reading whatever I wanted or watching grown-up movies with her or listening in to gossip. Although I didn't know anything about sex, I understood what there was to understand about lovers. People fell in love with people while married to other people. When that happened, they wanted to kiss those other people, instead of their spouses, but they had to lie about it so that their spouses wouldn't be hurt. Most of the movies we watched and most of the books on our bookshelves had this plot twist, so I assumed that the situation was fairly common. It was clearly upsetting, since the people involved often cried or screamed or even engaged in physical fights, but it was nothing out of the ordinary. In fact, I'd now gathered enough clues to suspect that this was exactly what had happened to my father before he left us.

And now it had happened to Olga. I wondered if she and the man had already kissed.

"Okay," my mother said. "That's not the whole story. Olga's lover is deaf and blind."

Now my grandmother did have to sit down.

"How can you be both deaf and blind?" my grandfather asked.

"Easy," my mother said. "You can't hear, and you can't see."

This was when I started to laugh. I laughed and laughed and laughed, until my mother had to slap me.

There were more questions.

My grandfather wanted to know if Sasha was all right mentally. "Yes, more than all right—he has a Ph.D. in philosophy," my mother said.

My grandmother wanted to know when and where Olga had met him. A month earlier. At a conference in St. Petersburg on the philosophy of perception. Sasha had been the keynote speaker.

"Speaker? How?" my grandfather asked.

"He hand-signs, Dad!" my mother said.

"How?"

My mother looked as if she were about to slap my grandfather the same way she had slapped me, but instead she answered him. "You take a person's hand and you touch it in a certain way. Different movements mean different letters."

My grandfather shook his head. "Her poor husband," he said. "To have your wife cheat on you is bad enough, but to cheat with a deaf and blind man!"

"We don't choose who we love," my grandmother whispered.

"This is just another of her whims," my mother said. "I give it a month."

But, of course, it wasn't over in a month. Or in six months. Or in eleven months.

We didn't see Olga in all that time. She didn't come to Moscow often, and when she did she spent her free time with Sasha. But she called my mother now and then, and they talked on the phone for a long, long time. My grandparents and I would hang about waiting for my mother to finish so that she could recap the conversation for us. My mother always started by saying, "Apparently, it's still going on."

Whenever she could, Olga would beg her boss to send her on a business trip to Moscow. He wouldn't do this without a bribe. One time she gave him theater tickets, another an expensive bottle of cognac, and then he demanded that she give him her place on the waiting list to buy an imported dining room set. What did she care about tables and chairs, anyway? She cared only about Sasha. Didn't she care about her husband, too? Of course she did! She felt affection and respect for him! It was very painful to have to lie to him. There were times when she'd return from Moscow on an overnight train, and he'd be there, waiting for her at the station with a small bouquet of flowers. This made her feel just awful!

" 'That man is crushing me with his kindness,' " my mother said to us with a mocking smile. She was quoting Chekhov's "The Grasshopper," not that I knew that at the time.

No, Olga's husband didn't suspect anything at all. Olga didn't understand how this was possible. His wife was crazy in love with another man and he didn't see any signs? Sometimes this made her angry. Because didn't it mean that he didn't really know or understand her? If he truly loved her he would notice that something was wrong! Sometimes Olga would get so mad at him that she felt like physically hurting him, like slapping him across the face with that pathetic bouquet.

Once, my mother said that she had a theory, a theory about why Olga had picked a deaf and blind man. It wasn't love. Not really. Olga had always wanted a child, so she'd gone and found a man who would be fully dependent on her. Like a child, you see? My mother sounded mean when she said this, and I could see that my grandparents weren't buying her theory.

During that year, I often pondered what it would be like to love a deaf and blind man, or, rather, what it would be like to be one. I'd close my eyes, put my hands over my ears, and try to walk. It was easier than I'd imagined, but inevitably I'd bump into a bookshelf or a corner of the dining table. I'd cry out in pain and open my eyes and my world would be safe and normal again. But Sasha couldn't do that. He couldn't just open his eyes and uncover his ears and be able to see and hear, no matter how scared he was in his dark silence. I thought that deaf and blind people had to be exceptionally brave.

"I don't think I can stand it much longer," Olga told my mother one day in early March. What really killed her was how difficult it was to communicate with Sasha when they were apart. Sasha couldn't call Olga, because of her husband, but Olga called him often. Usually, they were assisted by Andrei, Sasha's alcoholic roommate, a blind but not fully deaf man, who would hand-sign with Sasha and then translate to Olga. But he could convey only certain information, not the feelings! He was filthy minded and rude, and he was often drunk! He made fun of Olga when she asked him to translate how much she missed and loved Sasha, and he never said that Sasha missed her, too. Olga wasn't sure if Andrei was choosing not to translate that part, or if Sasha didn't say that he loved her because Andrei's presence made him shy. At the end of a phone call, Olga would ask Andrei to pass the phone to Sasha so that she could listen to his breathing. Sometimes Olga would sing to him. Sasha said that, even though he couldn't hear her, he could feel the vibrations. Olga knew a lot of weepy ballads, and she would sing them as loudly as she could. This was often more eloquent than Andrei's dumb translations. If only the phone connection were better. There were times when the call was disconnected midsong. Olga would find herself all alone, hundreds of miles from Sasha, sitting on the low wooden stool in the dark hall of her apartment with that greasy old receiver beeping at her like an angry siren, making her want to die.

"It's about to end," my mother said after telling us about the hostile receiver. But it didn't end.

A couple of weeks later, Olga called my mother again, this time from Moscow, and announced that she had quit her job and left her husband and come here to be with Sasha for good.

"You'll all meet him in two weeks," my mother said, her voice high-pitched and trembling. "Olga's bringing him to dinner."

"Deaf and blind! Deaf and blind! Deaf and blind is coming to dinner!" I started to scream.

Coincidentally, my father called to say that he wanted to take me skiing on April 7, the very day that Olga and Sasha were coming to visit. I said no. Who wanted to ski? A deaf and blind man was coming to dinner!

I can't and I won't describe the pleasure of delivering that "no." For that alone, I'll be grateful to Olga forever.

On the day of their visit, our entire apartment was filled with reverberating bangs. This was the sound of my mother whacking a beef filet with a meat pounder. We had decided to serve Sasha and Olga the most festive dishes we knew: Salad Olivier and Meat the French Way. The meat needed to be pounded very hard to work the French Way. I really wanted to pound the meat, too, but my task was to cut up potatoes and eggs for the salad.

My grandmother was polishing the silver and giving the cognac glasses an extra shine.

"Is it safe to use the good glasses?" she wanted to know. But my mother only groaned and gave the meat another whack.

"Is he neat with the toilet?" was my grandmother's next question.

"Please, stop!" my mother begged her. But my grandfather thought this was a valid concern. He said that after he used the toilet my grandmother often asked him if he was blind. And that man really was blind!

But the toilet issue wasn't what troubled my grandfather most. "How will we talk to him?" he asked.

"Well, Olga knows sign language," my mother said. "So I assume she'll hand-sign what we're saying to Sasha, and then translate his responses to us."

That didn't sit well with my grandfather. What he loved above all was impressing new people. He wasn't especially informed about politics or culture, but he loved to express his opinions on these subjects in a booming voice and with a stern lowering of his right eyebrow that demanded attention and respect. My grandfather was justifiably worried that, without the added power of his eyebrows and his voice, he wouldn't be able to impress Sasha with the mere content of his opinions. He ended up taking a leisurely dump while perusing recent issues of *Pravda*, hoping to build up his opinions so that they could stand on their own.

Then it was my turn to ask a question, and I used a child's license to speak what was on everybody's mind. "Is he scary?"

"No! Of course not!" my grandmother said without much reassurance.

And my mother said, "You should be ashamed of yourself!"

I was ashamed. I decided that even if Sasha was scary, I'd pretend he wasn't, for Olga's sake.

Don't you just hate those endless minutes between the time that your guests are supposed to arrive and the moment that they actually ring the doorbell? The women in my family are famous for being ahead of schedule, so all the preparations had been made. The Meat the French Way was resting in the warm oven. The salads were mixed and decorated with slices of boiled carrots. The cold cuts were carefully arranged according to a strict color scheme. The people were washed and combed and dressed in their best clothes. All we had to do was wait.

These days, I have social media to fill such moments. I just refresh my feed again and again, killing minute after nasty minute. But back then what was I to do? I kept running in circles between the kitchen window, from which I could just glimpse the stop where Olga and Sasha would get off the bus, and our front door, where if you pressed an ear to the frame you could hear if the elevator was coming up. This was what I always did when my father was supposed to come and pick me up. "Stop it! You look pathetic," my mother would tell me then, but she was the pathetic one. Trying on different dresses before my father's visit, combing her hair this way and that, applying and reapplying her makeup, and then invariably running to hide in the bedroom as soon as she heard me yell, "He's coming!"

I managed to miss the first sight of Sasha and Olga. The doorbell caught me unawares, sitting on the toilet, with my underpants around my knees. "No!" I screamed. "Don't open until I come out!" Few things were more embarrassing for me than being caught on the toilet by our guests. Especially by guests of such magnitude. But, of course, my mother opened the door. Who ever listens to a child begging for something from the toilet?

I used my grandmother as a shield and came out of the bathroom hidden behind her. By the time we made it to our tiny entrance hall, Sasha and Olga had taken off their coats and were vigorously wiping their feet on the doormat. Sasha was shorter and bulkier than Olga, with a soft square face. His eyes were half-shut; he seemed to be squinting. Olga was holding his left hand. Everybody took turns shaking his right hand, and he sounded out everybody's name in a strained, bellowing manner.

I stepped forward. Olga leaned in to kiss me and said that she had told Sasha that I was her favorite person in the whole world and he was eager to meet me. I saw that she wasn't just holding Sasha's hand, but playing with his fingers. Then it dawned on me that this was sign language. That Olga had been talking to Sasha that whole time.

Sasha put his right hand forward, and I put mine into his. He closed his palm over my fingers and smiled at something behind my back. I turned around, but there was nothing there, except our gurgling fridge with a pile of empty boxes on top of it. Olga took his left hand and put it on top of my head, and he lowered his gaze and almost met my eyes. There's an expression people use when someone is blocking their view: "Hey, you're not made of glass!" But Sasha looked through me and beyond me as if I were, in fact, made of glass. I got scared and wanted to hide, but I caught Olga looking at me, so I smiled and squeezed Sasha's hand. He bellowed my name and signed something to Olga. She translated that Sasha was really, really happy to meet me. I knew that this was true, because she was beaming as she said it. Or perhaps she had been beaming to begin with.

"You look radiant, Olga!" my grandfather said in his booming voice. My grandmother agreed with him. And my mother asked everybody to follow her to the table.

Salad Olivier turned out to be less than ideal food for a blind person. All those hard slippery cubes of vegetables and meat, bouncing off the fork, scattering on the plate. Sasha had to chase those cubes around, tapping his fork against the surface of the plate like a cane against the sidewalk. Whenever he managed to hunt down a cube, he'd take a sip of his cognac, as if in celebration. I couldn't take my eyes off him, even though I knew that this wasn't polite. "You should be ashamed!" I kept telling myself.

At first, Olga let Sasha focus on his food while she took on all the talking.

No, Sasha wasn't born deaf and blind. He'd lost his sight and hearing at the age of four, after a long battle with meningitis. His parents had refused to treat him as an invalid. They'd taught him to be as independent as possible. Then they'd sent him to a special school for deaf and blind children. This was a really excellent school, and Sasha had proved to be a brilliant student. He had been one of only four graduates who were invited to study at the Moscow State University. Olga said this with exactly the same proud expression that my mother had when she told people about my achievements. All four of those students went on to get their Ph.D.s in philosophy, but Sasha's achievement was especially remarkable, because he was the only fully blind and fully deaf person in the group. Sasha's roommate Andrei, for example, could hear just fine with the help of a hearing aid. Imagine how much easier studying must have been for him! It wasn't really fair to compare his career with Sasha's.

"Of course, it's not fair," my grandfather said with an impressive lowering of his right brow. "In fact, I recently read in *Pravda*—"

But just then Sasha, who couldn't have known that my grandfather was speaking, interrupted him. He made a series of urgent motions with his fingers, and Olga said that he wanted to thank us for the food. Everything was delicious, but especially the meat. He wanted to know the secret ingredient.

"The secret ingredient is a lot of whacking," my mother said.

Olga translated this for Sasha and even punched his hand with her fist several times. That was when he laughed for the first time. His laughter sounded like a series of rumbling groans, but we were all very happy that he appreciated both the food and my mother's humor. (Not everybody did.)

By the end of the meal, Sasha had started to talk more. If alcohol loosens your tongue, perhaps it loosens your fingers as well. He poked his fingers into the flesh of Olga's palms with amazing speed, and she translated for us. He talked about smells and how important they were for him, how he knew that we were good people just by the warm, homey smell of our apartment. "It's the smell of the meat," my mother whispered, but I saw that she was pleased. He talked about the woods his mother used to take him to when he was a child. She'd lead him to a tree or a bush and ask him to touch it, and she taught him how to pick berries. He knew how to find wild strawberries with his hands. Olga had never tried wild strawberries. Last July, when Olga had visited Moscow, Sasha had taken her to the woods and taught her how to find them.

Then he said something else, and I wanted Olga to translate, but she said that she couldn't, that this was too much and most of it was private. There were tears in her eyes. Suddenly she grabbed Sasha's hands and kissed them.

At that moment, we all felt the presence of something in the room. Well, I can't be sure about my grandparents, but I felt it, and I know that my mother felt it, too. It was as if something enormous and grand were growing out of our dinner table, reaching up, up and up, like a cathedral breaking through the sky.

It was like nothing else in my life up to then.

I wish I could say that I recognized what it was, but I didn't. What I felt was pure awe, unburdened by understanding.

"Love is blind indeed," my grandmother said after they left.

"Deaf and blind," my grandfather quipped.

But my mother didn't say anything. She went into her room and closed the door behind her. I went after her. She hadn't turned the light on, so I couldn't see, but I could hear that my mother was crying. I walked over to her bed and put out my hand hoping to find and touch hers. What I found instead was her face, all wet and slippery with tears.

"Get in," she whispered. I climbed into the bed and hugged her from behind as tightly as I could. I was crying into her shoulders, which were warm and shaking. I tried to squeeze them even tighter to stop the shaking, to console her.

I pitied her. But I loved her more than I pitied her. I loved her so much that it was hard to breathe. And another thing: at that moment, I felt close to my mother in a completely new way. Not as a child but as a fellow woman, an equal.

Sasha and Olga got married later that year, as soon as Olga's divorce came through. As far as I know, they lived happily ever after until death did them part. Olga was the one who died. She was only forty-two. Cancer. It's usually cancer when women die that young. Sasha remarried within a year. Strangely enough, his second wife also left her husband for him.

But my mother—my mother never remarried.

Jenny Zhang

Why Were They Throwing Bricks?

"I LOST HEARING IN THIS EAR when a horse jumped over a fence and collided against the side of my face," my grandmother told me when she arrived at JFK. I was nine and hadn't seen her in four years. "In Shanghai you slept with me every single night. Every week we took you to your other grandmother's house. She called incessantly, asking for you. 'Can't I see my own granddaughter?' I said, 'Sure you can.' But—let's not spare any feelings—you didn't want to see her. Whenever you were at your waipo's house you cried and called my name and woke up the neighbors. You hated her face because it was round like the moon, and you thought mine was perfectly oval like an egg. You loved our house. It was your real home—and still is. Your waipo would frantically call a few minutes after I dropped you off asking me to come back, and I would sprint all the way there. Yes, my precious heart, your sixty-eight-year-old grandmother ran through the streets for you. How could I let you suffer for even a second? You wouldn't stop crying until I arrived, and the minute I pulled you into my arms, you slept the deep happy sleep of a child who has come home to her true family."

"I sleep by myself now. I have my own bed with stickers on

it," I told her in Chinese, without knowing the word for stickers. I hugged my body against my mother, who was telling my father he would have to make two trips to the car because my grandmother had somehow persuaded the airline to let her bring three pieces of checked luggage *and* two carry-on items without any additional charges.

"And did you see that poor man dragging her suitcases off the plane for her? How does she always do that?" my mother said. She shrugged me away and mouthed in English to me, "Talk. To. Grandma."

My father threw his hands up. "You know exactly how," he said, and went off with the first two bags.

"You remember how uncanny it was," my grandmother continued, tweaking her hearing aid until it made a small shrill sound and then a shriller sound and then another even shriller sound. "They called me a miracle worker and I said, 'No, no, I'm just her nainai,' but everyone said, 'You're a miracle worker. You're the only one who can make that child stop crying.' They said there was no need for me to be modest. 'This child prefers her grandmother to even her own mother and father! Why sugarcoat the truth?' I had to stop myself from stopping other people from saying it after a while. Was I supposed to keep insulting everyone's intelligence? Protesting endlessly? Your nainai isn't that type of person. And the truth is, people don't make things up out of nothing. There's truth in every widely believed saying, and that's just true."

"What?" I said. "I don't understand Chinese that good."

"I knew you wouldn't forget a moment of your real life, your real home—the place you come from. Have you learned English yet?"

"That's all I speak. It's America."

"Your nainai is so proud of you. One day your English will catch up. It's such a gift to be here now with you. You don't know how many lonely nights I've spent dropping tears for you.

It was wrong of me to let you go. Remember how you called for me when you let go of my hand and boarded the airplane with your mother? Remember how you howled that you wanted to take me with you? Four years ago, your father wrote to me, 'You can't keep my own wife and child away from me any longer. I'm sending for them immediately.' I wanted to know if he ever considered maybe you and your mother simply didn't want to go to America? In those days, you would've rather eaten a basement full of rats than be separated from your nainai. Your father's also stubborn, but I'm not the type to insult the spoonful of food nourishing me. You see what I mean? I won't say any more. I'm living in his house now and even though he has only made fatally wrong choices, we still have to listen to him. But remember how at the airport you cried and said, 'Nainai, I love you the most of everyone. I want to stay with you. I don't want to go to America.'"

"I don't remember that," I said to my grandmother. "Sorry."

"You remember everything, don't you? But it hurts too much to dredge up bad memories." Her hearing aid buzzed again and she twisted its tiny hidden knob with her thumb and index finger. "This thing works for a moment and then it goes dead for days. Your father said he would get me a proper hearing aid so I can hear your beautiful voice. You speak up now and let your grandmother look at you. She's only missed you every minute of every hour of every second of every single iota of a time unit that's elapsed since you last slept with your nainai every night, refusing to even close your eyes unless I was in the bed with you. You know what everyone's favorite joke was? 'Who's the mom? You?' Oh, I laughed."

"That's not a joke."

"That's right. It was the plain truth," she continued. "They all asked me, 'Doesn't your granddaughter ever want to sleep with her mother and father?' And I had to tell them—not in a bragging way, just in an informing way—'No. Her father is in America learning how to build computers and her mother works late at the factory and even if her mother didn't come home from work so late, my granddaughter has made it clear she can only sleep with me. I know it's not proper while her mother sleeps alone in another room under the same roof, but when a child wants something, how can you look her in the eye and deny her?'"

My grandmother lived with us in America for a year. She taught me how to knit, and after school I watched her make dinner and do dishes and sew curtains. At first I wouldn't let her sleep with me in my bed. She cried and came every night to my bedroom and sat at the edge of the bed saying nothing. She had small red eyes and no teeth at night, except for four on the bottom row and a couple in the back. She ate daily bulbs of garlic so she'd live to be 117 and see me grow for another forty-five years, and the first few times she brought it up, I imagined myself running away from home just to get a few years to myself. But after a month, the smell was comforting, and I needed it near me before I could close my eyes, and just when I started to call for her more than she called for me, my parents announced that she had to move back to China to be with her dying husband. "Your grandfather," my grandmother said with disgust, "says the only proper way for a man to leave this world is in his own home with his wife by his side. Have you ever heard anything so spineless?"

My grandfather had been begging her to come back for six months. He had been diagnosed with lesions in his throat and he didn't want to die without her. For a year, I had slept in her bed, pressed up against her like she was my bedroom wall, and after she left, I stayed in her bed for two weeks, refusing to return to my own bed even after my mother threatened to push me off if I didn't get out.

"This room reeks," she said. "It smells like several people have died. You still want to sleep in here?"

I nodded.

"On sheets that haven't been washed for weeks?"

I nodded. "She said she's coming back after Grandpa dies."

"She also said you'd learn English in middle school. She said she learned to drive in her dreams and that's how she'll pass the driving test and take you to Mount Rushmore for your birthday. You believe everything she says? Have you gone back in time and lost all sense?"

I shook my head. Finally, she and my father dragged me out, my arms wrapped around the cheap white lacquered bed frame as my father held my legs and my mother pried my fingers free.

"You're going to sleep on your own," my mother said. "Like you did before she came around."

"You hear your mother?" my father said, wiping the tears from my face and blowing softly on my hot red cheeks. "Just a day at a time."

"Don't indulge this," my mother said.

"You want to beat the sadness out of her?" my father said. "Because that's what your mother wants. For us to be the bad guys and her to be the hero when she comes back."

"I'm not inviting her back," my mother said.

My grandmother came back two years later. I was in middle school, and my pathetic puberty struck like a flash of lightning in the middle of the night—I suddenly saw all my surroundings for what they were: hideous and threatening. I had no friends, social life, interests, talents, breasts, straight teeth, likability, normal clothes, or charm, and every day I came home weighed down with dread. I started to fake illnesses so I could stay home with my two-year-old brother. I followed him around everywhere, crawling when he crawled and walking on my knees when he learned to walk so that we were the same height.

When my grandmother moved in for the second time, she told us that this time she wasn't leaving. She was going to apply for a green card and raise my brother until he was old enough to be on his own—eighteen, maybe nineteen.

"We'll see about that," my father said in Chinese, and then to me and my mother in English, "Let Grandma believe what she wants to believe. My gut says we'll be back at the travel agency in March, or my name is not Daddy, problem solver of this house."

I laughed at him. "But that isn't your name."

I made a point of telling my grandmother that I'd been sleeping by myself this whole time. "I also know how to cut my own toenails and braid my hair and make my own snacks." My mom was looking at me without pleasure. "Hi, Grandma. I missed you," I added.

Then she was babbling, hugging me up and down and side to side. "*Nainai xiang ni le*," she said. "Grandma missed you, oh, Grandma missed you, oh, Grandma missed you—"

"'Kay, got it," I said.

She stepped back and took my hand. "Baobei, you can sleep with your nainai if you want, but your brother will, too. I don't know if three will fit, but I'm very happy to try. Does anything make your nainai happier than having her two grandchildren by her side? Your brother will sleep with me until he's old enough to sleep in his own bed. Most people say thirteen is the age when a child learns to sleep on their own but most people are selfish and looking out only for themselves. Not me. I say sixteen. I say seventeen. I say eighteen. And if he needs me to, I'll gladly sleep with your brother until he's twenty-one!"

I laughed. "Allen's not going to do that. It's different here. We wrote you about this."

My grandmother pulled me in so close I faked choking noises to make my point known. "Oh, baobei, I missed you. My hearing has gotten worse. In China doctors are crooks and charlatans. They take your money and make everything worse, or if you're lucky, exactly the same. I lost my hearing in this ear running away from boys who were throwing bricks. Why were they throwing bricks? Who knows. There was a violence back then no one can understand now. And where did those boys get the bricks? That's the real question. In those days no one had brick houses. Everyone lived like animals. You wouldn't have been able to tell your nainai had skin as white as a porcelain doll because she was covered in dirt. These rotten boys chased me until I tripped over a fence and a sharp spike of wood pierced my eardrum. I lay there for a night until the shepherd's daughter found me, curled up like a child."

"I thought you lost your hearing when a horse ran over a fence and trampled you."

"They took me to the village doctor and he grafted skin from my knee to my ear. I was bleeding so much I thought I would die. That was the worst I've ever experienced, and I've experienced awful things. Your nainai has lived through two wars and saw her own mother gunned down by Japanese soldiers. No child should see their mother die. But do you know what was worse than lying there in the mud with blood in my ears? Worse than seeing my own brother come back from war with only half a leg and no right arm? It was living in China with your grandfather, who didn't have the decency to die like he said he would, and being thousands of miles apart from you and your brother. I was hurting for your brother so much I told your lowlife grandfather that unless he died right this instant, he would have to learn to leave this world just as he came into it—without me. What could he do? Stop me from going to America? I said to him, 'Come with me if you need me around so badly.' 'But no,' he says. 'I'm comfortable here. This is our home. You should want to live in it with me. These are our golden years.' Blah blah blah. My home is where you and your brother are. Oh, I've missed him like I miss the skin from my knee."

"You just met him today."

"Speak louder, my heart, so your nainai can hear you."

"My mom says I can only call my grandmother on my dad's side nainai, and you're actually my waipo."

"Your father said he's going to replace this hearing aid. I might as well have kept that spike of wood in here. They wouldn't know technology from the inside of their asses in China. And it's filthy over there. Can you imagine some illiterate doctor with dirty hands touching your nainai's ear? This is why I couldn't stay in China. I missed your brother's birth because your grandfather said he was dying, and then I go back and guess who isn't dying? Guess who's walking around the garden and smoking? Every day he goes to the *lao ganbu huodongshi* to gamble. Does that seem like a man on his deathbed to you, my sweetheart, my baobei? Do you think your grandmother will forgive your grandfather for making her miss the birth of her one and only grandson? Will your grandmother fall for his bluff again? Not ever. I'll be here until I pass to another realm, my baobei."

"I'm not going to call you nainai."

"All of my grandchildren call me nainai because nainai is the dearest, closest name you could call a person in your family. You refused to call me waipo when you were little. You said to me, 'You're not my waipo, my waipo is that strange lady over there who feeds me food I don't like and who has a cold bed.' Remember how you said that? Where's your brother now? I missed him so much. I pray hummingbirds peck my eyes and leave their droppings in my pecked-out sockets before I have to experience this heartbreak again. But I'm healing already. When I see your brother's precious face, I'll never know sadness again. My heart will be overrun with joy until my last dying breath. Where's your brother, baobei?"

.   .   .

The third time my grandmother came to live with us, I was fifteen and my brother was five. "Please don't let her get to you again like last time," I said to him. "You were obsessed with her."

"No, Stacey. Was not."

But soon he was sleeping in her bed again and talking back to my parents and getting mad when I wouldn't let him have the last Rice Krispies Treat. Whenever he was upset with me, he ran to my grandmother, and she would come into my room and pretend to spank me in front of him, when really she was just clapping her hands near my ass.

"Your sister is crying so hard from my spanking," my grandmother said to my brother. "See? Nainai is punishing your sister for taking what's rightfully yours. You hear how hard I'm spanking her? Her tears are everywhere."

"I'm not crying," I said over my grandmother's clapping. "I'm not crying," I repeated until I was so frustrated that I actually did start crying.

My brother cried on the weekends when my grandmother went to work at a factory where she folded dumplings for five cents apiece. Most of the other workers could do only fifty an hour, and when the owner noticed my grandmother typically clocked in at a hundred and was teaching her trade secrets to the other ladies during their fifteen-minute lunch break, he instituted "quality control" rules, mandating a certain amount of flour on each dumpling and folds at the edge between 0.4 and 0.6 centimeters. My grandmother pointed out that he was arbitrarily docking pay for "unfit dumplings" without any real inspection, and all the dumplings she folded, including the unacceptable ones, were thrown into the same freezer bags, and that was exploitative. She persuaded the other workers to collectively demand back pay for all the rejected dumplings, and even organized a walkout one morning for higher wages. "Six cents a dumpling!" they chanted. The owner caved, and that day my grandmother came home pumping her fists like she was at a pep rally. Listening to her recount the day's victory, even I had to admit that she'd done a great thing.

"Don't you worry," she said, "you'll grow up to be just like your nainai one day."

"See, Grandma's a hero," Allen said. "She can do anything."

"Ugh," I said. "She just did it to get paid more. What's so great about that?"

I tried to save my brother, but my grandmother was too cunning. When we walked around the neighborhood at night, he hid inside her big, long nightgown. If I tried to ignore them, my grandmother would tap me on the shoulder until I turned around and then she would ask, "Where did your brother go?" and I'd begin to say, "Oh God, no, please no," but it was always too late—by then, my grandmother had already flipped her dress up to expose my brother, tumbling out from under her and onto the grass.

"I'm alive," he shouted. "I'm born. I'm born. I'm zero years old. I'm born. I'm suddenly born."

"That's how you were born," my grandmother cried out. "It was beautiful and majestic and everyone cried, and I cried the most. When you fell out of me, you awakened the gods and made them turn this world from an evil, corrupt world into one that is good and beneficent, eliminating poverty and hunger and violent death."

"You have to stop doing this with her," I said to him. "That's not how you were born and you know it."

"Grandma says it is."

"She's wrong," I said.

"And when your brother was little," my grandmother shouted with her hands in the air as if waiting to receive something promised to her, "he suckled on my breast because your mother's milk dried up, but my breasts have always produced milk whenever my grandchildren were born. Your cousin drank from my nipple too, but no one drank as hungrily as your brother. He drank until it was all dried up. And when it hurt for me to produce any more, he would cry out in anguish for it. I had to pray to the gods for more milk so your brother could go on."

"This is disgusting. This never happened," I said, but as usual no one was listening, not the trees that bent away from me; not the road ahead that sloped up and curved into a C; not my grandmother, who only heard what she wanted to hear; not my brother, who was being slowly poisoned by her; not my parents, who didn't listen when I said they'd lose my brother if they didn't start spending more time with us. What time? my father demanded. Yes, what time? my mother asked. Should we stop working and paying our mortgage and saving for your college fund? Should we go back to sleeping ten people to a room where someone's kid was screaming all night about needing to scratch her legs? Should we stop eating and stop owning clothes and a car for this "time" you speak so highly of?

But I knew what I knew. One day, he'd be sixteen and still cowering underneath our grandmother's dress, clinging to her before she woke him up, waiting for her to make lunch or clear away dinner, curled up around her like a twisted vine in the living room. Don't you want more than this? I would ask him. Don't you want to make friends and kiss someone you aren't related to? And he would say, No, I just want nainai, and then I'd see her next to him, with her toothless nighttime smile and small, satisfied eyes, and the outrageous lies she inserted into our lives until they became strange trivia in our family history, and there was nothing any of us could do to stop it from being that way.

One afternoon I came home to an empty house. An hour later, I saw my brother and my grandmother walking down the street, hand in hand. He was sweating even though it was still winter.

"Why are you sweating like that?"

"I was jumping."

"Jumping?"

"Grandma did it too."

"She was jumping with you?"

"Yeah. On that bouncing thing."

"What bouncing thing?"

"There's a purple bouncing thing and Grandma said it was okay to play on it."

"You mean a trampoline?"

"What's a trampoline?"

I drew him a picture of our grandmother in her nightgown suspended over a trampoline and, in the distance, five cops with their guns raised and pointed at her. Over their heads, I drew a collective dialogue bubble: *Kill her! It's the LAW!!!!!*

"Oh yeah, that's the bounce thing," he said, ripping the police officers out of the picture. "It was at the purple house."

"Let me get this straight. There's a purple trampoline in that purple house down the street where no one lives?"

"Not *in* the house. In the backyard. Grandma said I could jump on it. She did first."

"She jumped on the trampoline?"

"Like thirty times."

"Did you tell her to?"

"No, she just did it on her own. Then she was like, 'Allen, come jump on the trampoline with nainai.'"

"My God. You two are criminals. How many times did you do it?"

"Jump on the thing?"

"How many times did Grandma take you there?"

"I don't know. Every day."

"Jesus," I said. "Didn't you see my picture? You're breaking the law."

"No, we're not."

"Yes, you are, and you're going to go to jail if someone finds out. I could call the police right now," I said, walking toward the kitchen phone.

"Stacey, don't. Please don't put Grandma in jail."

"Who cares if she goes to jail?"

"I don't want her to. Please, Stacey."

"Who would you rather go to jail, then? Someone has to go. Mom or Grandma?"

"Mom."

"I can't believe you just said that."

"I don't know."

"This is stupid," I said.

"Don't call the police, Stacey. Grandma didn't do anything."

"Grandma didn't do anything," I said, imitating him.

She left that year after a neighbor's dog knocked her down against the asphalt. She split her head open and had to get stitches, several CAT scans that turned up inconclusive, and an MRI. She had overstayed her visa and we didn't have insurance for her, so the hospital bills ended up burning through several months of my parents' savings. They were never able to diagnose her with anything, but she complained of frequent headaches and started sleepwalking. Once, our neighbor down the street, a retired judge who'd fought in Vietnam and walked on crutches, returned her to us. "She knocked on my door. Now I'm knocking on yours."

"We have to send her home or we'll have to sell our home just to keep her alive," my father said to my mother, later.

"I know," she said. "She won't go. But I know."

Things reached peak crisis mode when one night my grandmother sleepwalked her way to the main road and stepped out into oncoming traffic, causing a four-car pileup and several police to show up at our door.

"I won't send her back in a body bag," I overheard my mother say to my father.

"We'll have to tell her that she either leaves on her own accord or INS will have her deported and banned from ever coming back."

"I'm not going to lie to her."

"Do you think she agonizes like you do every time she tells a lie? Look, I know you want to be fair to her, but this isn't the time to be virtuous."

The night my grandmother left, I told my brother she was never coming back and he tried to hit himself in the face with closed fists.

"You have to get used to this," I said, holding his hands together. "I know how you feel. I felt this way once, too. I thought I was going to die without her. But it's not so bad. You think it is now, but it's nothing. You just have to get used to it. Every day you'll miss her less. And then one day, you won't even think about her at all. I promise. And you can always talk to me if you feel sad."

He wasn't listening. His face was red all over like someone had slapped every part of it. The only time I had ever heard someone cry so violently was in a documentary about the Vietnam War. This village woman had jumped into her dead husband's freshly dug grave. She wanted to be buried with him. The sight and sound of her crying, seized-up body being dragged out of her husband's grave haunted me for days.

"This is a good thing, Allen. It's not even the worst thing you'll ever experience. Honestly, I'm happy. I'm happy she's gone, and you know what? I won't let you ruin this moment for me," I said, my voice cracking a little.

The fourth and final time my grandmother came to live with us, I was seventeen. My brother had forgotten her in the two years that had elapsed. He and I were close again. He slept on my floor or in my bed whenever I let him and played computer games with headphones on while I did my homework. He asked me to sit with him when he practiced the violin, which he was terrible at, though it wounded him if I laughed. When my friends came over, he lurked in the corner pretending to check the doorframe for bugs. I told him he couldn't always attach himself to someone, even though I liked it. I liked his small body leaning on mine in restaurant booths, and the way he pulled his chair up close to mine at home and sat with half his body on my chair, and how he often said he wished I didn't have homework or friends so I could spend all my time with him.

My grandmother tried to get him to sleep with her at night again, but he only wanted to sleep in my room. He taunted her sometimes, like when she asked if he would get under her dress like old times, and he did, but then punched her between her legs and scurried out and into my room. That was one of many days when she came and sat on the edge of my bed, waiting for my brother to apologize and tell her that he loved her and never meant to hurt her, but he never did.

This time around she was deafer than ever and wore hearing aids in both ears. They were a new model my father had purchased at Costco but worked just as poorly because she'd only use five-year-old batteries. Sometimes I saw her in her bedroom taking old batteries out and putting new old batteries in. She'd developed new interests and was teaching herself calligraphy and the history of American Indians. "America belongs to the Chinese," she said. "We were the first to settle North America."

"I thought the Native Americans were first."

"The Indians are the Chinese. Christopher Columbus saw Chinese faces and called them Indians. We invented spices and gum and paper; block painting on wood and then movable type for paper; paper money; gunpowder; fireworks; tea; silk spinning; alchemy, which later became modern chemistry;

navigational tools for maritime exploration; weapons for war and machines for peace. That is why China sits in the center of the map."

"Not in American classrooms."

"This is why you should be proud to be Chinese."

"Nainai, the Chinese aren't Indians."

"The first Africans were Chinese. The first South Americans were Chinese. No one lived in Australia for a long time. The civilization there was and is backward. Just think—all of North and South America, all of Africa, and most of Eastern Europe, all of Russia, Siberia—all first settled by the Chinese."

All of her was laid bare now—I saw her. She was just an old woman, raised in the country without education, who'd been told as a girl that women had been put on this earth to give birth and rear children and not be a burden in any way but to live as servants lived, productively, without fatigue or requirements of their own, yet had been resourceful and clever enough to come up through the feminist movement that Mao had devised to get women out of the house and into fields and factories, who had been given more power than any of the women in her lineage, who alluded to all the people she "saved" but never the people she turned in during the Cultural Revolution, whose hearing loss fed her fears of becoming useless, and who to counter those fears adopted a confidence that was embarrassing to witness, an opinion of herself so excessively high that it bordered on delusional. She tried to make her children believe they would perish without her, and when they learned better she tried the same with her grandchildren. But we were learning better, too, and it would be years before we had our own children, and by then she would be dead. My grandmother's unwillingness to be a victim was both pathetic and impressive, and she deserved compassion. But fuck, why did she have to be so greedy for it? It repulsed me that she wanted my brother and me to love her more than we loved our own parents, more than we loved each other, more even than we loved ourselves.

So I taunted her. I ignored her. I told her that she spoke Chinese like a farmer, the deepest cut I could make. "Here comes the Trail of Tears," my brother and I would say whenever we heard her whimper and sniffle. We bet on how long she could hold out, sitting on the edge of my bed and being ignored by us, before she went downstairs to practice her calligraphy. She had a third-grade education and was teaching herself characters so that she could write a book about her grandchildren.

"The world needs to know about you two," she said. For a moment, I was moved. But I knew that for either of us to grow up into the kind of people other people would ever want to know about, we had to leave her behind.

"You should write about your own life, nainai," I said. "People should know about you, too."

"You and your brother are my life," she insisted, tracing the strokes of my Chinese name in the air.

After I graduated high school, my parents took my brother and me on a cruise to Canada with some other Chinese families. The night before we left, my brother started crying and wouldn't tell my parents why.

"Are you worried Grandma will be alone in the house crying a Trail of Tears?" I asked him when we were alone.

He nodded. "Don't you feel bad for Grandma, Stacey?"

"I mean, it sucks to be alone in the house, but she can handle it. I know she can. That's life. Not everyone can have everything they want."

"But Grandma doesn't have anything she wants."

"That's not true. She got to go to America four separate times and live with us each time. Some people don't get to come even once. Ever think about that?" Allen's lip was trembling again. "Look, why don't we find her something really cool to bring back from the cruise. Wanna?"

The cruise was so much fun we forgot to get her a gift. On the car ride back, I rifled through my backpack and found an empty mini Coke can with a bendy straw stuck in it. We tossed the straw and wrapped the can in a food-stained pamphlet about onboard ship safety.

"We got you a present, nainai," Allen said.

"It's a souvenir we bought from Ontario," I added.

"Sorry we drank it already."

"Oh, my two precious baobei. You have given me a gift fit for kings." She hugged Allen, then hugged me, then hugged both of us in an embrace so tight that all three of us started crying for different reasons.

That summer, my grandfather wrote to tell her that he was about to be diagnosed with lymphatic cancer. It was real this time, he wrote, and she had to go home and be with him.

"He's a liar, you know," she told me and my brother.

"We know, nainai."

"He's jealous that it's my fourth time in America when he's too chickenshit to come even once. Why should I leave my grand-children and my real home for that worthless sack of bones?"

She returned to Shanghai shortly afterward. At the last min-ute, as my father was dragging the last of our grandmother's suitcases to the car, I said that I wanted to go to the airport with them.

"There's no room for both of you," my father said.

"Who said I wanted to go?" Allen said.

"Well, you can't stay alone," my mother said. "I suppose Daddy can stay with Allen."

"Forget it," I said. "It's too complicated."

My grandmother was kneeling next to Allen, who was on the

couch playing *Super Smash Bros.* She was trying to turn his body toward her but he kept shrugging her off.

"My own grandson won't even look at me because I've let him down so completely," she said. "I'm so ashamed. I'd rather die by his side than live a long life in China without him."

"He doesn't give a shit," I mumbled in English.

When we finally got my grandmother into the backseat of the car, she reached through the open window and grabbed Allen's arm. My father started the engine.

"I said I don't want to go," Allen said, and started to cry.

"Oh," my grandmother wailed. "And now he's crying for me."

My father nodded at me, and I stepped between them. It took all my strength to pry her fingers off his arm.

"It'll be too sad for him, nainai," I said quickly. "We love you, have a good trip, see you next time." Allen ran back into the house without looking back or waving. I heard my father raise the windows and engage the child-safety locks. My grandmother was trying to open the door, banging on the window with her fists like an animal. My father backed the car out of the driveway and drove up the C-shaped hill out of view. I heard a familiar low whine by my feet and looked down to see one of her hearing aids on the ground.

"It's like you just won't go," I said. I kicked it away from me, then ran to pick it up. I cradled it in my hand and tenderly brushed the sediment away, just like I did when I found my grandmother three years earlier, fallen on the asphalt, bleeding from her head.

The night my grandmother told me she was leaving again for the third time, I felt strange inside. My father reassured me she would have the very best doctors back home, who would figure out what was going on with her headaches and sleepwalking, and once she was healed she could come back again. I wanted her to get better but I didn't necessarily want her to come back. I lay in bed until everyone was asleep and then crept downstairs and out of the house, as I often did back then. I circled the neighborhood under a sliver of moon and imagined being born to a different family. On the walk back, I stopped in front of the purple house and followed the stepping stones to the backyard.

I had a feeling she would be there, and she was, crouched by the chain-link fence, facing the purple trampoline. "Nainai," I called out, even though I knew she could not hear me. I wanted to jump with her. Though I would forget in a few days, though my resistance to her would rise again, I felt her loneliness and it scared me.

She stepped forward and then she was running, so fast that she looked like a young girl, no longer saggy and round in the middle. She was a straight line—something I could understand, something I could relate to. I closed my eyes, afraid she would trip. When I opened them again she was high in the air, her dress flying up. I knew there might come a time in my life when I would want to sleep next to her again, return to her after the uncertain, shapeless part of my life was over, when no one would mistake me for a child except for her. Her children and children's children were children forever—that was how she planned to become God and drag us into her eternity.

I was about to run to her, to reveal myself, when I realized she wasn't awake.

"Mother," she said, as she jumped on the trampoline. "Mother, I didn't want to leave you, but I had to go with Father into the mountains. Mother, you told me to take care of my brother and I let him fight and he lost his legs. Mother, I let you down. Mother, you said you wanted to die in my arms and instead I watched our house burn with you inside as I fled to the mountains. I told Father I wanted to get off the horse and die with you and he gripped me to his chest and would not let me get down. Mother,

I would have died with you, but you told me to go. I should not have gone."

I took a step toward her. Her eyes were open but they did not see me. In the dark, I thought I would always remember this night and be profoundly altered by having seen her this way. But it was like one of those dreams where you think to yourself while the dream is happening that you must remember the dream when you wake—that if you remember this dream, it will unlock secrets to your life that will otherwise be permanently closed—but when you wake up, the only thing you can remember is telling yourself to remember it. And after trying to conjure up details and images and coming up blank, you think, *Oh well, it was probably stupid anyway*, and you go on with your life, and you learn nothing, and you don't change at all.

Lauren Alwan

An Amount of Discretion

H ER HUSBAND'S INSTRUCTIONS WERE CLEAR. Within a year of his death, the sum of his collected work—the notebooks, drawings, prints, and paintings—would go to the institute where he'd taught painting for nearly five decades. As Jonathan's executor, Seline was entrusted with the task, charged with inventorying the studio and dispatching the gift to the provost (the same provost who at the wake informed her, Scotch on his breath, that there would indeed be a posthumous retrospective with color catalog and scholarly overview). Knowing his art would have a home at the institute was Jonathan's comfort in those final months. It meant the collection would not be divided and sold off, but remain intact, stewarded by an institution that knew and understood his work. Once the immediate legal and personal matters were settled, Seline's work commenced. But as it happened, she'd only just begun her inventory when she came across her husband's field journals.

It was summer, a glum Los Angeles June, and sitting cross-legged on the studio floor she studied the journals. There were eight in all, and some she was seeing for the first time. Most contained notes on the weather, varieties of light and shadow, observations that couldn't be made with a drawn line, even one as good as Jonathan's. But there was one notebook, bound in green, she'd never seen before, and opening it, she found it was filled with marvelous sketches—deer, quail, details of lupine and monkey flower, globed brown hills with scrub oak clustered in the gaps. Her first thought was to make the green journal a gift to Finn. But then she couldn't bear to break up the lot, and soon resolved that her stepson should have all eight. He was Jonathan's only child and he'd spent countless weekends hiking the foothills with his father. While mindful of Jonathan's instructions, Seline believed her executorship gave her the latitude, and the notion quickly became an imperative, not just for Finn, but for her, too. In those first months without Jonathan, Seline had wanted to reach out, but felt she had nothing to offer, and her wish to do so didn't seem like enough.

Now it was July, and Finn, a music major at San Francisco State, was about to start his final year. She planned to ship the notebooks by FedEx, but on the morning she sat down to write the e-mail found a message from him. He was coming to Los Angeles, he wrote, for his mother's birthday, and asked if he could stop in on the way. Reading that, her eyes lifted from the screen. Finn was twenty-two, and she'd been his stepmother for nearly sixteen years, but she'd always relied on Jonathan for their connection. Might she yet have some closer bond with her late husband's son? She replied to Finn saying yes, of course, to come, and mentioned she had something for him. Something she thought he might like.

Maybe she should have stated her intention up front—she'd never been one for surprises herself—but her reasons for the gift struck her as too personal for e-mail. Better, she decided, to simply present the books in person. That way, she could explain herself, assure Finn that the gift conformed with his father's wishes, and see firsthand his response. That point in particular was important, since the gesture expressed what she could not—her regret at the distance she'd put between them when Finn was young. There had been so many chances for them to be close.

She'd never had much of a maternal temperament, yet on those weekend visitations and the annual two weeks each summer, she'd found surprising pleasure in the Lego building and story reading and the cooking of macaroni and cheese. Finn had been an even-tempered, pleasant child, with an independent nature that made her task easy. Still, it was always a relief when the visits were done, and, released from having to care for a child not her own, she could return to her life with Jonathan and her work in the studio. On Sunday afternoons when they dropped Finn back at his mother's, Seline would watch from the car as Jonathan walked him to the door and never once felt the pang her unmarried friends did, of being deprived of the bliss of babies and children. Instead, how unencumbered she felt! How free to return to her own needs and wishes.

Her change of feeling had not come all at once. Not in those final, difficult days when she'd called Finn to his father's side, or at the memorial, when he'd spoken about their hikes in the hills, how Jonathan taught him the names of the grasses and varieties of oak. It happened gradually. A few e-mails, an occasional phone call to discuss the gift of cash or transferring ownership of his father's Volvo. With each exchange, Seline felt more at ease, as though a knot were loosening inside her, one she hadn't known was there. In one call, Finn confessed he'd always thought she and Jonathan were cool parents, an admission that prompted in her a strange mix of guilt and pleasure. She told him how much she'd enjoyed their summers together, which was true. She simply left out the part about her relief.

In another call, Finn mentioned a girlfriend, Anna. He'd known her since his freshman year, he said, but the friendship had turned romantic that spring, not long after Jonathan died, and they'd been living together since June, in a flat on Octavia Street. Anna had a child, he added, a four-year-old named Chloe, and she was living with them, too. There was no mention of the child's father, and Seline did not ask, but the responsibility struck her as too great, the relationship moving too fast. On both points, there was little she could say. She'd met his father at thirty-two, a student in his graduate seminar, and soon after, they'd begun living together in her rented warehouse space. What right did she, Seline, have to express concern? And when, a few days after his first e-mail about the trip, she learned Finn's visit would include Anna and Chloe, she was crestfallen. It meant the afternoon would be one of polite exchanges and small talk. It meant the gesture intended for Finn alone would be shared with strangers.

The night before his visit, she worked late in the studio. The fall term would begin in three weeks, and for Seline would bring a full schedule at the institute. Normally, summer was reserved for her own work, but the recent weeks had been spent cataloging Jonathan's work, leaving only the nights to complete a series promised to her dealer, and she was already behind schedule. That left only the morning hours to prepare for Finn's visit.

She'd offered to make lunch, and by ten o'clock the capon was roasted, only in need of warming before the meal. In the dining room, she set down a favorite blue madras cloth, pottery carried back from a trip to Portugal, heavy goblets bought secondhand in North Hollywood.

There was a round of bread, olives from the Syrian grocer, and from the Italian bakery, a sacripantina. The dessert was Jonathan's favorite, layers of cake and voluminous cream. "A cake my wife could never bake," he liked to say.

In the living room, sunlight burned through the sliding glass doors in a blinding sheet. Seline stepped forward to close the drapes, heavy linen lined with cotton duck. The southern exposure was intense, typical of Los Angeles, a high desert sun that parched the wood paneling and bleached the furniture and throw pillows. Jonathan would pull the drapes each day at this time to prevent damage to his books and paintings. Today, she decided, the drapes would remain open. She wanted the sweep of space and light, a mood that was uncluttered and airy.

In the bedroom, she pulled a dress from the closet, a garnet column that grazed her ankles.

The color was striking, but the simplicity called for embellishment. She twisted her unwashed hair into a tortoiseshell clip, found a lipstick, and ran it across her mouth, a deep color that gleamed on her lips. What kind of woman wore lipstick at home, she thought, capping the lid on the case. "Don't overthink it," Jonathan would say. Even with the effort, she felt unkempt.

From the bureau, she took what she called the Damascus bracelet. She'd bought it at the Near East Bazaar in Glendale when she was a young art student, the bracelet a stand-in for the genuine jewelry she couldn't afford. Made of silver alloy, the piece had eight filigree strands caught in an oblong clasp. It was a hinge clasp, with a pin that threaded through two tiny barrels, and fastening it had always required Jonathan's help. She made several attempts, but the catch was impossible to work alone. Setting it aside, she took up a string of glass beads, a gift Jonathan brought home from a conference in Florence. Against the dress, the beads looked as she'd hoped, milky and lustrous.

On the bed, the notebooks waited, wrapped in archival paper and packed in an acid-free box. That morning, Finn had called from the road. They'd been passing the aqueduct south of Modesto and expected to arrive on time. Seline opened the box, examined the row of eight spines in pale gray paper. The books looked anonymous, hardly the kind of thing you pinned your hopes on.

She closed the door behind her, catching sight of her bare wrist. It was a shame, she thought as she left the bedroom. The bracelet was a trifle, cheap costume jewelry, but she would miss wearing it today. She always felt more like herself when she looked down and saw it there.

Outside, Jonathan's Volvo rounded the hill. Hearing the familiar engine, Seline stepped out in time to see the car pull forward, the blue exterior and headlights clouded like old eyes. Finn eased into the driveway with Anna in the passenger seat. Already they looked like tired parents, she thought, with empty chip bags and juice boxes on the dash. In the back, the child was asleep in the car seat, her head listed to one side.

"We were just saying if we should wake up Chloe," Finn said, coming around the car to meet her.

Anna emerged from the passenger side. She was nothing like Seline imagined. A girl born and raised in San Francisco, she'd thought, would have a certain formality and polish, but Anna was tall and ungainly, wearing a faded shift and scuffed sandals. A pair of incongruous, oversize sunglasses were pushed atop her head. Her eyes were lovely—almond shaped and green—though her close-cut dark blond hair gave her a severe, unforgiving look.

Seline extended her hand. "The drive down okay?"

"Just long."

Anna reached into the back and unbuckled the car seat. A moment later the child appeared, her hair a soft brown nest, face still bearing the gloomy look of sleep. Anna directed her toward Finn, and the child made her way obediently. Dressed in overalls cut off at the knee and faded pink tennis shoes, she clutched a plastic bag of broken graham crackers. She took no notice of Seline, but went directly to Finn and slipped her hand in his.

"Chloe, say hello to Seline." The girl refused, and Finn waggled her hand, but she said nothing.

Seline's heart went out to the child, wakened in a strange place, made to speak to a person she didn't know. "Let her be. She's still sleepy."

Anna returned with a large canvas bag, and Finn led them inside, still holding Chloe's hand. They stepped down into the carpeted living room, and Seline saw she was right to leave the drapes open. Daylight filled the room to its open-beamed ceiling, and outside, the view stretched into the haze.

"Look," Anna said, "at all this space to play."

The canvas bag was set down, and Chloe, with the bag of crackers in one hand, removed its contents with the other: an assortment of plastic fruits and vegetables, scruffy stuffed animals, and half-dressed dolls. The bag emptied, she pulled off her shoes, revealing the polish on her toes, cherry red and chipped to a series of ragged patches.

"You look good, Seline," Finn said.

"No I don't. I've been in the studio every night this week."

"I heard you're a painter, like Finn's dad," Anna said, sweeping up Chloe's shoes and setting them beneath the coffee table.

"When I'm not teaching."

Anna turned to the glass sliders. "You can see quite a ways up here."

"Yes, my husband often—"

"Don't play with that." Anna hurried across to Chloe and took an abalone shell from her hands.

"She isn't hurting anything."

"She knows better than to touch other people's things."

"Here," Finn said, crouching beside Chloe to examine her toys. "Let's see what you brought. A horse, good. The blue dog."

"Sorry—your husband?"

"Oh, I only meant—he loved the view."

"I never know where I am in LA," Anna said, turning back to the window. "Is that downtown?"

"No, it's over the grade. You can set your bearings by those mountains." Seline nodded to the east. "That's inland. The coast is opposite, over the hills."

"Things are so far apart here. I guess I'm used to the city."

Seline had been to San Francisco only once. One frigid July years ago, Jonathan met with a dealer in one of the small galleries off Union Square. After, not knowing where else to go, they'd headed toward Chinatown. On the unfamiliar street, they pressed forward along the stone facades, feeling stray and small as children, and the chill penetrated her coat as though it were made of the thinnest cotton. She'd never been more grateful to slip into the dark recesses of a bar, where her frozen hands encircled an Irish coffee. Jonathan had smiled wearily—the meeting had not gone well—and noted the end of her nose was reddened to a perfect shade of alizarin crimson.

"Can I get you anything?"

Anna dropped onto the couch. "Nothing for me just now."

"I'll take a beer if you have it," Finn said.

"I want a drink," Chloe cried.

In the kitchen, Seline pried the cap off a bottle and a waft of cool air curled out. In the back of the cupboard she found a plastic cup, filled it halfway with orange juice, and placed everything on a tray. She thought of Finn, and the knack he seemed to have with the child, despite having been an only. Seline had been an only, too, but unlike Finn, she'd been a defiant child, one who was made to stand in corners, who peered through the narrow cracks of closed doors, who lied and cheated as though it was her right. She'd never cared to please adults, let alone entertain them, and knew at a glance who had something to offer and who didn't. Perhaps Chloe saw her in the same way.

"Pacifico," Finn observed, taking the bottle. "Thanks, Seline."

He passed Chloe the juice. "What do you say?" he asked, but the child only looked blankly at Seline.

"I hear you're going to a party," Seline said, thinking that might engage her. The child smiled to herself, a secret smile that said she found the attention pleasing. "I bet you have a new dress."

"She does. From Mom," Finn said.

"Delivered personally," Anna added.

"Oh?"

"She's been up a few times. To see clients in Sunnyvale."

Seline didn't mind discussing Eva, her art consulting trips north, or the birthday party she was throwing for herself. From the start, Seline had to cultivate a good relationship with Jonathan's first wife. On weekends when Jonathan was on deadline for an exhibit, Seline was the one to drive Finn back, making the long return trip to Santa Monica.

"Annie," he said, nodding in the direction of the shelves. "Some of Dad's pictures."

"I saw. They're amazing. So realistic."

The comment was the sort that, for Seline, could be trying. An outsider's view, as though realism were nothing but a contest of appearances. Jonathan believed not in factual accuracy, but the visual experience of texture and surface, an interest not in exactitude but the way light moved through layers of underpainting and glazes. Finn had never expressed much interest in his father's work, but he knew something of its technique and demands. And like his father, Finn knew the foothills of San Fernando and Big Tujunga Canyon—the orange groves and ravines beyond the first ridge, Little Tujunga Creek running full and fast in winter—that served as the landscapes in his Northern European–inspired pictures.

It was puzzling, why Finn had chosen this young woman who appeared to know little about art and the place he'd grown up. Seline took note of the way Finn distracted the child with another toy, the way Anna seemed to rely on his patience and good nature, and saw already how involved Finn had become. Whether Anna proved temporary or not, Seline told herself the field journals would remain, something of Jonathan's that could belong to Finn, that Seline was at liberty to give. She needed only a moment with him to explain. *I found something*, she would say, *in the studio. You'll remember these.*

"It smells great in here," he said.

"That's the capon. The thyme and oregano."

At that moment, Anna and Finn looked at each other.

"Lunch," Anna said, in a way that struck Seline as odd, even evasive.

"There's no hurry," Seline put in. "We can eat anytime." Then she understood. The wrappers on the dash. It would have been early when they left San Francisco, and they couldn't have made the trip without stopping. And there the capon sat in its serving dish, the ornate rub trumpeting her effort, her anticipation.

"Sorry," Finn said. "We ate on the road. Junk, mostly."

Anna added, "But I'm sure we'll be hungry again soon."

The table was visible in the shadows of the dining alcove. The olives, drizzled with lemon, glistened in a shallow bowl. It was a trick of Jonathan's, doctoring store-bought olives to resemble ones he'd eaten in Rome. Seline had added parings of the rind, something he never bothered with, and of course there was the cake in the refrigerator, the cold preserving its impossible shape. The madras cloth hung with dread formality; the flatware was marked by scattered flashes, the goblets with shining hairlines at their rims. Sandwiches, she thought, would have been better, but nothing could be done about that. Seline had set the table. She'd prepared the meal. Whether it would be consumed or not, there it was.

At lunch, her guests poked at the food. The capon lay snipped apart and heaped on a platter, its anatomy jumbled and untidy. The bread and cheese were broken into but scarcely eaten, and the Spanish wine taken in sips, as though by invalids. The food was not sustenance, but diversion, and when it was apparent the novelty had been exhausted, Seline gathered the plates and took them to the kitchen. She couldn't bear to serve the sacripantina, fearing it would be left to melt, and in its place she brought out a plate of dried figs and walnuts, a nutcracker that was to be used in turn.

"I want to try!"

"Here," Anna said to Chloe. "I'll start one for you."

Seline passed the plate to Finn. "How's school going?"

He shrugged. "I may take a semester off. It won't be an academic hiatus. Just a hiatus hiatus." He smiled wearily. "I'll probably take more shifts at the restaurant."

The news was unsettling. "But why? There's your father's gift."

"It's not that—"

"I want to do it," Chloe cried.

"No," Anna said. She'd been passing a handful of nutmeats to Chloe when the child grabbed the nutcracker from the table. Before Anna could take it away, it slipped from Chloe's hand and crashed against a dish. A chip the size of a quarter flew from its rim.

"Chloe!" Anna cried. "I'm sorry. Your plate."

"It's nothing," Seline said. "Really, nothing to worry about." The chipped plate wasn't from the Portuguese set, and in fact, now that it had happened, she felt relief—as though the inevitable had finally occurred.

Finn plucked the chip from the cloth and grimly set it aside. "She's been sitting too long."

"Let's go play," Anna said, helping the child from the chair. They settled on the living room carpet amid the scattered toys.

He leaned back, took the nutcracker from the table, and studied it. "Sorry about your plate."

"It's nothing. It's not easy, adapting to a new place."

"Ha. For Chloe it is. She's too adaptable."

"How do you mean?"

"Everything's easy for her. Nothing fazes her." He shrugged. "Anyway, I think a little discomfort keeps you in check."

The observation was one of those odd theories Seline had herself contrived at that age—youthful philosophy that explained nothing. That was the problem with being twenty-two. You did things for reasons that were temporary, like take a semester off to wait tables. And he'd been so anxious to finish school, to begin teaching.

Like Finn, Seline herself had abandoned her studies when pursuits seemed more vital than her courses. Yet Finn's character was nothing like Seline's at that age. She'd been rebellious for the sake of it—she had taken off not just one, but two semesters, skiing and traveling—eager for the grand gesture, to show she could be unexpected and cocksure. Finn, on the other hand, had always been a thoughtful student—never one to be rushed or put off course. Even when he was young, she'd seen that quality in him. She liked to think she'd seen him as a peer might, or the colleague who glimpses promise others can't yet see.

"Where's Chloe?" he spoke to Anna, who was sitting cross-legged on the living room floor. At that moment, the child appeared from the shadows in the hall and stuck her tongue out.

"See?" Anna said, holding up the doll. "I peeled off the stickers."

The child came forward and examined the doll's arm. "She's not pretty anymore."

Seline knew well that response. Back talk. *Lip*, her parents used to call it, as in, *Don't give me any lip*. But the way that Chloe pushed away the doll suggested a heartlessness that was both unnerving and electric. This child was her own person, Seline knew, and unafraid.

"Hang on, Seline," Finn said, and stood to speak to Anna. "Maybe you should take her outside."

"Come on," Anna said, standing as well. "Birds like nuts. You can give the birds some nuts."

Chloe bounced on her toes. "You don't feed them, I'm feeding them!" And as she continued jumping, Anna led her outside, onto the deck. Finn followed them as far as the slider and closed the door behind them.

Only then did it occur to Seline that Chloe had appeared from the shadows outside Seline's bedroom door. Where had she been? Fearing the notebooks had been tampered with, Seline crossed the living room. Looking into the bedroom, she saw the box on the bed just as she'd left it, apparently undisturbed. She was still at the open door when Finn came to where she stood on the landing.

"Seline, while Chloe's outside, there's something I need to tell you." She couldn't bear it if he asked for money. Please, she thought, don't ask.

But then, the expression on his face was altogether different, astonishing in its openness—as though he were about to confess some long-held secret. "Anna's pregnant," he said. His voice was light and clear, animated. "We just found out. I could have told you over the phone, but I wanted you to meet Anna. And Chloe."

Seline's hand was still on the doorknob. She'd been about to show Finn the notebooks, but now felt frozen. He meant the news to be good, she knew, but she kept thinking of the irreversibility, the obligation it would mean, taking responsibility for Anna and her child. The wine thrummed at her temples. "It's unexpected news."

"Yeah," he laughed. "But it's okay. We're glad."

Seline's mind was blank, and she grasped at what to say next. "Your mother must be thrilled."

"She's getting used to the idea."

"It won't take long." All of a sudden, Finn's future played out clearly in her mind. "Soon she'll be flying up all the time. Or asking you to move down."

"I doubt that. Anyway, we need to be in San Francisco. Her parents are there." He glanced back to the sliders, where through the glass doors Anna could be seen leaning on the rail. Nearby,

Chloe was saying good-bye to eucalyptus leaves as she dropped them through the redwood slats.

In the silence it came to Seline, a clearer sense of what this all meant. "Your father would be so pleased."

"Yeah," he said. "Dad told me to have kids young. Not to put it off like he did."

"I don't follow."

"You remember. He'd say that being an older parent sucked. Not those exact words, but something like that."

She'd never heard Jonathan say that. True, he was fifty-six when Finn was born, but Jonathan had always been a person of focus and energy, who loathed sleep and vacations, the kind of person who did the things he wanted, regardless of where or when.

"He was so hardworking." Even as she said this, the words seemed beside the point, yet there was a connection, a vital one, between her husband's work and the son he bore in middle age. "He never stopped his hiking, until nearly the end, and even then he had his notebooks with him, always making entries." Finally, she'd somehow broached the subject.

"I meant to ask . . ." Finn's tone changed in color, more somber, less assured. "Do you still have the foxtail painting?"

The question caught her by surprise, hearing the name they'd used when Finn was small.

The title was in fact *Hare with Green Glass*, painted the summer Finn was nine. Jonathan had exhibited the picture frequently since, and it was one he always intended to keep. A model of his late style, a still life set on a rough-hewn table, the picture featured a cluster of wild barley, a glass globe, and the carcass of a rabbit. Foxtails were what they called the awns on the barley tips, bristles that turned barbed and sticky in the dry months of summer and fall.

"Yes, of course. It's here." The painting had hung in the dining room until this summer, when Seline moved it to her studio.

She spent most of her time there now and liked looking up from her work and seeing it on the wall.

"I remember those stickers got caught in my socks."

Seline remembered that, too. Though she hadn't explained it to Finn, *Hare with Green Glass* wasn't going to the institute, not yet. Jonathan had wanted Seline to have the picture. It was one of his most personal, and meant more than any of those that posed technical challenges of subject or color or composition. Simpler in design yet more intimate, with objects that referenced their life in this place: The pale grass that covered the hillsides of the northern San Fernando Valley, the glass globe they'd bought one night they spent drinking bad margaritas on Olvera Street. The weathered table Seline moved with her through the places she'd lived before Jonathan, despite its loose joinery and splintered surface. Finn knew those things, the pieces of family lore. But he didn't know she was keeping the painting. When they'd discussed Jonathan's gift to the institute, she'd left out that part.

Finn glanced at his phone. "We've got a little time. Do you think I could see it?"

Originally, Seline's studio was a walk-out basement overlooking level ground that quickly descended to a slope of oleander and pampas grass. The space had been dank and unfinished, but Seline painted the exposed framing and concrete floor white, covered the two small windows in Tyvek to soften the south-facing glare, and installed lighting of a wattage and temperature identical to that of the gallery that annually showed her work.

She stepped inside first and switched on the lights. Traces of turpentine and stand oil hung in the air. The large table was covered with sketches and notes; an old clay pitcher held her bristle brushes. Three glass palettes lay where she'd left them last night, gleaming with dark orbs of pigment: burnt umber, lampblack, alizarin crimson. When Seline was still Jonathan's

student, he'd showed her his method for organizing a work surface, how to arrange the tubes of paint in rows of warm and cool
colors, to use sable brushes only in a work's final stages, and how
to wash them properly, with soap in her cupped hand.

The child ran in from outside and went straight to the table,
to one of the glass palettes. "No," Anna said, following her.
"That's not for you." Calmly, for Seline knew the lay of her
worktable, the location of each stray cap and lid, she closed the
tubes and jars. With large sheets of newsprint, she covered the
palettes of still-wet paint.

Standing beside the drafting stool, Chloe asked to be lifted
up. Seline obliged, surprised by the child's weightlessness and
the bony column of her ribs. Chloe settled on the seat and Seline
saw her up close for the first time. She took in the child's sleek
complexion, the color of tea with milk, and the pale floss at her
hairline. Her coloring is so like Finn's, she thought. They must
often be mistaken for father and daughter. Just then, Chloe
reached forward to Seline's necklace. She examined the glass
beads, fingering one, then another. As she did, Seline took in the
miracle of her hands, perfectly formed miniatures; her extrava-
gant eyelashes; and the flecks of blue in her hazel eyes.

"Pretty," Chloe said.

From a drawer, Seline took another sheet of newsprint and a
red lithography pencil. With a fingernail, she pried away a sec-
tion of the cedar wrapping, and a ringlet unwound to reveal the
nub of red crayon inside. "I want to paint," Chloe said.

"I know," Seline said. "Here." She held out the pencil.
Entranced, the child took it and began to draw.

Last night, Seline had preemptively turned her pictures to
the wall, leaning canvases against tables, chairs, and along base-
boards. Only the pigment-stained back of the linen was visible.
There were two dozen pictures in all, each the size of a picture
book. It was new work, solemn and enigmatic, and none of it
was ready to be seen. Each painting depicted a tiny figure ren-

dered with heavy impasto strokes. She herself didn't know what to make of them, but had kept on, sometimes adding the suggestion of a door or window—not quite an interior, but an askew portal by which the figure might enter, or exit, to some equally ambiguous place. The only picture on display was Jonathan's, hanging on the wall above her desk surrounded by postcards, photos, and memos pushpinned to the wall.

"This is the one," Finn told Anna. "I pictured it bigger, somehow."

"A collector in New York wanted it," Seline added, coming to stand beside them. "But Jonathan felt he should keep it."

Anna moved closer. "Look at that rabbit fur." To render the hare's coat, Jonathan treated the pale underfleece with dry brushwork, and for the outer bristle coat, set down hundreds of strokes with a one-hair brush.

"He got those foxtails right," Anna said. "They grow on Diamond Street. In summer, they'd get stuck in the cats' eyes and have to be pulled out with tweezers."

Finn turned to Seline. "Is this going to the institute?"

"Of course. With the others." The picture would be going there, eventually. But standing with Finn before his father's painting, it occurred to her that the notebooks would seem small by comparison. In Finn's eyes, she might have used her executor's power to see that Finn got something more significant—this painting, for example—but she hadn't.

"If it were me," Anna said, "I'd keep it. I love the fur on that rabbit."

Finn studied the picture and Seline watched him, aware now that the picture must have been on his mind. He stepped close to the surface. There was so much tactile in it: the animal's fur, the twiggy quality of the grass, the grain of the table, all of which stood in contrast to the smooth expanse of sky. Did Finn notice, she wondered, the redwood in the distance? The tree was invented. No redwoods grew on these hillsides, and the detail was one Seline loved, a glimpse into Jonathan's mind. The hills and the foxtails, the sky and the landscape. The picture spoke not just to her own life, but to a part of Finn's, too.

Finn turned and spoke to Anna, but Seline did not catch the words, so caught up was she in her own stream of thought. What, she wondered, would happen if she told Finn the painting could be his? Couldn't he as easily be its provisional guardian? Might Finn see her differently then? She could speak to the attorney, find out if such a thing could be arranged, and under what terms.

"Actually," Finn was telling Anna, "it's a desert cottontail."

Seline, still caught in her thoughts, said, "I don't recall."

"That's what it is. Dad was curious, so when we got back, he looked it up."

"Got back?" Anna said.

"We found it on the old road. In Traeger's grove."

Jonathan had known Kit Traeger nearly all his life, and in those final weeks, he'd telephoned the man to ask if, when the time came, his ashes could be scattered at the grove's property line. At the time, Traeger agreed, but days before it was to take place, Traeger called Seline to say he'd changed his mind. He'd thought it over, he said, and in the end, he had acreage and crops to consider.

"Dad said the hare was hit by a car," Finn was saying. "Thrown back into the mud. He didn't want to paint the fur like that. He wanted it to look like a Dürer. So when we got home, he washed it under the hose."

"What's a Dürer?" Anna said.

No one answered. The room was silent except for Chloe's humming. A sensation came alive in Seline's chest, somewhere beneath the glass beads. It was the feeling of Jonathan's physical presence, engaged in an act that, until this moment, was unknown to her. She saw him vividly, not in memory, but anew. His large hands pushing the carcass into the sack, his determined footfalls on the trail. She could see him in the driveway, turning the nozzle on the hose, the streams of water mixed with Traeger's precious soil running in inky lines to the gutter. The streams snaked past his shoes, which, like Finn's, would have been covered in pale barbs.

From the drawing table, the sound of paper rustling. Only Seline seemed to hear it; Finn was pointing out some aspect of the cottontail to Anna. Seline turned and saw Chloe kneeling precariously on the stool, reaching across the table as the red pencil rolled away. Seline took a step forward, but it was too late. Chloe's arm knocked against the pitcher of brushes. It crashed to the floor, but not before colliding with a trio of Seline's paintings propped on a low bench.

In an instant Seline was at her side. She grasped the child's arm, still outstretched, and held it firm. Startled, Chloe looked up. She fixed a fearless gaze on Seline, her eyes wide and lips glossed with spittle. They were so near, Seline could feel the girl's warm breath, see the sticky remnants of orange juice on her chin. The paintings lay facedown on the concrete floor, but Seline couldn't bear to look at them, couldn't feel anything but her own heart racing.

"You don't reach," she said. The child tugged and tried to pull away, but Seline tightened her grip and held her. "Things break if you're not careful."

Anna slid past and swooped Chloe into her arms. The child pressed her face to her mother's neck and broke into sobs.

"It's not the place for a child," Anna said, gently raising Chloe's arm to inspect it. For injury from the pitcher, Seline told herself, certain she had done no harm.

"It's okay, it's okay," Finn said, though the look in his eyes was hard, protective.

Another of Seline's paintings had fallen faceup, and its surface was littered with clay fragments. As the child sobbed, Finn picked off the shards one at a time. Seline ignored the scars left on the tacky paint. She could see Finn was upset with her. "There doesn't look to be any harm done," she said.

Anna shot a look at Finn.

"Take her outside," he said, and Anna stepped out, Chloe's legs wrapped around her waist. In the high glare of the afternoon, they dropped into silhouette, a single, indeterminate shape.

Seline gathered the brushes from the floor, her grip tight to keep her fingers from trembling. The damage to her paintings was minor and could be repaired, but Jonathan's picture had nearly been lost. And the field journals lost, too: the trove of notes and images given away in a lapse of judgment. She knew better now. She knew sentiment could not influence her. She would follow Jonathan's wishes and keep the collection together. There was no room for discretion, not even hers.

Upstairs, Anna gathered Chloe's toys and blanket and the bag of graham crackers and placed everything in the tote bag. "Let's go to the potty," she said, and led the child to the half bath off the living room. In the kitchen, Seline made coffee while Finn watched, leaning against the counter. She opened the bag of grounds and considered the sacripantina, but she couldn't imagine presenting that airy lightness, as though nothing were amiss.

A prickling danced along the back of her neck. It was the residue of losing her temper. Her temper: a part of her long hidden and suddenly exposed, as though under a rock that the child had unwittingly kicked away. Still, she aimed to appear at ease.

"You'll be going against traffic. The 405 should be fine."

He looked sidelong at the coffeepot. "I hate the freeways in LA."

The words stung, as though she was the place, and the hated roads a part of her. "How's the traffic in San Francisco?"

"Not like here."

She checked the coffeemaker, which was brewing at a pathetic rate, and took three mugs from the cupboard. "Your father never mentioned you were with him when he found the hare." She reached into the refrigerator for the half-and-half. That sounded disapproving. "I only meant, I'm glad to know you were there."

Just then Anna came from the bathroom and stood beside Finn. Leaning against the counter they were nearly the same height and made a striking pair. The baby would no doubt be good-looking.

"Chloe's going on her own," she said, and Finn nodded.

Anna turned to Seline. "How are your paintings?"

"They'll be fine. Wet paint is forgiving. The child—"

"Chloe."

"Yes, Chloe. She'll be in school this fall?"

"Pre-K."

"She's bright. She should do well." Finally, the coffee was finished, and Seline poured three cups.

"She's *very* bright," Anna said. "She understands more than most kids her age."

"That must be a challenge."

"In fact," Anna said, reaching for a cup, "she's just asked me why you don't like her, and I couldn't think what to say, so I told her I didn't know."

"She misunderstood."

"I don't think so."

"I'm sorry if she didn't like being interrupted. It had to be done."

"Not that way, it didn't."

Seline glanced at the bathroom door. From inside, there was the faint sound of singing. "Children have to have rules," she said.

"It's just . . ." Finn struggled. "Anna and I don't think it works, being harsh."

"We think adults should follow rules, too."

"I don't disagree."

There was a pause. Chloe's singing grew quiet, then suddenly rose again. "Finn," Anna pleaded.

"Don't, Annie."

"It's just, you've got rights, too." She turned to Seline. "Fine then, I'll say it. It's wrong that Finn's father didn't leave him any of his paintings. Why give them all to strangers and not his own son?"

As she spoke, Anna's features took on a taut quality, one that, Seline now understood, had been there all along, from those first moments she emerged from the car, and in the living room, and over lunch. Perhaps, Seline thought, these were the words Anna had meant to say since the first moment of her arrival.

"The situation, it's complicated." Seline felt compelled to say more, but there was no explaining the situation to someone like Anna, a person who knew nothing about the obligations and duties an artist had to his work.

"He should have thought about his son. But all he thought about was himself, his own reputation. That was obviously more important."

"Annie, that's enough."

Seline turned to Finn. "These decisions were not mine to make."

"I know that. I—"

The bathroom door opened and Chloe jumped into the living room. She was shouting a song, a made-up one without rhyme or rhythm. She swayed with her head thrown back, singing to the beams. The song overtook the room, and Seline watched with a curious detachment. As Chloe saw it, the empty space was hers alone. Like Seline at that age, she saw a world that belonged only to her, one in which adults were necessary inconveniences, obstacles who stood in the way of true desire.

.   .   .

To ensure nothing was left behind, they searched the rooms a final time. Seline checked the washroom. When she opened the door, she found the soap dispenser overturned and its contents smeared along the basin. The mess had been hastily wiped away, but traces were still visible. She righted the soap dispenser, nearly empty now when she had filled it only that morning. Nearby, the wastebasket was overspilling with clumps of wadded tissue. There would be time after they were gone to empty the wastebasket, to refill the dispenser again, but for now, she closed the door behind her. She was about to return to the kitchen when she saw the door to her bedroom was open.

She stepped to the box, still waiting on the bed. Checking it now, she found each book in place and the seals on the wrapping unbroken. She replaced the lid carefully, and after opening the closet doors set the box on the upper shelf, pushing it deep into the shadows. Soon she'd return the notebooks to Jonathan's studio, where they'd be cataloged along with the rest of his work.

She was about to go when she saw a string of amber beads on the carpet. So the child had been here, though not for reasons she'd expected. After collecting the beads, Seline caught sight of herself in the mirror. Too thin now, with ample room in the dress that was once snug, gray showing in her dark hair. More unsettling though was the haunted look in her eyes, as though living alone was too difficult. Being alone was bearable now only when she was at work, when the earbuds were in and she silently laid down paint, keeping vigilant for something wild and abrupt in the only form that still mattered.

On the bureau top, the tube of lipstick was open, its cap removed and tossed aside. The top drawer was ajar, and its contents had clearly been rummaged through. Quickly, she replaced the cap and shut the drawer, as if that would erase what had happened. Then it came to her. The Damascus bracelet was gone. She reopened the drawer, didn't see it, then went through the others. She checked beneath the bureau, then the bed. With its ornate clasp and glittering tracery, it was the kind of fancy object a child would covet. And the overalls, with all those small pockets. How easily it might slip into any of them.

"Chloe, sit still." Seline heard Anna's voice in the next room. "I can't tie your shoes."

It wasn't so outrageous an act. As Seline well knew, children took things. She could ask for it back, but thinking of Anna's words, how could she, Seline, ask for anything? If one day she traveled north to see the baby, Jonathan's grandchild, she might inquire in an offhand way if anything was found, but even that seemed impossible now. Seline stepped from the bedroom and closed the door.

"Nothing here," she said.

She saw them off, standing in the driveway until the Volvo's brake lights disappeared.

After, she went inside and pushed the door closed. Her face felt like a board. She thought of Finn in the moments before he left, leaning over the car seat, ensuring the child was safely buckled in. By spring he would be father to two, swallowed up by a job, by San Francisco, and by Anna's people, who would take him in as their own.

She stepped down into the living room. All was in order except for a stray throw pillow on the floor. Later, she would clear away the remaining dishes, gather the tablecloth, and throw it by the back door where that night it would go into the washing machine. Once the house was in order, she'd go to the studio and put that in order, too. She would examine her pictures and see what, if any, repairs were necessary. She'd straighten the worktable, return her tools and tubes of paint to their customary places, and all would be as it was before the visit. She'd return to her cataloging, to the work of going through each of Jonathan's drawings, listing them for the provost to approve. She had an obligation to fill on Jonathan's behalf, and the balance of a year in which to fill it.

In a single movement, she pulled the drapes closed. Too late for the sun, not that it mattered. In the darkness, she took the string of beads from her neck and let them pool in her hand. She thought of the Damascus bracelet, the way it felt on her arm, the metallic filigree moving as she moved, grazing and light, so familiar. She imagined it plucked from the bureau, held by a small hand. How irresistible it must have seemed. How unexpected. The child must have marveled at her luck, that she had found something she could pretend belonged to her.

Brad Felver

Queen Elizabeth

MANY YEARS LATER, knots of grief cinched intractably within her, Ruth still urged her memory back to their first evening together: drinks at a posh restaurant on the shores of Lake Erie, how Gus offered to pay long before the bartender even noticed them, how he spoke so earnestly of dovetail joints. He wore a flannel shirt and carpenter's jeans with fabric gone thin at the knees. He was wiry as a cornstalk and always would be. That night he spoke of how he wanted to make desks. "Desks!" he said, smiling as if he knew how absurd it sounded. For now he had his union card and worked what jobs came his way.

Ruth was working on her Ph.D. in applied mathematics at Case Western, studying stochastics. She spoke at length about her research, which involved probability theory, random variables, and chaotic systems. Gus listened with genuine interest, and when she finally paused to say, "Does that make sense?" he admitted that he wasn't a graduate student, wasn't a student at all, had in fact never been to a college campus. "I doubt I can even spell stochastic," he said, "but I love listening to you talk about it." The only fancy bit of math he knew was about Euclidean planes requiring three points, and this only because he felt strongly that all desks—all tables of any kind—should have only three legs. Two legs could not balance a load, but four created wobbles. Three created a perfect Euclidean plane.

His knowledge seemed so practical compared to her own— how to fix squeaky floorboards, what made a diesel engine different, why oak leaves fell later in the season than maple leaves. She had never met anyone like him at Case or back home in Boston. He was wholly without pretension, frequently offered remarkable compliments but quickly grew embarrassed when similar compliments were returned. Even that name of his, Gus, seemed clipped short, as if his mother and father considered extra syllables an extravagance.

When the bartender did finally bring the check, Gus reached for his wallet and realized he didn't have nearly enough money. Who had ever heard of $6 bottles of beer? Cold shame spread over him, and he knew immediately that such a gaffe would quash the small, snug world they had built during their evening together. But Ruth thought little of it, pulling out a wad of cash while Gus went quiet like a penitent little Catholic boy, which of course he was. What Ruth never told him—never told anyone—was that it was his mortification over such a small trifle, so utterly sincere, that made her love him immediately.

He visited her family before she visited his. Theirs was a three-and-a-half-story house of deep maroon brick and cream trim in Beacon Hill and boasted a view of Boston Common. The sidewalks were of cockeyed brick, framed by cobblestones, and the shrubs were manicured into perfect moons.

They sat on a back veranda and ate eggs Florentine. Gus never did see the kitchen or who had prepared the meal. Her father flinched when they shook hands—just a small twitch, barely perceptible—and only later did Gus realize this was because he was a vascular surgeon of some note, ever afraid of rough calluses and strong grips. Her mother had tight gray hair and picked at her food with a single tine of her fork. Gus felt her eyes that morning as he reached for what was almost certainly the improper cutlery.

After brunch, the men separated from the women in a way that felt mannered and Edwardian. Gus stood next to her father on the front stoop and drank down a glass of coconut rum. They watched dog walkers wander the Common. His eyes cruised around all the sights. He had never been so far east, had never experienced the extravagance of an old city. For a long while they didn't speak, and he felt as if he was being tested. Who could maintain the silence longer? Eventually, her father said, "Desks." He nodded ever so slightly. "Is that a growth industry?" It wasn't entirely clear what the suggestion was. Was he afraid he would have to support them himself if they got married? Embarrassed that his daughter was dating a man who owned more than one hammer? Or was this just the easy contempt that New Englanders reserve for Midwesterners?

"They didn't know what to make of you," Ruth said on the drive back to Cleveland.

"Unfortunately, I think they knew exactly what to make of me."

"Well," she said, "that's their problem."

Ruth wanted arguments to resolve things, but Gus just needed them to end as soon as possible.

"Stop apologizing," she would say. "You're allowed to disagree."

"But I'm sorry. I hate this."

"If you want to sit in a booth instead of a table, you have to say so."

"I don't have an opinion. You choose."

"You need to have more opinions."

"About tables and booths?"

So Ruth would always win the fights, which was somehow worse than losing them. He made her feel spoiled, not by anything he did or said, but because she was and he wasn't. She had never realized it before then. It made her feel cold, like a bully.

Gus's father lived at the end of a long lane in Medina County. Charming Ohio farm country. Ruth searched the cabinets until she found the hand mixer and started making her special pepper-biscuit recipe. She chided his father for eating with a napkin tucked into his shirt but in a way that felt playful, like some ancestral joke that ranged back over the decades.

His mother had been dead long enough that they didn't think to explain what had happened. It was clear enough that they both liked having a woman in the house again.

"A doctorate," his father said, shaking his head. "Must be a lot of work."

"I guess I've always known I would have to do it," Ruth said. She then drank off the last bit of her coffee and stared out the window at the flat green fields.

Later, while Gus hand-washed the dishes, Ruth sat at the table with his father. "That sounds like some house you have there in Boston," he said. They hadn't been speaking of home or her family. It was obvious how close Gus was to his father.

"It's so lovely here," Ruth said. "The quiet, I guess I mean. And there's something about always being able to see the horizon that's comforting."

That afternoon, Gus walked her the length of the property, down long fencerows where he showed her how to scare up rabbits from their dens until she told him to stop being mean. She wanted to pet a chicken but lost her nerve at the last instant. They tried to reach around the ancient bur oak in the barnyard, the largest tree she had ever seen, but even together their arms were swallowed up by its girth. "We call her Queen Elizabeth," he said, explaining that the tree was roughly the same age as Shakespeare. She had always thought New England was old. Such grandeur, she thought, and such different grandeur than what she was accustomed to. How could something be so regal and so unassuming at the same time?

He led her through the outbuildings full of equipment. Where the wood siding met the ground it had mostly shriveled up with rot. Finally he guided her into the workshop, where she quizzed him on what each tool did, and he explained it to her, carefully and without a trace of smugness. The planer and the table saw and the jointer—they had all been his grandfather's, had been made in Germany. Nothing even approached their quality anymore. She pulled open drawers and fingered drill bits and awls and rasps. "There's a tool for everything," he told her, "and most of them are good for only one very specific thing."

"This will all be yours one day," she said, and he said, "Not soon, I hope."

In the middle of the floor sat a magnificent desk, wood still raw and unstained. Clean lines, trim like Gus himself. Not a trace of excess flourish to be seen. Solid, squared legs, tapered to a slender tip. Three legs only, always three legs, he said, again referencing the perfection of a Euclidean plane. Old-growth walnut, he went on, taking her hand and tracing it over the grain pattern, all harvested locally. He pointed out the dovetails in the lap drawer, the through-mortises on the legs. She felt she understood him better then, the artist lurking underneath those flannel shirts of his.

"It's for your father," he told her.

They had each other there on the desk. He was slow and deliberate, polite even in lovemaking, his callused hand never leaving the curve of her neck. It smelled of sawdust, and for the rest of her life, when she smelled that smell, flickers of arousal would warm her from the inside out.

. . .

A growing swell of energy between them, they each felt it, the way it lashed them together. Slowly they wormed themselves into each other's lives, not always the grandest moments—holidays or great traumas—but the smaller, daily gestures: kissing with bad breath, boiling hot dogs for dinner, changing flat tires in the brutal Cleveland winter.

They talked about how happy they were as if afraid that they must decipher it daily, how astonishing it all was, or risk its diluting right in front of them.

"I don't want to take your name," Ruth said. "I've had this name all my life and I'm used to it now."

"You don't have to."

"But what about our kids? It'll be too confusing."

"Your mother wouldn't understand," he said.

"Yes," she said. "Her." She looked out the window, squinting into the sun. "We both know I won't hyphenate."

"We could make a new name. Both of us."

"Something fun?"

"Something tough."

They each wrote down their choices. She chose *Ivers*. He chose *Bazooka*.

In the end, she took his name because they didn't want to spend the rest of their lives explaining it at dinner parties.

Ruth miscarried deep into her second trimester. A problem with the umbilical cord. For a week they stayed in their little apartment, curtains drawn, the air thick like after rain. Sometimes she wanted to be close to him, nuzzling into his chest, and other times she just needed him to not look at her. These waves came suddenly, and he learned how to recognize them. He didn't understand them, but he knew it wasn't important that he did.

"I'm okay," she insisted, "but I just can't stop picturing the cord like a noose around his little neck." For a long while she went back to the diaphragm without telling Gus. She was terrified of her own body and didn't want him to know. Sex changed from something they did together into something that was done *to* her.

They spent weekends with his father on the farm and never told her parents at all. She took the rest of the semester off, technically to finish her dissertation, though she accomplished little. They adopted a dog, which generally brought more agony than joy. When it pooped on the carpet, Gus chased it around with a drywall hammer; when it ran away he stapled signs to telephone poles. He had wanted an Irish setter, but Ruth wanted a Pomeranian. He joked with friends that they compromised by getting a Pomeranian.

A few months later they went out to dinner and drank too much wine. She laughed like a teenager and sat cross-legged in her chair. They tossed bits of uncooked macaroni into each other's glasses and then apologized to their waiter. When dessert came she got quiet again as if some shadow had descended. She stared into her glass and picked at the polish on her forefinger. "I'm so, so sorry," she said, and he knew then they would haul this on their backs for the rest of their lives.

Her father died in March, and his father died in June. They both realized then that the last traces of childhood were gone. She thought the wakes would be dramatically different, but they weren't, hushed voices and hollow platitudes for rich people and poor people alike. She wasn't terribly sad but had to pretend she was; he was devastated but had to act like he wasn't. And so for several months it seemed as if they weren't talking to each other so much as to the emissaries they sent out into the world.

One night she found him sitting on the toilet lid. The door was closed and the light was off, but she knew he was in there. "What are you doing?" she asked.

"I don't know," he said. "I guess I'm trying."

She sat on the floor in front of him. The Pomeranian stood in the doorway, guarding them, like it knew things weren't right. "He told me once that your desks were his favorite things." His father had never really said that to her, but she inferred a great deal from his long proud looks.

They writhed together there on the cold tile floor. He was manic, desperate, even a bit rough with her, which he never was before or after.

They named her Annabelle. They had never been so exhausted or so happy. Gus could scarcely bring himself to take on jobs that stole him away. Ruth officially abandoned her dissertation, all those years of work that suddenly seemed frivolous.

Gus built Annabelle a crib of cherry, with lovely tapered spindles and long finger joints. He was afraid of SIDS, it was all you ever saw on the local news, and so he often slept in the chair next to the crib. He strummed a toy ukulele for her. It wasn't long before Annabelle learned how to smile. D-minor and G were her favorite chords, and for hours he would play them, the D-minor hovering like a Frisbee in flight, just out of reach, until he would finally resolve it with the G, and little Annabelle would smile and kick.

One evening when Gus was working late, Ruth was alone with Annabelle. They hadn't eaten yet, and she was trying to apply for jobs. Their budget had become frighteningly thin. She stirred a pot on the stove and held Annabelle and scrolled through a list of academic positions, then secretarial ones. It was all too much. She wanted to scream and chuck rocks through the windows. Here she was: A mother, but was she anything else? Anything at all? Motherhood had seized her destiny while she had been too busy to notice. Fathers were somehow exempt from this fate. She hated Gus for being gone, hated herself for quitting her dissertation, hated Ohio most of all. Then Annabelle threw up on her shoulder, and before Ruth could clean it up or set her down, her daughter had started gumming up the vomit.

She told Gus about it when he got home.

"She ate her own puke?"

"Sorry. Jesus."

"What color was the puke?"

"I don't know. Purple maybe? I think we had plums earlier."

Gus held Annabelle up and looked at her. "Hi there, my little puke-eater. Next time we could cook it for you first. That seems like our job. Your mother can do wonders with garlic and a little olive oil. You could have yourself a nice puke fritter!"

He gave her a bath and read her one book after another before bed. Ruth listened from outside the bedroom door as Gus made his outlandish voices and Annabelle giggled. It often worked this way: all day she fought off a manic craving for a break, only to find that when it finally came, there was little joy in it. By the time she got back to her job applications, the toyish strums of the ukulele pulsed out from the bedroom, washing over her like a sleeping serum.

Gus would sometimes lay playful traps for her, which made her feel young and loved:

"If you had to change one thing about me, what would it be?" he asked.

"That's not fair."

"That's the point."

She thought for a moment. "I'd make you twenty pounds heavier."

"I'm serious."

"I am, too," she said. "It would make me feel thinner. I gain weight like a normal person and you just keep on looking like some teenage bronco rider."

Years later, when she emptied the trash bin in his workshop, she found dozens of empty Archway cookie packages. At first she was terribly confused—he had virtually no sweet tooth to speak of—and only after some thought did she remember.

Annabelle started preschool, and suddenly every wall in the house grew crowded with crayon artwork. Their friends became the parents of Annabelle's classmates, their free time split between swimming lessons and playgrounds and the zoo. Ruth took a position as an office manager for a pet food distributor. Gus began selling a few more desks, working late rehabbing grand staircases in Cleveland Heights and Willoughby and Hudson. They bought an old Craftsman home with pipes that knocked when they flushed toilets. They put rugs over the old oak floors and let Annabelle chase them from room to room while she screamed like a Viking. Blanket forts dominated their living room for weeks at a time. They raked leaves and jumped in the piles. They became experts about dinosaurs and then seashells and then paper airplane design.

Without noticing it, they had created an entire country with its own language and customs and mythologies and even defensive perimeters. Their own lines allowed few breaches. Their country was complete on its own. A wide world existed beyond their borders, they could still hear its bustling chaos, but they were content to ignore it, and to be ignored in kind.

. . .

The doctors found the tumor in Annabelle's brain when she was four years old. It was the size of a robin's egg, malignant, and needed to come out.

"But you can do surgery, can't you?" Ruth asked.

"We're not sure yet," the doctor said. That phrase—*We're not sure yet*—became an oft-heard refrain through months of consultations, and they learned it had a very specific meaning: *We are quite sure, and it's bad news.*

They saw specialists in a dozen cities: Pittsburgh, Orlando, Denver, Los Angeles, Toronto. Ruth was ferocious in her research, in her preparation for each appointment, bringing with her pages of questions that she asked like accusations. The numbers gave her something to focus on, though quantifying bad luck in such a way also made her want to murder the universe.

"Do you know the odds of this happening?" Ruth asked one time. "Sixty-eight million to one," she said. "Sixty-eight million."

Gus looked down at her legal pad, the scratches and strange symbols, Greek or Latin, perhaps. He sometimes forgot about her imposing mathematical pedigree, which now became a prison, intellect stunting emotion. What was the point of calculating probabilities or the effects of random elements? Gus wanted to know. They were here already. These calculations served only to make him feel like a helpless victim. What he didn't understand, of course, was that they allowed Ruth a respite, precious moments of cold, abstract thought. Through them, she could quarantine her despair so that it would not pollute everyone around her.

They drove to Boston to see a specialist her father had known at Mass General. She was from Mumbai and had a long name that Gus could not pronounce. The doctor paged through Annabelle's chart, frowning and shaking her head without speaking.

When she finally looked up, she smiled at them, but it was the kind of smile offered to a dear friend at a funeral.

"No more bad news," Ruth said.

This specialist was aiming to lead a trial of an experimental treatment that involved first inducing a coma and then utilizing a special cocktail of drugs that would, perhaps, still target the ravenous tumor.

"She's a good candidate, isn't she?" Ruth asked, not completely a question.

The doctor leaned in with a bowl of candy and told Annabelle to take as much as she could hold. Ruth realized then that this doctor had done this many times, was as expert in delivering bad news as she was in the operating room.

"I won't presume to understand what you are going through," she said. She spoke with that peculiar British-Indian accent, which, Ruth imagined, meant she had likely been educated at Cambridge or Oxford. "My father was a particle physicist and my mother died when I was a teenager. He could be a harsh man, largely devoid of human sentiment. He forbade me grieving over my mother's death because he believed there was no reason, scientifically speaking, to do so. According to the Law of Conservation of Mass, she was still with us. Mass cannot be created or destroyed, of course. In fact, he pointed out, the very atoms from my mother's body were now repurposed in our own bodies. This is true of every human who has ever lived. Every human currently alive is composed of the very atoms of every person who has ever lived. Every person! Billions of atoms from each person. Can you imagine? A billion atoms that make me a person once made Shakespeare a person, and Cleopatra and Gandhi and Einstein."

"Also Hitler and Stalin," Ruth said. "Genghis Khan, Oliver Cromwell, Caligula, Attila, Jeffrey Dahmer."

"Ruth."

The doctor ignored this and handed Annabelle another sucker.

"So, scientifically speaking," Ruth said, "we cannot be sad."

"Ruth," Gus said, more pleading than scolding.

"Well," the doctor said, but then said nothing else.

Gus insisted on making the casket himself, long hours alone in the workshop, and he was unable to see the strange selfishness of this. It was a refuge he refused to share with her. He fixated most on the casket dimensions, hardly larger than a laundry basket.

"Why are you punishing yourself like this?" Ruth asked.

"She'll be in there forever."

"Come home," she said, but he had already gone back to work.

They couldn't even hold hands at the funeral or feign unity at the wake. They each faced the same choice at this moment—anger or sadness—and each opted for anger. Perhaps this was not a conscious decision. The world had drained them of compassion until no residue remained. Anger seemed easier, cleaner, almost tangible. But in the coming years, each of them would look back at this time, searching for the precise moment they pivoted away from each other, because if they could isolate the fulcrum, the singularity, perhaps some wormhole would sprout and revive a conduit to the past.

Ruth said awful things and then felt horrible about them, but then she would say more awful things. It was an addiction she could not kick, as if discarding her grief and forcing him to bear it instead. *You can't play ukulele and fix this, you know. You always wanted a boy anyway. She'll never need one of your desks now.*

If Ruth said awful things, Gus said nothing at all. He retreated to the farm, to the workshop, where he could easily make her feel like an interloper. He spent whole days there, while Ruth sat at home, waiting for him to return to her, though he never truly did. She began to spend weekends in Boston. For months they lingered on this way, trapped in a stalemate.

Ruth appeared at the workshop one afternoon. Gus had been mindlessly sanding the tapered legs of a desk for several hours, his arm ached from it, and as he stood to look at his work, he realized he had sanded so much that the third leg was now noticeably thinner than its counterparts.

Ruth sighed. "I need a break."

"Me too," he said.

"From you. From all of this. I don't expect you to understand."

Gus dropped the sanding block, and it rattled on the concrete floor.

"Do you have to act like this?"

"How am I acting?"

"Like the spoiled little rich girl."

He'd never once spoken to her that way. Halfway through saying it he already felt horrible. He didn't love her any less now, but everything around them had changed, as if they were standing still while a storm swept through around them.

Ruth sat down on the cold concrete and suddenly looked very young and very fragile. For a moment Gus had some hope, the smallest breach. But her face was drawn, had grown tighter, menacing.

"We can use a lawyer we know," she said. "Charlie's brother, I guess. Keep it all simple."

"Simple," he said.

It was stunning how quickly their country could crumble. Civil war. A dozen years to construct but only a few months to collapse.

· · ·

Gus started moving his things out of the house the next week. At first Ruth was still there, but by the time he was nearly finished, she managed to be absent. The last hours he moved slowly, one small box at a time, adding in extra, unnecessary trips. What did he hope for? A change of heart at the last minute? A dramatic reconciliation where they fell to the wet ground and kissed?

He found a note on the kitchen counter, just a small Post-it, as if Ruth did not even care if Gus found it: *It's different for mothers.*

He stared at the note. It demanded that he develop a fresh emotional response, one that hadn't yet been charted and classified by scientists: profoundly sad and confused and resentful and sad again around the edges. Such hardness in her. Jesus, he thought, halfway wishing he were capable of such hardness also. How easily grief could mutate into something else entirely. She was right, of course: there were things that only mothers were capable of, like lifting cars off their children during tornadoes. Like this.

He left the note where it was. He needed her to wonder for the rest of her life if he even saw it. Initially, he had planned on leaving her the Pomeranian, but the note stopped him. He made room in the front seat, where it curled into a ball and fell asleep as they drove away.

Gus moved back to the farm. He leased the land: soy, wheat, corn, hay. Days he worked jobs in Cleveland—elaborate built-ins, mantels, newel posts and hickory spindles on wide staircases—and evenings he built desks, the glow of the old workshop spilling into the barnyard late into the night. He ate microwave dinners in his underwear and left the telephone off the hook. He became a ghost, the sort of man that people in a small town recognize, though no one can recall ever speaking to.

Ruth sold the house to the first offer. She couldn't be in Ohio any longer. She moved back to Boston, where her mother still lived, and soon she was attending fund-raisers and charity auctions in the ballrooms of the most elegant old hotels. She found herself surrounded by people so wealthy they had no need to locate Ohio on a map. The city offered as many distractions as she needed, faces new to her and those whom she had known many years earlier when they were thinner and more eager.

Ruth eventually settled in with a man named Harold Gutman. He had worked as an intern under her father and kept a trimmed beard, mostly gray now, and had a single bumper sticker on his BMW, which read, very simply, "DOCTOR." Ruth found this a strange and gaudy touch for a man who, otherwise, largely passed through the world undetected. When he started speaking of marriage, she would turn away and tell him that she wasn't so sure, not yet. She still had so many things to sort out, tangled linkages in her brain. It was always in the evenings when Harold Gutman would invariably make such hints, always after a few drinks. He never proposed outright, only took her temperature, which was icy for many years, though he was convinced a thaw would eventually come.

"I'm just not *sure*," Ruth would always say if he pressed her. Of course, she was perfectly sure, perfectly sure she did not want to marry Harold Gutman, did not want to marry again, ever.

It was this incessant talk of marriage that pushed her back into her dissertation. She needed something to occupy her evenings in order to avoid Harold Gutman's affections, and so she holed herself up in the wood-paneled study, finally finishing eight years after Annabelle's death. She declined to walk at the commencement ceremony because she did not want to travel back to Cleveland. Instead, she strolled the Back Bay streets alone, and when she returned to their apartment, she found on her desk a sticker of the letter "S," which Harold Gutman had left for her. Together they would be "DOCTORS" for all the world to see.

When the Pomeranian died, Gus buried it behind the barn. He stood in front of the old rotary wall phone, ready to dial Ruth and deliver the news. It was all he could think to do. Should he or not? They hadn't spoken in years. He wouldn't even know how to say hello. Old lovers were far worse than strangers. Should he use her name or not?

Hello, Ruth.

Ruth, hello, it's Gus.

Hi there, it's me.

Ruthie, dear, I'm sorry to deliver such bad news.

When he finally dialed, a man's voice answered, and he hung up immediately.

Ruth took an adjunct position at a local community college, teaching a course or two each semester. It felt like a concession, but she ended up liking her students, most of whom were bright and engaged. Some days she would stay on campus for eight or ten hours, teaching and meeting with students. She loved most how they would stomp into her office, breathless and full of absurd excuses. She would come home and tell Harold Gutman about them. "Even when they say ridiculous things, they're so enthusiastic about it," she said.

"What about children then?" Harold Gutman asked her one evening after a benefit at the Park Plaza. He'd allowed himself an extra glass of wine and was feeling warm and confident.

She squinted, though it was dark in their bedroom. "We're too old for that, Harold." She was only forty-six but felt much older.

"We could adopt."

"It's nice of you to say that, but no, we couldn't."

Harold Gutman didn't pursue it after that. No marriage, no family of their own. Instead her students would become her children, in a way that was common but not terribly healthy.

When a full-time teaching post opened up, Ruth took it. "If your father were still alive," was all her mother would say to the news, which was the harshest sort of admonishment she could muster at the thought of a community college. Harold Gutman, too, seemed perplexed. "Isn't it terribly repetitive?" he asked, and she told him that of course it was. "I don't like surprises or changes the way I used to."

At a conference in Phoenix, she slept with a young assistant professor of statistics. He was barely thirty and played video games on his cell phone. He was aggressive in bed like an upperclassman in a fraternity. In the morning, when she woke and saw him there splayed atop the covers, naked and hairy, she immediately thought of what a horrible thing she had just done to Gus. How would she admit this to him? Would he ever forgive her? It was only at breakfast, when they sat in relative silence, that she realized she meant Harold Gutman. It was Harold Gutman whom she had betrayed.

Several years later Ruth took a stroll down Newbury Street, not so much interested in buying anything as in walking the promenade the way people do after a harsh winter. She was just about to turn back for home, when she saw in the front window of a store a three-legged desk. That unmistakable aesthetic: austere, unassuming, clean.

"It's a gorgeous piece, isn't it?" the salesman said. He wore a tailored vest, no tie, buttons undone through the hollow of his chest.

"It's beautiful."

"A relatively new artist, just breaking onto the scene in the last few years. He lives in Iowa, I believe—Iowa or Ohio—and crafts everything individually, which is unheard of anymore."

"It's beautiful," she said again.

"This desk is made from bur oak and features through-mortises and a tripod—all of his desks do." He eased out the lap drawer. "The artist does all the dovetails by hand, no jig. You can see the Shaker and Pennsylvania Dutch influences, of course, but he has carved out new territory. Remarkable work, lines as distinct as I've seen since Tom Moser."

Ruth traced her fingers across the edges of the desktop. She could smell the workshop, the arousal taking shape in her. Sparks that had hidden themselves away, dormant for many years.

"We're thrilled to have some of his pieces here," the salesman said. He was young and very fashionable and seemed afraid of Ruth's silence. "Ordinarily our New York and London stores get first crack, but they've done remarkably well here. All the young students, perhaps. People want smaller, cleaner desks now. Computers are smaller than ever. No more of those shelved, multi-level monstrosities of the eighties and nineties. That's the trend, anyway." He slid the lap drawer back in. "Quite the visionary."

The pain from this encounter was real, and yet so was the excitement. Ruth was alternately sad and angry, though she couldn't deny she felt more alive than she had in many years. She became convinced Gus's aim was to torture her. He could have sold desks anywhere. Why Boston? Why so close to her parents' old brownstone? Clearly, he wanted to force a confrontation between them where he would reveal to her . . . what? His children, his beautiful new wife? How he had survived and moved on? He would not say a word, but he would parade them in front of her. That was very like him, the quietest possible revenge.

But then other days she thought that perhaps Gus simply wanted to see her and did not know how. He would kiss her on the cheek, tell her how he had missed her, how differently his life had ended up without her. And then he would look down and say: "Could we just talk about her now?" And she would cry, and he would cry, and they would talk about her all night.

She found herself distracted during her lectures, and more than once she had to excuse herself into the hallway. For months this happened at regular—and then increasing—intervals. Harold Gutman noticed the change in her, but she told him it was just the stress of teaching.

Gus had burrowed his way back into that small nook of her brain where the trauma still lingered, quiet for many years but never truly dormant. His appearance had disturbed a system at rest, jolting it back into a slow but accelerating orbit that would slowly consume her. But Ruth surrendered to this freely, as if leaning into a strong wind, considering for the first time in many years that perhaps memory can exist without despair.

Harold Gutman didn't understand why he needed a new desk. His old one worked perfectly well, and besides, he was used to it.

"This one is just better," Ruth said.

"I liked all the drawers and nooks in my old one. Where will I put everything now?"

"You'll get rid of things. That's the point."

He frowned, unconvinced. She sauntered over to the desk, leaned against its edge, and slid off her heels. She unbuttoned her blouse and leaned back, trying to appear seductive but feeling ridiculous.

"What are you doing?" Harold Gutman asked.

"I'm showing you how much better this desk is."

"But we have a bed, a big comfortable bed. And I don't think it can support us both. It seems to be missing one leg."

She bought more desks, at first just to furnish guest bedrooms, then two more for the house Harold Gutman kept on the Cape, then more that she put directly into a storage bay. Eventually, the young furniture salesman asked what she'd been hoping he'd ask. "I'd be happy to arrange an introduction," he said. "For such a generous fan of his work. He's in town occasionally."

"Oh, I don't know," Ruth said, suddenly feeling diffident as a teenager.

"I haven't met him myself, but he's supposed to be a very modest, quiet sort of man. With all his success, he supposedly still lives in an old farmhouse in the middle of Iowa."

She told him it wasn't at all necessary, there was no need to go to such trouble. She just adored his desks was all. The salesman shrugged, unconcerned. Later that night, though, she dialed the number on his business card and told him that she had changed her mind. She would like to meet the artist the next time he came to Boston.

It was a Saturday in October when she arrived at the store to see him. She told Harold Gutman she had an appointment with a student, and he nodded, suspecting a lie was hidden somewhere. He had noticed her fussing in the mirror far longer than usual. They both knew they were clinging to the threads of whatever they had, like the last day of a vacation that is spent mostly on travel.

Wet leaves painted the sidewalks on Newbury Street. When she entered the store, Gus's back was to her, but he was the same as ever. Hadn't gained a single pound, though he'd gone fully gray. He wore carpenter's jeans and a flannel shirt. As she drew nearer she realized that the pants weren't just of a style; they were the exact pair he often wore years earlier. She recognized a stain above the left pocket.

How long had it been? She'd become horrible with dates. Twenty years? That sounded about right.

"Jesus," he said when he turned around. It took him several moments before he could compose himself. Ruth felt absurd. She had hoped that he knew, that he had actively targeted Boston, but Gus seemed truly shocked.

They strolled down Newbury Street. Gus clasped his hands behind his back and took long, loping strides. He glanced over at her and smiled that calm smile she remembered. Strangers often took this for arrogance, but she knew it was just his quiet nature. *Silence is something that should be protected*, his father used to say.

"How's the farm?" she asked.

"The same." He stopped walking and looked up at the roofs of the buildings, tarnished copper and clay tile. He frowned. "That's not true. I don't know why I just said that. Queen Elizabeth died," he said. "Came down in a bad storm a few years ago."

"No!" she said.

He nodded. "More than a few years ago now, I guess. I built a kiln next to the barn and cured all the lumber I could, some thousands of board feet."

"And the desks?"

He nodded. "Bur oak is just about all I've worked with ever since."

"I could tell you still use the handsaw for the dovetails. You always did hate those jigs."

"You do something one certain way for long enough and you become incapable of doing it any other way." It was just like him to say something like that. But it made her feel more like a client than the mother of his dead daughter.

He stepped off the curb to allow a mother with a stroller to pass. Ruth watched the woman and child move away from them, then disappear around the corner.

"I suppose Queen Elizabeth is still in our bodies, isn't she? Or her atoms anyway."

Gus looked at her quizzically for a moment, and then he remembered. He nodded but said nothing.

They walked on in silence for several minutes, and then Ruth said, "I hated that doctor. But her story stuck with me. I guess that's obvious, isn't it? When I went back to my research after all those years, I tried to calculate it. How many atoms from the dead might migrate to the living. It became this strange obsession, not at all related to my dissertation. It took a long time, but I eventually worked out a reasonable prediction and asked a scientist on campus about it, and he pointed out that my math was generally good, but I'd overlooked one basic error of physics."

"That it takes far too long," Gus said. "Centuries for them to dissipate."

"You, too?" Ruth asked, and Gus touched her arm, telling her yes. She froze, his hand warm on her skin, afraid that the smallest movement might dislodge them.

After a few moments, they noticed they were blocking the sidewalk and had to move on. "So, Queen Elizabeth isn't actually in us," Ruth said, and paused. "Never will be."

"No," Gus said, "but she'll end up in someone eventually."

They started walking again. He dug his hands into his pockets and gazed around. She felt a sadness in him that had never been there. A hollow look in his eyes. Whether it was all the talk of death or long-term loneliness or just the general cruelties of life, she couldn't know. The truth was they had been apart far longer than they'd been together. Could she even claim to know him anymore?

They ended up at an outdoor café, drinking tea. Ruth warmed her hands on her mug and sipped slowly. Gus noticed that the table wobbled on the uneven bricks, and so he shimmed one leg with a folded napkin. They both felt uneasy, wishing they'd gone to a bar instead, where it becomes easier for old lovers to ignore how well they know each other's bodies.

"I can't believe no one else snatched you up," she said.

"Well," he said, "I doubt I made it very easy." His eyes were trained to all the commotion on the street. "When Queen Elizabeth died, it was strange at first not having a tree there, like a pulled tooth when all you can do is trace the gap with your tongue." He set his tea down. "Then I found myself sweating all the time. It took me over a year to realize that the house itself retained that much more heat with the tree gone. No more shade." He paused and for a moment seemed ready to weep, but then he coughed and looked away.

"I know what you mean," Ruth said. "It felt so strange when I moved back to Boston, like I didn't actually grow up here." She didn't tell him how for years she would think about him in the middle of the day, how some silly little thing would happen and she would make a mental note to tell him when she got home, only to remember hours later that she couldn't.

They went back to their tea, their own thoughts. It hurt Ruth to see the many ways Gus was still the same man, how her absence had not changed that, but it also hurt to see the many ways he was now different, to know that she'd had no hand in shaping his new quirks. He still palmed his mug rather than using the handle, but he took smaller sips now, probably because he moved slower. He was older, but he was also successful, could accomplish fewer things each day. He probably appreciated success in ways that she never would.

"It's strange seeing me, isn't it?" she asked. "I can tell it's strange for you."

He squinted at her for a long time, and she began to worry that he would never respond. She was thinking of that terrible note she had left him, though she wasn't certain if he'd even seen it. Finally, he said, "Not strange, no." But then he stopped talking and grimaced. "It's like having phantom limb syndrome. I feel you over there, and I know you belong over here, but you're there and I'm here and there's no changing that."

A warmth crept into her limbs, like muscles being stretched. She had forgotten how his words could puncture straight through to her core. All these years separated hadn't changed him in the important ways. She cried then. It was a dirty, messy sort of cry, not at all dignified. All the grief of her life seemed to surface: a loveless mother and father, an unfulfilling career, dead children, dead relationships. She couldn't look at Gus. He didn't reach for her or offer a tissue, just let her have it out as privately as possible.

"I just worked," he said, hoping to give her more time to recover herself. "Eventually, I could go five minutes without thinking about her, and that was a revelation. I learned how to function without pressuring myself to find joy in anything. But five minutes is as long as I ever got. Never more than that, not even now."

She already knew that Gus was the only one she could ever talk to about Annabelle, but she realized then it wasn't that simple. It was all they would ever be capable of talking about. But she also realized that it was the only thing she wanted to talk about, and that would be true for the rest of her life.

When she'd composed herself, she said, "It's hard to know that you've used up all the good parts of your life so early."

She wanted him to disagree but he nodded. "Thank God we're still young," he said, perhaps as a joke, but perhaps not.

They didn't speak for several minutes after that, and neither of them had any intention to. It was the silence of age, if not of wisdom, and also the silence of those who have weathered the worst long before and now have little fear of the world's residual cruelties. Occasionally their eyes met and lingered, but they managed only to grin at each other as if they shared some private secret that they would never try to articulate, not even to each other. Eventually, the waiter approached and silently placed the check between them—perhaps he saw that neither of them wore a wedding ring and wanted to be proper—and there it would stay, each of them ignoring it, hoping that they might sit together just a few moments longer.

Dave King

The Stamp Collector

LOUIS HAD A FRIEND who collected stamps. Years ago, I won a small pot in the Massachusetts lottery and took Louis to Europe, and in every country we visited he bought sheets of postage to mail home to his friend. In Paris, I watched him from a hotel reception desk, choosing a table at an outdoor café, raising two fingers at a waiter, sliding his friend's stamps into an envelope and addressing the envelope in his big loopy scrawl. By the time I'd paid our bill two coffees had arrived, and when I sat down beside Louis he was humming a club tune. This was Europe to me: sunshine and all the national coffees and Louis humming as he did his mail.

Louis addressed the envelope to his friend, then he wrote postcards. He asked me to pick out a card for his mother, and even sixteen years later, I remember the Seine river scene I chose; it was the one I thought he'd have chosen himself. "Picturesque," he remarked, then he suddenly kissed me—on that broad French street! I closed my eyes and took his hand under the table, and he sang me a love song to the tune of the French national anthem: "Je t'aime je t'aime, je t'aime, je t'ai-aime, Joe . . ." In those days I hadn't yet learned to fear Louis's mom, and I didn't know the friends he wrote to at home. I barely knew Louis.

We'd only been seeing each other five weeks when I won my money. Nothing like that had ever happened to me, and I'd never had a steady boyfriend, either, and between Louis and the sudden wealth, I believed life had changed. Louis had a fancy dining guide, and in Europe I spent a fortune on expensive dinners, after which we checked out the clubs, most of them just like places in Boston, but exciting nonetheless for being overseas. Then we came home, and I gave Louis fifty-five thousand dollars toward a salon on Newbury Street. It was the best thing I ever did, because it made me a partner, and through all the bad years, I've depended on that stream of checks, each with PRE-VALA printed fancily at the top. And giving him money tied me to Louis, too. Otherwise, how long would he have lasted after I drank up his goodwill? But Louis was loyal. He got me in a program and tried to watch out for me, and sometimes we still had dinner, once, twice, even three times a year. He knew how I felt.

I remember saying the money wasn't going to affect me, and perhaps it didn't. Perhaps it simply heightened existing defects. For a while, I kept my job with City Cyclists, humping along as I always had, repairing flats and talking jargon with weekend athletes, but it was hard to convince myself that I *needed* to work, and even harder to resist squandering the sudden deluge. Besides the cash for the hair salon, I wrote checks to every gay charity in Boston and hired a muscle-bound design queen to fluff up my small apartment. I stood rounds of drinks all over town and bought Louis bouquet upon bouquet of flowers.

I've never been good at planning for the future. Eleven months after I won my pot, I screamed at my boss and lost the bike shop job, and the thing with Louis barely made it to two years. And sometime between those two points, the money finally ran out. As I'd told myself again and again without believing it, even $237,000 can't last forever.

. . .

When the phone rang, I was wondering what small tidy gesture might make the place clean. I'd been struggling to stay dry, but I'd had my slips, and it was weeks since I'd closed up the fold-out couch. On the night table, perched like a tea bag on the handle of a coffee mug, lay the wrapper from a condom I barely remembered using, and when things reach this point I start to get worried. I watched Mr. Navy jump to the ficus plant and squat, and when I hollered at him he hopped down and rubbed my leg. I'd been out walking most of the night, approaching, then avoiding the usual taverns, and I still had on yesterday's button-down shirt and briefs.

The man on the phone said, "Mr. Meegan, Officer Lee McCabe of the Rhode Island State Police. Regarding a Louis Prevala, of Boston, Mass?"

I said, "Yes, sir."

There's a notion that such moments bring you to your senses, but the effect on me was to turn up the static. Louis had once called me a sports car with a headlight misaligned, and as the trooper explained the nature of his call, that crooked, unpredictable beam was hard to resist. I went to the kitchen and poked around for Excedrin, and as I knocked back the tablets I noticed my hand was shaking. I opened a Dr Pepper and wondered if I'd fed Mr. Navy, and through it all, the cop described the collision. He said Louis's mother had turned into the wrong lane, and I pictured East Duffield as it was when I visited: the shingled storefronts, the chunky green window boxes. How inconspicuous I'd felt there! The officer said Mrs. Prevala had not survived—but she never thought I was right for her boy. Then he said Louis had not yet regained consciousness, and all I could say was, "Who gave you this number?"

The officer paused. "Mr. Meegan, you do know a Louis Prevala . . ." Of course: handing him that fine piece of change was my crowning achievement. "Because his wallet listed you as emergency contact."

"We're in business together."

"Well, at your business, it seemed you were closed for the holiday." He paused again, then said, "Columbus Day," and I nodded. Louis often spent long weekends with his mom.

I bent down to pick up Mr. Navy, who gave a cry and leapt from my arms, and perhaps Officer McCabe thought I'd cried out myself, because he said, "Sir, are you all right?" I said I was. "You might want to get down here ASAP," the trooper said, and it was a good thing he told me; I might have stood there all day.

I took down the names of the hospital and Louis's emergency room doctor and the garage in East Duffield that had towed Mrs. Prevala's car. "How long before he comes to?" I asked. The cop said the doctor would answer my questions and told me to drive safely.

I fed Mr. Navy and lay down on the crumpled sheets. I could hear him dropping kibble on the floor, then there was a thump as he joined me on the bed. Years ago, Louis had had a calico that woke him each morning by licking his scalp. "Doing hair's just an interim thing for her," he used to joke. "Until her big break in entertainment." But I've never liked being groomed by a cat, and as I pulled away from Mr. Navy I rolled onto a black boot folded into the bedclothes and jumped up in a panic.

Louis was in a small county hospital, in a jarringly quiet ICU. To his right lay an old man with some kind of plastic device on his mouth; to his left was an empty bed. Louis had a plastic thing in his mouth, too, and an oxygen tube running under his nostrils. His face was swollen and padded with bandages, and his body hung limply, like the tail of a kite. He looked awful.

I whispered, "Hi, Louis," and a minute later added, "Joe

here." After that I was at a loss. When Louis broke up with me he said he had nothing left to give, and I yelled that it was funny because that was how *I'd* felt since the money ran out. Now, standing beside the hospital bed, I reached for his hand, then noticed a tube running into a vein and thought I'd better not touch anything. Behind us, a nurse in a blue sweater was moving about a small, glassed-in office. I tapped the door and asked if the doctor would be around soon.

"We're real shorthanded here on holidays," the nurse said. I took a seat on the empty bed and didn't trouble her for anything else.

Louis had two black eyes, and his cheeks were so swollen that the skin dimpled over his nose. It was a while before I realized the nose might be broken. Poor old Louis! In our twenties he'd had all the vivacity, but I was the one who got cruised when we were out together, and it made my passion for him seem like our secret. And then, how everything changed. I lost my hair and whatever small confidence made me attractive, and when I stopped racing bikes I got heavy. But Louis only got younger. A beauty salon is, after all, a fountain of youth. Even at forty, his hair was lustrously dark and his skin taut and nicely tanned. And though he never conquered the pudginess that made him a bit like a large hairy infant, I know he hit the gym regularly and had some baby fat removed from his tummy. But pudgy or not, he still made my mouth water, so it was heartbreaking to see that after all that cosmetic work he now looked so much more beat down than me. Me, with my gut and my desperation shirt.

A tiny man stepped to the bedside and touched a stethoscope to Louis's neck. "You friend of Mr. Pervawa? We just waiting for him to wake up."

"How long?"

The guy glanced at the machines behind the bed, then reached out and hit a button. "His numbers very good," he said, smoothing the blanket over Louis's feet. "Brain activity, normal range. Maybe *li*ttle, little depressed if you consider antiseizure meds . . ."

"His face looks crappy."

"No! Not crappy. Not so crappy at all, really." He patted my hand. "Not bad. Doctor tell you the same."

I nodded back. I'd thought *this* guy was the doctor. "Where's his stuff?" I asked. "His clothes and all, whatever he was wearing." They had Louis in a gown that tied at the neck.

"Oh. ER orderlies generally . . . Yep. Right here." The man reached for a bin attached to the bed's undercarriage. "Of course, valuables usually set aside for safekeeping, although—oops!" He passed me Louis's fancy watch. "Very shorthanded today."

Louis had been wearing a white shirt of some silky knit. His blood had soaked into it in ragged brown stains, and as I drew the fabric from the bin I felt sick. Beneath the shirt lay his folded socks, his expensive loafers and black designer jeans; also gray cotton boxers. Sometime, while my back was turned, he'd stopped wearing briefs. I let the foreign guy drift away, then dug around in the jeans until I found Louis's billfold. And there was my name, after his mother's and the name of the shop. As the officer had said: "In Case of Emergency."

I put a hand on Louis's shin, and the next I knew it was evening, and nothing had changed. What on earth was I thinking as the sun slowly set? I was wondering if Louis's recovery would be a long one, and if he'd let me take care of him while he got well. In the silence of the ward it was easy to imagine what a fine nurse I'd make; to dwell on my chance for regaining what I'd lost.

The tiny man appeared again and touched me on the shoulder. "You can speak to him, you know," he said. "Go 'head. Speak, sing. Important to let him know that you here." He picked up the hand with the tube running into it and slapped at the fingers. "Mr. Pervawa! You friend is here. Time to wake up!

You friend—" He said, "What you name?" and I told him, and he called out, "You friend Joemeegan!" and offered me Louis's palm.

"Hi, Louis," I said. "It's Joe. I'm still here. You had an accident, but you're gonna be fine." And then, to the foreign guy: "That's right, right? He'll be okay?"

The guy nodded. "You wait. Mr. Pervawa's doctor tell you everything. But . . . Maybe tomorrow. You go home now, get some food, shave, some rest. Conserve you stren'th." He patted my hand again, and I stood to go. The old guy in the next bed hadn't budged, and the thought of him lying like a stone made me queasy; but of course, Louis was just the same. "Go on!" said the foreign guy, and moved me toward the bed. "Go on, you can kiss him. Mr. Pervawa!" he called out, slapping Louis's fingers. "You friend Joemeegan giving you good-night kiss!"

Except for Mr. Navy, no one was waiting for me in Boston. I had a temp job I was expected at in the morning, but I could call and say I'd had an emergency, or I could let them figure it out for themselves. It wasn't the first time I'd let someone down. The roads had changed since I'd visited Rhode Island, and I wandered blindly for a while, then took a chance and turned toward the coast. Rounding a curve, I saw a frame house where a lantern shone on yellow clapboards and a gravel road led up a hillside, and I knew I'd seen the place before. Sure enough, a mile further, East Duffield's streetlights began. A motel called the Franklin Arms looked shabby enough to be cheap, and as I passed over my card I realized that if I blew off the temp place I'd be short of cash, and I wondered if I should have borrowed something from Louis's wallet. I found a fish place on the main street, but when my meal came I couldn't eat. I can always drink, though.

I haven't been around much. Other than one miserable season house-painting for an AA acquaintance in Key West, I've lived my whole life in Boston. And though Louis continued to travel as he made money, that trip to Europe was my only time abroad. It might have been years since I'd set foot in an unfamiliar establishment, and when I caught myself watching the barkeep handling the tap I lit out lickety-split. I stopped at Cumberland Farms for a six-pack of Dr Pepper to take back to my room, and as I pulled up to the motel it began to rain.

By morning, I felt I'd conquered something. Unlocking the car, I drew deep breaths of sea air, and if I hadn't wanted to see Louis I'd have gone to the beach. I drove out of town the same way I'd come, and as I passed the yellow house I realized why it was familiar.

Two men were in the front yard, running an American flag up a pole. The older man was thin and gray haired, and as he unfurled the flag, the stamp collector tugged at the rope. The stamp collector was in his thirties, but as I came into view he waved vigorously, letting go of the line, and the flag dropped into his father's arms. I waved back.

Louis's mother had been advised to walk, for her heart, and she insisted on company. When we visited, we walked to the bottom of her hill before breakfast, and where her gravel road met the main one we'd find a neighbor and his developmentally disabled son puttering about their yellow house: putting up the flag or weeding or once, in the wintertime, shoveling a path to the street. Louis would shake the kid's hand, which he seemed to love, then he'd chat about chores or stamps or some small pet that was always getting out of its cage or even what the kid had eaten the night before. Louis was good at this. Small talk is, after all, a hairdresser's trade. But Mrs. Prevala had limited patience for the son, and if Louis kept talking she could get rather edgy.

Once, as we made our way back up the gravel road, she said tartly, "I'm really not interested in Stevie's *meals*." Her hair, newly colored by her son, shone in the summer light, and she wore green dangling earrings that matched her shift, but her face was puffy and the color of oatmeal. I knew she kept a bottle of scotch in a drawer in her bedroom, and I knew what it meant to be thirsty in the morning. But Louis's mom had a black belt in facade; it was one of the differences between her and me. Each day she got done up and behaved like a duchess.

Louis did not take his mother's bait, and after a moment she said she felt for the boy's parents. "I don't know what I'd *do* if I had a child like that."

"I'm sure Stevie feels the same," Louis muttered, eyes fixed on the road. Mrs. Prevala stopped short.

"What's that supposed to mean?" she said. It was a good question, and I'm not certain Louis had any answer. He trudged grumpily forward, leaving me wondering whether my role was to soldier on with him or remain like a chevalier at his mother's side. Then the roadside bushes rustled in a breeze, and Mrs. Prevala inhaled dramatically. "Mmm. Smell the bayberry!" she said, and when Louis still didn't turn she said, "Ex*cuse* me, Joe," and bumped me aside as she ambled after him—though as far as I knew I'd been sniffing the breeze and hadn't crowded her at all. But Mrs. Prevala had a black belt in condescension, too.

It must have been one of my dry weekends late in our time together, when Louis convinced me to join him in East Duffield and avoid the temptations of the Boston bars. The pressure of me and his mother together could make Louis snappish, but we did pretty well when we slipped off alone, so we spent an hour at an animal shelter looking at puppies, then took our sweet time with his mother's many errands. At dinner I visualized a big tub of Maker's Mark instead of Louis's famous chicken, but I kept to my seat and ate what was before me.

Mrs. Prevala, though, barely touched her dinner. Louis had banned wine on account of my struggle, and his mother made numerous trips to that drawer in the bedroom, growing slightly more querulous each time she returned. Taking her plate to the kitchen, she'd heat it in the microwave, then set it on the place-mat and disappear into her room. Louis and I remained at the table, and for an hour he urged her to come and sit down, but at last he snapped. "For the love of God," he cried, balling up his napkin. "What does it cost a person to act civilized?"

Mrs. Prevala stared widely at him. "Aren't you lucky, Louis. You have such freedom." She let her gaze pass coolly over me, and I felt so unmanned that I tore a banana from the fruit bowl, just to put something, anything, in my mouth. "Beholden to no one and so free to judge," she said. "Well, maybe you think life is easy for everyone."

"Mom," said Louis, "I'm gonna help you to bed. Joe and I are—"

"*Civilized!*" Mrs. Prevala said bitterly. "Like it's an *at*titude. Or some chic hairstyle!" She took a step toward the bedroom, and I thought she might fetch that bottle and wave it about, as I'd certainly have done, for once I'm drinking I can't pretend that I'm not. But even three sheets to the wind, Mrs. Prevala acted as if she was only high-strung, and Louis never acknowl-edged his mother's alcoholism the way he did mine.

Mrs. Prevala pointed a manicured finger. "*Get* yourself a little dog, Louis! So you can monitor its behavior. Buy stamps for the retarded neighbor boy, whose actions can't possibly disappoint. Or find some—" She glared nakedly at me. "Get some hapless hanger-on to follow you around!"

Mrs. Prevala went into her room, closing the door with surprising softness. Louis stormed to the kitchen and noisily attacked the dinner dishes, and I could perhaps have followed, whether to show my skill with a dish towel or fuck him hard on the floor by the range. But by then I was mentally halfway to

Boston, more than halfway to a package store. And it was only years later, on my way to that hospital after the accident, that I realized the stamp collector wasn't even a boy when I first met him, but a man not much younger than Louis and I.

The little hospital had lost its Columbus Day sleepiness, and the lobby was bustling. I ducked into the men's room to put on a shirt I'd picked up at an outlet place, and as I did the buttons I imagined Louis up and counseling nurses about their hair. But he was just as I'd left him, under the beige blanket, and the sight of him lying there made my head ache. Even worse, April, the Prevala Salon manager, was by the bed, and I almost snuck off before she spotted me. There are those in his circle who view me as a nuisance.

But April flung her arms around my neck. "Oh, Joe! Thank you for being here yesterday! Why didn't you call me?"

I shrugged. "They say when he's gonna wake up?"

"Not much change, I guess. The doctor will be around soon."

"Could be the swelling's down."

She nodded, slipping an arm in mine. When Louis first hired April, she had a look that was down-the-line New York City: black outfits, spiked hair, tough-tough mouth. But over time she'd made an asset of her pixie qualities, and now she cuddled against me. "Joe's here," she called out wistfully to Louis. "He just arrived. It's Joe and April, honey, who love you very very very much." With her free hand she stroked Louis's fingers.

There was a step behind us, and we turned. "The family of Carole Prevala?" A man in a tight suit stood at the foot of the bed. He had a Rhode Islander's ruddy complexion and sun-lightened hair, and he looked like a dressed-up lobsterman. "I'm sorry for your loss," he said.

"Thank you for meeting us here," said April. "Joe, we have decisions to make."

The man stuck out a hand. "Al Flaydon, funeral services. Very sorry, sir, for your loss."

"We've had no loss," I said. "He's *this* close to coming to."

"For Carole, Joe." April squeezed my elbow.

I turned away. Louis had a coterie who moved in his orbit, who called his mother *Carole* and weren't ashamed of their behavior, but I was not in that club. Still, no one knows drunkenness as well as a drunk, and Mrs. Prevala was driving drunk—of that I was certain. And here was Louis, a plastic breather on his face! I let out a sob, and April's pixie voice trilled my name. The pixie fingers scampered over my arm, but I'm not a salon patron, and I will not be managed.

"This was her fault," I said at last. Who else would say it?

"Joe!"

I felt April's grip tighten, but something was caught in the beam of my wayward headlight, and I drove right at it. "It's her *fault*!" I cried—as if they all didn't know! "And you thought I was trouble." Turning to the lobsterman, I said, "You want a decision? Take her down to the beach. Leave her for low tide, for the fishes, what do I care?" Recalling those dangly earrings, I could have wept in despair! The facade, the hauteur: I could have torn off my ears! "I came here for Louis, April. Certainly not for fucking *Carole*—" From their glassed-in office, the nurses stared.

April shot the undertaker a look, and he stepped away. "Joseph," she said. "We do not know what caused this tragedy."

"I mean it!" I wailed. For the moment, everything I'd done since I'd won my big money seemed like only a failure to watch over Louis. Louis and me. "You think it's coincidence they called me yesterday? After sixteen years?" I grappled for his pants with those emergency contacts. "Take a look in his wallet! He respected my *judgment*!"

April jerked me by the collar. "You fucking sociopath, don't make me laugh. And get your fat ass off the floor." I stood up, wiping my nose, and she said, "If you want to be part of this, cut the crap. Sit down and think of what *Louis* would want. For his mother's burial. Which is no picnic for anyone." She slid a chair across the linoleum. "*Sit!*"

I sat down and stared at Louis. His skin still looked like it was brushed with yellow, but his nose was reemerging in his swollen face. I sniffed, laying my hand on the bedside rail, then set my chin on my fingers. Before me, Louis breathed in and out. I reached down and touched the crook of his elbow, which was warm and a bit moist, then I moved my fingers to the sleeve of his hospital gown, where I could feel his biceps, more pumped than when he'd belonged to me. "Mmm," I said, and remembered that I could talk to him. I ran my knuckles down the hairs of his arm, and as the skin pebbled to goose bumps I said, "Mmm," again; he'd always loved it when I moaned. I reached over and rubbed his stomach, and my dick jumped.

The doctor arrived, accompanied by the foreign guy from the night before. "Morning, Joemeegan," bubbled the foreign guy. "Mr. Pervawa seem much better." He and April had met already; she called him Ricky and said he was a love. Flaydon was gone.

The doctor was pudgy and pink and could have been Louis's overachiever brother. He said he was optimistic, then said it again in various other phrases, but my only question was when would Louis wake up, and I'd already figured that was one thing they wouldn't discuss. The doc said, "Remember, it's only the second day. These things take time," and Ricky nodded. "I gather there was another party in the car," the doctor said. "So sorry for your loss."

We watched him examine Louis's chart and do everything Ricky had done the night before. At last he picked up Louis's hand and pinched the palm, and the four of us watched the fingers contract. "That's good," said the doctor. "Response to pain stimulus is normal, in fact."

"So he's miles ahead of me," I said. The doctor grinned.

I drove up to Boston to get some clothes and see Mr. Navy, and I decided to bring him back with me. All down the interstate he sat on my lap, but at the exit he stood and began to meow, then he disappeared under the seat and continued his complaining from there. "Psst," I said. "Pss-pss-psst." It was midnight, and no one else was on the road. I'd stayed longer than I intended at my apartment, always planning to stand up and get moving, but really just lingering on the fold-up couch. It wasn't April who'd made me feel helpless, but Louis, lying stonelike until visiting hours ended.

I turned toward the coast, and the yellow house looked cozy, lit by its single lantern. I slowed for the curve, then suddenly braked, and instead of continuing to the Franklin Arms I turned up the gravel road.

Louis's Miata was parked in a turnaround; the top was down. I caught my breath, thinking for just a moment that—but of course, it was Mrs. Prevala's car that had been in the crash. I got a flashlight from my glovebox and peered at the leather seats, which held puddles from last night's rain, and as I poked around for something to soak up the water there was a whish of fur, and Mr. Navy darted into the blackness. I called, but heard only crickets, and as I waited for him to come back I took off my sweatshirt, then my shirt, and sopped up the water in Louis's car.

The house was unlocked. I went around turning on lights, and as I passed the pantry I saw two fifths of Mrs. Prevala's cheap scotch peeping from behind a half-open louvered door. In Louis's room, one twin was unmade, under the same poster of Diana Ross that had always hung there, and on the bedside table sat the same clock radio beside the same book of movie-star portraits. Louis's dirty laundry was on the floor, and on the second bed a weekender contained his clean clothes: Calvin Klein underwear; nylon running shorts; a cashmere sweater. The sweater was too small for me, but I draped it over my shoulders and hugged the sleeves to my bare chest, and suddenly I was thinking about that scotch.

The first pull was like heaven, and I let the bottle touch the back of my throat like a glass dick, until it made me gag. A little stream ran down my chin and onto my stomach, and I dabbed at it with the sleeve of Louis's sweater. Another slug, and when I screwed the cap on I was gasping for breath. I leaned my forehead on the cool kitchen counter and knocked a dirty cereal bowl into the sink. It landed with a terrible clatter.

I picked up the bottle again and called for Mr. Navy and felt very sorry for myself. Outside, the crickets were still making their deafening pulse, but I stood on the deck and said, "Pss-pss-psst," as loud as I could, and when nothing happened I said, "Well, fuck you, then." On the patio was an ashtray with a couple of Mrs. Prevala's butts in it, and I said "Fuck you" to the ashtray and then "Fuck you" to the porch furniture and the half-open kitchen door and the gabled roof of the bathroom and Mrs. Prevala's Polident and ugly toothbrush and Metamucil inside on the sink and the little area of cleared lawn and all the overgrown bayberry and honeysuckle bushes that crowded the hillside: "Fuck you. Fuck you, fuck you fuckyoufuckyoufuck-you." I spun around a couple times and flung the bottle into the night, thinking as I waited for the sound of the crash that if it would make Louis wake up this would be my last taste of alcohol forever, despite that second, unopened fifth still waiting in the pantry. But the bottle just bounced on the hard ground without breaking, and I walked over and picked it up. "Fuck," I said. The air was cold, and I forced my head through the neck of Louis's sweater, letting it sag around my shoulders like the neck ruff in some old-fashioned painting.

I went around to where the Miata was parked and reached down to feel the upholstery. It was damp and flabby, but I didn't use Louis's sweater to mop it up. Instead, I had another drink, and then another, and then I decided to see how quickly I could finish the bottle, and I did the best I could. After this I could no longer stand, and I got down on my knees and pressed my face to the fender, which was wet with condensation and felt delicious. I crawled the length of the car with my cheek to the metal, imagining the swath as my face slid along the side panel, and when I reached the rear bumper I lay down in the dirt. The ground was damp and a bit soft, and I inched myself under the trunk, putting my arms at my sides and getting in tight behind the rear wheels, until I was pinned there and could no longer move. I pressed my face to the ground and rubbed my nose back and forth until it seemed I'd abraded the skin, then I picked my head up and slammed it against the undercarriage, and though I wasn't quite sobbing yet, I started to heave. I knocked my head around until stars fluttered before me and all I could manage was a few whimpery squeaks, then I opened my mouth and bit the soil, scooping up all I could with my tongue. I've done this before, this wallowing in abasement, and it always feels good. There's a theory that a drunk won't clean up until he hits rock bottom, so each new incident might perhaps be the one.

Sometime in the night I moved my face out of the dirt, and I woke to feel something soft strike my cheek. I opened my eyes and saw a limp mouse in front of me and the gray-yellow morning shimmering beyond the car. In a patch of sunlight sat Mr. Navy. "Hello, there," I said, and he stepped toward me with a new kind of proud chirp and reached out to bat the mouse, and when the corpse hit me in the face again it was time to rise and shine.

It wasn't easy climbing out from under the Miata; I'd wedged myself in with the kind of ambition I only muster when I'm wasted. Louis's sweater caught on a bolt and nearly choked me, and I slid out of it and left it hanging from the undercarriage; and as I emerged I saw the scotch bottle a few feet away, with two fingers of amber liquid capped in like a message. I didn't drink it. Instead, I took it into the house and replaced it on the pantry shelf, and I was in Mrs. Prevala's bedroom rummaging for Excedrin when I heard knocking on the screen door.

It was the neighbor from down the hill. He nodded at me, and when I stepped outside I saw the son trying to sneak up on Mr. Navy. "I'm a friend of Louish," I said. "Been at the hoshpital, got in late." The man leaned back, and I realized my breath must be something. My face was undoubtedly pretty bad, too, and I hoped it would make him take his kid and go. "It'fine. I won't break anyfing." My mouth was so dry.

Mr. Navy scampered under a bush, and the stamp collector ambled toward us. He had short, very black hair and a large mouth, but he wasn't ugly or crazy looking. He eyed me deliberately, then said, "You got in a fight."

His father said, "*Stevie.*"

I looked myself over. My pants were streaked with dirt, and there were patches of mud in the hairs on my stomach. Rubbing my hand over my face, I felt the sting of torn skin, plus some crustiness on my stubble, and I wondered if I'd spat up during the night. I nodded at Stevie and tried to think of what to say, and at last I stuck out my hand. "I'm Joe."

Stevie shook my hand enthusiastically. "Your kitty caught hisself a mouse."

"Probably his first. Mr. Navy's an apartment cat."

"What's that mean?" he said.

The old man sighed, shaking his head. "I hear Carole's viewing is today, over to Flaydon's. Terrible thing." He pushed up the sleeve of his jacket and picked a scab from his forearm. "She was some lady, for all her frailties."

"I'll stay with Louis," I said. "I won't go to the viewing." I started to tell him I'd never bought into Mrs. Prevala's gentility, but my mouth was too cottony to say very much. And of course, the man was just being polite. How people do that I really don't know.

"Louis is *my* friend," put in Stevie. "I like him better than her." The dad laid a hand on his shoulder. "He brings me stamps and cuts my hair."

"Looks good," I said, wetting my desiccated lips. "Quite a handsome cut." The bayberry trembled, and I rubbed my arms: goose bumps. "You know, you could visit him. It's supposed to be family in ICU, but nobody checks. And Louis has got no family now." Then I was overcome by the dryness.

The old man said, "You ought to have some clothes on," and reached for the screen door, and I pushed past him and rushed to the kitchen and put my mouth under the tap, and the water that came out wasn't nearly wet enough. It poured into my mouth and burbled down my face, and I swallowed as much as I could, then turned and let it wash over my head and ears, finding sensitive zones all over my scalp. At last I just let go, and my face hit the bed of the sink. The cold water poured over my neck, and when I opened my eyes I could see the dish I'd knocked in the night before. Then the tap was turned off, and someone was patting my head with a cloth.

"Good idea," the man said. He moved the cloth to my back and went on patting, gently patting, and said nothing about my heaving and sniveling or the way I rocked back and forth and dug my chest with my nails. "A quick visit to Flaydon's, pay our respects. Then off to the hospital to tell Louis hello. How's that sound, Steverino?"

"Good."

"Get yourself cleaned up." He tapped my shoulder blade. "We'll wait."

I stood up, running a hand through my wet hair. I hadn't

changed my opinion of Louis's mom. She'd had nothing for me, not even friendship, but I'd addressed all that yesterday, or meant to, and now, with my face raw and my belly muddy, I hoped I would never think of it again. And of course, Louis's mother was never the point.

I watched Stevie stick a finger in a dried flower arrangement and thought how Mrs. Prevala would hate having him here, then he opened the door, and Mr. Navy strolled in. "I just don't know," I told whoever was listening. "I can't make up my mind."

"What you want . . . ," the father said thoughtfully. "You want to be able to tell Louis about it. How respectful it was, all the little details." He'd had thirty-plus years, I guess, of guiding the stamp collector, and he did it very well, speaking very slowly and holding my gaze. " 'Cause you bet your life savings he's gonna ask." He scratched his arm again and asked if I had a razor, and I realized that if this was the day Louis woke up, I'd better be at my best. And I *had* a razor, so the first step was easy.

I went to my bag and dug out a can of cat food. "Do something for me?" I wondered if there was anything that might do me some good, and I thought of the years I'd spent looking after myself. I didn't do a good job, but I endangered only me. How long did it take to become one of those guys who'd hit rock bottom and bounced back?

I handed Stevie the can and gestured at the bathroom. "I'll be quick."

"Come on, fella." The man took his son's arm. "Why don't I help you with that, then you'll give it to the nice kitty. And I'll make a pot of coffee."

"Be my guest," I said.

The day Louis and I were scheduled to leave Venice, our flight was canceled. We'd had our last cappuccino in the sunshine, and Louis had mailed Stevie his Italian stamps, and we'd already checked our luggage when the airline canceled the flight.

In the little tourist kiosk where two young Venetians were making hotel reservations, Louis pretended we'd only just arrived. "No, no, just the one night. Our first!" he said. "I'm excited already." And on the ferry into the city he continued to pretend it was all once again new, and I played along. "Look, babe, the canals! Do you think we can ride around in one of those boats?"

I put my arm around him. "We'll do whatever you like."

Our new hotel was on an island across from the main square. In the years since, I've forgotten the name. Our room was on the top floor and had a single high window, and Louis and I went to bed and made love in the light of the window, and when we were finished he stood on a bench to look out. I climbed up behind him and held his waist. Across the water, the city was lit by sunset, and the cathedral looked like a cluster of bright balls dropped down among blocks. In the main piazza we could see tourists photographing each other with the pigeons, just as he and I had done the day before. "Let's come back every year," I said. "Every year an annual first visit."

Louis said, "I might have my salon by next year. I'm really ready to set up on my own."

"But you'll take vacations." He said he would.

Louis said, "I have a place in mind. You know on Newbury, with the big white planters?" I didn't, so I kissed his neck. "It's got kind of new fixtures, but the guy wants to sell. Of course, it's an old queen's shop now, and I want soft lighting. Maybe an accent color, greenery, orchids . . . Very friendly and genteel, no attitude."

While Louis was talking, I stepped down from the window and sat on the bench with his feet between my thighs. He always had great legs, and when I touched his shins he shifted his feet so my dick fell between his heels. I wondered if he expected me to speak of my own ambitions, and I almost told him it was my dream to take over City Cyclists, though it certainly was not. The fact is, I'm no good at imagining the future, and all I wanted was for everything to go on forever: the vacation, the money, the amazingly relaxed camaraderie that was just beginning to become love. Even the very moment itself! Yes, if everything had stopped then: if I'd been compelled to spend eternity sitting on that bench with my forehead against the backs of Louis's thighs while he gazed at the Venice skyline and contemplated his plans—if that had happened, I'd have been perfectly happy, because that was truly all I expected at that moment of my life.

Michael Powers

More or Less Like a Man

IN THE SECOND HOUR of a six-hour flight, the woman sitting next to me looked up from the book she'd been reading, or pretending to read, and said, "I am fleeing."

We were on our way from New York to San Francisco. I had a cousin there who was trying to start a landscaping business, planting native succulents to replace the lawns people were tearing up because of the drought. He had called to ask if I wanted to go in on this venture with him. We had never been close, but I think he knew I didn't have much else going on at the time.

"I'm sorry?" I said to my neighbor.

"I am in flight," she repeated, as if annoyed that I had not been paying attention when she said it the first time, "which is the noun form of the verb *to fly,* but also *to flee.*"

Okay, I thought, here we go.

"For a long time, in fact," she said, "and until quite recently, *fly* and *flee* were used interchangeably, to mean *run away, escape.*"

She spoke with an accent that to me sounded central European—Czech, Bulgarian, something like that, but really I had no idea. I didn't know what history she might have been speaking from.

The *Fasten Seat Belt* sign was illuminated, and so accordingly my seat belt was fastened low and tight across my hips. The *No Smoking* sign was also illuminated, as it must always be, because it exists—because the possibility that one might be allowed to smoke has already been written into the language of airplanes and cannot be unwritten except at a cost of many millions of dollars, and so now the airplanes must continually remind you that no, you will not be allowed to smoke.

"To fly:" she was saying, "to escape the earth."

How was I supposed to respond to that? Like all normal people, I go to great lengths to avoid striking up conversations with strangers on airplanes. I keep a book open in my hands, my eyes trained on it at all times, even if I am not actually reading it. A hardcover is best, something thick and heavy, preferably Russian. Tolstoy is ideal. At the slightest stirring from my neighbor I stare intently at the page before me and furrow my brow in a way that I hope conveys that whatever they are about to say to me had better be more important than the collapse of traditional morality and the question of what it means to lead a good life. I keep earbuds in my ears, music playing just loud enough to let my neighbors know that I can't hear them, but not so loud that they will want to ask me to turn it down, since then we would be talking, and who knows where that might lead? Nothing is worse than knowing exactly how long you'll have to continue to be charming, to smile and make sounds of empathetic agreement, to think of new questions to ask so that the conversation can continue. Well, one thing is worse, and that is that the conversation does not continue. The silence you enter into then is not at all the happy, innocent silence you had foolishly left behind a moment ago. It is strained, awkward, full of guilt and unuttered apology. You are two human beings who have been forced to admit, without even being able to say so aloud, that you have no interests in common. The embarrassment is total. You are staring at the miniature television screen in front of you as if into an abyss.

The flight clock displayed on that miniature screen said three hours, twenty-eight minutes to San Francisco. Here we go.

"What are you fleeing?" I said. I thought since she had brought it up that she would want to talk about it, but in fact she was oddly cagey.

"The earth," she said, "as I told you." She turned back to the window, but a moment later she added, as if realizing that, having interrupted my reading, she owed me a bit more than that, "But more specifically, New Jersey."

"Ah," I said, aiming for the sound of empathetic assent. "What's in New Jersey?"

"You haven't been?" she said. "Oh, it's a big and diverse and fascinating place. There are old faded industrial cities, immigrant communities from all over the world, rolling, meadowish countryside full of horses and horse people, the Pine Barrens, a mythical creature called the Jersey Devil—"

"No," I cut her off, "I've been to New Jersey. I meant what's in New Jersey for you? What is it that you feel you need to flee from?"

"Excuse me," she said. "You don't flee *from* something. You just *flee* that thing. *To flee* already implies the idea of going away, so the preposition is unnecessary. It's redundant."

A voice came over the intercom, perhaps the pilot's. "Ladies and gentlemen, we'll be experiencing some mild turbulence for the next several minutes. We ask that you please remain seated with your seat belts fastened."

A moment later the body of the plane began to shudder and pitch slightly from side to side, like an insomniac trying to find a position in his bed that will allow him to sleep. There was a lightness in my stomach that meant we were falling perhaps hundreds of feet down the back of a wave of air, and then a heaviness in my legs as we rose up the face of the next wave. All of this was routine. No one that I could see looked even slightly alarmed, but my neighbor became silent and looked out the window, which meant, since she was in the middle seat, that she had to look across the body of the sleeping man to her right.

She was older than I had thought—maybe forty, maybe a little older even. She had fine but deep creases at the corners of her eyes and her mouth. Her hair, which she wore in a guileless ponytail, was going gray along the temples, but was so pale anyway that it was hard to tell the blond from the gray.

She might have been married or not, might have had children or not. It might have been her husband or her children she was fleeing.

The outfit she wore looked almost American but not. I don't know what it was exactly. Her boot-cut jeans maybe, a little too artificially distressed at the hips and the backs of the knees.

She was fleeing New Jersey, and she wanted to talk about it but did not want to talk about it.

How readily the slightest coincidence leads us to believe what we want to believe anyway: that the world outside ourselves corresponds with whatever is going on in our minds. In the paper that morning I had read that the Department of Justice was investigating some three hundred Bosnian immigrants on the suspicion that they had in fact participated in the atrocities committed against Bosnian Muslims and Croatians in the 1990s. Thousands of people had *fled* in those days, had arrived in the United States and in Western Europe *in flight* from the nightmare that had arisen in the place that had been their home, and amid this chaos it had been impossible, apparently, to sort with perfect accuracy the perpetrators from the victims. In the article there was a photo of a middle-aged woman being led in handcuffs toward a white police van. The caption said that her name was Cvetka Basíc, that for twenty years she had worked as head cook in the cafeteria at Colonial Middle School, in Conshohocken, Pennsylvania, that in 1995, in Srebrenica, she had tied men to chairs and forced them to drink gasoline, to drink the blood of their friends and neighbors, before she shot them.

How old would my neighbor have been in 1995? Twenty, twenty-five? She looked so slight, so unintimidating, but give her a gun. Let her stand in the company of others who also have guns and who are on her side. Easily she was old enough to have poured gasoline down someone's throat as he sat helplessly praying, waiting for the bullet that would kill him.

On the other hand, easily too she might have had gasoline poured down her own throat, seen it poured down the throats of the people she loved.

I thought of what frozen fields she might have crawled through on her hands and knees at twilight, all her family trailing behind her, the hills rising over them as if they were already bodies wombed in the body of the earth, the edge of the woods dark as an open mouth. How the place that had been her home might have become alien to her, and she to it.

In the dark she might have whispered the names of her children, her sister, her mother and father, just to hear them reply in their own voices, "I am still here."

Maybe then in the last light sparrows rose from the grass on the hilltops above and flew over them, and it was as though the birds were trailing black thread behind their wings, to sew up the gaps in the earth where the sky showed through.

How bound she would have felt to the earth then.

To flee, to fly.

"I had an affair with my sister's husband," my neighbor said. She touched the back of my hand with the tips of her fingers as she said this, but the gesture was not romantic. *We are two human beings*, it meant, *and we have interests in common. I am trusting that you will understand me.*

I didn't know what I had done to make it seem as though I deserved that kind of trust.

She had moved to New Jersey three years ago, she told me, from Ljubljana, Slovenia. She had come with her sister and her sister's husband. Her sister was a geologist—"a little bit famous," my neighbor said—and had taken a faculty position at Rutgers.

I told her I understood why the husband would have had to move, but why then had she herself left her home and moved across half a continent and an ocean in the middle of her life? Surely not only to follow her sister. At this point she had already told me how beautiful her city had been, how much she missed it.

"I have not always been the best at organizing my life," she said. "I had lost another job, broken up with another boyfriend. Our mother had died the year before, two years behind our father. I thought, 'Why not try a new place, a new language?' It seemed the right time."

The plane shuddered slightly, then settled back into the calm of its sleep.

"And also yes," my neighbor said, "she is my sister. I have never been apart from her."

It wasn't that she had been jealous of her sister. She herself had never wished to be married, and in Ljubljana she had not even liked her sister's husband.

"I thought him boring," she said. "He was too nice."

But in Newark my neighbor's sister was often away from home, and my neighbor and the husband spent a lot of time alone together, looking for work, speaking only in English in order to master the language.

"We knew English already, of course," my neighbor said. "When there are only two million people in the world who speak your native language, you learn English. But we wanted really to speak it well."

She blamed the change in language for the change in her feelings. "He was someone else when he spoke in English," she said. "Someone I loved. I was someone else, someone who loved him."

My neighbor had told me that she was fleeing New Jersey. What did it mean about me that I had imagined her fleeing the memory of violence, the nearness of death, when in fact what she was fleeing was an excess of life, a love that had simply been allowed to grow in the wrong place?

To her sister, though, it had meant death, or something like it.

"She tried to kill herself," my neighbor said. "She swallowed Drano. She had to have surgery to repair the damage to her small intestine."

My neighbor realized that she could not continue the affair, but also that she could not see her sister's husband again, that her presence would be enough to destroy their marriage.

"At the time when it was happening," she said, "I thought, 'What does a marriage matter?' Do you know what the word *husband* means? What it used to mean? In Old English it meant a manager, a steward. It comes from the combination of the word *hūs*, which meant a house or household, with the word *bōndi*, which meant one who cultivates or tills the soil. These dead words, these dead ways of being hanging around like ghosts, poisoning our lives. 'Why should she have a husband?' I thought. 'Why should anyone?' Let our desires be wild plants instead of tame ones."

Now, having seen the damage her desire had done, she was fleeing. "I have committed a transgression I cannot undo. It is just the sort of thing for which, in very ancient times, one might have been put to death, or banished from one's home forever."

She wanted to escape the earth, but she didn't want to die, so she was going to San Francisco, to sit beside an ocean she had never seen before, and to be far from those she loved.

In San Francisco you have to take off your sweater and put it on again twenty times a day. What else is there to say about it?

Something about the fog? It's crawling with assholes. It would be a beautiful place to live if you had a time machine.

I am trying to date again. It's been a while, and the modes of courtship have changed. My phone shows me the faces of women who are physically near me, and I decide whether I like these faces. The owners of the faces decide whether they like my face. If we like each other's faces, we type messages to each other. I try to think of things to say to the owners of these beautiful faces that will be different from the things everyone else is saying. I tell them that I grew up in New Jersey, that I've seen the Jersey Devil in the Pine Barrens. It was late at night, and I was eating a hamburger with a friend at a diner, on this long stretch of empty road where there was nothing else around but the dark woods growing out of the sandy soil. I looked up from my hamburger and saw him through the window, but he was pretty far away. He was naked, covered in short, stiff hair like the hair of a dog, but shaped otherwise more or less like a man. He was standing at the edge of a beam of light from a streetlamp, at the border between the woods and the parking lot, just staring in at us. I could tell by the way he held his tail in his hands that he'd been alone a long time.

Jo Lloyd

The Earth, Thy Great Exchequer, Ready Lies

The companions

Hm has been deceived by the dainty manners of first acquaintance, when Cassandra nibbled his fingers and blew nose kisses into his palm. Now she flattens her ears, twitches at the reins. Every hoof she sucks from the ground aims another clot of water at her rider. HM happens to know that horses, like all creatures intended to run for their lives, can observe their full compass round, so when she turns her head back, it is not to look but to make by-our-lady sure he sees her look. Raindrops have beaded on her lashes and whiskers, transforming her into some frosted basilisk of the great northern ocean, risen to recite the charges against him.

Behind HM rides Shiers, also sulking, on a cow-hocked bay. Shiers has tunneled deep into his habitual melancholy to uncover a seam of stygian gloom. With every new set of accounts or assay report, his head has sunk further between his shoulders, threatening to reduce him to one of those nipple-eyed monsters of Ethiop. He may not even have understood the fine details. His mind is blunt, a maul at best, or a crowbar. For this reason, he has been HM's most trusted employee yet tedious companion, the more so right now for his rheumatic affliction. He sniffled and sneezed through a passable supper at the inn and then again through a more doubtful breakfast. Aeolian fanfares accompany their progress along the puddled track.

At the front of this small cavalcade rides the man who calls himself Tall John, his feet dangling past the belly of a gray pony that is first cousin to a sheep. Tall John wears a short hood or perhaps a long hat of coney fur, which covers his neck and his ears and merges around his face into a grizzled ruff where, HM surmises, the coney stops and the man begins.

Since leaving the highway, they have slithered up and down and around so many hills that every six yards ridden marks one gained. Each ascent reveals more hills—bare, treeless wastes of sorrel and mauve, rain clouds tumbling down their slopes like the smoke of burnt villages.

The bay slips, and Shiers curses. "How much longer must we wade through this by-our-lady swamp?"

"Pish!" says HM, to assure anyone listening that in him, at least, dwells the true spirit of an Adventurer. "Pash!" he adds, more quietly, because perhaps Tall John, with his fur-coddled ears, has not heard.

But Tall John looks back at them, with an expression that suggests their exchange has disturbed the grasshoppers in his head.

"A journey is as long as it is long."

"Indeed," agrees HM, noting that once again this could be the wisdom of a rustic savant, the subtlety of a cozener, or the rambling of a lunatic.

It was Shiers whom Tall John approached first, with a tale that he could not be persuaded to elaborate or even repeat. When Shiers explained the finder's fee and its conditions, Tall John stipulated that HM must be of the preliminary party, plus Shiers, and no one else.

So here is HM, founding director and deputy governor of the Company of Mine Adventurers, former comptroller of the Middle Temple, former member of Parliament, knighted by His Royal Majesty King Charles II, in sodden garb on a sodden horse trailing through the sodden by-our-lady wilderness after either a simpleton or a crook.

It is clear to HM that Tall John belongs to that most disagreeable class of humanity, those who refuse honest employment, choosing instead to scrape a living off the land, like animals. They take anything they can eat or burn or sell: berries, acorns, bracken, scraps of fleece, leaves, peat, sand. They trap and fish, empty birds' nests, pull the very stones from the ground. And with all this, account themselves a second Adam, more free than a freeborn gentleman.

This morning, in the stable yard of the inn, Tall John observed the preparations in silence. HM still prickles from the smirk he recognized as he took up his reins. A look-at-you-fine-sir-in-your-fancy-sleeves-and-neckcloth smirk.

Smirk while you can, Mr. Coneyhead, HM thought, we'll see who is fine in the end.

Tall John looks back again, and HM sits up straighter, like one who has studied not only horsemanship but also fencing and archery (has Tall John studied fencing and archery? HM thinks not), and reminds himself that before getting mixed up with the Mine Adventurers he had single-handedly restored the fortunes of his wife's family and hauled the estate into the modern age. He has put occupation into the hands of the poor and gruel into the mouths of their young, even provided them with ministers and teachers at his own expense (that is, at the expense of the Company, yet is that not the same thing, almost?).

He brings to mind, as he is wont to do in moments of doubt, his favorite poem, a lengthy ode on the subject of HM and his mineral pursuits (is there an ode to Tall John? again, HM

thinks not), certain flattering lines of which he has committed to memory: "a genius richer than the mines below," "with
virtues bless'd and happy counsels wise," "commanding arts yet
still acquiring more."

It is comforting to remember, as the rain pools in the toes
of his boots, that he is "with virtues bless'd." For it is common
knowledge, among Adventurers as among rustics, that the signs
they seek are reserved for the righteous.

HM wishes, above all, to be seen as righteous. Everything he
has ever done has been for the good of his children, the nation,
the deserving poor. It wounds him when his altruism is not
acknowledged. When, instead of "Thank you very much, HM"
or "HM has done a fine job," he must suffer, "Where are the
receipts?" "Where are the accounts, the evidence?"

But if today's expedition finds nothing, then he has been
cheated, and will look a fool. And there is nothing he hates more
than to look a fool.

An unwelcome apprehension teases at the edge of HM's
vision—a familiarity in the shape of the hills, in the contours of
the valley through which their horses wind, and now a row of
hovels, thatched like sties. With consternation, he realizes they
are approaching one of the Company's sites.

He has passed here once before, on a tour of inspection with
Waller. It is among the smaller mines, not greatly different, at
casual glance, from the surrounding dents and hollows and
tumbles of rock. The entrance resembles a crude lair, clawed out
by some night-skulking beast to evade a fiercer one.

A number of men and women and children are lolling
about on the surface. They have the yellowed skin of subterranean creatures, and when they raise their heads it is with
the single movement of a startled herd. HM tries to adopt a

deputy-governorial posture but is conscious of how he must appear—mud spattered, squelching, his entourage a blemmye, a sheep, and a coney-headed clown. The opportunity to retreat has passed.

Yet again he is to be tested. Not Hercules, not even Job himself, has had to overcome more obstacles.

Hardships of his early life—he achieves success

When his mother died, he mourned a shade that had moved now and then across his sight, seeming always to be attending to someone more important. Four years later, he lost his sister, Louisa, who had petted him and carried him and played with him, teaching him his letters, helping him to fashion shiplets of paper and muskets of blackthorn.

"What a blessing it wasn't one of the boys," said Aunt Verity, shaking dust from her little-used head, and HM said that he would happily trade, for Louisa's life, that of his elder brother Richard, whose preferred pastimes included kicking, smacking, tripping, pinching, and twisting.

He was beaten for this sentiment yet did not recant.

HM's role was to be audience to the parade of his brother's talents. Richard was quick and strong and courageous. Richard was accomplished in Greek, Latin, rhetoric, ancient history, and the use of arms. Richard went up to university with a princely allowance and a small household to attend him.

HM, meanwhile, had to scrimp his way through Oxford and the Middle Temple on £80 a year. And it was not enough that he had to live like a pauper—his father denied requests for loans or expenses, even the necessities required to secure a royal appointment and thereby HM's legal career (not to mention pay off a number of debts).

In the end, however, he didn't need his father or his aunt or his brother or any of his weak-livered relatives, only his own industry and excellent judgment.

Mary was very young when he met her, pale and thin like her mother, with the same prominent bones. The family had made its money initially in salt, which might account for a certain redness, as if from crying, about all their eyes. Still, wise investors are tempted not by the sparkle of an object, yet rather by its use. In her hair was the black of coal, in her irises, the gray of ore. She was the wealth of nature in the shape of a girl.

Mary was the sole heir to the mineral leases her grandfathers had bought up a century before and earlier, times so primitive that a man scratched what he could off the surface and then scrabbled to the next seam to repeat the process. HM's new family, despite their tenuous claim to nobility, had shown uncanny foresight, first in acquiring the leases, then in holding on to them as proceeds fell, and finally in preserving this girl, alone of all her dead sisters, for him, the most fitting man in the kingdom to exploit the opportunities of her inheritance. (What had HM's own grandfather left? His treasonous bones to be, at the Restoration, removed from Westminster Abbey and thrown into a common grave.)

In the span it took Mary to produce three boys so very like their father that her part in the matter seemed negligible, and then pass away, HM had revived the neglected mines, turning £60 annually into £500. He toured the northern coalfields, where the latest technology was squeezing profit from land otherwise useless, and came back eager to introduce the ingenious new ideas he'd discovered—gunpowder, devices of fire and water, systems of draining and ventilating.

But he found himself obstructed again, this time by his mother-in-law's new husband, one of those doddering curmudgeons stuck in the fifteenth century who thought gentlemen should not dirty their hands with commerce or anything else that he did not understand. Jealous of HM's success, he blocked plans for expansion, even further investment in the current facilities.

HM was in London when the news of the man's death arrived. In the privacy of his chamber, he danced a little jig (for the sake of his dear children). And when his mother-in-law wrote, begging him to return and take control of the estate, he allowed himself a hornpipe.

HM had seen, by then, that his ambitions had been too small and local—even a peasant could dig and sell. It was transformation and manufacture that generated real advantage. He set about creating what he liked to think of as a vast, modern machine of industry, his sundry projects like its cogs and levers, each fulfilling its own purpose while contributing to the functioning of the others, every part more profitable for its communication with the whole.

He blasted adits and sank shafts. He constructed horse gins. He renovated the abandoned smelting works, employing artists from the Continent to prepare ponds and dams and engines of iron. He cut a dock and built floodgates, established battery mills, rolling mills, brickworks, manufactories.

Taking a lesson from the plantations, he imported men from other regions and bonded them to his service, conscripted convicts to work out their sentences. He was able to move labor between his concerns as required, so that no man need ever stand idle. Day and night, in shifts of eight hours, he mined and smelted and swadered and lantered and shined. While the farmers still lazed in their beds, before even the rooster opened his eyes, HM worked.

Deep in the earth, he carved shining black streets of coal, lit with candles and drained of much of the water, ensuring his laborers were almost as comfortable belowground as above. He lined these streets with wooden rails, so that trained men could haul the coal to the shaft in great wagons bearing eighteen hundredweight. He laid more tracks between his mines and his works, his works and his docks, over highland and lowland, over (for all the squawking of envious neighbors) common land and public highways. To these surface wagons, he fitted sails. A horse could replace ten men, but a sail could replace even the horse. His terranauts skimmed over the skin of the earth, merry as a flock of small birds put to harness.

Master of the elements, HM schemed once again for expansion. The royal monopoly on silver had been lifted, and in the next county were rumors of rich ores—the wealth of three kingdoms.

That was when it all started. Waller pouring poppy and poison in his ear. The founding of the Mine Adventurers. His present troubles.

An unpleasant encounter

HM recognizes the foreman yet is unable to recall his name. He prides himself on knowing such things, likes to think of his men as a kind of extended family, akin to lesser relations or servants, who roost and thrive in the spreading shelter of his generosity. (It is true that it is easier to think of them this way when they are at a distance.)

The foreman's memory proves quicker, and he greets HM with accurate deference. He seems unsurprised by the party's arrival, and reports, as if it were expected, on the progress of the work ("Very good," says HM), the length of the drift ("Very good"), the quantity of ore raised (so little?), the days of rain and the days of frost, the injured and the sick.

"Very good, very good," says HM, nodding, as if he has ridden all this way in this foul by-our-lady weather to learn about Samuel David's leg or Edward Morgan's burns. He gathers the reins to move on, but the foreman stops him.

"If I may, sir," he says.

HM cannot think of anything in this wasteland so urgent as to give plausible excuse to leave.

"The men, you understand, sir, are anxious. If there is anything you could tell us, sir."

"There is no reason for anxiety."

"We have heard talk, sir. Of closure." At this point the foreman—is his name Jennings?—looks at Tall John. "Or sale."

Can he think that the coneyhead is here to invest? Are all these people simple?

"Nothing runs faster than false rumor," says HM, with a memory of Latin and all the authority he can retrieve from beneath his dripping hat.

The yellow people, without seeming to move, have somehow crept closer.

Jennings is closer, too. "So there is no truth in it?"

It can be hard, HM has found, to determine the sentiments of common men, lacking, as they do, the gestures and expressions of gentlefolk. At this moment, however, he has no difficulty in interpreting the glinting eyes and parted lips of the miners. This is the face of the mob at a dogfight or a baiting.

But they are on the ground and shoeless, and he is in the air and booted.

"Look at me," he says to Jennings. "Do I look like someone who needs to sell?"

Jennings drops his eyes and murmurs something that HM decides to take for an apology.

"Perhaps," he says, "you would be better served working than spreading gossip."

And with that, he jabs Cassandra in the ribs. Startled from

a dream of carrots, she springs forward, all four feet leaving the ground at once, almost unseating HM, who hangs on by reins and mane and jabs her again for good measure. Summoning to his face the expression of a man who has studied horsemanship and fencing, he rides past the crowd, past Tall John, and on up the track. A trot, he decides, is an acceptable pace. A righteous man rarely needs to canter, but the importance of his affairs justifies a trot.

Soon enough Tall John catches up and jogs beside him (the gray pony judging its distance from Cassandra's bite), looking at HM like a schoolmaster expecting the square of the hypotenuse.

"Lead on, man," says HM. "You know the path."

"We all follow the path we have chosen," says Tall John, like a sage of Bedlam. And he leers, showing all five teeth.

HM can conjure no reply, and would give half his purse to put a wall between himself and his appraiser at that moment.

This whole unfortunate incident, he adds to the list of things for which Waller is to blame.

An opportunity—the conspirators

His first meeting with Waller came about, it seemed at the time, by chance, when they found themselves in the same inn, one journeying north, the other south. Waller introduced himself, expounding in the most gratifying manner on HM's achievements and innovations, before progressing to the opportunities in that county. This was a new world for the new century now beginning, Waller said, a second Eden, a vast, untilled garden of minerals waiting to be cultivated by a man of wisdom and experience, a man of energy and insight, a man with the genius to raise the necessary capital.

It was a barbarous region, the natives without schooling,

without speech almost, clothed in rags. The land was rock and fen and bog, not worth enclosing. The rain fell unceasingly, turning gullies to streams and streams to rivers, making marsh of every flat place.

Yet here thrifty nature had chosen to lay up her stores of silver and copper and lead, stacked and sealed and ready for use.

The numbers were beguiling. In the great mine that Waller compared to Potosí, the sun vein was eleven foot wide, with seven foot six inches in ore, yielding more than fifty ounces of silver to the ton. The east vein was four foot wide at its narrowest, and in places eight foot in solid ore. The bog vein, of potter's ore, was four foot wide. There were further veins, each at least a yard wide, of silver lead, green copper (three tons of copper to every twenty of ore), and brown copper (five tons to every twenty).

And that was but one mine of more than a score available for leasing.

Waller had calculated that in the first year, having drained the water from the main veins, fifty miners would raise one thousand tons. By the fifth year, eight hundred miners would raise sixteen thousand tons. The washed ore was merchandisable at 3s. and 7d. a ton. After subtracting the cost of bone ash, casks, candles, buckets, storage, and the mending of bellows, the lessees would clear an annual profit of £171,970 9s. 9d.

HM brought in his cousin and a number of other gentlemen with whom he had done business, and the Company of Mine Adventurers was formed. Like conspirators of less worthy causes, they exchanged letters and documents, met in inns and private rooms, the flames lighting their faces as they plotted ways to fund their enterprise.

"A prospectus," one would say, "advertising the benefits to the investor and to the nation."

"Stating the portion to be set aside for charitable uses," another would add.

"A plan of the mines."

"Accounts to show their future value."

"A lottery," said one—later they wouldn't remember who.

Lotteries were the entertainment of the age. The crowds flocked to them as to fairs and executions. The more distant the prize, the more certain they were of winning.

The Company would issue twenty-five thousand tickets. Prizewinners would receive shares. Those who drew blanks would be entitled, when the mines ultimately turned a profit, to their original outlays. There was no risk, no loss.

The Company advertised the scheme in newspapers and handbills. Subscribers included nobles and aldermen, a former lord mayor of London, a director of the East India Company, grocers, cobblers, widows and orphans, the poor of the village of Empingham. A fifth of the tickets were sold on the first day, all within two months.

And there, nature put her pert nose in the air and turned her back on them.

In this wild country, it was the dead work that was the problem: blasting, tunneling, propping, draining, draining, always draining. Whole years were spent pumping water. Even the newest, most costly engines struggled. The floods always returned.

A little ore was raised here, a little there. But after the drilling and the draining, certain necessary payments to friends and accomplices, and such transfers and long-term loans as, having examined his conscience, HM judged himself entitled (only those purchases required by his position: minor lordships, a second, very modest estate), there never seemed to be anything left to repay the investors.

He did what he could to put good news in place of bad. There is a difference between lying and presenting the best possible outcome, which no reasonable man could call fraud. Yet even HM, feeling queasy, found himself pleading with Waller to somehow speed the works—employ more men, buy more engines, open more levels, any by-our-lady thing.

As the creditors started to bleat, the Adventurers conspired again. They made more shares and sold them to more share-holders. They borrowed money. They lent money. They set up their own bank to issue bills (hadn't the Goldsmiths and the Hollow Sword Blade Company done the same? Hadn't the king himself when he needed money for war?), scant months before the Bank of England, like a jealous wife, seized all such activities for herself.

They were left with one bleak calculation: To raise ore required money. To raise money required ore.

He faces more troubles

The bay drops a forefoot in a hole, throws Shiers to the ground, and pulls up, trembling, on three legs. Shiers is bruised and pet-tish, but the horse is useless and must be shot. It is decided that Shiers will follow the path back to the mine, where he can find some conveyance to the inn. HM will continue on alone. That is, with Tall John.

In the very moment they part company with Shiers, it seems to HM that the rain becomes wetter, the wilderness wilder, himself more mortal. He feels a greasy sweat beneath his cold clothes and considers that he may have a touch of fever. He reminds himself again that he is an Adventurer, a genius richer than the mines below, knighted by His Royal Majesty, et cetera, et cetera.

As they climb again, the track fades into the surrounding thin tapestry of moss and sedge. Soon there is nothing more to see than the subtle byways left by savage creatures on their errands.

Tall John marches ahead as if a line of beacons blazes before him, leading HM down a hill so steep that Cassandra and her rider grunt, and along a valley where the marsh coalesces into a small river. Raindrops stipple the surface, reminding HM of the flies dancing at evening over the fishing pond on his father's estate, and then of the time Richard pushed him into that pond and ran home laughing. HM, green with duckweed, dripped slowly after him, intending to creep in unseen. But Richard had forethought him. Every member of the household who could be called from his duties was assembled to point and mock.

They ascend to a high plateau where reeds huddle in slaty pools. Cassandra's mood has become stoical, with a touch of resentment, like one of the less successful martyrs. When Tall John drops back to ride beside HM, she barely bothers to flick her tail.

"The mare thinks herself too good for our paths," says Tall John.

"The mare cost nearly thirty guineas," says HM (rounding up from twenty-two).

Tall John gives a fancy-gentlemen-and-their-fancy-horses shrug. "The best servant is a trusty companion," he says. "Spratt knows where to put his feet. Does not mind getting them wet."

HM glances at Spratt's woolly round flanks and decides not to pursue this topic. "How much farther is it?"

"The farthest point of a journey is its end."

"And what is that in by-our-lady miles?"

"Have no fear. I have led other gentlemen to a just reward."

HM chews on this for a moment. "A well-lived life is its own reward."

"I've heard that in the city, merchants catch the rain before it falls to the ground. That the poor must pay for even the air in their streets."

"What low people do in their muddy hollows is of no concern to me."

"There may be mud on the highest mountain," says Tall John, and, before HM can conceive of any kind of retort, moves on ahead, Spratt putting his wet feet wheresoever he chooses.

As they advance, the vegetation is alchemized to bronze and pewter, ocher and lead. Dwarfish worts and spurges drown in every hoofprint. Great plashy expanses of dark bog grass are topped with quivering white flags. If this is not the realm of goblins nowhere is.

And these goblins are well known among miners and Adventurers—the tapping of their hammers signals the vein. A modern man like HM may scoff at such superstitions, but the method is proven. There are many cues that a rustic is more fitted to detect than a gentleman. Underlying minerals influence the spring herbage, planting directions for those who live close to the ground—just as in winter, heat rising from the ore to the frost writes letters only the unlettered can read.

And HM needs to believe that, with or without the help of goblins, Tall John has made a find. Because even such ore as the Company has been able to raise is yielding a paltry four or five ounces a ton. Because the debts are thirty times the remaining capital. Because the creditors will not accept promises, pleas, or yet more shares, but, like overindulged children, demand everything right now. Because they are taking their case to Parliament. Because HM's defense is to lay the blame with Waller, who plotted from the beginning to cozen him. Because Waller has in his possession correspondence containing certain unwise statements that might, if made public, throw a poor light on HM's actions, on his knowledge, and on what he has subsequently said about his actions and knowledge. That might, if taken in an ungenerous spirit, cast HM as unscrupulous, crooked, a liar, a thief even. Because if he is found guilty, he may lose the Company, his sons' inheritance, his very freedom. For all these reasons it is essential that Tall John has located a seam of finest ore, right on the surface, fat and firm as floorboards.

The mist descends—the other realm

The rain has thickened to a dense curtain. If there is danger ahead, it will arrive without warning. Spratt seems eager to meet it, is speeding up, pulling away. HM spurs Cassandra, who for a few begrudging moments concedes a faster amble. (She will be ambling to market next week, HM vows.) The gray pony glides on, a two-headed centaur, round a ridge and out of sight.

When HM rounds the same ridge, he pulls up short. A few yards ahead, the land plummets into a great bowl of white mist. There is no sign of Tall John.

HM cannot see any path down into the bowl and is not keen to improvise one. He nudges Cassandra forward to take a closer look, but she digs her front feet in and, when he whips her on, wheels her rump around, stating that she has no intention of venturing that slope.

"Halooo!" he calls. And then again, "Halooo!"

Cassandra rolls an eye at him, contending that his shouts are as likely to attract wolves and footpads as Tall John.

"They will reach you first," he says. All the same, he checks his pistol and regrets leaving the musket with Shiers.

He calls once more.

Tall John cannot be out of earshot already. This is some knavery. The man has tied cloths through the pony's harness, as tinkers do, and is creeping away, leaving HM to face an unknown peril.

The list of his enemies is long. Waller. Those in the Company who support Waller. The Company's creditors. Its rivals.

The laborers. The ex-laborers. His envious neighbors, who, not content with digging up his wagonways, went so far as to plot an attempt on his person.

He calls yet again, anger propelling his voice a little farther.

It occurs to him then that perhaps he is misjudging Tall John. Perhaps the lout has merely fallen to his death. Perhaps he and the gray pony lie at the bottom of an abyss with broken necks.

The mist is surging over the ridge behind him, islanding him on this shelf like a mariner on a foreign shore, with only his wits to guard him from death or humiliation.

He listens. He hears Cassandra's breath, her creaking harness. The primitive croaking of a moorland bird that has never apprehended music. Water seeping from every surface, oozing and dripping and trickling, and a gurgling like the laughter of small children setting nutshells to sail and watching them bob and founder. Grasses sighing, and beetles and worms crawling among the stems and burrowing down between them. Roots pushing into the thin soil and sliding around pebbles and rocks and seams and veins, knotting them in place, hoarding them, hiding them.

HM did not achieve his current position by sitting impotently, waiting for deliverance. He will not succumb. He has taken "paths before untrod." It is his right and his destiny to enter nature's abode, "the smiling offspring from her womb remove, and with her entrails glad the realms above."

He points Cassandra toward the rim of the bowl and unleashes upon her such an almighty thwack that his whip slips from his grasp. For a moment it seems she will resist again, but she is too tired or bored, too habituated to complying with decisions from on high.

Down they go, through a white tunnel that leads to more white. The mist rolls and buffets, like a jeering crowd. The slope is steep and faced with loose, wet scree. The mare skids, recovers, skids again.

"You must be kidding me," says Cassandra.

It is clear what has happened. Like those travelers of tales old who bargain with the devil, they have crossed to another realm, an enchanted, purgatorial kingdom where men babble and beasts speak, where time moves by inches. Outside, years pass, then centuries. Wars are fought, empires spread and contract, fortunes are lost and recovered. The world is changed utterly.

But HM knows how this future will be, for it is he who has molded it, he who can see it even now, through the billowing drapes of tomorrow.

His accusers are buried with their lawsuits in long-neglected graves. His sons and his sons' sons have nurtured his legacy through the generations and carried it to every corner of the domain. Forests and pastures and all such wastes as they have passed through today are sown with mines and mills and workshops. Nature herself is employed to break open her treasury. No rock is too hard to breach, no material too elusive to extract. Her engines run day and night, needing only one man to oversee and perhaps a few boys to carry messages. Every valley, every mountain, every high street is lined with rails carrying kettles and coins and candles. Where wind is lacking, great bellows worked by lungs of fire blow into the canvas.

And where are the idle wastrels and the coneyheads? All such men are properly employed now, not in mines and fields, where nature's powers have supplanted them, but in countinghouses and chanceries and stockrooms. Every village and hamlet has its school and library and coffeehouse. Every manor house has its university. Even the poorest are provided with all the learning necessary to make them useful. In well-tended rows, they bow their heads to their tasks.

And past their windows, at the command of her masters, the earth's wealth flows. No longer curbed by whining investors or petty regulations, commerce runs swift and smooth and ceaseless, unfeeling, untiring, a machine of perpetual and profitable motion. The rails gleam in the dawn like spiderwebs, and the song of gears drowns the birds. At night, the stars, the planets, the moon herself are dimmed by the glitter of furnaces.

Faint noises can be detected through the mist, and an enticing, almost familiar scent. Cassandra lifts her muzzle, cheered by the possibility that their destination may be near. She had a stableboy once who, in lieu of good-bye, gave her warm bran mash with cider and sliced apples, and ever since, she has hoped for such reward at the end of each journey. In her narrow skull, experience and speculation are pressed together, the days that have disappointed layered with those more frequent imaginary ones that have not, and compounded by increments into a single substance in which the main element is sweetened, hallucinatory mush. She lengthens her stride and hurries toward whatever lies ahead.

Tristan Hughes

Up Here

T HE DECISION HAD BEEN MADE the night before, though I'd played very little part in it. We'd been lying in bed and she'd said it had to be done. And because the day had been long and we were tired and a bit drunk, I thought it might not stick, and hoped it wouldn't. It seemed like the kind of thing you decided at night and safely forgot in the morning. But it wasn't forgotten. We were going to shoot the dog. Or rather, I was going to shoot the dog.

That didn't have to be spoken of at all. Up here, it was the kind of thing you did for your lover. In other places, you might be expected to do other things. I had never shot a dog before, but I was determined to now because I'd never done any of those other things in those other places. I wanted to show—to her, to myself—that I was getting better at being in love. I wanted to show her how committed I was. I couldn't bring her twenty-thousand-dollar bills, but I could shoot her dog for her. "I'll do it," I'd said, before she'd even had to ask. That was my part of the decision.

. . .

The sun wasn't fully up yet and the mosquitoes were bumping frantically against the screens on the windows. They were always at their most bold, or desperate, during these early hours; it gave an added, grating octave to the high, whining hum of their wings. My girlfriend, who worked as a naturalist in the park that surrounded us, had explained to me they were mainly crepuscular insects. "*Crepuscular*," I'd said. "They use that word in biology?" Up until then I'd never heard it outside of a poem. It was like that with words here sometimes: they turned up in ways and forms you didn't expect. For instance: what exactly did *park* mean in a place where they were as big as countries?

"Fucking crepuscular insects," I whispered.

My head was hurting. I'd been more than a bit drunk.

"They're only doing what they have to do," my girlfriend said, turning around to face me.

She must have been awake for a while, but I hadn't noticed because she'd been lying with her back to me. Now I could see she'd been crying and knew that what she'd decided had been remembered, and that it had stuck. After a second or two, she turned her back to me again and I reached over and gently touched her head and we ended up making love in that slow, muffled morning way, at once coy and intimate, where your bodies touch but your stale breath is carefully exhaled in other directions. It began slowly, but then she started pushing herself back onto me, strongly and roughly, as though it was after midnight and we were making a different kind of love. Afterward, she jumped out of bed and held up her hand so I wouldn't follow her.

"Give me fifteen minutes," she said. She wanted to say goodbye. And for the first time, it dawned on me that I actually would have to shoot the dog.

"Okay?" I said when she returned.

"Okay," she said, returning her head to her damp pillow.

We lay there for another few minutes. I went to brush a strand of dark hair from her forehead.

"I said okay," she said.

I got up.

"Make sure you feed her first. I just couldn't."

For a moment I hesitated. A knight picturing the thundering hooves and quivering lance as his lady ties the ribbon onto his arm.

"We could take her to the vet?"

"We decided," she said.

Up here, even mosquitoes did what they had to do.

The dog was standing beside the kitchen table. She took a long time to get onto her feet in the morning, so once she was up she tried to stay that way as long as possible. The world she stood on had become a thin wire. Her body was slowing, her insides were failing, her bones were going: she had to be careful about each move she made. Every morning, my girlfriend crushed painkillers into her food, as well as pills for arthritis—both of which I think were meant for humans. Sometimes she gave her a few tablets of her depression medication too.

I placed a bowl of kibble by the door and she teetered over to it, looking confused; it wasn't me who usually fed her. After she ate, her hips and back legs began to judder and tremble. Her nails made a doleful clickety-clack on the wooden floor until she could no longer sustain herself and collapsed into a sitting position. Every day the wire got thinner. She looked up at me, her eyes sorrowful, perplexed, ashamed, until I could no longer bear it. I have always been moved by the eyes of old dogs.

She remained sitting as I went to fetch my girlfriend's rifle. It felt strange in my hand (I didn't come from a place where people owned them) and for a moment (there were often these moments) I felt that strangeness extend outward to take in my whole situation. Here I was, living in a house beside a lake, in the middle of a great forest, holding a gun. When I returned, I tried to keep it out of sight behind my leg, but as soon as the dog saw it, she dragged herself painfully back up. Her expression had altered. She looked suddenly delighted, restored. It was excitement her legs trembled with now. Sometimes, in the autumn, my girlfriend would take her out to hunt grouse on the logging roads, and this is what she must have associated the gun with. When she followed me out the door, she didn't even notice the greenness of the leaves.

And how very green they seemed! Up here the summers were short. There was so much to be packed into them. The colors, the warm air, the sun, the smell of fresh sap and sweet gale, the glitter of light on the lake, all of them felt concentrated, intensified—a hallucination through a magnifying glass; a glass of bright cordial whose sweetness sometimes left you feeling a little sick.

The dog stopped on the deck to sniff a stale hot dog bun. There were empty bottles of beer strewn everywhere, and saucers full of cigarette butts, and pieces of burnt meat—who knew what they'd once been—on the barbecue. A white sun hat lay bedraggled at the edge of the shoreline. On the dock was a pair of shattered sunglasses. It had been a long day.

None of it had been planned. Some of our neighbors—a couple about our age—had come by after lunch to borrow my girlfriend's generator. Another couple (there were only three houses on the bay) had been driving past in a boat and seen us and stopped by to say hello. They were also about our age and had two children, and in no time at all these children had changed into bathing suits and were jumping and diving from the dock.

And pretty soon we adults were running back and forth from house to house, fetching cases of beer and searching through freezers for meat. And pretty soon after that we were all jumping and diving from the dock, happily addled by the heat and light, as reckless as the children under the high sun. At one point, I slipped away from the others to sit beneath some red pines and hold my own happiness to myself for a minute or two. I watched my girlfriend dive and swim. The elegant arch of her back, the easy grace of her swimming strokes—how beautiful and unencumbered she appeared, uplifted by the light and water. How lucky we were to live on a lake like this! How golden our lives seemed, lived so far away from anywhere! What a wonder it was, this magic trick of distance, that could conjure you so effortlessly into another existence. In a different far away my other life stuttered and failed, and here it meant nothing. It was no great fall, hardly a topple really (though up close it might have felt that way). I'd published a few books and not many people had read them. Twice a week I drove into the little town down the highway and sat at the computer in the library and looked at my emails as though they were the flickering of some nameless, inconsequential star. I saw its light but not its slow implosion (which was maybe the kind of expression that had meant not many people had read those books).

Later on, we all sat on the deck and drank. I found myself standing with the men by the barbecue, burning the mysterious meat. They were talking mostly about hunting and fishing and other things I didn't know that much about yet. But my enthusiasm felt boundless. I told them I was very keen to learn about these things. I told them I wanted to share in the kind of stories they told. One of them ran an outfitting business, the other one fought forest fires, and I told them I admired and envied them for having such a practical purchase on things, for being so solidly enmeshed in their world. I think that may have been the phrase

I really used. The firefighter smiled indulgently, and surreptitiously put the beer he was about to hand me back in the case.

At some point, quite a few drinks later, the outfitter took me aside and said I should marry my girlfriend, that she was a truly wonderful woman. I agreed wholeheartedly and said I'd like to do that very much and he thumped me on the back and we clinked beer bottles and I felt like a stand-up guy among stand-up men.

We threw horseshoes. We swam some more. We lit the sauna and sweated and drank and said all manner of things. My girlfriend told a story about spending a year homeless in a city when she was a teenager, and everybody laughed as if it was funny. That was the way she described it. But I knew it hadn't been funny and wondered why she'd brought it up. Maybe she'd thought if she told it here, at this time and in this place, she'd be able to laugh at it all like the others had. It felt like the kind of day you could think things like that.

She left the sauna soon after and I waited a second or two before following her out. She'd walked to the rocky shoreline near the edge of the property and was crouching down toward the water. I thought she was upset because of what had happened in the sauna.

"Hey there," I called out to her.

"You've got to help me," she called back to me.

And I ran toward her. Everything felt possible that day.

It was the dog. She must have gotten excited about everyone leaping into the lake and followed them in, forgetting in a euphoric instant the thinness of the wire beneath her. She was trying to get up over the rocks, but her hind legs had failed and she was scrabbling pitifully against them with her front paws. She was half drowned. It was a terrible sight.

"Please, you've got to help me," my girlfriend said. She was trying to pull the dog over the rocks but couldn't get a proper hold of her. She was a big dog.

Once I'd hauled her out of the lake, I carried her into the house and dried her with a towel.

"She could have drowned," my girlfriend kept saying.

"But she didn't," I kept replying.

By the time the others returned from the sauna, the light was beginning to fade and it was something of a relief when they made their excuses and began to leave.

It had been a long day, in a short season.

The dog followed me along the dirt road that curved around the shore of the bay. Now and again, she'd stagger a few feet off the dirt and sniff the trunk of a tree, trying to pick up some scent that to her failing senses must have seemed as faint and fleeting as grains of pollen in a breeze. We passed through stands of birch and cedar and pine, past outcrops of lichen-mottled granite, along the sides of lonely pools edged with sphagnum and cattails. We could have walked a hundred miles and seen no more—or no less—than this. She suited these wild places. I was never sure what mix she was, but there was definitely husky in there—and I'm sure some wolf too. She'd been out at the lake for almost five years and had her routes and territories. It was the reason my girlfriend had not wanted us to drive the many hours it would have taken to get to a vet. The journey would have been traumatic for her. She wanted her to die where she had lived longest and happiest.

About half a kilometer or so down the road we came upon my neighbor's daughter. She was searching for wild asparagus. It was the kind of place where that's what children really did. Although in actuality my girlfriend had planted the asparagus a few years before just so the girl could search for it. It was the kind of place where that's what grown-ups really did.

She looked up from a blueberry bush. "What are you doing with that gun?"

"I'm hunting grouse," I lied.

"But it isn't the season yet."

"I'm practicing, for when it is the season."

The second lie came even more quickly and effortlessly than the first. Being a killer—or being about to become one—seemed to help in that way.

"Have you seen any asparagus?"

"No," I said. "But I did see some back near your house."

"Really? I looked around there already."

"It's easy to miss."

"Are you *sure*?"

"Oh, I'm sure," I said. "I'm one hundred percent sure. I'm one thousand percent sure. The dog here sniffed it out."

"That dog's too old to sniff anything out."

"You'd be surprised what this old dog can smell."

"Okay," she said. "If you *promise* it's there."

"I promise."

The dog and I waited until she was long out of sight before we carried on. I didn't want her wandering anywhere near where we were going. I wasn't experienced with guns. Who knew what accident might happen? It was bad enough I was killing this dog.

We'd walked about a kilometer and a half and the dog was beginning to tire when we came to a narrow side road. It led up to a small clearing where my outfitter neighbor kept a reefer truck to hang deer and moose carcasses during the hunting season—which had made it seem an apt enough place for what I had to do. What I hadn't taken into account was that every hunting season the dog snuck up there in search of scraps of meat, and every season my neighbor had to go up there and chase her away. The dog knew she wasn't supposed to go up this road with people watching and didn't trust me when I tried to coax her.

"C'mon, old girl," I pleaded.

She looked at me. She knew her territory.

"It's okay," I said.

"Please," I said.

Things weren't going that well. It wasn't the executioner who usually begged.

Fortunately, before leaving the house, I'd stuffed a handful of Milk-Bones into my pocket—for a sort of last supper—and so I started up the track dropping one behind me every few steps. Now she followed me. It was like the very worst kind of fairy tale.

Occasionally, on sunny days, I'd go down to the park's visitor center—this park that was as big as a small country—and bring a picnic lunch for my girlfriend. Often, after we'd eaten, I'd stay on and watch with the other visitors—mostly families and campers, and various outdoors people—while she delivered talks about the natural history of the park. She was knowledgeable and charming and it made me proud to watch and listen to her. She told better stories than me. The ones she told for the visitors were of appointed times and seasons; of cycles; of a world where everything fitted together and carried on. The turtles laid their eggs at this time, the bears hibernated at another. In the autumn, the trout spawned, the walleye in the spring. She rolled it all out for them like a more upbeat Ecclesiastes.

But in private she told me different ones. The seasons sometimes didn't arrive when they were supposed to. And the animals tricked by them fared badly. When the snow came late, the snowshoe hares, white nuggets in the dun landscape, were taken easily by hawks and foxes. When the spring came too early, the moose, still wearing their winter coats, would overheat and die of stress. Ice stayed too late and thawed too early. Rivers dried up and then overflowed. Fish couldn't lay their eggs. Frogs perished in multitudes. And when she told me these stories, it seemed as though being a naturalist was more like doing PR for a Greek god. There was no absolute where or when or how. It could do whatever the fuck it liked. It didn't really give a shit about anything. It was a wanton boy with a fly.

It's hard trying to live between different stories, ones that will not fit together. Sometimes at night my girlfriend locked herself in the bathroom to cry. Sometimes she made love with me so roughly, and then so sadly, it wasn't like love at all. And outside the window the sap would drip down the bark of the black trees and the loons would keen and the mosquitoes would fly berserk through the dark like miniature warlocks on their broomsticks.

And the next day, she'd have to talk to the visitors again, while they took pictures of turtles sleeping on logs, and lifted their faces to the bright sun, and spoke of beautiful sunsets.

I remember once we journeyed deep into the park together. The place we went to was so remote we had to get flown in there by boat plane. It was my birthday and she'd arranged it all as a gift. The plane landed us beside a long sand spit that stretched across the narrow bay of a lake. The whole place was unusual for up here: the water was almost turquoise, the sand soft and fine and white, as though it had been miraculously transported from somewhere closer to the equator. It was like a tropical pearl in a boreal oyster. After we put up our tent, we swam naked and lay together on the hot sand. We'd brought a thermos of gin and tonic and as we passed it back and forth, she told me she wished she'd met me ten years before, and I laughed and said what mattered was that we'd met at all. Maybe it would have made a difference back then, she said. A difference to what? I asked. She never answered that. When the thermos was empty, I got up and ran to the end of the spit, tipsy and exhilarated, my bare skin still warm from the sand. On returning I told her this was one of the most beautiful places I'd ever been. Come with me,

I said, getting ready to run back along the spit. I'm so glad you like it here, she said. I really am. She began to lift herself up but then paused and dropped back onto the ground. She looked at me, and then she looked past me toward the end of the spit, as though she were calculating the distance.

"Wherever you go," she said, "wherever you end up—there you are."

This time it was I who could offer no answer, even though it had not really been a question. I felt my tipsy joy begin to evaporate, the gin and tonic settling flat and cold in my stomach. I already missed the warmth of the sand.

The clearing was a dreary place, even in the summer. It was shaded by a stand of tall pines. The outfitter stored his retired boats there, and various pieces of broken and abandoned machinery. There was an old tarp covering the floor of the reefer truck, to catch the blood of the hanging carcasses, and it occurred to me it could be useful for carrying back the dog. How could it be that I was now somebody who had such thoughts! Was this what being practical was? Was this being happily enmeshed in the world?

I was pretty sure the dog's hearing was mostly gone, but when I pulled back the bolt on the rifle, she looked up. She was expecting to see a grouse. But seeing none she returned to her Milk-Bones. She chewed them slowly.

After a while, it was as though I could see every one of the gray hairs about her muzzle and hear each separate poplar leaf flicker and the wing of every fly beating in the air, and even feel the slight tremor in the earth beneath my feet as the worms began their hungry ascent toward the surface. I would experience this same sensation later—at bedsides and in white corridors and in certain recollected minutes and hours—but I will never know more vividly the terrible intimacy and clarity of last moments than I did in that clearing, watching an ancient dog eat Milk-Bones.

I ended up sitting down on the grass beside her. I rubbed her ears.

"Hey there, old thing," I said.

I didn't know exactly how old she was. My girlfriend had told me how this dog had been her one constant companion— through failed love affairs and family estrangements and brief lives in other places. And then as we'd lain in bed the night before, she'd told me how she felt her love for it had morphed into a cruel and selfish desire to eke out its dwindling life, one she could take no pleasure in. She's suffering, she'd said, and there's only one thing that can stop it. But how can you tell how much she's suffering? I'd asked. Why decide now? Because if I don't decide, then I'll just keep on not deciding, she'd said.

"What are we going to do with you," I whispered to the dog.

I scrabbled for alternatives, some useless, some cowardly. I would walk her far into the woods and abandon her. I would ask the outfitter or the firefighter to shoot her.

The Milk-Bones were almost done.

"What are we going to do," I shouted.

The dog looked up at me and I held her around her neck and pressed my face deep into her matted coat, which was rank with all the years that had gone and all the ones that would not be. "And so here we are," I wept. "Here we are." And when I released her from my arms, she bent down to the bones again and I picked up the rifle and shot her in the back of the head.

Afterward, I wrapped her in the tarp and dragged her back to the house.

My girlfriend had already decided where she wanted the dog to be buried: on a rocky point at the edge of the bay. She hadn't wanted to see the body, and so I rowed it out there on my own. A breeze had begun to blow across the lake, and the boat thumped gently over the crests of the small waves. One of the dog's paws had come loose from the tarp, and her nails scraped across the aluminum bottom, in almost the exact same rhythm as they'd done against the floorboards in the morning. When I arrived, I removed the tarp and laid her down on the moss between two cedars. There was too little earth for a burial.

I would return there only once. I had not been up here for some time—an amount I could not then bring myself to properly measure or calculate, to unpick from the blurry gray knot it had all become. At first there was no sign of her at all, but eventually, I dug my hands into the moss and found a few small bones. The eagles and vultures and foxes had left nothing else.

I rowed out there on my own that time too. I'd had to borrow a boat from the outfitter, and as I returned past the dock, I could see the winter ice had warped some of its boards. I'd promised myself I wouldn't stop off at the house, but in the end I couldn't help myself. I'd noticed one thing before I reached the door, and that was enough for me. Even though it was getting toward evening, there were no mosquitoes on the window screen. There was no longer anything inside to draw them to it.

And that was because of another decision. And how did you learn to live with a decision like that? What was it that you had to do? And what here was there where you could do it?

Brenda Walker

The Houses That Are Left Behind

ONE SUNDAY AFTERNOON the intercom buzzed, just as I was setting out the things I needed to cook a meal for my husband's children. I'd already set the table. I wasn't expecting them so early. My husband was barefoot, reading a newspaper in a cane chair in the sun. I laid down my knife and went to the screen, which showed an image of the caller, shot from a vantage point above her head. It was a stranger, a girl in ugly sunglasses. When I greeted her, she began to talk, immediately, about a cell phone; she thought we had given her a phone or she had our phone. Her voice was metallic, an electronic interruption in an afternoon of low, winter sunshine. We were going to have to investigate.

I waited for my husband to pull on a pair of shoes, looking at the girl as she folded her arms and twisted miserably from side to side. I could see her shoulders clearly, her cheap sweater, her dark springy hair.

We didn't plan to invite her upstairs. We could deal with whatever she wanted in the foyer quickly. When she took off her sunglasses to speak to us, I could see that she was crying. She told us she'd bought a mobile phone from a couple in our building. They made the transaction in this foyer, and they said they lived in our apartment, number ten. She paid them a thousand dollars, then the phone stopped working.

Her hands were dirty. She must have been digging hard, bare-handed in the earth, to get that amount of black dirt under her nails. We live in a region of parks. Opposite us was the park that overlooked the Parliament building. It's planted with specimen trees, none belonging to this country. A little above us, on our side of the street, following a high escarpment that is one of the few scenic places in this flat city, lies a vast expanse of orderly lawns and monuments. We often walk along the escarpment paths in the early evening. In the dimming park young girls in hijabs play football with their textiles flying; babies are photographed on pale small rugs; lovers talk, frowning, in the privacy of lawns beyond earshot of the paths. As twilight deepens, teenagers occupy a Victorian gazebo, and the smell of cannabis, syrupy with natural oil and boyish saliva, drifts over memorials to fallen soldiers, over the whispering wall and the eternal flame.

There were so many places near where we live where the girl in the foyer could bury something or dig up whatever had been left in the earth for her to recover.

She said that she'd come to plead with the phone sellers to unblock the phone. My husband suggested the obvious things: she should contact the telco company, then the police. I suspected that just one of the things she told us was true: she'd lost some money.

After we said good-bye and watched her stumble, still crying, across the road towards the Parliament building, my husband said no, it wasn't money she'd lost, it was love. She'd fallen in love with a man, he lived in our building with his wife, he gave her the wrong apartment number, she was trying to force a confrontation. The man had given her the phone so that they could talk privately, then he decided to end the affair and cut her off.

We had some experience with this kind of thing.

When we arrived and unpacked, he noticed a long, fair hair on one of the sofas. We'd bought some of the furniture that was already in the apartment; we were busy and it was easier than going shopping. The hair belonged to the previous owner, we decided, although we knew the owner was a man and unlikely to have long, fair hair. A visitor, then. A woman who visited that man and lay on the sofa. A passing woman, not a wife. We had the sofa cleaned. We were away often, at work, or at another house belonging to my husband. The cleaners were no good. Time passed and more hair drifted from the sofa: fine and fair. I picked it up and disposed of it, absentmindedly, until one day my husband called a locksmith. After that there were no traces of strangers.

Sometimes I wonder about the woman who met a man in our apartment. How they must have rushed past our things, hand in hand, how she flung herself beneath her lover, overjoyed, laughing, both of them laughing at love and trespass.

I reminded myself that the woman we met in the foyer had dark hair.

I thought her crisis had to do with something that was supposed to be buried, something she scrabbled for with her desperate hands, until she admitted to herself that it wasn't there.

The children came for their meal, they ate plate after plate of rich food, because they lived in a student household and this cooking was one of the small pleasures of their week. It was almost possible to forget the crying, dark-haired girl. Our dining table was lit with a row of candles on a shelf behind my eldest stepdaughter. A person sitting on a park bench near the Parliament building could see right into the apartment, despite the dim candlelight. They could watch my stepdaughter's careful laughter and see her proud, slim dress; they could see her father, or the other children, or me.

I left the table and went into an adjoining room and closed the door. The only light in this room came from the streetlights below, which illuminated a wide margin of the park. There was no one on the benches. No dark-haired girl, not even one of the sad women who often crept away from an expensive rehab clinic on the far side of the park to sit among the trees in the darkness. But I had reason to be vigilant about all witnesses, man or woman.

Because of Neil and his long campaign of threats against me, I was always slightly afraid. Neil stalked his targets, gathering domestic information that he interlaced with his threats. He was capable of taking up position opposite the Parliament like a military officer on duty, motionless, guarding the small personal hinterland of his resentment. I was always slightly afraid, but I was also defiant, determined to be seen, even if the viewers were barking men or solitary lying girls or sad alcoholics, and I never drew the curtains.

In daylight the reflections of the big windows along the front of the apartment make it hard for anyone on the outside to see in. The view from inside, a view of sky and the crowns of trees, is bright and clear. I cook a great deal. I pause, in the kitchen, to stretch and look out through the windows. Herons fly over rooftops from some interior wetland to the feeding grounds on the river. Crows move about singly, or in groups. Wagtails land on our balcony, showing themselves to our elderly house cat, which mews behind glass. Parrots fly in pairs, and so do small brownish-gray birds fast as darts, one leading and the other following a wing beat behind, gliding or climbing and dipping very fast. The second bird lags slightly, so if the first flies through a gap in a moving obstacle — traffic, for example — the second might not be quick enough to follow. Then the first climbs, bewildered, circling back over a mate crushed on the road.

I thought of these birds as I followed the taillights of my husband's car in heavy traffic one evening. My car is smaller, less powerful. He accelerated through a change of lights. Then he pulled over and waited for me, but I swept ahead of him and found myself on a freeway, the tarmac lit by high, majestic orange streetlights, each light at the end of an arc of steel, alone with the giant dark, green and cream traffic signs announcing directions to the airport. I turned back across many empty lanes to where he was waiting for me.

The next day I saw two crows high on the bend of the arm of a streetlight, one upright and the other bent toward it, bowing its head in what seemed to be a moment of worship. Crows make courtship gifts. Woven balls of grass or twigs, presented to one another with some kind of formality, before their love can begin. Crows are not easily led; they don't fly in formation; believing in the joy of speed, they don't take passionate and fatal risks.

Neil was a gardener, a professional, expert with complicated watering systems, which he installed for the very rich. He always wore the casual costume of a senior lawyer on holiday: sockless boat shoes, Bermuda shorts, a soft white T-shirt, a light tan. I thought I saw him recently when I returned to my old suburb to collect my mail. A man was texting intently outside the post office. I thought: Neil will look like that when he gets old. Suddenly I realized it was Neil; he was looking at his phone to avoid meeting my eye and this pleased me, this small act of avoidance, which might have been a moment of shame. I hoped it was shame. No, I hoped it was fear.

I was distracted because the moment I saw Neil I also saw a woman I knew, Juliet, who was walking toward me with a small dog in her arms. It was a chihuahua. Juliet was a lean woman, lean from yoga but not calm; she looked tired, in fact. The dog and Juliet lived next to the railway line. But each day they walked to the river, the zone of the extremely rich, which was surprisingly close to the railway and the sanitation lanes. I knew her history. I liked her, and I hoped she never had cause to run into Neil. Her story had plenty of premium high-grade grief. She didn't need the grief an old low troll could cause. Juliet. Her life ended at the airport in Nice. Or before that, on the drive up from Monaco, watching the clipped hair of her husband's driver from a rear seat in a big car. Now all that is left of that life is the knowledge of how to be very thin. Yoga, walking, a lifelong refusal of fine food, because it is important to be thin. I have to remind myself: the man who dismissed her wasn't her husband. He was just a man, a rich man whose children she bore.

Juliet passed me with a narrow smile. I took a step toward the door of the post office and Neil looked up, then he quickly looked away. I guess he was on his way to his own post office box. He kept a Gmail account in a fake name for the hate mail he sent out from an Internet café in the next suburb. He kept a post office box for correspondences he set up with women. The death threats and hate mail, the weird letters to and from women—it's how he pulled himself together. Some men buy a pint after work, and then they buy another one for a mate and both men relax with their elbows on a bar. Neil had his hate mail.

You didn't have to do much to get mail from Neil. If you cut him off in a merge lane on the freeway, he'd take down your number plate and work his way through his system of contacts until he found your address, and then he'd threaten your life. If you said you wouldn't go to bed with him, you needed a wide margin of regretful flattery, otherwise the hate mail went on for years and years.

It was unlikely that he feared me. The suburb was populated

by addicts, painters, the very rich and so on, but there was no one else, I hoped, like Neil. Neil, that great swearing, barking man, hunched over his phone, unable to meet my eye.

For fifteen years I lived in a series of bad houses, on both sides of the country.

The first house was a long way from our apartment and the spacious parks. It had the sweet smell of wood rot. I was there for a long time, thinking myself blessed, breathing the strange, musky perfume of the house, until a friend visited and told me what the smell really meant: the stumps under the floorboards were decomposing. The house was entirely made of wood, from the rafters to the crumbling stumps, and as it turned out this rotten timber burned like newspaper.

The terrace at the back of the house was shaded by an old fig tree, which produced huge crops of sweet dry figs, year after year. I watched that house burn; the fire brigade came minutes after I first saw smoke pouring from the ceiling. By then it was too late.

All my life I have been protected by my own stupidity, unable to see malice until it was directly in front of me, on paper, in my hand, unable to see flames until they formed above me, creeping along the rafters. I thought I lived in a place of bees and honey. This stupidity has bought me whole seconds of dull happiness, while around me ordinary things ignited fiercely.

The second house was on the other side of the country. My publisher was in the East, and I took leave from my job to work with her on a new book. This house was old and pretty, sitting squarely above a steep road where boys roamed in the early hours, breaking into cars wherever they could. My car was Swedish: solid, with a tough windscreen that never cracked, although it was covered in big boot prints most mornings. Jets flew low in the sky, and at certain times there was a light precipitation of something foul smelling, chemical dew or aviation fuel, most noticeable in the garden when washing was being unpegged from the clothesline.

It was also haunted. How was I to know? I spread out my rugs and arranged my furniture. At that time I was not aware of the lawlessness of the street outside, I had not seen the staunch little car with the tough windscreen covered in angry boot prints, morning after morning. On the day I took possession of the house I just saw bright rooms that gathered themselves beautifully around my belongings.

Something in that house didn't submit to being dead. I woke each night in my bed, and cool air blew down inexplicably on my face, as if a very cold person had closed his lips and blown steadily on my own mouth, my forehead, my shoulder, the back of my wrist. I still remember the feeling when I'm flying and the air-conditioning nozzle is pointing directly at my face. That's exactly what it felt like. When that happens, now, I put down my in-flight magazine, I reach up, twist the nozzle aside and order something steadying: gin. Something to flood the body with false warmth. And I comfort myself: I am flying, I am in flight.

I haven't mentioned the third house, where I lived after I left the haunted house, before I married and moved into our apartment. My book was finished and removalists packed my things for the journey back across the continent. The largest and most fragile item was a dining table, very old and extendable, which had somehow survived the fire, although it was made of wood.

The third house was built of stone; it would never burn. It was the most unhappy place I ever lived. The worst thing about this house was Neil, somebody's husband, polite and handy, at first, willing to hang paintings and lift tubs of house plants from the boot of my car.

But there were other, lesser problems. It had a garage that faced a sanitation lane. A long time ago these lanes were dusty, tufted with long grass and wild fennel, traversed by carts collecting shit and urine from backyard privies. Then they were scraped flat and surfaced with bitumen and issued with the names of English trees. Yew Lane, Linden Lane. Garages and high walls replaced the original fences. Small infill houses appeared among the garages. Green rubbish bins on wheels were drawn up untidily against the walls, which were painted bright shades of gray.

Cars drove slowly past the infill houses, dodging bins, each on their way to a pad of oily paving, and these cars began to trouble a woman who lived in the lane. She spoke to other mothers who lived in the laneway about the dangers of the cars. A child could be killed. She began to make barricades across the laneway with rubbish bins. Drivers had to leave their cars and wearily clear a path for themselves when they returned from work. This woman was not the only problem with the third house: one of the neighbors was a painter, who turned up on my doorstep at odd hours.

Upstairs one of the long bedrooms had a small balcony overlooking a paved courtyard. You could hear the sound of the sea at night in winter. A railway line ran next to the highway at the top of the street, carrying passengers to beach-side stations. Sometimes, in the early morning, the air outside the windows was white and sticky with sea mist. I thought all this was beautiful, or beautiful enough to make me want to stay. I lived there for a long time, without ever really wanting to.

When I arrived, I put my suitcase down inside the front door, thinking suddenly: gardenias. The front path needs a hedge of gardenia. In the meantime a bottle of good wine, a gift from a friend with a vineyard, had broken in my luggage and everything was flooded with wet sweetness, the smell of must. I didn't want to admit to myself that this was a disaster; I told myself it was almost worth the damaged clothes, to smell the old grapes fermented in the climate of a life that had gone. And new clothes could easily be bought; buying new clothes would be an additional pleasure.

Small trees grew in the courtyard. In spring their leaves came, brownish and transparent at first, then broadening, quite quickly, into solid green. I thought of cicadas bursting from their shells, their wings elongating, turning hard in the sun. The courtyard was a sun trap. I began to make a garden. Someone I knew bought a block of land with a derelict orchid house. I asked to see it before it was demolished. Inside I found poor makeshift treasures: a moonflower cactus overflowing the cracked porcelain bathroom basin it had been planted in, succulents flabby from water deprivation and scabbed with old injuries. The orchids were all dead. I carried off the cactus and replanted it, I rescued the succulents, and Neil helped me to lift them from the boot of my car and position them in the courtyard. I carried water to my garden in the early morning, a long sip for every plant.

The gardenias grew tall, making a glossy, broad-leaved hedge. The painter lived on the other side of the hedge. She painted big, realist pictures that I could not afford. If the painter kept her studio windows open, if the night was warm, there was a composite scent: little gardenias and vapor from the turpentine she used to scrub down her failed canvases, cleaning up, starting, more hopefully, again. Then the painter decided that the hedge must be cut down. She was convinced that the wind carried gardenia leaves up into her gutters; she tried to persuade a local addict to clear them. The pitiful and unpaid addict was in no condition to climb a ladder, let alone work at the edge of the painter's roof; I feared for his life.

The gardenias would have to go. And when the gardenias went, all that was left was the occasional wash of turpentine drifting in the air, saying *clean up, start again.*

. . .

When I came to the apartment with my husband, it was hard to believe that I lived there. We met our neighbors in the elevator with brief eye contact and soft greetings. We knew nothing about the neighbors, and we were not keen to learn. We were relieved to be with one another; we weren't sociable. Months after we moved I remembered that my old dining table, then a square shape, suitable for two, was extendable. The extra leaves and the detachable handle that fitted into a delicate bolt under the ledge of the tabletop were in storage, as they had been for many years, but when I retrieved them and wound the stiff handle the top opened out, creaking, like a hidden door opening in an ancient house. I slipped in the heavy wooden leaves. Then I reversed the handle, anxiously, waiting to see if the rods that locked each leaf into its neighbor aligned. The rods slid into sockets that had been prepared for them over a century before, the handle corkscrewed for a final time, and the table was tight, whole and long enough for many guests.

We still kept to ourselves; we invited only the children to eat with us. Like myself, the table had been through fire. It may have been one of the things Neil looked at enviously, as he hung paintings in my previous house, gathering pieces of information, pretending to be a lawyer on holiday and a man with community spirit who was helping a woman establish a home.

Not constantly, just sometimes, I feel a sense of dread. Doesn't everyone? Even Neil, especially Neil. His first life ended when he left his mother's arms for the people who were going to be his new parents. He was given away. When he met his birth mother, he was in his thirties and they had nothing to say to one another. He was practicing his impersonations of the wealthy and his mother was old, stained with cigarettes, a battler from a life long past.

Those past lives. Like houses filled with breath and even laughter until the point where a key no longer fits a lock, the blond girl is left waiting tearfully by the door that no longer belongs to her lover. Her lover will shrug when he arrives and finds his key doesn't fit, and they'll decide to meet in hotels, or not at all. Babies are suddenly handed over, women—and by this I mean myself—fly across a continent, about to begin a long period of solitude, not realizing that that solitude will end and they are just one move away from lying on a sofa with their own hair untied, and laughing and talking softly to a man while the light fades with the traffic noise far below.

Stephanie A. Vega

We Keep Them Anyway

I KNEW HER WELL—and I barely recognized her picture in the paper. In black and white, the colorful shawl and red tablecloth looked ghoulish, the shattered glass around her, otherworldly.

I knew her before she became a sensation at the San Juan fairs. We called her Ña Meli. The woman lived in my neighborhood, in La Chacarita, before they kicked us out and built the fancy park flanking the river that they now call Costanera. It was just a bunch of cardboard boxes and corrugated metal back then. It clung to the lip of the river—muddy, smelly, filled with mosquitoes—like a howling, injured beast.

Ña Meli wrote letters at festivals and fairs. She wrote horrific letters that left you staring at the paper shaking like a leaf. She had a second-grade education and terrible handwriting, but when she wrote the letters, her handwriting changed. Sometimes she used words she didn't even understand. Once I saw her write an entire letter in Portuguese. It was creepy, before we got used to her.

The woman arrived out of nowhere. Running from God knows what, as we all do. She built her home out of burlap, sticks, and Styrofoam—a shelter out of nothing. She was poor among the beggars.

Not a week after she arrived, Ña Meli showed up at my house and said, "I have a letter to write for you."

I stared at her like she was crazy, which I honestly believed she was. I was trying to take a siesta on a bunk I had made out of old tires and plywood from the junkyard where I sometimes worked. I had a second job as a guard at a nightclub and had gotten in late the night before. In shorts, covered in sweat, using my T-shirt as a pillow, I was trying to catch a sliver of shade under a weathered cardboard awning.

She stood firm as if she were a government official or something, with a threadbare pink towel on her head like a turban.

"Give me a piece of paper and *quinientos guaraníes*," she said.

I threw a half-eaten guava at her. Five hundred guaraníes in those days bought you an empanada and maybe even a bottle of Coca-Cola.

She shrugged.

"I guess this Fulvio guy doesn't mean anything to you then," she said over her shoulder as she turned and walked back down the dirt path between our houses.

That first time, after I threw the piece of fruit at her, I stayed put. I didn't give her the satisfaction of sitting up from my nap and calling after her, much less following her, but I wanted to. How the hell did she know about my brother?

It goes without saying that everyone in La Chacarita was poor. Who would pay five hundred for a crazy woman to write a letter? But she would goad us with hints until curiosity got the better of us. We all resisted, as best we could, but no one ever fully walked away.

People would try to negotiate with her, but she held firm at five hundred. The letters were eerily precise. If you don't believe in these things, you probably have your reasons, but the hand-writing, the very phrasing—it was as if someone else had taken her hand.

We got used to it. We would see her running over to some-one's house to sell a letter, like her purse was on fire. She would call out and say, "So and so wants to write you a letter!" She would stand there with her plastic Bic pen and ask for paper and *quinientos guaraníes.*

It had to be done right then and there though, or the moment was lost. "The visitor left," she would say. And if you didn't have money, "Too bad." She was disciplined, that Ña Meli; she walked away. The poor person who had denied her was left with the doubt.

Ña Meli was not that much older than me, maybe thirty when I first met her, but she acted like my grandmother. She acted like she had already been through it all and back, and she didn't take nonsense from anyone.

It wasn't all that frequent at first, the letter-writing. How Ña Meli made her living back then, I don't know. But we all managed.

A few days after I threw that guava at her, curiosity got the better of me. I waited to see if she would come by, but eventually I walked over to her shack.

"Ña Meli," I called in through the little window in the front.

She whistled first and then called me over from the back. She was washing clothes in a plastic bucket on a wooden plank.

"Ña Meli, about that letter." I wasn't sure how to go about asking her.

She wiped her hands on her shirt, a colorful man's shirt, and said, "Watch out for the mud over there," as she led me to a couple of stools next to her house. "There's no way to keep this place dry . . ."

Once we were seated in the little patch of shade next to her house, she asked me if I had brought paper. I said I didn't have any but I did manage to get five hundred guaraníes. I showed her the money and she smiled.

"I don't have any paper either," she said.

We sat there for a while, not saying anything. Swatting at flies, we followed the neighbor's chicken with our eyes as it pecked at the dirt.

Finally, she said, "I have a pen. I'm sure we can find cardboard or something around your house. You have anything to eat?"

Ña Meli was very scrupulous. "I tell everyone," she insisted, before she took my five hundred guaraníes, "you pay to see if someone answers. If no one does, I can't help that."

When we got back to my house, I gave her off-brand cola and leftover soup. She was hungry. She wrote a short note for me on a piece of cardboard, but it wasn't from my brother. I never told anyone.

Most of the messages—and this I know firsthand as well as from her telling me—most were not of great importance. Nothing life-shattering. Most.

But she wrote lots of letters.

Where Ña Meli eventually made her money was at the fairs leading up to the feast day of San Juan, selling letters to adolescent girls. They came in pairs and bought letters for laughs, for the thrill of dabbling in the occult. Those kids had money to burn. Ña Meli would charge two thousand per letter outside the neighborhood, sometimes more, and people paid. She made a good living after a while.

After the first year working at San Juan fairs, people started coming to see her year-round, at the little house she had pieced together just down the dirt path from mine, and she always produced something that either delighted or horrified them. Either way, it kept them coming back.

Even fancy people came after a while. Some drove cars as far as the dirt road would allow them and then continued on by foot. A pregnant woman once paid me a thousand guaraníes to watch her car, just like that, as if I had been standing there waiting for a car to watch. I was waiting for the bus. I pocketed the money and went on my way.

The feast day of San Juan falls on the twenty-fourth day of June, but there are celebrations, fairs, carnivals, and processions all over the country for two or three weeks leading up to it. As soon as it gets cold we look for the traditional foods and the games with fire—*pelota tatá*, *toro candil*, things like that. Finally, on the night of San Juan proper, we burn the effigy of a man; we light a San Juan of rags and kerosene on fire and we cheer as we watch him burn.

These days it's all very modern, and it's harder to find the real, traditional games, but back then when Ña Meli and I started working the fairs, almost every San Juan had a real *toro candil*, a live bull with real fire burning on its horns, and people of faith or good drinking walked over hot coals without burning their feet. Boys waited in line to impress the girls as they climbed greasy poles for prizes and kicked the *pelota tatá*, a ball of cloth lit on fire.

We crossed paths frequently in the month of June. I had some experience as a mechanic and picked up work setting up the Ferris wheels that were all the rage at the time. I piled on whatever job I could get.

The whole month, Ña Meli would work at two or three different San Juan fairs every day, one after the other. She had a cardboard sign that read, "Madame Melie Labé," but everyone knew her as "Ña Meli who writes the letters."

At the fairs, she would set up with a red tablecloth and wear a shiny turban and a colorful tasseled shawl. As her fame grew, she invested in a stack of envelopes and letter-writing paper. Over time she added things to her stand. I have to admit it had a certain flair.

Ña Meli wrote me a dangerous letter once, an ugly, painful letter. The ghost was not all that literate so it was all jumbled up with terrible handwriting. Still, I knew who it was. I knew what he was trying to tell me. In truth, I had known all along. He was a small-time agitator in a forsaken town; it didn't take much imagination to guess what happened.

When they caught my brother, a neighbor tipped me off. I left my drunk father to fend for himself and abandoned the tall bushes of yerba mate I knew he would never get around to harvesting.

As Ña Meli wrote the letter for me I thought, *What good does it do me to know it was muddy after the rain and he slipped?* And I told her. I said, "Ña Meli, be careful. You can't go around writing things like this."

She smacked me on the head with her purse and said, "*Imbécil!* It's not me. They visit me."

I didn't know what to tell her.

"Read it if you want to, burn it if you don't, I don't care," she said. "Just don't leave it lying around, you incompetent *badulaque . . .*" She gave me another smack with her purse for good measure and continued the string of insults as she walked away.

Once, she found a round glass light fixture on the side of the road and brought it home on the bus. She showed it to me.

"What do you think it looks like?" she asked.

"I don't know, a glass light fixture?" I answered.

"No, you idiot," she said. "A crystal ball, don't you see?" She lifted it so I could see it up close. "No?"

It did look like a crystal ball in her hands. It was a kind of white frosted glass, and I could see it getting milky or dark with the light.

"Supernatural," I said.

She showed it to me later, after she had made a Styrofoam base for it and covered it in scraps of tinfoil. It looked like a legitimate crystal ball.

What really made her name, though, was her seal. She sealed her letters with red wax and a stamp. The stamp, I know for a fact, was a small wooden block with the letter "M" in relief. She saw it on the street one afternoon while she was running to catch the bus. She missed the bus for that stamp and had to wait another hour and a half for the next one, but she said it was worth it. She said she believed it was "sent." I believe it was dropped by a distracted nanny hoisting some pampered baby's bag into a fancy car. But what do I know?

The point is, she sealed her letter with her "M" in red wax, and handed it over for the person to read on their own time. Anyone could recognize one of her letters with that red "M."

Ña Meli always wore a colorful turban when she worked at fairs. She took it seriously. From time to time, she would change them. She said the thing would begin to weigh on her, as if she had been standing for hours in a light rain.

She never told me this herself, but I heard that sometimes ugly things came to her, ugly spirits. "Bad visitors," they called them. But she felt that, having given her word and having charged up front, she could not deny even these "bad visitors" their time. She would write down the message and seal the envelope and ask the addressee not to read it.

"Burn it," she would say. "Don't read it."

Knowing that people are curious, and once they pay they want their money's worth, she would write at the end of these letters a second warning in her own handwriting, simply stating, "Burn this. Do not keep it."

But even then, I doubt anyone followed her instructions. Everyone wants souvenirs, even of the worst things.

I often saw Ña Meli in her element, sitting behind her red table with the fancy turban and her homemade crystal ball. Whenever she was at a fair, hers was, without a doubt, the longest line.

But that last San Juan season before she died, the whole month of June, she looked like she could evaporate. Like she could disappear.

There were a lot of bad letters that season—not evil spirits, but spirits who had suffered, and the suffering weighed on her. She changed her turban four or five times a day. She told me she felt like it was raining all the time.

"You don't look good, Ña Meli," I told her one night as we waited for the last bus back to La Chacarita.

She was carrying a heavy bag with the tablecloth, the turbans, and the crystal ball, and I offered to help her. I guess I was getting soft.

She didn't even put up a fight.

It was almost midnight, bone cold and humid. We could see each other's breath, and hers came out like tiny bursts of nothing.

"You have to take care of your health, Ña Meli," I said, just to have something to say.

There was no point in telling her to stop with the heavy letters, with the string of detailed accounts from souls that had been imprisoned, tortured, and raped. Who wanted to know for sure that their loved one had been gunned down or stripped naked, electrocuted, and submerged in a filthy pool? What good was it to know the names of the officers that did it?

Maybe all that rattling about of their names in documents had lured the poor souls back. The "Archives of Terror" had been all over the news, recently discovered in a pile in the back of a minor police station. I saw the picture in the newspaper. It was a mountain of yellowing paper, taller than the armed guards that surrounded it. The picture itself took up half the front page.

Some journalist had heard a rumor that the torture files of the Stroessner government, which had been hastily moved out of Investigaciones, the intelligence headquarters, after the dictator was deposed, were still intact. They had been dumped in the back shed of a remote police station. They only survived, almost four years later, because no one there knew what the stacks of files were. The leadership had been shifted around and the conscripted eighteen-year-olds on mandatory military service that manned the police station had simply not gotten around to burning them.

These files offered a meticulous log of method, application, time, and duration, mechanically typed, in addition to the lists of names of the tortured and killed. It was all over the radio and the TV—you couldn't turn the channel without someone commenting on it. After a while, the thing, like all things, was dying down.

But there was evidence now. There were files and lists for people with money and lawyers to look through. I could guess that much of what Ña Meli transcribed in letters from spirits could be corroborated in the newly discovered Archives of Terror. If I were a spirit, maybe I would also want to tell my story now.

I wanted to warn her, to tell Ña Meli that she was on the losing side, the side of the souls of the tortured, the ones who had already lost. What good was their clamoring for some sort of recognition when we, on this side, were just trying to get by, just trying to get on with our lives?

I knew enough. What good does it do me to know who shot

Fulvio as he ran away from the church shed? What good does it do me to know he slipped in the mud? What good does it do me to know who threw the first punch, breaking his jaw, once he was tied to a chair in Investigaciones? And everything that came after? My brother was a nobody. He never stood a chance. I knew everything I needed to know before she wrote a single word.

I thought, as I watched her shivering at the bus stop, that those letters, heavy with pain and suffering, they didn't do anyone any good. Nothing had changed. Maybe they would show a little restraint, maybe they'd be better at covering up, but the same people were still there. I wanted to tell her, *Be careful, these are powerful people, and someone is bound to come across a letter of yours sooner or later.*

She smiled and looked out at the distance. She knew what I meant. I knew there was no deterring her.

Poor Ña Meli died one night, not long after that, at a San Juan fair at a school for rich kids. They said it was an evil spirit, a "bad visitor" from the other side that possessed her. But there are more evil demons on this side. In the neighborhood, where no one had the luxury of being innocent, we all knew.

I wasn't there but I was told that she began to tremble, then to shake violently, and that her eyes went completely white. She clawed at the tablecloth before the folding chair gave out and she fell back pulling her red tablecloth and with it her whole display, sending the crystal ball flying before it shattered into a burst of sparkling stars around her.

A few days after she died, they came around asking questions. They shook a few things up, made a real mess, tried to find letters she might have left lying around, but they didn't find anything. That part never made it into the papers.

But the death of the medium at a San Juan fair was immediate, sensational news. The whole country was talking about it. As soon as I saw the black-and-white picture in the newspaper, I found that letter she had written from my brother and I burned it in a barrel a good distance from my house. I had memorized the names and places, but I wished I hadn't. I knew what Fulvio wanted me to know. That was enough.

The first message Ña Meli had written for me, that was from my mother. A few days after the incident with the half-eaten guava. My mother told me that she loved me and that it had pained her to leave Fulvio and me behind when we were still so young. Nothing I didn't already know.

Eventually the cardboard with my mother's message became a replacement shade for my window. Then, when the whole place was razed, it was lost along with everything else. I didn't miss it, or the letter from Fulvio that I burned. I had loved my brother and I had cared in my own way for Ña Meli, the woman who wrote the letters. When they razed La Chacarita, I moved on. I don't need souvenirs.

Anne Enright

Solstice

IT WAS THE YEAR'S TURNING. These few hours like the blink of a great eye—just enough light to check that the world is still there, before shutting back down.

Sometime in the midafternoon, he had an impulse to go home, or go somewhere, and when he lifted his head, of course, it was dark outside. It just felt wrong. Two hours later, he was in the multistory looking for his car and he couldn't find the thing. It was like a lost dog. He clicked the key fob over and over, but there were no answering lights flashing orange on Level 2, where he usually parked, or on Level 3. He went up the little stairs to Level 4, then along the tiny path on the side of the ramp to 4A, brushing against the live cars that were stuck on the slope, nose to tail. He glanced into the windows as he went past and there was a gone look to the drivers' faces; they'd already left for home.

Out there, it was Christmas, but he did not think it was Christmas inside the multistory, the only place in Dublin that had no fairy lights. He walked the last ramp to Level 5. Above him, the black concrete angles of the car-park roof gave way to the night sky, and the car was right there, out in the weather.

He took a moment to glance up and around him at the longest night of the year.

It felt like the end of things. Made you want your religion back. He looked out over the landscape of west Dublin, the square industrial units set among dark young trees, and he entertained the possibility that it would not work this time. This time, the world would spin deeper into shadow. And, because the exit ramps were still jammed, he stayed a minute to check the solstice on his phone. For some reason, it didn't always happen on the same day, but in 2016 it came just when you thought it should, on the twenty-first of December. Not at midnight, though—"the event," as the Web site called it, would happen at 10:44 a.m. Irish time. Somewhere in that moment, whether he believed it or not, the sun would pause in the sky above him, or seem to pause. It would stop in its descent and start its slow journey back to summer and the middle of the sky.

Or this year, he thought, it might not bother.

The M50 was at a crawl, and there was the usual nightmare getting off at the Tallaght exit. He could see the red taillights running in a sequence toward him until he pushed his own brake pedal down. It would be stop-start all the way to Manor Kilbride.

A full forty minutes later, the dual carriageway turned into the old Blessington Road, and oncoming traffic shot by so close he flinched in the glare of the lights. This was the part of the journey that he loved best: the streetlamps gave way to the idea of countryside, and there was a song on the radio as the road opened up ahead. The music made him feel like he could keep driving forever. It was a love song, or a sad song. It reminded him of a time in his life, some town he was in, he could not say where. The loss of that place made him unsure of this one. Or indifferent—as though he could clip an oncoming car and it wouldn't matter. And he didn't know what he was thinking, until a truck bellied past, sucking the air from the side of the car.

It gave him a fright. He checked all the mirrors and shifted in his seat, set his hands more deliberately on the steering wheel. After the turnoff, he followed his own headlights down a country lane, and when he got to the house he sat in the parked car for quite a while.

The night was very big out here. There were three texts on his phone; ten, fifteen minutes apart.

When home?

Will I put yr name in the pot?

Food anyway, half-seven.

When he comes in the door, there is the smell of cooking, the sound of pans and of water pouring into the sink. His daughter is failing to set the table and complaining about the Dakota Access Pipeline. "It's, like, so unfair," she says, and her family neither agrees nor disagrees, because that's just asking for it. Ruth is fifteen. She is arguing with her own shadow, her mother, her teachers, none of whom care about the Dakota Access Pipeline, or not enough for her. "We live in County Wicklow," her mother sometimes likes to remind her. But Ruth does not see what *location* has to do with anything, and he would admire this more, he might even take up the discussion, but she is back on her phone.

He glances over her shoulder and, for once, she lets him see. "What's that?"

"Just," she says. A person called chikkenpenis has sent a funny picture to do with Kanye's breakdown, a video clip that jerks and repeats, endlessly. It's hard to know what the joke is.

And what kind of person spells "penis" right and "chicken" with two "k"s?

"Is that someone you know?"

Ruth just rolls her eyes, types with two thumbs. Cracks up laughing, saying, "Oh, my God. Oh, my God!"

He looks into the kitchen, where his wife is trying to serve up stir-fry out of a too-heavy pan. She is in her track pants. Upstairs all day, at a guess, translating some car manual for solid German euros. Her hair is in a scrunchie, which does not suit her. He tries to remember the song he heard on the radio as he goes over to help, but "Go, go. Out!" she says, and it is gone.

Halfway through dinner, he becomes aware that Ross, his son, is talking to him about something or someone called Stripey. His son says that Stripey knew about death because he always went to Tiger's grave. After a moment, he realizes that Stripey is a cat and so is Tiger. The ones at the childminder's, when Ross was little. Cats from many years ago.

"Animals believe in death," his son says.

"You think?" This is a big statement for a ten-year-old. "Maybe he was just waiting for the other cat to come back out of there. I mean, maybe he doesn't know what the ground is. Maybe he doesn't believe in the ground."

The boy's face goes still, and he looks at his plate.

Ruth goes, "*Kcchchhhh,*" does a Carrie hand out of the grave. And there is an immediate fight. Shouting, pushing.

"Hey, hey, that's enough!" he says.

When they are settled, his wife casts a baleful look at him, and he shoots one back. *What have I done now?*

"I think the cat was sad," she says to Ross. "I think Stripey missed Tiger, don't you?"

She has put her hand on the loose fist his own hand makes beside his plate. This is one of the things they fight about. *Stop undermining your own son.* Which irritates the hell out of him.

Because the boy has to learn how to roll with the punches. "Could have been hungry," he says. "Yum yum. Dead cat."

Ruth starts to laugh. And Ross obliges him with a crooked smile.

His wife pushes back from the table, starts collecting the plates, though they are only just finished.

"Sorry that was so," she says. "It was just a rustle-up."

"Lovely," he says.

Oh, *great*, he thinks. On the longest night, his wife with that look in her eye that says, *Christmas is coming and it is all turning to shite.*

Correction. His wife with a look that says, *Christmas is coming and it is all your fault.*

He pours a glass of wine and almost spills it on himself falling asleep on the sofa after the news. He was dreaming about weather, or discussing the weather with his dreaming self: all autumn it had been so dry, high pressure, clear skies, the leaves drying to dust on the trees, falling like smoke, they'd hung on so long. It occurs to him that Tiger was Stripey's mother. The cat's mother, no less. He says as much to his wife, who is sitting across the room. She looks at him.

"Yes," she says. And he suddenly remembers that his own mother is dead—a fact he manages to forget for days at a time.

"You'd think they'd make a better go of the names," he says.

Later, he mutes the TV to check on a noise, and hears his daughter singing upstairs. She has her headphones on, her voice half in her head, half in the room.

"Goddamn truck," he says. "Nearly had the wing mirror. You know the bend."

"Be careful," his wife says. "This time of year, they're all drinking."

"They're all wrecked," he says. "I was half asleep myself. No, not asleep." She looks slightly shocked. "Just a bit."

Unmoored. That is the word he is looking for. Recently he feels—he has felt—unmoored.

He used to have a place in his mind where he could go. Hard to say where it was, but his mother has been dead since April, so maybe this was the place she used to occupy. Because he can't go there anymore. It was the song reminded him.

"I was listening to the radio," he says.

"The radio?"

It wasn't like an inner monologue or anything; he did not sit around talking to his mother all day. It was more like a silence. He had lost a great and wonderful silence. The traffic came against him, and he felt unprotected, bullied by the lights. Because he had no one on his side anymore. Not even his wife.

"Yes, the radio. In the car. You know, I wish, for once, you'd let me say something without repeating it back at me, like some kind of gom."

She lets this sink in for a moment and then gets up out of the big armchair and leaves the room. He can hear the sound of her starting to unload the dishwasher in the kitchen.

And "Mutual!" he wants to shout after her. "Fucking mutual!" He wants to tell her how he sat in the car, outside his own house, thinking, Whatever happens when I walk in the door, that's the thing. When I walk in the door, I will find it. The answer or the question, one or the other. It will be there.

And what did he find? These people. This.

Even in her sleep she is affronted, her body straight in the bed beside him, her head twisted to face the wall. The earth spins them toward morning, and he cannot close his eyes for the vertigo; he has to urge it on. He wakes without knowing he has slept, and the house is busy around him—the sound of the front door, finally, and silence. It is after nine o'clock, but when he comes into the kitchen Ross is still at the table, stuck on his phone.

"It's the Christmas concert," his son says, as if that explains something.

The office is closed but he still has a mad number of payments to process before the end of the year, so he takes a coffee back to bed and opens his laptop there.

He clicks on a spreadsheet, then he starts reading the news instead and wandering about online.

Ross comes in to show him something. He climbs across the duvet, bringing the phone screen so close that his father has to push the thing a distance away. It is a video of two tigers, play-fighting in the Siberian snow.

They are pretty impressive, the tigers.

"Fantastic," he says.

And Ross is so pleased his cheeks glow with it.

It is 10:38 and, outside, the sun has not cleared the tops of the winter trees.

"Look up 'solstice,'" he says, spelling it out for him and then typing it on his own keyboard, because he is running out of time now. He has six minutes to do this, to tell his child that the world will keep turning. No matter what happens, the sun will always rise in the morning, the planet's orbit will tilt them toward the light. He finds a video clip of a cartoon earth circling a harmless, small sun, but Ross says he already knows about the solstice. They covered it at school.

It is 10:42.

The boy is sitting cross-legged on the bed beside him. Ross shuts his eyes, and "Sh-h-h," he says. "Is it happening?"

"In a minute."

"Is it now?"

The seconds pass. The boy squeezes his eyelids tighter.

"Now?"

"Yes."

Ross keeps his eyes shut for another moment, then punches the air. He turns to his dad and they look at each other, full of mischief and amazement. Because it happened. Nothing happened, but they know it was there. The tiny stretch of daylight that will become summer.

His wife is home. She is standing in the doorway watching them. They look up and smile at her.

"What?" she says.

Reading *The O. Henry Prize Stories 2018*

The Jurors on Their Favorites

Our jurors read the twenty O. Henry Prize stories in a blind manuscript. Each story appears in the same type and format with no attribution of the magazine that published it or the author's name. The jurors don't consult the series editor or one another. Although the jurors write their essays without knowledge of the authors' names, the names are inserted into the essay later for the sake of clarity. —LF

Fiona McFarlane on "The Tomb of Wrestling" by Jo Ann Beard

From among these remarkable stories I've chosen Jo Ann Beard's "The Tomb of Wrestling" as my favorite. In twelve thousand words it manages to include all the large, small, secret, shameful, silly, gorgeous, terrible parts of a life. Many lives, in fact: furious, funny Joan with her embarrassing cheese who saves turtles from the highway; Roy, who, with a marvelous series of stepladder jumps, leaps into life; the stranger, whose brain flickers in and out of ordinary horror. Not only human lives, but those of sweet Spock and clever Pilgrim, the dogs whose tender, animate worlds coexist with snakes and frogs and coyotes and also Joan's world, which relies on them. And just as, in the story, Joan remembers the advice to let the weight of the hammer work for you, Beard allows the story to work its own terrible swing: here is a woman alone in her own house with a man, a stranger, who means to do her harm. Here is every part of that violence—large and small, past and present. The story focuses on the minute twitch of a hidden finger; it expands to take in past marriages; it narrows to the parasols and roses of old wallpaper and expands until the shadow of a heron flying past a kitchen window is part of the world in the same way a man breaking a woman's nose is part of the world. It manages to ask questions about art, violence, men and women, animals, weapons, and bodies, and to do this on a scale that is horrifying for being so conceivable. This story makes me laugh, and gasp in astonishment and admiration, and see the world, and check the lock on my door. And it's generous, too: it closes with an awful gift. It's a story for this year, and this century, and all the centuries before this one.

Ottessa Moshfegh on "Counterblast" by Marjorie Celona

Rarely can I read simply for pleasure. When I do, the book is usually the autobiography of a swami or the journals of a creative genius—always a text that is deeply personal, apparently careless in its form, and effortless in its persuasion. I like when secret truths are revealed, insights are conveyed coolly, with grace and distance, not boastfully or aggressively. I like a relaxed narrator. And I like when the narrator speaks directly to me. It's easier to listen that way.

With fiction, however, I often have trouble. I am always peeking behind the veil of the prose, asking the text to show me its seams. I can't easily relinquish my seriousness around craft and relax into the world on the page. I study stories and novels with the obsessive acuity of someone trolling the beach for diamonds. Most days I find none, sadly. So reading fiction feels like work with little reward a lot of the time. And to be honest, I'm usually watching out for the writer's mistakes: Where did he start to go wrong? Where is she being sloppy or delusional? What would I have done instead? What kind of person wrote this? Does he know anything new about life? Would I want to talk to her at a party? What does this fiction have to teach me about myself?

When a story can shut me up, I fall in love.

"Counterblast" by Marjorie Celona is a perfect story. Not perfect in its uniformity or flawlessness—that's for factory-made products. Not perfect in its characters—the people in the story aren't "perfect" by any means (who is?). But the personalities are drawn with expert strokes, not too many of them, so that I see perfectly who these people are without extraneous details to distract me. Grace in economy is one mark of a mature and humble writer! The subjectivity of this story's narrative voice dances between sarcasm, self-awareness, and self-deception. That is extremely hard to do while maintaining continuity of personality, not to mention an air of vulnerability and firm perspective. Praise God, subtlety is not a lost art! The emotional range of the story is both deep and narrow: I feel what the characters feel and not much else. Although that may sound limiting or limited, controlling the emotional experience of the reader is precisely what a writer must do. I was more than ecstatic to relinquish control to this author. "Counterblast" inspires in me only exclamations of awe, no questions: that is how true it feels.

It would be silly for me to try to analyze its fictional content or say what is exciting about the plot. Read it and find out what happens between the characters. And when you do, look at how you lose yourself in the story. You are in deft hands, but you won't see them in the text. They are invisible hands, like the hands of all great writers of fiction.

Elizabeth Tallent on "The Tomb of Wrestling" by Jo Ann Beard

If this can be said of prose, "The Tomb of Wrestling" doesn't mind getting its hands dirty—a good thing, since it's fascinated by violence's ability to mess with reality, to walk in through the door of an ordinary afternoon and take our breath away. Violence is such a big deal that it arranges stories around itself, pretty often; it's not that violence is exalted, it's just that the story is always, in every adjective and image, aware violence is coming; its importance is irresistibly manifest. But what "The Tomb of Wrestling" does is different: violence gets only the most necessary slice of its impartially beautiful attention. The rest belongs to—is devoted to—life.

The story disenchants violence by depriving it of its usual prideful immanence. Instead it's dispensed in the story's first verb, *struck*. The pronoun before *struck* has a similarly unemphatic strangeness: *she*.

*She*s don't usually *strike*, certainly not *in the head with a shovel*, but it's where the sentence goes in the wake of *struck* that's really remarkable, because instead of blood or struggle or any what-happens-next-ness the narration turns to the shovel and from the shovel to snapping turtles and Joan's habit of rescuing them from the road, and thus—that fast!—Joan becomes for the reader, as she is for herself, a likably conscientious person, inclined to rescue creatures who, without her intervention, often enough end up "strewn like pottery shards across the road." The question I would have thought inevitable—Isn't there a human skull she's just struck, and is *it* in shards?—is coolly sidelined. *In times of hard trying, nonchalance is good*, wrote Marianne Moore, and I've often wondered if what she esteemed was nonchalance's indifference to aim and ambition, an indifference that loosens up focus and lets in errancy and drift and diversion.

A note scribbled in the margins of my first reading of "The

Tomb of Wrestling": "ADRENALINE." I was amazed to find the narrative's quantum nimbleness, its irregular but searching interiority, infusions of memory, bits of ekphrasis, spontaneous point of view shifts, and offhandedly lacerating absurdities in complete harmony with the terror and seriousness of its mortal stakes. Under investigation are many shadings and kinds of consciousness, which the narration tenderly, mercilessly inhabits. The erratically obsessive terrier cognition of Joan's smaller dog, Spock, is funny and real, as is the reverie of a coyote gnawing a deer bone, as is the lethal cerebration of a heron stalking a frog. Panicked by the possibility of her attacker's regaining consciousness, unable to find rope to tie his hands with, Joan finds her own kitchen "strangely beautiful. [She] looked down and saw flowers foaming at her feet last week as she took a shortcut through the Queen Anne's lace. . . . [Time] was swirling instead of linear, like pouring strands of purple and green paint into a bucket of white and giving it one stir. Now was also then was also another then." Who writes "one stir"? It's beautiful! Uncensored attention garners not only beauty but a whole lot of weirdness and incongruity, this story proves—it's like life, having fun with even the darkest stuff.

Honoring its title's nod to surrealism, the weird and wrongful deployment of objects and bodies fascinates "The Tomb of Wrestling." The abuse of a child is chronicled, and errors in erotic improvisation, too; tools are misappropriated, and so are lives. Knocked out by the shovel blow, Joan's would-be murderer is returned to a childhood classroom where the teacher "had used a pencil to lift a human skull. . . . He had felt an illicit jolt right at the moment the pencil disappeared into the eyehole; the deep, almost shuddering pleasure of it." In the next paragraph he feels he is "wedged somewhere . . . the big hollow dome of his head resting against something hard. Wherever this was, it felt like he was filling the space completely." His "oversized and momentous" head evokes the flaring scarlet rose facing the viewer from a plain room scarcely big enough to hold it in Magritte's painting *The Tomb of the Wrestlers*. The rose, like consciousness, is mysteriously *there*. Given the smallness and plainness and permeability of its room, its vividness feels hazardous, about to spill out of bounds.

Magritte: "Everything we see hides another thing, we always want to see what is hidden by what we see." What I love most about this story is how deeply it lets us see into what we can't see.

Writing *The O. Henry Prize Stories 2018*

The Writers on Their Work

Lauren Alwan, "An Amount of Discretion"

My grandmother was fairly young when my father was born, and of those child-rearing years she often said, "We grew up together." I feel the same about "An Amount of Discretion." The story has been with me from nearly the beginning, from the time I first began writing. That was about eighteen years ago, and since then, the story has traveled with me to writing conferences, workshops, online classes, and grad school. During that time, other stories were drafted and finished while work on "An Amount" continued. The long process has to do, in part, with coming to know the character of Seline. People who hold their feelings in reserve are hard to know, and it was the same here. Her character was for so long a mystery because her actions were nonactions—the important things weren't said or done. It took time to understand and to build a situation that would draw out responses that felt correct to her nature. Yet as the story changed, and characters came and went, I always felt a commitment to Seline, to the yearning she feels for the incomplete nature of her relationship with her stepson, Finn, and the loss she feels at the story's conclusion. Even when I knew little else, I knew I was writing toward that finality.

And while the story is founded on that loss, to me it's also a story about art-making. Before I began writing, I was a figurative painter. I come from a family of artists and grew up drawing and painting. In college, I studied at the Art Institute in San Francisco and in the graduate program at San Francisco State. But in my thirties, I began to feel the limits of that visual form. Slowly, the paintings became more narrative, then words began to creep in. Soon after, I set the pictures aside altogether and began to write. So I like to think that part of this story comes out of that intersection of painting and writing.

Lauren Alwan was born in New York City in 1955 and grew up in Pasadena, California. Her work has appeared in *ZYZZYVA*, *StoryQuarterly*, *Alaska Quarterly Review*, and *Sycamore Review*, among other publications. She is the recipient of *Bellevue Literary Review*'s 2016 Goldenberg Prize for Fiction. She lives in Northern California.

Jo Ann Beard, "The Tomb of Wrestling"

The first sentence of this story came to me when I was cleaning out the trunk of my car—it was summer, past turtle time, and as I held the shovel, trying to decide whether to put it in the barn or back in the trunk, I noticed the heft of it. For just a moment I had a great urge to swing it really hard and smack an imaginary person's head with it. I was not at all in a bad mood, by the way, and had no urge to do it to a real person. There's where writing a short story comes in, so I sat down on the front porch—I still remember just how I was sitting, computer on lap, feet up on railing—and wrote the first sentence. Then, oh joy of joys, I had to figure out why Joan had done such a thing and who she had done it to. The story took a long time to finish, not because of the writing, but because there were key questions I couldn't answer. Like, why didn't she run away and why didn't she call the police. I was committed to only going forward and never going backward, making it a challenge for myself, and I knew there was a mistake on the first page that I would have to make right by the end, which was kind of interesting. Along the way, someone sent me a postcard of the Magritte pipe painting, and it happened to be propped where I could stare at it while thinking. The deepest mystery in the story—why she didn't run and didn't call the police—was answered for me eventually, though I didn't put it in the story. If I did, then a pipe would just be a pipe.

Jo Ann Beard was born and grew up in Moline, Illinois. She is the author of *The Boys of My Youth*, a collection of autobiographical essays, and *In Zanesville*, a novel. Beard has received fellowships from the John Simon Guggenheim Memorial Foundation and the New York Foundation for the Arts, and a Whiting Award. She lives in upstate New York.

Thomas Bolt, "Inversion of Marcia"

Many ingredients have gone into "Inversion of Marcia," including the Italian highway sign that gave me the title, news clippings about wild boar encounters, the kiss timer from a charm bracelet I assembled for my wife, unsupervised libraries, some of my own adventures as a teenager (along with those of several young informants and old friends), and a long and fruitful study of the names of lipsticks. Add to that an actual villa with none of the drawbacks of the one in the story, a dash of *Alice's Adventures in Wonderland*, a glass or two of Greco di Tufo, a couple of volcanoes, and the scene is set. Though, for me, the only essential ingredient is Mary, a young woman who has the adventure of paying attention.

Thomas Bolt was born in Washington, D.C. His writing has appeared in *BOMB*, *Epiphany*, *Southwest Review*, *AGNI*, *The Paris*

Review, The Yale Review, Nuovi Argomenti, and *Poberezh'e. Night-maze,* a multimedia work for live instrumental ensemble, spoken voice, and video projection, created with composer Sebastian Currier, has been performed in Philadelphia, Chicago, and New York City. Thomas Bolt's past awards include Ingram Merrill Foundation and New York Foundation for the Arts fellowships, and the Rome Prize for literature. He lives in West Virginia and Toronto.

Marjorie Celona, "Counterblast"

The opening scene of this story is true: my husband did lose his wedding ring on an airplane, and we did find it, eventually and improbably, in another passenger's backpack. I'd never done that before—dramatized a scene from my life—but it was too funny not to write about, especially the desperation with which my husband searched his shoes. Of course my husband insists I tell you that he *isn't* the husband in this story—and he isn't—and I'm not the wife, though we have similar anxious thoughts. I wrote this story in a panic. My daughter had just turned one, and we'd put her in day care for the first time. I'd never felt so guilty, leaving her in a brightly lit room on the other side of town. I lasted three weeks, then pulled her out. But those mornings—eight a.m. to noon, I think it was—were enough to get the story out. I wrote it because I was angry at all the wrongheaded advice I was given about babies—stuff I found cruel, much of it from doctors. This story, to me, is a kind of corrective—a way of saying, I hope with humor, that any move away from love is a move toward ugliness and a move toward sorrow. And, I guess, a warning to married people everywhere not to take their rings off on a plane.

Marjorie Celona was born in Victoria, British Columbia, in 1981. She is the author of the novel *Y,* which won France's Grand Prix Littéraire de l'Héroïne for Best Foreign Novel. Her work has appeared in *The Best American Nonrequired Reading*, *The Southern Review, Harvard Review, The Globe and Mail*, and elsewhere. Her second novel is forthcoming in 2019. A graduate of the Iowa Writers' Workshop, she lives in Oregon.

Youmna Chlala, "Nayla"

"Nayla" began as a way of making sense of a friend's very sudden loss. Hers was among many during a time when it felt that most people I knew were either in crisis or experiencing a collective loss. Were we all destined to now exist because of absences? How could I write about the scale of what I was feeling and witnessing? I set the story in the not-so-distant future as part of a novella I had been working on but put aside because it felt too close to what was happening around me. As the characters transformed the spaces of confinement, the story became about recognition, intimacy, and friendship. These are the ways we not only survive but also find ways of breathing and moving.

Youmna Chlala was born in Beirut. She is the author of *The Paper Camera*, a collection of poetry, and the recipient of a Joseph Henry Jackson Award. She is the founding editor of *Eleven Eleven (1111): Journal of Literature & Art*. Her writing has appeared in publications such as *BOMB, Guernica, Bespoke, Aster(ix), CURA*, and *The MIT Journal of Middle East Studies*. She is an associate professor in humanities and media studies in the Graduate Writing Program at the Pratt Institute. She lives in New York City.

Dounia Choukri, "Past Perfect Continuous"

I was an anxious child, and I think that anxious people tend to gravitate toward the past, rather than the future. The past was my treasure chest, and the stories from my German mother's side were like the ornate rings and necklaces she never wore but took out of the jewel box once a year. Growing up, I didn't feel connected to the town my parents had moved to, but, listening to these family stories, I could conveniently and comfortingly connect to a fascinating past simply by being my mother's daughter and my grandmother's granddaughter.

As a teenager, I realized that the rigid collective family memory didn't leave much room for me to grow. The vast past magically stopped at the margins of my own memory, like a sea licking at the shore, teasing, never quite reaching my toes. The past became ambiguous. It had the power to connect and to isolate, to soothe and to constrict.

I chose the fall of the Berlin Wall for the ending of this story because it is such a powerful image of liberation and offers a peaceful contrast to the horrors of World War II. Children have vivid imaginations, but even as a child, I never dared to dream that the Wall might come down in my lifetime. It was a fixture, one side painted, the other gray, a little like my German grandparents' past and present.

Many aspects of "Past Perfect Continuous" are based on real characters and events. I rearranged these and invented parts to join the fragments to create a story that is like life itself—highly subjective and continually reinvented.

Dounia Choukri was born in East Berlin in 1976 and grew up in Bonn, where she attended the Lycée Français. She has studied in Germany, France, and the United States, and holds an MA in American literature. Her fiction and poetry have appeared in *The Cincinnati Review*, *Green Mountains Review*, *Folio*, and *The Bitter Oleander*. She lives in Bonn.

Viet Dinh, "Lucky Dragon"

"Lucky Dragon" is based on a true event—there actually was a fishing vessel, *Lucky Dragon No. 5*, that got caught in the fallout of the Bikini Atoll nuclear test. I wanted to blend the story of that boat's crew with a love of mine: Japanese *kaiju* films. I grew up watching an unholy number of horror movies (around 666, to be exact), so the concept of the monstrous has always fascinated me. Indeed, the *Lucky Dragon No. 5* incident was dramatized at the start of *Godzilla*. Although I had always intended for my fishermen to be similar to the Creature from the Black Lagoon, I discovered the legend of the *ningyo*, the Japanese mermaid (generally depicted as a hideous creature, as opposed to the seductive beings of Western myth), which gave their transformation a more definite shape. Furthermore, I came across an article that detailed the reception of the returning Japanese POWs in Japan itself. Upon learning the struggles they faced within their own society, I was able to connect the men's increasing monstrosity with a metaphor that was both personally and culturally significant. Then, I simply let everything mutate.

Viet Dinh was born in Vietnam and grew up in Colorado. He attended Johns Hopkins University and the University of Houston, and currently teaches at the University of Delaware. He has received fellowships from the National Endowment for the Arts and the Delaware Division of the Arts. His stories have appeared in *Zoetrope: All-Story*, *Witness*, *Fence*, *Five Points*, *Chicago Review*, *The Threepenny Review*, and *Best American Nonrequired Reading*. His debut novel, *After Disasters*, was a finalist for the PEN/Faulkner Award. He lives in Delaware.

Anne Enright, "Solstice"

I wrote this story for a short-story event that I was hosting in Dublin on the night of the solstice, December 21, in 2016. It was many years since I had attempted a short story, and I thought about this failure as I drove home from town one evening in late November. It was a few short weeks after Trump was elected president of the United States. My children, who had spent the spring of that year in school in New York, were upset about the election result, as were their parents. These felt like truly dark days, and one way or another, it was an emotional journey home. I resolved to use whatever thing I saw or heard when I walked in the door of the house as the basis for a story. I would sit down after dinner and just write.

When I walked into the house, I found one child talking ecopolitics and the other talking about two long-dead cats. I also realized how wonderful they were. The finished story also contains the story of how it got written, and this pleases me no end. I changed everything about the little family—I flipped genders, ages, I changed the issues they faced—but I kept this essential insight about the end of darkness and the first glimmerings of hope.

Anne Enright was born in Dublin. She has published two collections of short stories, published collectively as *Yesterday's Weather*; one book of nonfiction, *Making Babies*; and six novels, including *The Forgotten Waltz*, which was awarded the Andrew Carnegie Medal for Excellence in Fiction; *The Green Road*, which was shortlisted for the Baileys Women's Prize for Fiction 2016 and won the Irish Novel of the Year 2015; and *The Gathering*, which was the Irish Novel of the Year and won the 2007 Man Booker Prize. She is the inaugural Laureate for Irish Fiction. She lives and works in Dublin.

Brad Felver, "Queen Elizabeth"

I had been working on this story for a long time before I stumbled upon its proper shape. It started as a series of fragments about a couple in love, which is to say boring and tedious fiction. Then my personal life intervened: my son was born. As a new father, I suddenly knew what story I had been trying, and failing, to tell. I was writing a grief story, but until then, it lacked a central trauma—the death of a child. I simply couldn't, and still can't, fathom how parents deal with losing a child. What I did know was that this trauma was the wedge I needed to separate my happy couple. Still, writing a grief story tends to be a foolish venture for anyone not named Chekhov. They so easily become tiresome, lethargic affairs. Grief depicted on the page often feels static. A story about a couple stuck in grief suffers from the exact same ailment as a story about a couple stuck in happiness. So I had to find ways to stimulate that grief, to animate it. Enter the beguiling magic of art: I had already been writing those short fragments, and they allowed me to slide through space and time. This kept me from letting my characters passively wallow and introduced a temporal component to the equation. Examining how grief mutates over long stretches of time ended up being fascinating work.

Brad Felver was born in St. Marys, Ohio, in 1982. His fiction and essays have appeared widely in magazines such as *Colorado Review*, *Hunger Mountain*, and *New England Review*. His forthcoming debut collection, *The Dogs of Detroit*, won the Drue Heinz Literature Prize. He lives in northern Ohio.

Tristan Hughes, "Up Here"

Occasionally, trying to recall the origins of a story can leave you feeling a bit like a hapless paleontologist, searching beds of shale and finding only frustrating gaps in the fossil record. But the origins of this story remain clear to me. I can trace them to a specific place and time; a single day, a single afternoon.

It was summer, and I was in love and living in a remote corner of northwestern Ontario. And I was at a party. Like the best parties, it was one of those impromptu affairs, where a few neighbors gather and the sun shines and you lose track of time and the world becomes a little golden. It didn't take much to make it an idyll: we were by a lake in the middle of a great forest. Late in the afternoon, I was talking to one of my neighbors when he told me, very matter-of-factly, that he had to get up early the next morning to put down his friend's old dog. We must have spoken about other things. I must have swum and laughed and drunk with everybody else. But the spell had been broken, and in its wake crept a nameless sense of disarray. That night I wrote "The day of the dog" in a notebook and didn't open it again for two years.

When I did, that unsettling feeling seemed to waft up from the page like the remembered scent of a pressed flower. Sometimes you know you have a story because something leaves you with a residue of feeling you can't shake off; it sits in the pit of your stomach, and you don't know what it is yet, or what it means, or what form it will take. And then, as I began to write, it took on a form: a love story—and a pastoral. All the original elements were there—a sunlit clearing in a forest, a lake glittering in the light, an old dog—but what came later was the animating pulse that brought them together, the realization of what had been there the whole time. An inky rippling across the water, a rustling among the green leaves. *Et in Arcadia ego.*

Tristan Hughes was born in Atikokan, a small town in northern Ontario, and brought up on the Welsh island of Ynys Môn. A winner of the Rhys Davies short story prize, he is the author of four novels, *Eye Lake*, *Revenant*, *Send My Cold Bones Home*, and *Hummingbird*, as well as a collection of short stories, *The Tower*. He is currently a senior lecturer in creative writing at Cardiff University and lives in Wales.

Dave King, "The Stamp Collector"

I wrote the first draft of this story in graduate school in 1998. It was a time (like all times) when gay guys were focused on seeming straight-acting, and because that's so irritating I came up with Louis, who's not at all straight-acting. Who in fact, with his hair salon, boxer briefs, and old disco poster, is a bit of a cliché. This led me to Joe, who's more conventionally desirable but who nevertheless thinks Louis is the cat's meow. I knew I did not want to justify Joe's passion—who knows how love works?—but I began to write about a relationship in which the two are unequal in a whole bunch of ways: sexiness, ambition, capability, wealth, joie de vivre, vulnerability, and so on.

I showed the story to the class, and one comment stayed with me. How come, a student wondered, my work usually included a somehow differently abled character, often skulking around the edge of the plot? It had to do with having a disabled brother, but I'd never registered the reflex myself, and it got me thinking about the structures we create intuitively.

More drafts got written. I changed Joe from a chronic drunk to a guy struggling with sobriety and recast Mrs. Prevala to make her less of a stage villain, but mostly I tried to figure out Stevie's function. This led to deepening the echoes among the Louis/Joe, Stevie/Louis, and Stevie/dad pairs, and when, several drafts in, the old man finally dried Joe's head with the dish towel, the cycle of compassion I was going for notched forward. I had found something that captured Joe's unrooted place in the world yet still advocated for his right to be as he was.

Dave King was born in Meriden, Connecticut, and grew up in a suburb of Cleveland. His work has appeared in *The Paris Review*, *The Village Voice*, *Nuovi Argomenti*, and elsewhere, and he's the author of a novel, *The Ha-Ha*, which won the John Guare Writer's Fund Rome Prize from the American Academy in Rome. He divides his time between Brooklyn and the Hudson Valley.

Jamil Jan Kochai, "Nights in Logar"

"Nights in Logar" was born of a brief memory. In 2005, when I was twelve years old, my family and I traveled back to my parents' home village in Logar, Afghanistan. At the time, the country was only a few years into the U.S. occupation, and Logar was still relatively safe. Then this one morning, my mother's family's guard dog, whose name was actually Budabash (bless his heart), got loose on the roads of the village. My older uncles frantically rushed after it, worrying the fierce dog might attack someone. Without asking permission, my younger uncles and my brother and I decided to follow them. At some point, I became afraid of the chase, and my younger uncles left my brother and me under a mulberry tree. We waited there for many hours until night fell, and then, worrying about bandits and soldiers and djinn, we walked back home on our own, almost getting lost in the process.

Ten years later, I was remembering this memory. I saw the dirt roads, the mulberry tree, and the black mountains in the distance, and I wondered what might've happened if I'd gone along on the chase. If I hadn't been afraid of the adventure. And so the story began.

Jamil Jan Kochai was born in Peshawar, Pakistan, in 1992. His family was from Logar, Afghanistan. He is a Truman Capote Fellow at the Iowa Writers' Workshop. His first novel, *99 Nights in Logar*, is forthcoming. He lives in West Sacramento, California.

Jo Lloyd, "The Earth, Thy Great Exchequer, Ready Lies"

This story began with a rain-soaked walk over Welsh hills where silver-lead mining has left pools and scars and ruined stone buildings. HM, who shaped and exploited and suffered this landscape, was going to be a few lines in a different story, but he kept expanding, by turns vain, ambitious, self-pitying, greedy, ridiculous, ruthless.

The story is set at a time when an almost medieval seventeenth century was turning into an almost modern eighteenth. On the one hand, it was widely believed that ore could be found with divining rods and required the warmth of the sun to grow. On the other, the Industrial Revolution was lumbering into motion, bringing not just gunpowder and the first steam engines, but a profit in moving people off the land and into mines and factories.

As I was working on this story, the Brexit vote was taking place in the United Kingdom and the election campaign in the United States. I had not set out to draw any kind of parallels, but they kept prodding at me. Sometimes I thought I saw HM himself popping up on Twitter. The story's ending crept out of the darkness on the morning after the U.S. election.

Jo Lloyd was raised in South Wales. Her stories have appeared in *Ploughshares*, *The Southern Review*, *Glimmer Train*, *Best British Short Stories*, and elsewhere. She lives in Oxford.

Michael Parker, "Stop 'n' Go"

Like most of the stories that make it off my desk, "Stop 'n' Go" is stitched together from other (failed) stories, as well as those stray and necessary fragments from which stories are compiled: my own puzzlement at the shifting narrative techniques of advertising, the experience of getting stuck behind pickups driving twenty miles per hour on a farm-to-market road where the posted speed limit is at least fifty-five, and some memories my ninety-three-year-old father shared with me.

The brunt of the story comes from my father, who fought—and, like the farmer in the story, was wounded—in World War II. Though he rarely spoke of those days, he did tell me once that after D-Day, his regiment was sent to supervise the cleaning up of Dachau. The detail about the Roma hanging around after the camp was liberated because they had no place to go seemed to haunt him more than being shot. (Or at least I choose to interpret it so, based on the way he told the story or the way I remember his telling it.)

As for the character of the retired farmer, I would like to think that he is not, in fact, merely spiteful of those motorists who are in a hurry to get somewhere for reasons he deems trifling. In his way, he is trying to regulate his memories, to bring order to all the things he saw in his youth that made no sense to him then and make even less sense now. His refusal to shift gears and speed up has nothing to do with where he's going and everything to do with where he's been.

Michael Parker is the author of six novels and three collections of stories. A new novel is forthcoming in spring 2019. He is the Vacc Distinguished Professor in the MFA Writing Program at the University of North Carolina at Greensboro, where he has taught since 1992. He lives in North Carolina and Texas.

Mark Jude Poirier, "How We Eat"

In my twenties, before eBay ruined the thrill of the hunt and turned everyone into experts, I spent too much time scouring Tucson's thrift stores and garage sales for pop-culture detritus (treasures). "How We Eat" is grounded in this period of my life. I used to imagine a subculture of scroungers—people who beat me to all the good stuff and resold it at antique malls and flea markets. As with all my writing, though, this story's seed is a character: Brenda. I don't know her specific origins; she's nothing like my mother. Her brand of selfish immaturity and savvy knowledge of all things collectible is unique, and it kind of scares me, but I lived with her in my head for months before I started typing this story. Like the narrator, I was a neurotic kid who feared that abduction, torture, and murder were waiting around every corner, and in eighties southern Arizona, there were plenty of lurid news stories to feed my anxiety. These stories continue to weasel their way into my fiction today.

Mark Jude Poirier grew up in Tucson. He's the author of two collections of short fiction and two novels, and the coauthor of a farcical graphic novel. Films he has written have played at the Sundance Film Festival, the Toronto International Film Festival, the Museum of Modern Art, and in theaters all over the world. He lives in New York City.

Michael Powers, "More or Less Like a Man"

I have in common with this narrator an almost paralyzing fear of being drawn into conversations with strangers on airplanes or really in any situation where I won't be able to make a polite exit once the well of small talk runs dry. I shouldn't be this way, I know. It's a bad habit for any fully grown person to avoid these kinds of chance encounters, but for obvious reasons, it's especially bad for a writer. In part the story grew out of an impulse—like the impulse that leads the tongue to prod an aching tooth—to put some inquisitive pressure on this irrational fear: Where does it come from? What is it about? To that end I did what just about every story, in one way or another, ultimately does: put two people together and get them talking, give them each a reasonable level of awe and trepidation at the enormous mystery of another person, give them each a history that they feel compelled both to share and to hold back, and watch to see what happens.

Michael Powers was born in Connecticut and raised there and in central New York State. He is at work on a Ph.D. in creative writing and literature at the University of Southern California. His fiction has appeared in *American Short Fiction, Bellevue Literary Review, Hayden's Ferry Review*, and *Barrelhouse*. He lives in Los Angeles, California.

Lara Vapnyar, "Deaf and Blind"

"Deaf and Blind" is the most autobiographical of my stories. When I was seven or eight, my mother's friend left her husband to be with a deaf and blind man. I was absolutely enchanted by this couple. I thought that their relationship was the essence of true love.

When they came to dinner once, I was bent on impressing that man. My mother's friend suggested that I sing for him. He couldn't hear the words or the tune, but she assured me that he would be able to feel the vibrations if I sang loud enough. So I walked right up to him and started to scream the Russian Christmas song into his ear: "A little tree was born in the woods, and there it grew and greeeeew!!!" I hope that what he felt was the vibrations and not hot spurts of my saliva. Afterward, he graciously hand-signed how much he had enjoyed the performance.

Lara Vapnyar emigrated from Russia to New York in 1994. She is a recipient of a fellowship from the John Simon Guggenheim Memorial Foundation and was awarded the Goldberg Prize for Jewish Fiction. Her stories and essays have appeared in *The New York Times, Harper's Magazine*, and *Vogue*. She lives in New York City.

Stephanie A. Vega, "We Keep Them Anyway"

It takes courage to name things, to write them down.

I first approached the story of Ña Meli, a medium working at small-town fairs, wondering about her. I wondered about her life, the social structures she was embedded in, and in particular what she had to say. What is the danger in saying things we already sense or suspect? Why do we write them down? Create a record? Why is it not enough to pass a knowing look and keep quiet?

The story came to life when I found the perspective of the neighbor, a person who both did and did not know Ña Meli well—a person for whom her words mattered. He also had something to say, and I listened. But the story only became complete once I pushed through the hints and oblique references and named the particular, horrible truth lurking in the background.

Ña Meli, the medium in my story, violates the expected silence, the complicity of both victims and perpetrators in trying to move on as if nothing has happened. For me the story, any story, has to violate the expected silence. The story has to name what we would rather gloss over if it hopes to speak truth.

Stephanie A. Vega was born in Paraguay and moved to the United States to study. She later completed graduate degrees in economics and Latin American policy at Oxford University. She spent time in Paraguay before returning to the United States to teach economics. Recently, she completed an MFA in creative writing at Chatham University. Her fiction has appeared in *The Normal School* and *The Capilano Review*. She lives in Pittsburgh, Pennsylvania.

Brenda Walker, "The Houses That Are Left Behind"

The story began with strands of long pale hair that my husband and I found on a sofa we'd bought for convenience when we acquired our apartment. This mysterious hair, we discovered, was not easy to eradicate, and in my mind it became an emblem of everything that ties my characters to the past or releases them into the future. It is an emblem, too, of romance and passion.

The central love in the story is conducted high up, at the level of passing birds, but it is shadowed by the provisional, since the lives that are visible at street level are marked by loss and ruin, and even the birds in the story can fall to earth. The story is about the strange alignments of different lives, about love and refuge, watchful judiciousness and, finally, unexpected happiness.

Brenda Walker was born in Grafton, New South Wales. She has written four novels, including *Poe's Cat* and *The Wing of Night*, and a memoir, *Reading by Moonlight*. Her work has won numerous awards in Australia. Her short fiction has appeared in *Stand*, *The Review of Contemporary Fiction*, *The Literary Review*, *The Penguin Century of Australian Stories*, and *The Best Australian Stories*. She was the recipient of the H. C. Coombs Creative Arts Fellowship at the Australian National University and the 1996–97 University of Western Australia Stanford Women's Fellowship. She lives in Western Australia.

Jenny Zhang, "Why Were They Throwing Bricks?"

Love seems simple, beyond debate—one should give and receive as much of it as possible. What is the harm, I used to think, in loving someone? But it was often fraught. Love became inseparable from demand, expectation, pain, baggage. Sometimes, it was suffocating, one-sided; the more someone demanded it of me and demanded me to accept their love, the more defiant I became, at times even cruel. As I got older, I began to be wary of those who were the showiest and most insistent with their love—why did they need me to love them? Why did they need everyone to love them? I began to realize that love, like everything else, could be weaponized.

I find childhood endlessly interesting because it's such a blurry time yet so easy to idealize through nostalgia. Still, others look back at that time and remember nothing, or only the nightmarish experience of being so helpless and reliant on adults for care.

"Why Were They Throwing Bricks?" tracks Stacey's relationship with her grandmother, who is both manipulative and inspiring, though as Stacey gets older, she brushes off the latter and clings to the former. I was interested in the ways children idealize and attach themselves to the adults who are tasked with caring for them and the painful process of growing up and realizing that some of these adults are not at all fit, some cannot help but imprint their own unprocessed traumas onto the children under their care. It's also a story of how trauma is passed down, inherited, rejected. For so long, I wanted to believe the world was cleanly cleaved into two kinds of people—those who have been traumatized and those who traumatize others. In other words, I believed some people deserved total sympathy and others none. How quickly that notion was destroyed for me when I realized that some people who have suffered the most can be insufferable to be around! How do we hold people accountable for the harm they cause when they themselves have been victims of violence? How do we reconcile the ways love and tenderness can be entangled with power and dominance? These were the questions I had when I began this story and still have years after I finished.

Jenny Zhang was born in Shanghai and grew up in New York City. She is the author of the short-story collection *Sour Heart* and the poetry collection *Dear Jenny, We Are All Find*. Her writing has appeared in *The New York Times*, *Harper's Magazine*, *Poetry*, *New York*, and elsewhere. She holds degrees from Stanford University and the Iowa Writers' Workshop. She lives in New York City.

Publications Submitted

Stories published in American and Canadian magazines are eligible for consideration for inclusion in *The O. Henry Prize Stories*. Stories must be written originally in the English language. No translations are considered. Sections of novels are not considered. Editors are asked not to nominate individual stories. Stories may not be submitted by agents or writers.

Editors are invited to submit online fiction for consideration, but such submissions must be sent to the address on the next page in the form of a legible hard copy. The publication's contact information and the date of the story's publication must accompany the submission.

Because of production deadlines for the 2020 collection, it is essential that stories reach the series editor by June 1, 2019. If a finished magazine is unavailable before the deadline, magazine editors are welcome to submit scheduled stories in proof or in manuscript. Publications received after June 1, 2019, will automatically be considered for *The O. Henry Prize Stories 2021*.

Please see our website, www.ohenryprizestories.com, for more information about submissions to *The O. Henry Prize Stories*.

The address for submission is:

Laura Furman, Series Editor, The O. Henry Prize Stories
The University of Texas at Austin
English Department, B5000
1 University Station
Austin, TX 78712

The information listed below was up-to-date when *The O. Henry Prize Stories 2018* went to press. Inclusion in this listing does not constitute endorsement or recommendation by *The O. Henry Prize Stories* or Anchor Books.

Able Muse
www.ablemuse.com
submission@ablemuse.com
Editor: Alex People
Two or three times a year

AGNI
www.bu.edu/agni
agni@bu.edu
Editor: Sven Birkerts
Biannual (print)

Alaska Quarterly Review
aqreview.org
uaa_aqr@uaa.alaska.edu
Editor: Ronald Spatz
Biannual

American Book Review
americanbookreview.org
americanbookreview@uhv.edu
Editor: Jeffrey R. Di Leo
Six times a year

American Short Fiction
americanshortfiction.org
editors@americanshortfiction.org
Editors: Rebecca Markovits and
    Adeena Reitberger
Triannual

The Antioch Review
review.antiochcollege.org/antioch
    -review-home
cdunlevy@antiochcollege.edu
Editor: Robert S. Fogarty
Quarterly

Antipodes
www.wsupress.wayne.edu/
    journals/detail/antipodes-0
antipodesfiction@gmail.com
Editor: Nicholas Birns
Biannual

Apalachee Review
www.apalacheereview.org
mtrammell@cob.fsu.edu
Editor: Michael Trammell
Biannual

Apogee
apogeejournal.org
editors@apogeejournal.org
Editor: Alexandra Watson
Biannual

Arcadia
arcadiapress.org
editors@arcadiapress.org
Editor: Roy Giles
Quarterly

Arkansas Review
arkreview.org
mtribbet@astate.edu
Editor: Marcus Tribbett
Triannual

ArLiJo
arlijo.com
givalpress@yahoo.com
Editor: Robert L. Giron
Ten issues a year

The Asian American Literary Review
aalr.binghamton.edu
editors@aalrmag.org
Editors: Lawrence-Minh Bùi
    Davis and Gerald Maa
Biannual

Aster(ix)
asterixjournal.com
Editor: Angie Cruz
Triannual

Baltimore Review
baltimorereview.org
editor@baltimorereview.org
Editor: Barbara Westwood Diehl
Quarterly

Bat City Review
www.batcityreview.org
editor@batcityreview.org
Editor: Nick Almeida Miller
Annual

Bellevue Literary Review
blr.med.nyu.edu
info@BLReview.org
Editor: Danielle Ofri
Biannual

Bennington Review
www.benningtonreview.org
BenningtonReview@Bennington
    .edu
Editor: Michael Dumanis
Biannual

Black Warrior Review
bwr.ua.edu
blackwarriorreview@gmail.com
Editor: Gail Aronson
Biannual

BOMB
bombmagazine.org
betsy@bombsite.com
Editor: Betsy Sussler
Quarterly

Boulevard
boulevardmagazine.org
editors@boulevardmagazine.org
Editor: Richard Burgin
Triannual

The Briar Cliff Review
www.bcreview.org
3303 Rebecca Street
Sioux City, IA 51104
Editor: Tricia Currans-Sheehan
Annual

CALYX
www.calyxpress.org
editor@calyxpress.org
Editors: C. Lill Ahrens, Rachel
    Barton, Marjorie Coffey,
    Judith Edelstein, Emily Elbom,
    Carole Kalk, Christine Rhea
Biannual

The Carolina Quarterly
thecarolinaquarterly.com
carolina.quarterly@gmail.com
Editor: Moira Marquis
Triannual

Carve
www.carvezine.com
azumbahlen@carvezine.com
Editor: Matthew Limpede
Quarterly

Catamaran Literary Reader
catamaranliteraryreader.com
editor@catamaranliteraryreader
    .com
Editor: Catherine Serguson
Quarterly

Cherry Tree
www.washcoll.edu/centers/
    lithouse/cherry-tree
llusby2@washcoll.edu
Editor: James Allen Hall
Annual

Chicago Quarterly Review
www.chicagoquarterlyreview
    .com
cqr@icogitate.com
Editors: S. Afzal Haider and
    Elizabeth McKenzie
Quarterly

Chicago Review
chicagoreview.org
editors@chicagoreview.org
Editor: Andrew Peart
Triannual

China Grove
www.chinagrovepress.com/china
    -grove-journal
chinagrovepress@gmail.com
Editors: Luke Lampton and
    R. Scott Anderson
Annual

Cimarron Review
cimarronreview.com
cimarronreview@okstate.edu
Editor: Toni Graham
Quarterly

The Cincinnati Review
www.cincinnatireview.com
editors@cincinnatireview.com
Editor: Lisa Ampleman
Biannual

Colorado Review
coloradoreview.colostate.edu/
    colorado-review
creview@colostate.edu
Editor: Stephanie G'Schwind
Triannual

Confrontation
confrontationmagazine.org
confrontationmag@gmail.com
Editor: Jonna G. Semeiks
Biannual

Conjunctions
www.conjunctions.com
conjunctions@bard.edu
Editor: Bradford Marrow
Biannual

Copper Nickel
copper-nickel.org
wayne.miller@ucdenver.edu
Editor: Wayne Miller
Biannual

The Cossack Review
www.thecossackreview.com
editors@thecossackreview.com
Editor: Robert Long Foreman
Biannual

Cream City Review
uwm.edu/creamcityreview
info@creamcityreview.org
Editor: Mollie Boutell
Semiannual

CutBank
www.cutbankonline.org
editor.cutbank@gmail.com
Editor: Bryn Agnew
Biannual

Dappled Things
dappledthings.org
wisemeredith@gmail.com
Editor: Meredith McCann
Quarterly

december
decembermag.org
editor@decembermag.org
Editor: Gianna Jacobson
Biannual

Denver Quarterly
www.du.edu/denverquarterly
denverquarterly@gmail.com
Editor: Selah Saterstrom
Quarterly

Descant
descant.tcu.edu
descant@tcu.edu
Editor: Matt Pitt
Annual

Driftwood Press
www.driftwoodpress.net
driftwoodlit@gmail.com
Editors: James McNulty and
    Jerrod Schwarz
Quarterly

East
east.easthamptonstar.com
chelsea@ehstar.com
Editor: Bess Rattray
Weekly

Ecotone
ecotonemagazine.org
info@ecotonejournal.com
Editor: David Gessner
Biannual

Emrys Journal
www.emrys.org
emrys.info@gmail.com
Editor: Katie Burgess
Annual

Epoch
www.epoch.cornell.edu
mk64@cornell.edu
Editor: Michael Koch
Triannual

Exile
www.theexilewriters.com
Editor: Barry Callaghan
Quarterly

Faerie Magazine
www.faeriemag.com
info@faeriemag.com
Editor: Carolyn Turgeon
Quarterly

Fantasy & Science Fiction
www.sfsite.com/fsf
fsfmag@fandsf.com
Editor: Gordon Van Gelder
Bimonthly

Fence
www.fenceportal.org
rebeccafence@gmail.com
Editors: Rebecca Wolff and
    Paul Legault
Biannual

Fiction River
www.fictionriver.com
wmgpublishingmail@mail.com
Editors: Kristine Kathryn Rusch
    and Dean Wesley Smith
Six times a year

The Fiddlehead
thefiddlehead.ca
fiddlehd@unb.edu
Editor: Ross Leckie
Quarterly

Fifth Wednesday Journal
www.fifthwednesdayjournal.com
editors@fifthwednesdayjournal
    .org
Editor: Vern Miller
Biannual

Five Points
fivepoints.gsu.edu
Editors: David Bottoms and
    Megan Sexton
Biannual

The Florida Review
floridareview.cah.ucf.edu
flreview@ucf.edu
Editor: Lisa Roney
Biannual

Folger Magazine
www.folger.edu/folger-magazine
magazine@folger.edu
Editor: Garland Scott
Triannual

**Fourteen Hills: The San
    Francisco State University
    Review**
www.14hills.net
hills@sfsu.edu
Editors: Bradley Penner and
    Danielle Truppi
Biannual

Freeman's
www.freemansbiannual.com
Editor: John Freeman
Biannual

f(r)iction
tetheredbyletters.com/friction/
leahscott@tetheredbyletters.com
Editor: Dani Hedlund
Triannual

The Gettysburg Review
www.gettysburgreview.com
mdrew@gettysburg.edu
Editor: Mark Drew
Quarterly

Glimmer Train
www.glimmertrain.com
editors@glimmertrain.org
Editors: Linda Swanson-Davies
    and Susan Burmeister-Brown
Triannual

Gold Man Review
www.goldmanreview.org
heather.cuthbertson@
    goldmanpublishing.com
Editor: Heather Cuthbertson
Annual

Grain
www.grainmagazine.ca
grainmag@skwriter.com
Editor: Adam Pottle
Quarterly

Gulf Coast: A Journal of
    Literature and Fine Arts
gulfcoastmag.org
gulfcoastea@gmail.com
Editor: Luisa Muradyan Tannahill
Biannual

Harper's Magazine
harpers.org
letters@harpers.org
Editor: James Marcus
Monthly

Harvard Review
www.harvardreview.org
info@harvardreview.org
Editor: Christina Thompson
Biannual

Hayden's Ferry Review
haydensferryreview.com
hfr@asu.edu
Editor: Cheyenne L. Black
Semiannual

The Hopkins Review
www.press.jhu.edu/journals/
    hopkins-review
wmb@jhu.edu
Editor: David Yezzi
Quarterly

Hotel Amerika
www.hotelamerika.net
editors.hotelamerika@gmail.com
Editor: David Lazar
Annual

The Hudson Review
hudsonreview.com
info@hudsonreview.com
Editor: Paula Deitz
Quarterly

The Idaho Review
idahoreview.org
mwieland@boisestate.edu
Editors: Mitch Wieland and
    Brady Udall
Annual

Image
imagejournal.org
image@imagejournal.org
Editor: Gregory Wolfe
Quarterly

Indiana Review
indianareview.org
inreview@indiana.edu
Editors: Tessa Yang and Su Cho
Biannual

Iron Horse Literary Review
www.ironhorsereview.com
ihlr.mail@gmail.com
Editor: Leslie Jill Patterson
Six times a year

Isthmus
www.isthmusreview.com
editor@isthmusreview.com
Editor: Ann Przyzycki
Biannual

The Journal
thejournalmag.org
managingeditor@thejournalmag
.org
Editor: Margaret Cipriano
Biannual

Kenyon Review
www.kenyonreview.org
kenyonreview@kenyon.edu
Editor: David H. Lynn
Six times a year

**Lady Churchill's Rosebud
Wristlet**
smallbeerpress.com/lcrw
info@smallbeerpress.com
Editors: Gavin J. Grant and
Kelly Link
Biannual

Lake Effect
behrend.psu.edu/school-of
-humanities-social-sciences/
lake-effect
gol1@psu.edu
Editors: George Looney and
Aimee Pogson
Annual

The Literary Review
www.theliteraryreview.org
info@theliteraryreview.org
Editor: Minna Zallman Proctor
Quarterly

Little Patuxent Review
littlepatuxentreview.org
editor@littlepatuxentreview.org
Editor: Steven Leyva
Biannual

Longshot Island
www.longshotisland.com
contact@longshotisland.com
Editor: Daniel White
Quarterly

The Long Story
www.longstorylitmag.com
rpburnham@mac.com
Editor: R. P. Burnham
Annual

The Louisville Review
www.louisvillereview.org
louisvillereview@spalding.edu
Editor: Ellyn Lichvar
Biannual

The Malahat Review
www.malahatreview.ca
malahat@uvic.ca
Editor: John Barton
Quarterly

The Massachusetts Review
www.massreview.org
massrev@external.umass.edu
Editor: Jules Chametzky
Quarterly

The Masters Review
mastersreview.com
contact@mastersreview.com
Editor: Sadye Teiser
Annual

**McSweeney's Quarterly
   Concern**
www.mcsweeneys.net
custservice@mcsweeneys.net
Editor: Dave Eggers
Quarterly

Meridian
www.readmeridian.org
meridianuva@gmail.com
Editor: Helen Chandler
Semiannual

Michigan Quarterly Review
www.michiganquarterlyreview
   .com
mqr@umich.edu
Editor: Jonathan Freedman
Quarterly

Mid-American Review
casit.bgsu.edu/
   midamericanreview
mar@bgsu.edu
Editor: Abigail Cloud
Semiannual

Midwestern Gothic
midwestgothic.com
info@midwesterngothic.com
Editors: Jeff Pfaller and
   Robert James Russell
Biannual

Mississippi Review
sites.usm.edu/mississippi-review/
msreview@usm.edu
Editor: Adam Clay
Biannual

The Missouri Review
www.missourireview.com
question@moreview.com
Editor: Speer Morgan
Quarterly

Moment
www.momentmag.com
editor@momentmag.com
Editor: Nadine Epstein
Six times a year

n+1
nplusonemag.com
editors@nplusonemag.com
Editors: Nikil Saval and
   Dayna Tortorici
Triannual

Narrative
www.narrativemagazine.com
info@narrativemagazine.com
Editors: Carol Edgarian and
   Tom Jenks

Natural Bridge
blogs.umsl.edu/naturalbridge
natural@umsl.edu
Editor: Mary Troy
Biannual

New England Review
www.nereview.com
nereview@middlebury.edu
Editor: Carolyn Kuebler
Quarterly

Newfound
newfound.org
info@newfound.org
Editor: Levis Keltner
Annual

New Letters
www.newletters.org
newletters@umkc.edu
Editor: Robert Stewart
Quarterly

New Madrid
newmadridjournal.org
msu.newmadrid@murraystate.edu
Editor: Ann Neelon
Biannual

New Ohio Review
www.ohio.edu/nor
noreditors@ohio.edu
Editor: David Wanczyk
Biannual

New Orleans Review
www.neworleansreview.org
noreview@loyno.edu
Editor: Mark Yakich
Annual

New South
newsouthjournal.com
newsoutheditors@gmail.com
Editor: Stephanie Devine
Biannual

The New Yorker
www.newyorker.com
themail@newyorker.com
Editor: David Remnick
Weekly

Nimrod International Journal
nimrod.utulsa.edu
nimrod@utulsa.edu
Editor: Eilis O'Neal
Biannual

Noon
www.noonannual.com
1324 Lexington Avenue,
    PMB 298
New York, NY 10128
Editor: Diane Williams
Annual

North Carolina Literary Review
www.nclr.ecu.edu
BauerM@ecu.edu
Editor: Margaret D. Bauer
Annual

North Dakota Quarterly
ndquarterly.org
ndq@und.edu
Editor: Kate Sweney
Quarterly

Northern New England Review
www.nnereview.com
douaihym@franklinpierce.edu
Editor: Margot Douaihy
Annual

No Tokens Journal
notokensjournal.com
NoTokensJournal@gmail.com
Editor: T Kira Madden
Biannual

Notre Dame Review
ndreview.nd.edu
notredamereview@gmail.com
Editor: Steve Tomasula
Biannual

The Ocean State Review
oceanstatereview.org
oceanstatereview@gmail.com
Editors: Tina Egnoski and
    Charles Kell
Annual

One Story
www.one-story.com
Editor: Patrick Ryan
Monthly

One Teen Story
www.one-story.com
Editor: Patrick Ryan
Quarterly

Orion
orionmagazine.org
Editor: H. Emerson Blake
Bimonthly

Outlook Springs
outlooksprings.com
outlookspringsnh@gmail.com
Editor: Andrew Mitchell
Triannual

Overtime
www.workerswritejournal.com/
    overtime.htm
info@workerswritejournal.com
Editor: David LaBounty
Four to six times a year

Oxford American
www.oxfordamerican.org
info@oxfordamerican.org
Editor: Eliza Borné
Quarterly

Pakn Treger
www.yiddishbookcenter.org/
    language-literature-culture/
    pakn-treger
pt@yiddishbookcenter.org
Editor: Aaron Lansky

The Paris Review
www.theparisreview.org
queries@theparisreview.org
Interim Editor: Nicole Rudick
Quarterly

Pembroke Magazine
pembrokemagazine.com
pembrokemagazine@gmail.com
Editor: Jessica Pitchford
Annual

The Pinch
www.pinchjournal.com
editor@pinchjournal.com
Editor: Courtney Miller Santo
Biannual

Playboy
www.playboyenterprises.com
Editor: James Rickman
Monthly

Pleiades
www.pleiadesmag.com
Editors: Phong Nguyen and
    Jenny Molberg
pnguyen@ucmo.edu
Biannual

Ploughshares
www.pshares.org
pshares@pshares.org
Editor: Ladette Randolph
Triannual

PMS poemmemoirstory
www.uab.edu/cas/
    englishpublications/pms
    -poemmemoirstory
poemmemoirstory@gmail.com
Editor: Kerry Madden
Annual

Post Road
www.postroadmag.com
info@postroadmag.com
Editor: Chris Boucher
Biannual

Prairie Fire
www.prairiefire.ca
prfire@prairiefire.ca
Editor: Andris Taskans
Quarterly

Prairie Schooner
prairieschooner.unl.edu
PrairieSchooner@unl.edu
Editor: Kwame Dawes
Quarterly

PRISM international
prismmagazine.ca
prose@prismmagazine.ca
Editor: Kyla Jamieson
Quarterly

Profane
www.profanejournal.com
profanejournal@gmail.com
Editor: Patrick Chambers
Annual

A Public Space
apublicspace.org
general@apublicspace.org
Editor: Brigid Hughes
Quarterly

PULP Literature
pulpliterature.com
info@pulpliterature.com
Editor: Jennifer Landels
Quarterly

Raritan
raritanquarterly.rutgers.edu
rqr@sas.rutgers.edu
Editor: Jackson Lears
Quarterly

Redivider
www.redividerjournal.org
editor@redividerjournal.org
Editor: Bradley Babendir
Biannual

River Styx
www.riverstyx.org
BigRiver@riverstyx.org
Editor: Christina Chady
Biannual

Room
roommagazine.com
contactus@roommagazine.com
Editor: Chelene Knight
Quarterly

Ruminate
www.ruminatemagazine.com
info@ruminatemagazine.org
Editor: Brianna Van Dyke
Quarterly

Salamander
salamandermag.org
editors@salamandermag.org
Editor: Jennifer Barber
Biannual

Salmagundi
www.skidmore.edu/salmagundi
salmagun@skidmore.edu
Editor: Robert Boyers
Quarterly

Santa Monica Review
www2.smc.edu/sm_review/
atonkovi@uci.edu
Editor: Andrew Tonkovich
Biannual

Saranac Review
saranacreview.com
info@saranacreview.com
Editor: J. L. Torres
Annual

The Saturday Evening Post
www.saturdayeveningpost.com
editors@saturdayeveningpost.com
Editor: Steven Slon
Six times a year

Slice
slicemagazine.org
editors@slicemagazine.org
Editor: Beth Blachman
Biannual

Smith's Monthly
www.smithsmonthly.com
dean@deanwesleysmith.com
Editor: Dean Wesley Smith
Monthly

South Dakota Review
southdakotareview.com
sdreview@usd.edu
Editor: Lee Ann Roripaugh
Quarterly

The Southeast Review
southeastreview.org
southeastreview@gmail.com
Editor: Alex Quinlan
Semiannual

Southern Humanities Review
www.southernhumanitiesreview
.com
shr@auburn.edu
Editors: Anton DiSclafani and
Rose McLarney
Quarterly

Southern Indiana Review
www.usi.edu/sir
sir@usi.edu
Editor: Ron Mitchell
Biannual

The Southern Review
thesouthernreview.org
southernreview@lsu.edu
Editors: Jessica Faust and
Emily Nemens
Quarterly

Southwest Review
www.smu.edu/southwestreview
swr@smu.edu
Editor: Greg Brownderville
Quarterly

St. Anthony Messenger
info.franciscanmedia.org/
st-anthony-messenger
samadmin@franciscanmedia.org
Editor: Christopher Heffron
Monthly

StoryQuarterly
storyquarterly.camden.rutgers
    .edu
storyquarterlyeditors@gmail.com
Editor: Paul Lisicky
Annual

subTerrain
www.subterrain.ca
subter@portal.ca
Editor: Brian Kaufman
Triannual

Subtropics
subtropics.english.ufl.edu
subtropics@english.ufl.edu
Editor: David Leavitt
Biannual

The Sun
www.thesunmagazine.org
Editor: Sy Safransky
Monthly

Sycamore Review
sycamorereview.com
sycamore@purdue.edu
Editor: Anthony Sutton
Biannual

Tahoma Literary Review
tahomaliteraryreview.com
fiction@tahomaliteraryreview.com
Editor: Joe Ponepinto
Triannual

Third Coast
thirdcoastmagazine.com
editors@thirdcoastmagazine.com
Editor: Ariel Berry
Biannual

The Threepenny Review
www.threepennyreview.com
wlesser@threepennyreview.com
Editor: Wendy Lesser
Quarterly

Tin House
tinhouse.com
info@tinhouse.com
Editor: Rob Spillman
Quarterly

The Tishman Review
www.thetishmanreview.com
thetishmanreview@gmail.com
Editor: Jennifer Porter
Quarterly

upstreet
upstreet-mag.org
editor@upstreet-mag.org
Editor: Joyce A. Griffin
Annual

Virginia Quarterly Review
www.vqronline.org
editors@vqronline.org
Editor: Paul Reyes
Quarterly

Washington Square Review
www.washingtonsquarereview
.com
washingtonsquarereview@gmail
.com
Editor: Joanna Yas
Biannual

Weber
www.weber.edu/weberjournal
weberjournal@weber.edu
Editor: Michael Wutz
Biannual

West Branch
www.bucknell.edu/west-branch
wired/print-magazine
westbranch@bucknell.edu
Editor: G. C. Waldrep
Triannual

Western Humanities Review
www.westernhumanitiesreview
.com
ManagingEditor.WHR@gmail
.com
Editor: Michael Mejia
Triannual

Witness
witness.blackmountaininstitute
.org
witness@unlv.edu
Editor: Maile Chapman
Triannual

The Worcester Review
www.theworcesterreview.org
twr.diane@gmail.com
Editor: Diane V. Mulligan
Annual

Workers Write!
www.workerswritejournal.com
info@workerswritejournal.com
Editor: David LaBounty
Annual

World Literature Today
www.worldliteraturetoday.org
dsimon@ou.edu
Editor: Daniel Simon
Bimonthly

Yellow Medicine Review
www.yellowmedicinereview.com
editor@yellowmedicinereview
.com
Editor: Terese Mailhot
Semiannual

Yemassee
yemasseejournal.com
editor@yemasseejournal.com
Editors: Laura Irei, Charlie
Martin, and Joy Priest
Biannual

Zoetrope: All-Story
www.all-story.com
info@all-story.com
Editor: Michael Ray
Quarterly

Zone 3
zone3press.com
zone3@apsu.edu
Editor: Barry Kitterman
Biannual

ZYZZYVA
www.zyzzyva.org
editor@zyzzyva.org
Editor: Laura Cogan
Triannual

Permissions